About

Helen Lacey grew up ... *Green Gables* and *Littl...* childhood classics insp... when she was seven years old, a story about a girl and her horse. She continued to write with the dream of one day being a published author and writing for Mills & Boon is the realisation of that dream. She loves creating stories about cowboys and horses and heroines who get their happily ever after.

Formerly a video and radio producer, **Christy McKellen** now spends her time writing fun, impassioned and emotive romance with an undercurrent of sensual tension. When she's not writing, she can be found enjoying life with her husband and three children, walking for pleasure, and researching other people's deepest secrets and desires. Christy loves to hear from readers. You can get hold of her at christymckellen.com

Abigail Gordon loves to write about the fascinating combination of medicine and romance from her home in a Cheshire village. She is active in local affairs and is even called upon to write the script for the annual village pantomime! Her eldest son is a hospital manager and helps with all her medical research. As part of a close-knit family she treasures having two of her sons living close by, and the third one not too far away. This also gives her the added pleasure of being able to watch her delightful grandchildren growing up.

Second Chance Under the Mistletoe

HELEN LACEY

CHRISTY McKELLEN

ABIGAIL GORDON

MILLS & BOON

First Published in Great Britain 2020
By Mills & Boon, an imprint of HarperCollins*Publishers*
1 London Bridge Street, London, SE1 9GF

SECOND CHANCE UNDER THE MISTLETOE
© 2020 Harlequin Books S.A.

Marriage Under the Mistletoe © 2012 Helen Lacey
His Mistletoe Proposal © 2017 Christy McKellen
Christmas Magic in Heatherdale © 2013 Abigail Gordon

ISBN: 978-0-263-29835-2

MIX
Paper from
responsible sources
FSC C007454

This book is produced from independently certified FSC™ paper to ensure responsible forest management.

For more information visit: www.harpercollins.co.uk/green

Printed and bound in Spain
by CPI, Barcelona

MARRIAGE UNDER THE MISTLETOE

HELEN LACEY

For Jacqueline
Who told me there was no Santa,
who always said I was adopted and
whose old clothes never really fit me right.
Because sisters really do make the best friends.

Chapter One

Evie Dunn pushed her feet from under the uncomfortable airport seat and let out a long sigh. Two hours of waiting in the arrivals terminal had stretched her patience. And she'd never liked airports all that much. There were too many people leaving, too many sad faces, too many goodbyes.

She looked at the cardboard sign in her hand and traced the outline of letters with her forefinger. Her soon-to-be sister-in-law's kid brother was on the twelve o'clock out of Los Angeles via Sydney, and she'd agreed to pick him up. Because that's what Evie did. She picked up, she dropped off. Rock-solid Evie. Ever-reliable Evie.

Boring-as-oatmeal Evie.

Not true. She made the correction immediately. She *wasn't* boring. She was dependable and responsible. Nothing wrong with that. Nothing at all. And today she was acting true to form after agreeing to make the four-hour road trip from Crystal Point to Brisbane and back again.

If Evie's nephew hadn't fallen from his bike and broke his arm, Callie would have been doing this. *I wish Callie was here now.*

She liked who she was. Most of the time. When the twinges came—those niggling little voices telling her to break out, to take a risk, to be wild and unpredictable for once in her life—she pushed them back to where they belonged. Which was not in her world. She had a business to run and a teenage son to raise. Taking risks wasn't on her horizon.

Passengers filed out of the gate, some greeting friends and family, some walked on alone. Evie stood up and held the sign out in front of her. As the parade of people dwindled, a tall, brown-haired man caught her attention. He moved with a confident lope, as though he was in no hurry, like a man with all the time in the world. And he looked a little familiar. Were they the same blue eyes as Callie's? He wore khaki cargo pants belted low on his hips, a black T-shirt and he had an army-style duffel bag flung over one shoulder. He was broad, toned and gorgeous.

This is no kid brother.

His pace slowed and his eyes scanned the crowd, clearly looking for someone. He met her eyes. He looked at the sign, then Evie, then back to the sign. Seconds later he smiled. A killer smile that radiated through to the soles of her feet. He stopped a couple of meters in front of her and looked her over. A long, leisurely look that made her toes curl. For one ridiculous moment she wished she'd paid more attention to her appearance that morning.

"Hey, I guess you're my ride?"

The soft, deeply resonant American drawl struck her low in the belly. She stuck out her hand. "Hi," she said, aware her voice sounded unusually high pitched. "I'm Evie—Noah's sister."

His hand was big and easily wrapped around hers. "Scott," he said. "Nice to meet you."

Scott Jones aka The Most Gorgeous Man She Had Ever Laid Eyes On.

And about a generation too young for a thirty-six-year-old woman.

She cleaved her dry tongue from the roof of her mouth. "Did you have a good flight?"

"Reasonable. I had a three-hour stopover in Sydney after getting through customs."

Evie ignored the rapid pump of her heart behind her ribs. "You can sleep some on the drive back if you like."

He shrugged lightly. "I appreciate the lift."

"No problem."

"I guess I should collect my luggage."

She nodded. "Sure. But first I think I should see your identification?"

"Huh?"

Evie squared her shoulders. "I need to make sure you're who you say you are," she said, ever cautious, always responsible.

He smiled and exposed the most amazing dimple in his cheek. "Okay," he said, and reached into his back pocket.

Evie didn't miss the way his biceps flexed as he moved. He pulled his passport out and handed it to her. She read his name—Scott Augustus Jones—and wasn't surprised to see he was photogenic, too. Evie returned the document to him.

He smiled again. "Do you want to frisk me now?"

Evie nearly burst a blood vessel. "I don't…I don't think so," she spluttered, feeling embarrassed and foolish. He was joking, of course. However, out of nowhere came the idea of running her hands across that chest and those thighs, and it made her hot all over. "Let's go to baggage claim."

He continued to smile and followed her down the escalators and she became increasingly aware of him behind her. And mindful of how dowdy and plain she must look to him in her faded denim skirt and biscuit-colored blouse. She smoothed her hands down her hips and tilted her chin.

It took about three minutes to find his bag and another five to reach her car. She was glad she'd borrowed her brother's dual-cab utility vehicle instead of driving her own small sedan. She couldn't imagine Scott Jones spending lengthy hours cramped up in her zippy Honda. Not with those long, powerful legs, broad shoulders, strong arms...

She sucked in a breath. *Get a grip. And fast.*

It had been forever since she'd really thought about a man in such a way. Oh, there'd been the odd inkling or an occasional vague and random thought. Mostly memories of the husband she'd loved and lost. But that was all. Acting on those thoughts was out of the question. She was a widow and mother, after all.

Ten years. The words swirled around in her head. An entire decade of abstinence. *That would almost give me a free pass into a convent.*

She looked at him again, as briefly as she could without appearing obvious.

Young came to mind immediately. *And Callie's brother. And only here for three weeks. And not my type.*

Gordon had been her type. Strong and sensible. Her first and only love. They'd been happy together. But dealing with his senseless death had been hard. After that, she buried herself along with her husband. Buried the part of her that screamed *woman* and got on with living.

Or so she thought.

"Thank you for the ride."

Evie didn't budge her eyes and drove from the car park. "You said that already."

He shifted in his seat and stretched his legs. "So, what happened to the kid?"

"Matthew fell off his bike two days ago and broke his arm. He's out of hospital, but Callie didn't want to leave him."

Evie admired her brother's fiancée. Callie had embraced her role as mother to Noah's four children and had quickly become the tonic the family needed. When four-year-old Matthew had his accident, Evie had quickly stepped in to taxi Callie's brother from Brisbane to Crystal Point. With her wedding only weeks away, the home she was selling in the middle of renovations and Matthew needing attention, Callie had enough on her plate without having to worry about her younger brother being stranded at the airport.

Only, Evie hadn't expected him to look like *this.*

And she hadn't expected her skin to feel just that little bit more alive, or her breath to sound as if it couldn't quite get out of her throat quick enough. *Okay, so that only proves that I still have a pulse.*

"So," she said, way more cheerfully than she felt, "what do you do for a living?"

He looked sideways. "I work for the Los Angeles Fire Department."

Evie's heart stilled. A firefighter? A hazardous occupation. Exactly what she needed to throw a bucket of cold water over her resurfacing libido. "That's a dangerous job?"

"It can be."

Evie's curiosity soared. *Ask the question.* "So why do you do it?"

"Someone has to, don't you think?"

"I guess." He had a point. But it didn't stop her thinking about the risks. She'd had years of practice thinking about risks, about dangers. A decade of thinking. Since the rainy night Gordon had donned his Volunteer Emergency Services jacket and left her with the promise to return, but never did. An awful night long ago. The night she'd shut down. She wondered about Scott's motives. "But why do *you* do it? Are you an adrenaline junkie?"

He chuckled. It was such an incredibly sexy sound that Evie's cheeks flamed.

"I'm sure my mom and sister think so."

"But you don't?"

"I do it because it's my job. Because it's what I'm trained to do. I don't think about the reasons why. Do you sit down and analyze why you're doing what you do?"

No. Because a shut-down person didn't question herself. A shut-down person was all about control, the now. But she didn't admit that. It was better to sound like everyone else. "Sometimes."

"What exactly do you do?"

"I run a bed-and-breakfast."

He nodded. "Yeah, I think Callie told me that. And you've got a kid?"

"Trevor," she replied. "He's fifteen."

Although she remained focused on the road, Evie felt his surprised stare.

"You must have married young."

Evie pushed her hair from her face. "By some standards, I suppose. I was nineteen."

She could almost hear him do the math in his head and felt about one hundred years old. While he, she knew, was just twenty-seven.

She pushed the CD button on, waited for music to fill the cab and resisted the urge to sing along.

"Do you want to share the driving?"

Evie looked sideways. "We drive on the other side of the road."

"I have an international license."

Of course he did. He was young, gorgeous, fearless and accomplished. "I'll let you know."

He didn't say anything for a while and relief pitched in her chest, although she felt the nearness of him through to her blood. What was it about men who looked like Scott Jones that made some women discard their usual good sense and want to jump their bones? But not her. Evie wasn't about to make a fool of herself over a great body and an incredible smile.

She cast a quick look in his direction. His eyes were shut. Good. If he slept she wouldn't have to talk. Besides, they had three weeks to get through, including the wedding, Christmas and New Year's.

And she could bet, right down to the soles of her feet, that they'd turn out to be three of the longest weeks in history.

Scott wanted to sleep. He longed for it. But he couldn't remember the last time he'd caught more than a couple of hours without being bombarded by dreams.

Yes, I can...

Eight months, he thought. *Give or take a day.* It had been eight months since his colleague and friend Mike O'Shea had been killed. And he'd lived under a cloud of guilt and blame and regret ever since.

Because despite being acquitted of any negligence involving the incident that had taken Mike's life, Scott *felt* responsible. He *should* have been able to save his friend. He should have tried harder, moved faster, relied on instinct rather than adhering to protocol. Mike had deserved that. So did the two young daughters and grieving wife he'd left behind.

It proved to Scott that a man with his profession couldn't have it all. The job he had, the job he loved…that job and family didn't mix. The wife-and-kids kind of family that meant commitment on a big scale. He'd been in love once, a few years back. He'd thought being involved with another firefighter would work, that she would understand the job, the pressures and the dangers involved. It lasted eighteen months before she'd bailed on him, their apartment and their plans for a future.

He should have expected it. Love hadn't figured in his life since. Lust…well, that was different. Since Belinda had walked out he'd dated half a dozen different women. He'd slept with a few of them but had no inclination to pursue anything serious. Because serious wasn't for him. Not while he was a firefighter.

Scott inhaled a deep breath and got a whiff of perfume. Something sweet…vanilla. He smiled when his brain registered how much he liked it. The woman beside him was extremely attractive; although she was so uptight he could feel the vibrations coming off her skin. But he liked the way she looked. He'd always been a sucker for long, dark, sexy hair. She had a nice mouth and big green eyes beneath slanting, provocative eyebrows. The type of woman he'd notice. *Lush,* he thought. And touchable in a way that could make a man's palms itch.

Maybe I should talk to her and break the ice a bit? Talking with women had never been a problem. He liked women. They usually liked him. But she didn't seem interested in conversation, so Scott kept his eyes closed and concentrated on the soft music beating between them.

Sleep…yeah…I can do that.

* * *

Evie had a headache. Probably from the tightly clenched jaw she couldn't relax. Acutely conscious of the sleeping man beside her, she gripped the wheel and looked directly ahead. An hour and a half into the journey and she felt the need to stop for a fix of caffeine. She pulled into a truck stop twenty minutes later and maneuvered the pickup into a vacant space outside the diner. Her passenger didn't stir as she turned off the engine and unclipped her belt. She looked him over and experienced a strange dip low in her belly. Really low.

Okay...so my body's not quite the museum I thought it was.

Evie wasn't sure how this sudden attraction made her feel. She wasn't sure she wanted to *feel* anything. She wasn't sure she even knew how anymore. Oh, she knew how to love her son, and her parents and her siblings and her nieces and nephews. And she was a good, loyal friend.

But a man? A flesh-and-blood man like the one in front of her—that was a different kind of *feeling* altogether. Memories of those kinds of feelings swam around in her head, like ghosts of a life once lived, a life that belonged to someone else.

The life of a woman who'd had a husband, a lover, a soul mate. When Gordon was alive she'd had those things. They'd laughed and loved. She felt passion and heat and sweat.

But Evie wasn't that woman anymore.

She took a breath, grabbed her purse and got out as quietly as she could. The restaurant wasn't busy and she quickly ordered coffee to go and a couple of prepackaged sandwiches. Evie hung around the counter until the order came, then stopped to collect sugar and plastic spoons from a small table near the door. She was just about to pocket some of both when she heard a voice behind her.

"How's the coffee here?"

She turned. Scott was close. Really close. His chest seemed like a solid wall in front of her. "I'm not sure." She held up a small cardboard carrier containing two foam cups. "It's hot at least."

"That's a good start."

Evie's skin prickled. "I wasn't sure how you liked it."

He smiled. "Black, two sugars and milk."

A funny guy. Great. She passed him four sachets of sugar. "Knock yourself out."

"Shall we sit?" he asked.

Evie handed over the coffee. "Sure."

She grabbed the food and followed him to one of the melamine tables and contained her surprise when he pulled out a chair for her. "How much do I owe you?" he asked once seated.

Evie shook her head and flouted the way her heart pounded beneath her ribs like a freight train. "My treat."

He smiled again and she got another look at the dimple. "Thanks." He took the lid off his coffee and poured in some sugar. "Callie tells me you're in the wedding party?" he asked, resting both elbows on the table.

She nodded and pushed a sandwich toward him. "And you're giving the bride away?"

"Yeah." He looked at her over the rim of his cup. "So, what else do you do besides run a B and B?"

Evie carefully sipped her coffee. "I paint."

"Houses?"

"Pictures," she replied. "Portraits, landscapes...that sort of thing."

"Talented *and* beautiful," he said smoothly.

Color rose up her collarbone and she felt like shaking

her head to refute the compliment. Evie knew she *wasn't* beautiful. She had even enough features and was attractive at best. Her sister Grace, on the other hand, was a classic beauty. And Mary-Jayne, the youngest of the three sisters, had always been considered the pretty one. Evie was just…Evie.

"And I teach art classes at my studio. What about you?" she asked, ignoring the compliment. "What do you do?"

"Besides what I'm doing now?" he replied, then shrugged. "The usual, I suppose."

"The usual?" she echoed.

He put down his cup and leaned back in the chair. "I work."

Evie took a breath. *Talk. Say something. I talk to people every day. I'm good at talking.* "And when do you play?"

It wasn't exactly what she'd planned to say. Because it sounded outright flirtatious. And she *never* flirted. Without warning, the sexy-as-sin Scott Jones had somehow tapped in to the female part of her she'd kept under wraps for a decade.

"I mean," she said quickly, covering her escalating embarrassment. "Do you like sports and stuff?"

"I like sports." He smiled. "Do you?"

"I like to *watch* sports," she admitted. "Even the macho sweaty kind like football."

"But you don't play?"

She shrugged, suddenly feeling like a couch potato. "I run."

"Me, too."

With that body he did more than run—Evie would bet her boots on it.

"Shall we get going?" she asked, changing the subject. Before he had a chance to reply she grabbed her coffee and food and made her way outside. The late-afternoon sun was settling toward dusk and they still had another three hours driving ahead. It would be well after dark by the time they arrived into Crystal Point.

She hopped into the driver's seat, started the engine and waited until they were both buckled up before heading off. They had a few minutes of silence before he spoke.

"Lacrosse."

Evie slanted a sideways look. "What?"

"You'd probably like it," he said. "It can be macho and sweaty."

"I thought it was badminton on steroids?"

He laughed, and the sound thrilled her down to her toes. "*Ouch.* You don't miss a man's ego with that aim."

A smile curled the edges of her mouth. "I'm guessing you play?"

"Yes. I still think you'd like it."

"The next time I'm in L.A. I'll be sure to catch a game."

"Have you ever been?"

"Once," she replied. "Years ago. Gordon and I did the whole tourist thing just after we were married."

"Gordon? That was your husband?"

"Yes, he was." Her voice automatically softened. "He's dead."

"Callie told me that," he said soberly. "You must miss him."

"Yes."

"Were you happy?"

She shot a glance sideways for a moment. It was a highly personal question from a stranger. *A stranger who would soon be family. Part of the Preston clan.* Except, she hadn't been Evie Preston for a long time. She was Evie Dunn, mother of one—*mother-hen,* her father often called her. The girl most likely to fade into the background and do whatever needed to be done. The sensible daughter.

"We were very happy," she said quietly.

"And does your son look like his father?"

"No," she replied. "Trevor looks like me."

"Lucky kid."

Another compliment. He was good at them. He had an easygoing way about him and a kind of masculine confidence she figured he'd probably possessed since the cradle.

Evie was tempted to say thank you, but she caught herself before the words left her mouth.

He stretched out his legs and she couldn't stop herself from glancing at his thighs.

I really need to pull myself together...and fast.

She went for a rabbit in a hat. "So, your girlfriend couldn't come on this trip with you?"

"I'm single," he replied flatly.

"Sorry," she said automatically. "I didn't mean to pry."

He looked at her again. She felt the burning intensity of his gaze through to her blood. He wasn't fooled, either. She *wanted* to know, foolishly, if there was a woman in his life. And she felt stupid. Incredibly stupid. Like a silly teenager gushing over the new boy in school.

She glanced at him, hoping he didn't notice, and wondered where all these sudden hormones had come from. Okay, so he wasn't a boy. He was the furthest thing from a boy.

But he's young. Way younger than acceptable.

Boy-Toy sprang to mind. Ridiculous. *Cougar* followed on its tail, racing around in her head like a chant, telling her to stop dreaming impossible dreams.

"I broke up with my ex-girlfriend over a year ago."

Evie looked at Scott again, slanting her gaze sideways while concentrating on the road ahead. "I'm sorry."

"Are you?"

She gripped the steering wheel. "I guess..." Her words

trailed, then stopped. "Actually I'm usually not one for platitudes. So I'll happily take that back and stop sticking my nose where it doesn't belong."

"It would be a shame to waste such a pretty nose, don't you think?"

Evie's skin tingled. He turned a good line. She pointed to a stack of CDs in the center console. "You can choose some music if you like."

He took a moment before flicking through the pile, and then Jack Johnson's voice filtered through the cab.

"Good pick," she said on a sharp breath.

"You sound surprised?"

Evie stared directly ahead. "My son tossed them to me this morning. I had no idea what he'd chosen. I expected—"

"That I'd go for something a little less mellow?"

"I guess."

"I was raised on a steady diet of jazz from my father, and classic bands like The Eagles and Bread from my mom, who was, and still is a seventies purist," he explained. "I like most types of music."

Evie felt distinctly put in her place. "Sorry."

"That's a favorite word of yours."

Around you it is. But she didn't say it. All she wanted to do was stop thinking about his washboard belly, unfairly cute dimple and nice voice.

"I'll just…" she began, and then stalled because she knew he was looking at her, summing her up and working her out. "I'm really quite okay to not talk if you'd prefer. You've had a long flight and I'm…"

He laughed softly. "Chill out, Evie," he said with a grin she couldn't see but knew was on his lips. "I can cope without conversation."

He settled back in the seat and Evie drew in a sharp breath, feeling like such a fraud. She wasn't sure why. She wasn't sure she wanted to know why. She only knew that in a matter of hours, her life—the life she'd lived for so many years—seemed a lot like a life half-lived.

It was as though she'd been asleep for years, not thinking, not wondering. But Evie was wondering now. And she was awake. *Wide* awake.

Chapter Two

Scott woke up in a strange bed. He rolled onto his back, blinked twice and took stock of his surroundings. A nice room with sloping walls. A comfortable mattress. Clean sheets that smelled like fresh-squeezed lemons. Another scent caught his attention. Coffee. And vanilla.

Green eyes, lips the color of ripe California cherries, dark curly hair dancing down a woman's back.

Evie Dunn.

Scott quickly remembered where he was. *I'm in Evie's bed.*

Well, not technically *her* bed. Although that idea unexpectedly appealed to him when he inhaled another whiff of coffee laced with vanilla. A bed in her house. And not in the B and B part of the big home. These were her private quarters. That had surprised him. But she'd explained how the rooms were fully booked over the holiday season and with Callie and Noah's wedding organized so suddenly she hadn't time enough to change her bookings.

He checked the clock on the bedside table. Six o'clock. He'd been asleep for over nine hours. When they'd arrived at Dunn Inn the night before, he'd pretty much crashed within half an hour of dumping his duffel at the end of the bed.

Scott's stomach growled. He was hungry. And his body ached. He swung out of bed and planted his feet on the floorboards. *I need a run.* He stood, stretched and then rummaged through his bag for sweats. *It's summer here, remember?* He opted instead for shorts and a T-shirt, pulled on socks and trainers, found his iPod and left the room.

He headed down the hall and took the flight of stairs. The rich scent of coffee hit him again as he got to the side door and the private entrance Evie told him he could use. He could hear voices coming from the guest area and main kitchen and fought the urge to follow the sound. She was obviously busy. But he looked forward to seeing those sparkling green eyes again.

Once outside, Scott got a good look at the house. It was huge and had long windows protected by timber shutters and a gabled roof. He walked backward out of the front yard to the garden. Then he turned and was struck by the most incredible view of the Pacific Ocean barely one hundred meters away. As kids he and Callie had vacationed in the nearby town of Bellandale a few times, where their father had been born. But Scott had never seen Crystal Point before. Callie had told him about it, of course, and he'd listened to his sister's stories about small-town life and the camaraderie among the residents and how she'd been readily accepted by the community. And Scott knew her marriage to Noah Preston would cement that bond and she'd never return to California.

He looked toward the ocean, inhaling deeply. The sea was as flat as glass and he spotted a couple of fishing boats on the horizon. He liked this place. Especially when he looked to his left and spotted Evie Dunn pounding the pavement on incredibly athletic legs. She jogged toward him, zigzagging across a wide stretch of grass between the road and the footpath. Black shorts flipped across her thighs as she moved. She wore a white tank shirt, bright pink socks and flashy new trainers, and her glorious hair was pulled back and tied up beneath an equally pink visor. Scott swallowed hard. She looked vibrant and wholly desirable.

"Hey," she said, coming to a halt about six feet in front of him. "I didn't think you'd be up this early." She took in big gulps of air and planted her hands on her hips.

"I told you I run," he said, trying not to look as though he was checking her out. He managed a smile and kept his gaze level with hers. "Perhaps next time we could go together?"

"Perhaps," she said. "Well, I'd better go inside. I've got hungry guests waiting."

She smiled and headed off past him at a slow jog. Scott turned instinctively and watched her until she disappeared around the side of the house. He liked the way she moved. He liked her curvy, athletic body.

A jolt of attraction ran through him, stronger this time. Not what he wanted. *Definitely* not. She wasn't the casual kind of woman like those he'd been seeing since he'd broke up with Belinda. Evie Dunn looked like the kind of woman who'd want permanence—and more than that—she looked like the kind of woman who'd *need* permanence.

And that's not me.

Commitment had no place in his life. He had his job—a job he had to prove to himself that he could do without distraction.

He put the earbuds in place and turned up the volume on the iPod. Stretching his travel-weary muscles for a few minutes, he then went for a long run and decided not to think about Evie's great legs, or lovely hips or bright green eyes. He would just have to forget all about her.

The Manning sisters had been coming to Dunn Inn for nine years. Both in their seventies, both widows who'd married twin brothers, they shared a profound camaraderie that Evie knew she'd have with her own sisters throughout the years. Her sisters were her best friends, her confidantes, her conscience, her troubleshooters. She wondered what they would think of her new houseguest—or the semierotic dream she'd had about him the night before.

Evie listened to Flora Manning explain her newest recipe for double chocolate fudge brownies while she served them breakfast in the main dining room. Sticklers for tradition, the sisters preferred to have all their meals in the bigger room, and forgo Evie's usual and more casual approach of breakfast in the kitchen. Most of her guests favored that particular meal at the long wooden table where they could chat among themselves and with Evie.

But the Manning sisters liked the good china and the pressed tablecloths and the fresh flowers Evie always maintained in the formal dining area. And because her next guests weren't arriving until that afternoon, Evie gave Flora and Amelia a little extra attention.

"Did we see you talking with a man outside?" Amelia asked as she sipped her tea.

Evie looked up from her spot at the buffet table. There was clearly nothing wrong with the Manning sisters' eyesight despite their recent protestations about their failing senses. "He's here for my brother's wedding."

"Ah," Flora said, nodding to her sister. "Told you so."

"Mmm," she replied, and placed a rack of toast and petite pots of marmalade on a serving plate.

"He's a nice-looking young man," Amelia said.

Definitely nothing wrong with their eyesight. "I guess he is."

"And he's staying until after the wedding?" Amelia asked.

Evie nodded. "Up until New Year's, I believe."

The sisters shared another look. "Is he a relative of yours?"

"No," she replied. "He's Callie's brother. As you know, Callie's engaged to my brother."

Two sets of silver eyebrows rose. "Is he married?"

"No."

Another look—this one a little triumphant. "Straight?" Flora, the more to-the-point sister, asked.

Evie smiled to herself. "Yes."

"You should find yourself a man." Flora again, never one to hold back, spoke as she smoothed out her perfectly groomed chignon. "Your son needs a father."

Heat prickled up her spine. "He has a father."

Flora tutted. "A ghost," she said. "The same ghost you cling to."

Evie's hands stilled. "Not a ghost," she said, probably a little sharper than she would have liked. But she knew the sisters' cared about her. Telling it how they saw it was simply their way. "Just memories of a good man."

"Just promise you'll think about it," Amelia said with a soft smile. "Now, when are you going to finish decorating the house?"

Good question. With Christmas only weeks away Evie

usually had all the trimmings up. Granted, the beautiful cypress tree stood center stage in the living room and looked remarkable with its jewel-colored decorations and lights. Noah usually helped her with the rest of the garlands and tinsel she always scattered around the big house. But this year was different. He and Callie had their own home to decorate, and Evie hadn't wanted to bother her brother simply because she wasn't tall enough to finish decking the halls.

"I'll get to it as soon as I can," she promised, thinking the ladder in the shed out back would do the trick.

She returned to the main kitchen and left the sisters with their breakfast. She was just stacking the dishwasher when the door connecting the guest quarters and the stairwell leading to her private residence opened. Her sleepy-looking son emerged.

"Good morning," she greeted.

"We're out of milk upstairs," he muttered, eyes half-closed.

Evie opened the refrigerator and took out a plastic carton of milk for her cereal-addicted son. "Try and make it last past this afternoon," she teased.

"Sure," he said. "Hey, can I have twenty bucks? There's a computer gaming party at Cody's tomorrow night and we all want to pitch in for snacks."

Evie raised one brow. "What happened to your allowance this week?"

He shrugged. "I could say the dog ate it."

"We don't have a dog."

"But we should get one," Trevor said, swiftly employing his usual diversion tactics as he draped one arm across her shoulders and grinned. "It could be a guard dog. Especially for those times when I'm not here and you're all alone."

"I'm rarely alone," Evie said. "We have a seventy-five-percent occupancy rate, remember?"

"I remember. So, about that twenty bucks?"

"If you help me put up the rest of the Christmas decorations tonight, I'll consider it."

Trevor rolled his eyes. "Well, I have to—"

"No help, no snack money."

Her son's dark hair flopped across his forehead. "Okay," he agreed begrudgingly. "But I'm not wearing a Santa hat while I do it like you made me last year."

"Spoilsport." She checked her watch. "You better go upstairs and finish breakfast. Cody's mother will be here soon to drive you to school." She took a few strides toward him and gave his cheek a swift kiss. "And don't forget the milk."

As one young male raced out of the room, another walked right on in through the back door. Only *this* young man set her pulse soaring. It should be illegal for any man to have arms like that. The pale blue T-shirt did little to disguise the solid muscle definition. She spotted a Celtic braid tattoo banding his right biceps. *Oh, sweet heaven.*

Scott smiled when he saw where he'd ended up. "I think I took the wrong door."

Evie managed not to look him over as if he were a very tasty hot lunch. He looked as though he'd been running hard. His hair, a kind of dark hazelnut color, stuck to his forehead in parts while sweat trickled down his collarbone.

"You should find yourself a man."

Flora Manning's words returned with vengeance. Should she? Was that what she wanted? Sure—Evie was attracted to him. Any woman would be, right? He was young and gorgeous and had somehow kick-started her sleeping sexuality. But it was just *lust*. Just attraction. And attraction was...well, pointless if it wasn't backed up with something more, wasn't it? With Gordon she'd had more. She'd had love and loyalty. *A marriage.* Happiness.

Evie swallowed. "It's a big house. You'll get the hang of it."

"I don't remember much of the tour you gave me last night, I'm afraid," he said, just a little breathless.

"Did you sleep okay?"

He nodded and took in a few gulps of air. "Like a baby."

Evie had a startling image in her head of long, powerful legs and smooth silk-on-steel skin wrapped in cotton bedsheets. She cleared her throat in an effort to stop her thoughts from wandering any further. "Breakfast will be upstairs."

"You're joining me?"

"Er—yes. I just have to see to my guests." She quickly explained about the Manning sisters.

"I'll see you upstairs, then," he said, and chose that moment to grab the hem of his T-shirt and wipe the sweat from his face. Evie's eyes almost popped out of her head as she caught sight of the most amazing abs she'd ever seen. A six-pack. *A twelve-pack.* She could swear he'd heard the rush of breath from her lips and felt the vibration of her heart pounding like an out-of-control jackhammer.

"Yeah…okay."

He disappeared through the door that led upstairs, and it wasn't until she heard his footsteps on the top of the landing that she left the kitchen and returned to the dining room. The sisters were still sipping tea and peeling the crusts off toast, and Evie collected a few dishes and told them she'd be back later for the rest. When she was done in the main kitchen, she headed upstairs. She could hear water running in the guest bathroom and relaxed fractionally. Trevor was placing his empty cereal bowl in the sink when she entered the kitchenette and pantry. They heard the familiar beep of a horn outside.

"That's my ride. I gotta go." Trevor grabbed his knapsack and left on fast feet.

Evie filled the jug and pulled two mugs from the cupboard. By the time Scott reappeared about ten minutes later, she'd chopped fruit and set the small table she usually only shared with her son.

Faded jeans fitted over his hips, and the black T-shirt did little to disguise the breadth of his broad shoulders and flat stomach. His feet were bare, his hair freshly washed. He smelled clean and extraordinarily masculine. The mood felt uncomfortably intimate and Evie suddenly regretted agreeing to allow him to stay in her home. Downstairs would have been better. Downstairs was about business. Upstairs was her private world. A world she shared with her son. A world no man had entered for ten years.

He looked around and then pulled out a chair. "This is an incredible house," he said easily. "You have good taste."

And I'll bet you taste good...

She cleared her throat and held up the jug. "Coffee?"

"For sure." He sat down. "Is there anything you'd like me to do?"

Desperate to change the subject, Evie grabbed a couple of slices of bread. "So, how do you like your toast?"

He smiled. "However you'd like to give it to me," he said, and looked at the bread flapping in her hands.

Evie did her best to ignore the inflammatory words and placed the bread in the toaster, set out two plates and grabbed the diced fruit. Once the toast popped and the jug boiled, she poured coffee and moved toward the small table.

"You didn't answer my question," he said, taking the

coffee she slid across the table. "About anything you need doing around the place while I'm living with you."

Evie felt the familiarity of his words down to her feet. She should have insisted he stay at her parents' house instead of volunteering to keep him at Dunn Inn. *Keep him?* She meant *have him.* No, that wasn't right, either. *I'm not having him. I'm not having anyone.*

"I've got it covered. Besides, you're on vacation, aren't you?" she asked as she placed the food on the table and shifted her thoughts from his fabulous abdominals to a more neutral topic.

"I guess," he replied, and placed toast on a plate. When she remained silent he looked up. "I'd like to earn my keep, though."

"You're a guest," she said quietly.

"And family," he said, and bit into a piece of toast. "We'll be in-laws soon enough."

Evie met his blue eyes head-on.

"So, family does stuff for one another, right?"

Ever cautious, Evie narrowed her gaze. "What did you have in mind?"

"You tell me," he said easily. "It's a big house—I imagine there are always things that need doing."

I need doing came to mind and color immediately rose over her cheeks. She wanted Sensible Evie to come back. She needed her to come back before she made a complete fool of herself. But Sensible Evie had deserted her. In her place was I Haven't Had Sex In Ten Years Evie, and she was suddenly a strong, undeniable force.

"I'll let you know," she said. "But like I said, I've got it covered."

"You don't like taking help from people?"

Evie sucked in a breath. "Sure I do," she said, lying

through her teeth. "But I'm well practiced at doing what needs to be done through both habit and necessity."

"So I'm not stepping on anyone's toes by being here?" he asked, watching her with such burning scrutiny she had to turn her eyes away.

Evie knew what the question meant, knew he'd probably wondered if she had a man in her life. "No. There's just me and my son."

"Hard to believe," he said quietly.

She returned her gaze to his immediately. "What? That I'm single or that I choose to be that way?"

He smiled. "That you're not beating them off with a stick."

"Who says I'm not?"

Evie tried to look casual, tried to make out as though her heart wasn't thumping stupidly behind her ribs. But it was. In fact, her entire body was thumping—like a runaway train, like a horse galloping out of control.

"I stand corrected."

He was smiling and that incredible dimple showed itself. Okay, so she wasn't exactly turning potential lovers away at the door. But she'd had a few offers over the years. None she'd pursued.

"Are you okay, Evie?"

No…but she wasn't about to tell Mr. Great Body And Gorgeous Dimple that she was hot and bothered because of him. "Perfectly."

But he wasn't fooled. And neither was she. Something hung between them. Something unsaid. She picked at the fruit in front of her to avoid saying anything else. Once breakfast was over he offered to wash up. Evie was about to refuse when she heard the downstairs door open and a familiar voice called her name.

"That's Callie," Evie said, and pushed out her chair.

Scott did the same and moments later the kitchen door opened and his sister entered the room.

Callie stood in the threshold and her gaze flicked over them. Evie felt the scrutiny through to her bones. The kitchen was small, cozy, intimate. Evie knew the other woman could feel the invisible current in the air as much as she could.

Callie quickly came into the room and flung herself at her brother in an affectionate hug. Noah wasn't far behind and once Evie returned the keys to his truck the two men shook hands, quickly summed each other up as men seemed to be able to do without even speaking and started a quiet conversation. Then Callie headed Evie off by the sink.

"I can't thank you enough," Callie said on a rush of breath. "I mean, for picking up my little brother."

Little brother? Sure. Evie was struck by the remarkable resemblance between the siblings. Her soon-to-be sister-in-law was quite beautiful and Evie knew how deeply Noah loved the spirited and passionate brunette.

"No thanks necessary," she said, and set the dishes on the draining board. "It's—"

"Family," Callie said. "Yeah, I know. But I still appreciate it. I can't believe all the connecting flights from Brisbane to Bellandale were booked up."

"There's the big air show on this weekend," Evie explained. "Every flying enthusiast from around the state travels here for it. Same thing happens each year." She grabbed her rubber gloves. "Are the kids at my parents'?"

"Yes. We dropped them off before we came over here." Callie leaned back against the melamine countertop. "Matthew's enjoying the cast on his arm. Crazy to think we're at the end of the school year already. But I'm so looking forward to Christmas."

Evie smiled. "You *are* getting married Christmas Eve."

"Self-indulgent, I know," Callie said with such a blissfully happy grin Evie felt a tiny stab of envy. "Speaking of all things wedding—you and Fiona have an appointment with the dressmaker next Thursday at ten o'clock."

"It's on my list," Evie replied. "Fiona called me a few days ago to confirm." Fiona Walsh was the other bridesmaid in the wedding party and a friend of both Callie and Evie. "I'll be there."

"And thanks so much for your help with the caterers," Callie said. "I can't believe we've managed to organize all this in a little over a month. You're a genius. And a good friend."

"It's a special day," Evie said, and grinned. "And I like planning things."

"Fortunately for me."

"It will be a perfect evening," she assured her, sensing a few bride-to-be nerves in the usually composed Callie. "My brother's a lucky man."

Callie smiled dreamily. "I'm the lucky one."

The stab of envy returned and Evie squashed it down in a hurry. She wouldn't begrudge Callie her happiness. "You're both lucky. So are the kids."

Her friend looked radiant. *Have I ever looked like that? Yes, of course. Absolutely. Without a doubt.*

She'd loved Gordon since she was seventeen years old. He'd been her first kiss, first lover…her only lover. They'd shared dreams, values and the joy of raising their young son. And something else, a bond between two people so in tune with each other's thoughts, so completely at ease with each other it was as if they were halves of the same whole. And Evie didn't expect to ever have that again. And she wasn't about to throw herself out there looking for it.

Evie settled her gaze on Scott again, and her pulse

quickened. *It's just physical.* But despite the warning bells going off in her head, the attraction she felt for him suddenly poleaxed her.

Sex clouded judgments, right? Sex made people do crazy things. Inappropriate things. She had no illusions. Fantasies about a man nine years her junior were completely off the Richter scale in the good-sense department. Of course he wouldn't be interested in her. He'd have his pick. And he certainly wouldn't choose a thirty-six-year-old single mother well past her prime.

Besides, he was a firefighter. And men with dangerous occupations had no place in her life. She'd already lost one man to the elements. She wasn't about to start fantasizing about a man who chose to run into burning buildings.

That settled, Evie announced she had a B and B to run and excused herself. She was quietly relieved when Scott arranged to leave with his sister and Noah. She told him she'd left a spare key on the armoire in the guest bedroom and said goodbye to her brother and Callie before returning downstairs.

She had a lot of work to do. And a gorgeous man she had to get out of her head. Somehow.

Chapter Three

Scott spent most of the day with his sister. Callie's property, Sandhills Farm, was a few minutes out of Crystal Point. The For Sale sign out front was new and Callie explained how she had plans to relocate her horse riding school to Noah's larger property within the coming months.

"It's a big move," she said as they walked up through the stables. "But I've only ten acres here and I can easily take about twenty acres at Noah's. Plus, I don't want to be commuting every day and I want my horses close to me. I'm working on the house renovations now and will try to find a tenant if it doesn't sell quickly."

Scott didn't think she'd have a problem finding a buyer. Sandhills Farm was an impressive setup for any equestrian enthusiast, with its stable complex, round yards and sand arena. "So, you're happy?"

Callie's eyes opened wide. "Blissfully," she replied.

"Noah's just so..." She stopped, smiled a silly sort of smile Scott couldn't remember ever seeing on his sister's face before and let out a long sigh. "He's *everything.*"

Everything? That was a tall order. Scott couldn't imagine being *everything* to any woman. Not even Belinda way back when he'd been convinced he was in love with her.

"I'm glad he makes you happy." *He'd better,* were the words unsaid.

Callie looped her arm through his. "What about you?" she asked. "Anyone special in your life at the moment?"

"No," he replied, thinking about Evie all of a sudden. He pushed the thought back quickly.

Callie smiled. "Are you looking?"

Scott raised both brows. "Not intentionally."

His sister gave him an odd look. "I wish you were staying longer," she said. "With Mom arriving in two weeks and the wedding just around the corner, I don't think I'll be much in the way of a tour guide while you're here."

Scott shrugged and looked around. "Don't worry about it. You've got more important things to think about."

Callie squeezed his forearm. "Well, I'm glad you're here. And you're in good hands with Evie."

Scott's stomach did a wild leap. Thinking about Evie Dunn's hands made him remember how she'd looked in her small kitchen earlier that morning. She'd looked... *beddable.* Was there such a word? In jeans and a white loose-fitting shirt that exposed just enough of her collarbone to raise his temperature a degree or two, Scott had barely been able to drag his gaze away from her. She had lovely skin. And that hair—masses of dark curls reaching way past her shoulders. He'd wanted to twist it around his hands, tilt her head back and kiss the smooth skin along her throat.

"Scott, about Evie..."

He shifted on his feet. Had Callie read his thoughts? "What about her?"

She smiled fractionally. "She's, you know, my friend. And Noah's sister."

"The point being?"

Callie expelled a breath. "The point being that she's *my friend.* And there seemed to be a fair bit of heat between you in the kitchen this morning."

"You're imagining things." His sister raised both brows again and gave him a *look*. Scott held up a hand. "I left chasing everything in a skirt behind in my teens."

Callie gave a grim smile. "I know that. But since you and Belinda broke up and then Mike's death, you've changed and I—"

"Belinda was a long time ago," he said, cutting her off. "And I don't see what Mike has to do with any of this."

Callie shrugged. "He was your friend."

"And?"

"And losing a friend like that must be hard. And Evie, well, she's like a magnet. Everyone feels it about her. She's warm and generous and so incredibly likable. Anyone who meets her gets drawn in. I would hate to see her get hurt."

"By me?" Scott pushed back the irritation weaving up his back. Callie was way off base. Sure, he was attracted to Evie Dunn. But he had no intention of acting on that attraction. He already worked out that Evie wasn't for him.

Okay...maybe I did flirt with her a bit this morning. But flirting is harmless. It won't go anywhere. I'll make sure of that.

"You're jumping to conclusions," he said to his sister. "We barely know each other."

Callie made a face. "I know what I saw."

"Just drop it, Callie."

She did, but the thought stuck with Scott for the rest

of the afternoon. By the time Callie dropped him off at Dunn Inn, it was past three o'clock. Evie's car was parked in the driveway and Scott was just fishing in his pocket for his key when he spotted a teenage boy shooting hoops near the studio out back. And shooting them pretty badly.

The youth stopped playing when Scott approached and spoke. "Hi."

Scott smiled and shook the teenager's hand as he introduced himself. Evie Dunn's son seemed like a nice kid. Of course, Evie's kid wouldn't be anything else.

"Wanna shoot?" Trevor asked, and tossed the ball to him. "It would be good to see the thing actually go in the hoop."

Scott laughed and swiftly dropped the ball into the basket. "You just need to work on your angle."

Trevor shrugged and smiled. "I'm not much of a sportsman. Take after my mother, I guess."

Scott remembered how Evie had looked that morning in her running gear. She certainly seemed to keep herself in great shape. "She's an artist," Scott said, and then felt foolish.

Trevor looked at him oddly, but continued to smile. "I guess. My dad was the sporty one."

"Mine, too," Scott replied, and passed the ball on.

The teenager grabbed the basketball, aimed, concentrated and shot it at the hoop. It missed and rebounded directly into Scott's hands. "My dad's dead."

Scott lobbed the ball back through the hoop once it bounced. "Mine, too."

Trevor grabbed the ball and took another shot. The ball curved around the edges of the hoop before dropping to the side. "Yeah…it sucks."

They continued to shoot hoops and talk for several minutes, until a taxi pulled up outside the house and two elderly women emerged. As they walked slowly up the driveway, Trevor groaned under his breath. The women approached on quickening feet and Scott watched their progress with a broad grin.

It took them precisely five seconds to persuade Scott to help them carry their bags from the footpath and into the house. Trevor smiled as if he'd been given a Get Out Of Jail Free card and went back to shooting hoops.

There were about a dozen shopping bags from various retail outlets, and Scott guessed the two women had spent the day scouting the stores in Bellandale. The perfectly groomed pair were obviously the Manning sisters who Evie had told him about on the long drive from the airport. They regarded him with such blatant curiosity it felt as if their two sets of eyes were burning a hole through his back as he walked up the half dozen steps and opened the front screen door while juggling the parcels.

Once they'd stepped over the threshold, Scott closed the door and followed them through the house. *Vanilla.* The scent hit him immediately. *Evie.*

The living room was large and immaculately presented, but it was the huge, ornately decorated Christmas tree that held his attention. It was a real tree—the kind he remembered from when he was young and his father was still alive. Memories banged around in his head. They'd go out together and find the perfect tree, strap it to the roof of his father's Volvo and make the trip home laughing, because they both knew his mother would insist on moving the tree around for hours before she finally settled on a spot to showcase her decorating efforts. And they laughed because, inevitably, the tree ended up in the same position every year.

Funny, he didn't think about those days much anymore. He tried not to think about how much he still missed his father. He'd been a good man, and a good dad. But reckless. And that recklessness had contributed to his death. A desk jockey by day, his father would pursue one adventure after another on the weekend. Sailing, skiing, climbing. Ultimately, it was the climbing that killed him. His death had galvanized something inside Scott. At eighteen he had been determined to join the fire department and approached the job responsibly. He didn't take risks. He followed the rules.

And those rules didn't include fantasizing about Evie Dunn.

A widow. A single mom.

Two very good reasons to keep his head.

The Manning sisters thanked him for his help, and Scott was just about to make a quick exit when Evie walked into the room. She smiled at him and his chest tightened unexpectedly. He smiled back, saw her cheeks flush and then quickly she diverted her gaze. His thoughts lingered on how pretty she was. *And all that incredible, seriously sexy hair.* She started talking with the sisters, but he could feel the vibration of her awareness of him like a drum beating. Because she appeared to be trying *not* to look at him.

Scott had placed the bags near the foot of one of the sofas, and Evie and the elderly sisters began unloading the contraband. He stood back and watched, amused by the clear delight the three women displayed as bags were opened and items unwrapped. Evie's animated expression was addictive and he couldn't look away. He watched her unload parcels and sigh her appreciation for the treasures as she unwrapped close to a dozen shiny glass ornaments and garlands and laid them carefully on the sofa. Scott snatched a glance at the tree behind him and quickly realized something. *Evie loved Christmas.* He could easily imagine her trimming a turkey, wrapping gifts with matching paper and ribbon, singing carols on Christmas Eve and doing all the things that made the festive season special.

A magnet, Callie had called her. Someone who draws people in.

Was that what she was doing to him? But Scott was convinced it was just physical attraction. He'd been attracted to women before. Some he'd dated. Some he'd slept with.

Evie looked across at him briefly and the smile curling her lips made his stomach roll over. Her cheeks flushed again, brighter this time. Scott's fingers itched with the sudden urge to reach out and touch her face, to trace the line of her jaw and her delicious-looking mouth. Her lips parted, as if she knew he was thinking about them…wondering, imagining if they tasted as sweet as they looked. Her tongue came out and moistened her lower lip. The kick of it rushed to his feet, traveled up his legs and hit him square in the groin.

With his heart hammering behind his ribs, Scott looked at the two elderly women still fussing over their parcels and knew he had to get away from Evie…and fast. He cleared his throat and quickly excused himself.

By the time he'd returned to the private quarters and headed for his room, his breathing was back to normal. He sat on the edge of the big bed, took a deep breath and clenched his fists. *I'm not going to get involved here. I'm going home soon—back to my life—back to everything I know. Three weeks, Jones…I gotta keep it together.*

Evie lingered in the largest downstairs bedroom later that afternoon. She had guests arriving soon—a newly married couple who were staying for a week. The bedroom was her favorite in the house—big and airy and decorated in the palest hues of purple, lavender and white. It had its own bathroom and small sitting area, and the enormous bed was scattered with half a dozen cushions in various shades of mauve. She fluffed a couple of pillows, straightened the white lace bedspread and fiddled with the vase of lilac-and-cream miniature roses that sat on the dresser.

She thought about Scott. Her blood pumped when she remembered how he'd looked at her. The air had smoldered with a kind of throbbing, consuming, slowly building heat.

This is so crazy...he's twenty-seven years old, for heaven's sake.

Evie took a deep breath, straightened the already straight bedspread and headed upstairs. Back in her own room she looked out the window and saw her son shooting his basketball into the hoop. Scott was with him. They were talking and throwing the ball. She heard a shout of laughter from her son and it tightened something in her chest.

Oh...no...I'm not going to like him. But seeing him with her son made her like him. Not just lust, she thought, something else, an awareness of him on another level.

And Trevor's laughter made Evie ache inside. She knew her son longed for regular male company, a man's influence...a father's influence.

Imagining Scott in that role was foolish. He'd be gone in three weeks.

Her guests arrived about ten minutes later. In their midfifties and obviously in love, Trent and Patti Keller were all smiles when Evie showed them to their room. A tiny stab of envy knotted tightly and she tamped it down.

Evie gave them a tour of the house, and introduced them to the Manning sisters, who were reading in the front living room. She told them dinner was at seven and left her guests together.

Upstairs, Evie showered, slipped into white cotton cargo pants and an emerald-green collared T-shirt and low-heeled sandals. She raked a comb through her hair, applied a little makeup and headed from her room. She stopped outside Scott's bedroom. *Dinner's at seven in the main dining room. Please join me and my guests.* Her knuckles hovered millimeters from the door. *Just ask him.*

"Evie?"

He was behind her. Not in his room. She turned around, took a deep breath and told him about dinner. "So, will you join us?"

"Of course. Do I need to change?"

Evie couldn't help licking her gaze over his tall, muscular body. Jeans and T-shirt were such a great look on him. "No. I'll see you at seven." She turned on her heel and headed downstairs.

Evie loved to cook and adored her big, well-appointed kitchen. She wrapped her favorite apron over her clothes, finished off the lemon meringue pie she'd whipped up earlier that afternoon and popped it into the refrigerator to chill. The mustard beef and assortment of roasted vegetables were done within the hour and she set everything ready in the kitchen before making her way to the dining room. She set the big table for six. There would be no Trevor tonight. He'd pleaded to go to Cody's to study and promised to be home by nine o'clock. Once the buffet was set up with chilled wine and imported beer, Evie returned to the kitchen.

At five minutes to seven, people began entering the dining room. Evie noticed Scott first. Before she could say anything, the Manning sisters arrived and quickly cornered him. Evie had to smile. He took their monopoly of him with a grin and appeared to be genuinely interested in their conversation. Evie relaxed when the Kellers entered the room. Once all the introductions were done, she brought in the food and invited everyone to be seated.

It was a relaxed, enjoyable evening—mostly because Scott Jones was so effortlessly charismatic he held the attention of all her guests. Evie was as seduced by his humorous anecdotes and stories as the three other women at the table. He talked NASCAR with Trent Keller, antique restoration with Amelia Manning and the dwindling power of the European monarchies with her sister. And Evie, normally the one to hold court with her guests, remained mute and ate her dinner and simply listened to the sound of his voice.

Once dinner and dessert was done and her guests moved from the dining room and into the front living area, Evie began clearing up the dishes and remaining food. Busy with her task, she didn't immediately notice how Scott had stayed behind and now stood in the doorway, watching her intently. Very intently. His blue-eyed gaze scorched over her as if they were linked by a thread of fire.

"Need some help?"

No. "Ah—sure."

"So," he said quietly as he grabbed a stack of dishes. "Flora tells me you need a hand putting up some decorations?"

Evie stilled. "Trevor's going to help me."

His brows rose over those remarkable eyes. "Trevor's not here, though."

He had a point. "Well, no. I can get to it tomorrow night."

"Trevor mentioned he had a party at his friends' place tomorrow night?"

And another point. "Oh, yes, that's right." She didn't want his help and didn't want to question why. "I'll do it some other time, then."

"No time like the present," he said easily. "Flora and Amelia are keen to see them up."

He was right. She had promised to finish decorating the house. Not accepting his help made her sound foolish and neurotic. "Well, okay. I could use some help later."

That settled Evie headed back to the kitchen with her arms loaded. Scott was close behind her and then made another trip to collect what remained. He stayed and helped stack the dishwasher, and Evie was so excruciatingly aware of his every movement she had to stop herself from staring at him.

Once the kitchen was cleaned up, Evie turned toward him. "There's a ladder in the shed outside. Perhaps you could—"

"Sure," he said quickly, and disappeared through the back door.

While he was gone Evie retrieved a box of decorations from the cupboard beneath the stairs. When he returned she was waiting in the front foyer, armed with scissors, double-sided tape, a packet of small nails and a hammer.

Scott held the ladder in the crook of his arm. "So, where do you want me?"

A loaded question.

Evie cleared her throat and pointed to the archway above. "I'd like this put up there," she said, and pulled a wreath from the box.

Scott placed the ladder in the doorway. He took the wreath and held out his hand for nails and the hammer. "Just tell me where," he said, and climbed up the steps.

Evie stood still and gave instructions. *Not so easy.* When he reached the top step, her eyes were directly in line with his groin. *Not easy at all.* She looked toward the floor and examined the rubber stops at the bottom of the ladder and counted the markings on the timber floorboards. She looked anywhere but straight ahead. But temptation grabbed hold of the blood in her veins and she looked up and almost lost her breath when he raised his arms to knock in the small nails and his jeans slipped fractionally, exposing that glorious, beautiful belly, and her breath suddenly caught.

"Evie?"

She jerked her head up so fast she almost snapped her neck. As he looked down at her, Evie knew she'd been caught staring.

He smiled. "I need another nail."

She pulled another from the box and dropped it into his outstretched palm.

"That should do it," he said, and came down the steps. "Anything else?"

Evie dived for the box and withdrew another green and bronze festive wreath. "This," she said, taking a breath. "On the front door."

While he attended to the door, Evie looked inside the box. *Mistletoe.* The everlasting plastic type sat in a bunch at the bottom of the box. The last thing she wanted were sprigs of the kissing plant hung up at every doorway. She shoved it back into the corner of the box and pulled out three lengths of long green garland instead. "This goes in the front living room," she explained. "Along the picture rail."

"Lead the way."

She tucked the box under her arm and walked toward the front room. There was no sign of her guests and she assumed they'd all retired for the evening. It took about fifteen minutes to hang the remaining garlands. When they were done she adjusted a few lights on the Christmas tree and pretended not to notice his movements when he folded up the ladder and placed the hammer and tape back in the box. The tree really was spectacular—now all she needed to do was begin her shopping and put some parcels beneath it.

"What about this?" He pulled something out of the box.

The mistletoe.

In his hands, the small plastic greenery seemed to be laughing in her face. She should have tossed the stuff in the garbage bin. "I don't think so."

He grinned. "You're sure?"

"Positive."

"Not even one piece?"

He was still grinning. *Probably amused by the look on my face.* Evie tried to keep her voice light. "If that goes up I'm sure the Manning sisters will be chasing you around the house for the next three weeks."

He smiled, showing off that dimple, making her head spin. He twirled the bunch of plastic sprigs between his fingers. "I guess it's fortunate I have a thing for older women."

"It's still not a good idea," she managed to say, and fought back the feeling she was treading into deep water. But she felt the awareness in the air—it pulsed between them, catching them both, fanning the flames of an attraction she somehow knew was unmistakable.

He smiled again and tossed the item back in the box. "It's your call."

Yes, it is. "Well, thank you for your help. Good night."

His brows rose fractionally. "Are you sending me off to bed, Evie?"

She colored wildly, feeling the heat, feeling the air thicken. "Of course not. I just—"

A door slammed at the back of the house. Trevor. Evie made a sound of almost palpable relief. "That's my son. I should go and see if he's eaten." She turned and walked away but stopped at the threshold. *I'm being such an idiot.*

When she turned back, he was still standing by the box. "Peppermint tea," she said loosely, shaking her shoulders. "I'm making some if you're interested."

He smiled and the lethal dimple showed itself again. "Coffee would be better."

"Sure…coffee."

Evie headed upstairs and felt him in her wake. Trevor was standing by the open refrigerator when she walked into the kitchenette. "Hungry?" she asked her son.

Trevor shook his head. "Not anymore," he replied before he shoved a piece of cold homemade pizza into his mouth.

Scott was behind her and she heard him laugh softly. Evie ignored the way her belly rocked at the sound and concentrated on her son. "I can make you some—"

"I think I'm gonna crash," Trevor said.

Stay. But she didn't say it. Didn't dare admit she needed her son's presence to shield her from her ever-growing awareness around Scott. She bid him good-night and waited until she heard his bedroom door shut before filling the jug. Scott sat in a chair, the same one he'd occupied that morning.

He looks so good in my kitchen. I could get used to him being in my kitchen.

Evie rested her hand on the stainless-steel appliance. She was appalled by her thoughts. And knew she had to say something. "Scott, I—"

"Evie, I—"

Both stopped, both looked, both had something to say. "You go," she said quickly.

He nodded and placed his elbows on the table. "Okay. Something is happening here."

She caught her breath. "It is?"

"You know it. Downstairs…and earlier today…it was there again."

Denial burned on the edge of her tongue. But instead she nodded. She wanted the truth out there. Truth always worked.

"So, what should we do about it?"

Evie's cheeks burned. "Do? Nothing. It's just…"

"Attraction," he finished for her. "Yeah…and it's powerful, Evie."

He *was* attracted to her? Evie could barely contain the emotions and feelings running riot through her entire body. She'd suspected it. She'd certainly felt it herself. But to suddenly know this gorgeous man felt it, too, made her head spin.

She drew in a breath. "We have to keep it in perspective," she said evenly. "I mean, you're only here for three weeks. And you're Callie's brother. And I'm hardly your type."

That made him smile. "You know my type?"

"I imagine someone your own age would suit."

"You're an ageist?"

"I'm a realist," she replied, feeling hot all over because she was sure he was laughing at her. "I'm… And you're… It's a crazy idea."

"Probably," he said quietly. "But sometimes crazy ideas are the most fun."

Evie skinned burned. "I'm not looking for fun."

His eyes widened. "What are you looking for?"

"Nothing," she said flatly. "I have everything I need."

"Then you're one of the lucky few."

"What does that mean?" she asked quickly.

"It means that most of us are looking for something— friendship, success, love, sex."

Evie swallowed hard. "And you're looking for sex?" she replied, and couldn't believe the words were coming out of her mouth.

"As much as the next guy, I suppose."

It was a fairly relaxed response—when Evie knew there was nothing relaxed about what was happening between them. A fire was building and they were both fanning the flames.

He wants me? My God, I've forgotten how it feels to be wanted.

For a second she thought about Gordon. About wanting him. About how good it had felt. And then her thoughts shifted again to Scott and suddenly she didn't want to think, or make comparisons or imagine for even a moment that what she'd had with her husband could ever be replaced.

"I'm not interested in…" She colored, felt the heat rise up her neck. "I'm not in a position to pursue something that's… What I'm trying to say is that I'm not interested in casual sex."

Scott linked his hands together and looked at her with such burning intensity Evie couldn't drag her gaze away. "Believe me, Evie, if I made love to you, there would be nothing casual about it."

I'm dreaming this…that's the only explanation. "But we—"

"But we won't," he said decisively. "Yeah, I get that." He stared directly into her eyes. "I'm not entirely clueless, Evie. I have figured out what kind of woman you are, even if my sister hadn't pointed out your virtues."

"Callie said something to you about me?" she asked, mortified, and not quite believing they were having this conversation. Her virtues? How dull and unexciting did that make her sound? "What did she say?"

"Word for word?" he asked, smiling. "That you were likable and generous."

Definitely dull and unexciting. "Damned with faint praise," she said, and cradled her mug.

"Not accurate, then?"

Evie laughed. "Oh, I'd say it's accurate. But it makes me sound old and boring."

Scott unlinked his hands and leaned back in his chair. "How old are you?" he asked quietly. "Thirty-five? Thirty-six?"

"Six."

"Which hardly qualifies you for a walker."

She liked how his words made her feel—liked the slight grin on his face, which teased the edges of his dimple. "I suppose not. But, you know, despite what your sister said about me, I'm not always as nice as people make out."

"Must be hard living up to the expectations of others."

Evie looked at him, tilted her head and smiled. "I guess you'd know a bit about that yourself?"

"I would?"

She shrugged and then narrowed her gaze, trying to focus her thoughts into words. "You're expected to race into burning buildings, climb up trees to rescue kittens and risk your life for people you don't know simply because of the profession you chose. Sounds like you've got the tougher gig."

"It's just a job," he said flatly.

"And you love it?" she asked.

"I couldn't imagine doing anything else."

"Because you're addicted to the risks?"

He looked at her a little warily. "Because I took an oath to preserve life and property."

"Someone else's life," she said automatically. "Someone else's property."

"You disapprove?" he shot back, sharper, as if she'd hit a button inside him.

Evie took a moment. She took a few steps forward and pulled out a chair. As she sat she considered what she was about to say. She didn't want to sound irrational—she didn't want to admit to something and give Scott a window into her fears and thoughts. She'd said too much already.

But suddenly she wanted to say it. She wanted to get it out. The words formed on the edge of her tongue, and before the sensible part of her kicked in, she spoke. "My husband was an Emergency Services volunteer. One night there was a cyclone moving off the coast and he went out to help evacuate the holiday park because the strong winds were overturning trailers and camper vans. He was killed preserving life and property. And I was left to raise our son alone."

Chapter Four

Scott heard the pain in Evie's voice, felt it through to the marrow in his bones. It rang in his ears over and over. And his career suddenly loomed like a red flag. Her husband had died serving the community and he knew without a doubt that a firefighter from California didn't have a chance of being part of her life.

Not that he wanted to get involved...he was just thinking, wondering. And as he looked at her and saw the pain in her green eyes, Scott felt compelled to tell her he was sorry for her loss, but he knew the words would be inadequate.

"You're angry?" he said, not quite sure where he was going.

She shook her head quickly, as if she knew it was what he'd ask. "It's difficult to explain. I...sometimes I feel... I feel like..."

"Like what? I'm listening," Scott assured her when her voice faded.

She met his eyes directly, and his heart knocked behind his ribs. Strange, he thought, watching her, waiting for her to speak. Everything about Evie called out to some kind of inner radar inside him. Despite her outer layer of easygoing friendliness, Scott knew, without being sure how, that she was a complex woman who felt things deeply.

She took a long breath. "I feel like I should have known something was going to happen."

There was guilt in her words. And Scott knew guilt all too well. "You couldn't possibly have foreseen the future."

"I'm not sure. Gordon and I had this connection. It was strong—unbreakable. We always knew when something wasn't right and when we needed each other."

His insides heated up. She'd obviously loved her husband deeply. The notion shouldn't mean anything to him. Strangely, it did. "But?"

She shrugged. "But that night it felt different. The cyclone had been upgraded three times in the twelve hours prior to the evacuation of the holiday park. We were taping windows and clearing the yard of potential flying objects, like garden chairs, when the call out came. He left immediately."

Scott's skin prickled. "He left you here alone?"

She shook her head. "No," she said quickly. "Noah was here. His ex-wife and eldest daughter were away at the time, so he came over to give Gordon a hand preparing for the storm. After Gordon left I went downstairs and sat by the front window, looking out into the dark, listening to the wind and rain."

"And waiting?" Scott asked, prompting her.

She nodded. "Yes. I waited for hours," she said quietly. "When he didn't come home, I knew. I knew before the police arrived. I sensed it. I felt it." Evie shook her head, as if she were shaking the words out, ridding herself of the memories. "I don't know why I'm telling you this." She sighed heavily. "I haven't talked about Gordon's accident for years."

"Maybe because you're always the listener?"

She looked surprised by his question. "How did you know that?"

"It's not hard to figure," he replied, toying with his cup, wanting to keep her talking because being around her reached a place inside him that suddenly felt a whole lot more powerful than simply physical attraction. "You run this place—it's the kind of job that makes you the one who gets to listen to the lives of everyone else. And generally people like to talk about themselves."

"That's true," she said. "Do you?"

He shrugged. "Depends on who's doing the listening."

"You've got my attention," she said quietly.

Scott looked at her. "And you've got mine."

The air between them changed again, shifting on some kind of invisible and powerful axis. He knew she felt it as much as he did.

"Which kind of brings us back to what we were talking about before," she said, smiling fractionally, though he sensed the last thing she wanted to do was smile. "I'm thinking we should just keep a lid on whatever is happening."

Sex was happening, he thought. Or at least the idea of sex. That's all it was, surely? But she didn't want it to happen. And he knew it *couldn't* happen. "Sure."

Evie took a deep breath. "Good. We both agree it's the sensible course of action."

He bit back a smile. "Very sensible."

Scott watched her, fascinated, as her skin flushed beneath his gaze. She really was remarkably sexy. There was nothing obvious about Evie Dunn. But she possessed a latent sensuality that brimmed beneath the surface and it had quickly mesmerized him.

"Do something with me tomorrow?"

She stared at him. "Do what?"

"Sailboarding," he said easily, not sure why he was suggesting it.

She shook her head. "I couldn't possibly."

"Why not? Do you already have plans?"

"I'm not exactly the adventurous type."

"It's not bungee jumping, Evie. It's a board, a sail, some wind and a bit of balance. Can you swim?" he asked.

Evie nodded. "Of course."

"Then you can probably sailboard," he said, and an idea formed in his head. "I'll teach you."

She didn't bother to conceal her surprise. "I don't think it's a good idea."

"Sure it is," he said easily, and smiled. "I'm on vacation, remember? You don't want to ruin it by refusing to help me enjoy the sights of your little town, do you?"

"No," she said after a long, cautious-looking moment. Finally she smiled back. "I guess I don't."

"If it makes you feel better, we could get Trevor to come as a chaperone?" he suggested, smiling to himself.

She frowned and he liked the way her nose wrinkled when she worked out he was teasing her. "We *hardly* need a chaperone," she said purposely, and her green eyes lit up with a kind of defiance. "Okay, I'll do it."

Scott wasn't sure what the feeling was that pitched in his chest. Relief maybe? The idea of spending time with Evie pleased him. Too much.

They said good-night, lingered over the words for a few moments before Scott left the kitchen and headed to his room. He had a restless night. The time zone difference caught up with him and he spent most of the night lying on his back in the big bed, staring at the ceiling. And he thought about Evie just a few doors away.

He'd planned to go into Bellandale the following morning and hire a car. He needed wheels—and didn't want to spend every day until the wedding hanging around the B and B like loose change.

He'd come to Crystal Point for his sister's wedding. Only he hadn't expected Evie.

Scott tossed in the bed, looked at the digital clock on the small table to his left and pumped the pillow with his fist. *I've had too much sleep...and too much coffee...and way too much Evie for one evening.*

He thumped the pillow again, dropped his head back and closed his eyes.

Why is there a motorcycle in my driveway?

And not the basic model, either. This was huge and powerful and clearly designed for cruising. Evie grabbed the pair of planet-friendly shopping bags from the passenger seat of her Honda and stared at the big, noisy-looking machine parked in front of her studio. She figured out who the culprit was once she went upstairs and spotted two helmets on the kitchen table and a leather jacket hanging on the back of a chair.

She didn't have to wait long for Scott to emerge. He stood in the doorway, one shoulder resting against the frame. He wore a pale yellow T-shirt and long navy shorts—the kind made from some filmy sort of quick-dry fabric that was designed for swimming. He had trainers on his feet and sunglasses and a hat in his hand.

"Will it take you long to get ready?" he asked lazily.

Evie dropped the bags on the bench top. "Not at all. Nice bike," she said. "Yours?"

He smiled and nodded. "Just for the next three weeks.

I made a call and we can hire a board from the surf club," he said, and looked her over. "You should get changed."

She placed the perishables in the refrigerator and excused herself. In her bedroom she sat on the edge of the bed and wondered what kind of madness had taken hold of her usual good sense.

Sailboarding with Scott... She was off her trolley. She'd spent the night tossing in her bed, wondering why she'd opened up and talked to him with such intimacy. Evie never talked about herself. She never let anyone in. Oh, she made all the right noises—that was her way—but the deeper stuff, the stuff that really mattered, she kept all that guarded close to her chest. But with Scott she'd let loose about her feelings. About Gordon. About...herself.

Evie got up and shook herself and then chose shorts and a top to cover a sensible one-piece bathing suit she'd pulled from her dresser. She changed her clothes, tied her hair back into a ponytail, slapped on some sunscreen and grabbed her sun visor.

When she returned to the kitchen he was gone. Then she heard the unmistakable roar of a Harley-Davidson. She grabbed a couple of beach towels from the hall cupboard and headed outside. Evie followed the sound of the engine, saw Scott perched against the side of the motorcycle and stopped dead in her tracks.

"No way," she said, crossing her arms.

He held out a helmet. "It's only down the road. You'll be perfectly safe."

Evie looked at Scott, then the motorcycle. "I'm still not—"

"Come on," he urged as he took the towels and placed them in the storage compartment at the rear of the bike. "I won't let anything happen to you."

The way he said the words, Evie would probably have

scaled a mountain without a rope with Scott Jones beside her. She stood still while he placed the helmet on her head. It was her first time on a motorcycle, and even though the trip was brief, Evie felt the exhilaration down to her feet. She hung on to his waist, feeling the hard muscles beneath her fingers with only a thin layer of soft cotton between her hands and his stomach. She itched to stroke her fingers back and forth to *really* feel him. But she didn't because Sensible Evie Dunn didn't do that kind of thing.

When they arrived at the surf club, Scott parked the Harley and held her hand while she swung herself off.

"It's a good day for it," he said quietly. "Let's hope the wind keeps up."

He didn't release her hand and Evie didn't move, either. She looked at their hands, felt the heat between them and knew she was crazy. "Scott, I've changed my—"

"Let's go," he said, and tugged her to follow as he began walking along the pathway that led inside.

The surf club, situated at the fringe of the tourist park, was in the middle of a much-needed overhaul. Scaffolding covered the front of the building, and most of the ground level had been gutted of fittings to make way for the renovations. But there was still a small office inside the front door. A volunteer lifeguard manned the desk and within ten minutes they had the sailboard and safety vests and were heading for the beach.

The river mouth was one of Evie's favorite places. The inlet was one of the most pristine waterways in the state, and the local residents association, along with the rest of the tightly knit community, ensured that it stayed that way with regular patrols and rubbish collection. Jays Island was two hundred meters from the beach and had once been a part of the mainland. Through erosion and sand trenching to allow sugarcane ferries to pass, the island was now home to nesting herons and returning sea turtles.

"This is a great spot," he said as he placed the sailboard on the sand and flipped off his shoes. Evie did the same and her eyes almost popped out of their sockets when he pulled his T-shirt over his head and dropped it at his feet.

He had a magnificent chest and was so well cut she couldn't pull her gaze away. His smooth, bronzed skin stretched over hard, defined muscles. Flawless pecs, biceps, abs...he had it all. And she kept looking, absorbed by the beauty of him and the sheer magnitude of such physical perfection. Her fingertips tingled, as if they knew, somehow, that she wanted to reach out and touch him, to explore the contours of his smooth chest and then trace lower, down his superbly flat abdomen and lower still, to where his...

"Evie?"

His voice felt like a bucket of cold water. She knew her cheeks scorched. He smiled and she wanted the ground to open up and suck her in. "I'm...ready," she said unsteadily.

"You'll be more comfortable out of those clothes," he said, and grabbed a safety vest. "And you'll need to put this on," he said, and placed the vest beside her feet.

Evie shook her head. "I don't think—"

"Trust me," he said, so easily, so quietly, Evie's resistance faded. She grabbed the hem of her shirt and slowly pulled it over her shoulders. Scott began maneuvering the sail and didn't watch her very unseductive striptease. Evie felt a mixture of relief and mortification. She'd watched *him* as if she'd been starved of the sight of a man's body, but he showed absolutely no interest in watching *her* remove her T-shirt. Her self-esteem spiked, dwindled and then crashed to her feet as her fingers hovered on the waistband of her shorts.

Flaws. She wasn't twenty-five anymore. She had thighs she worked hard to keep toned but hadn't quite managed to maintain, and a behind she knew was fuller than what was considered fashionable. She had the body of a thirty-six-year-old woman—a woman who'd borne a child, a woman who looked and felt every year of her age as she considered the gorgeous young man beside her.

"Ready?" he asked, still not looking at her.

Why did I ever agree to this? Sand, crystal-clear water, swimsuits…she was asking for trouble. "Yes, sure." She tossed her flip-flops aside, stripped off her shorts as mechanically as she could and quickly pushed her arms into the safety vest.

"And you said you could swim?"

Her hands stilled on the task of clipping the vest and she nodded. "Reasonably."

"Good," he replied, still not looking at her. "Let's go."

Humiliation morphed into a slowly rising indignation. Okay, so her body wouldn't win prizes on the catwalk—but it wasn't totally unsightly, either.

Look at me. The words burned on the edge of her tongue. *Look at me, or I'll…*

He turned, stopped his task and straightened. And he *did* look at her. The same kind of look he'd given her in the living room the day before—long, leisurely and with the purpose of admiring. For a crazy second Evie forgot her flaws. Her perfectly respectable one-piece swimsuit suddenly felt like the most seductive piece of fabric on the planet.

Something whirled between them. Her skin prickled with awareness, her breasts felt heavy and sensitive and they pushed against the safety vest. It was as if her body had suddenly taken on a life of its own, betraying her, laughing at her.

"Come on," he said quietly, tipping his attention back to the board and forcing Evie to pull her thoughts away from having a deep lip-lock with the gorgeous man in front of her. "We don't want to waste this wind."

Evie followed him to the water's edge. And he was right—it was a good day for it. The wind was up, but the water was enticingly warm. There were a few people on the beach, some swimming, a young couple playing fetch with their dog and a stick and a trio of teenagers burying each other in the sand.

Scott explained the board and sail and how to position her feet, and Evie was agonizingly aware of his close proximity. But he was a good teacher. He was patient and considerate and didn't push her to do anything she didn't want to do. Her first attempts were disastrous, dumping them both in the water every time. But after a while she managed to maintain some balance and work the sail. She felt him behind her, felt his arms touch hers every time she maneuvered the sail to catch the breeze, and felt his chest against her back as he supported them on the narrow board.

He's really something else, she thought vaguely. The little voice in her head—the one which had been taunting her for the past two days, continued its assault. She wobbled and lost balance. Scott quickly tightened his hold and straightened the sail.

"Concentrate," he said against her ear, and Evie felt the warmth of his breath against her skin. She shivered right down her toes, despite the hot sun beating down on them. "And relax."

"I'm trying," she said, way too breathlessly, and knew she would never relax while he held her.

His body was suddenly closer, his hold firmer, more intimate, and Evie leaned into the support of his broad chest. Scott's arms cradled her like a safety net, and his hands half covered hers on the boom as the board skimmed across the water. She could feel his thighs against her bottom, and a sharp pleasure arrowed deep down in her belly. Her long-ignored libido did a wild leap, heating her blood.

And then, as he held her, it somehow became more than lust, more than an unexpected physical awakening. *Something else was happening.* Her heart pumped wildly and she experienced a kind of silly giddiness.

She leaned back farther, felt his chin against her hair and the tension suddenly coiling through his body. *Now who needs to relax?* She almost said the words. But the wind blew up and Evie pushed her concentration back to her task.

Half an hour later he steered the board toward the shore and they stepped off.

"Incredible," Evie said, and took a few much-needed breaths as Scott pulled the sailboard onto the sand. "I can't believe how much fun that was."

"Now who sounds like an adrenaline junkie?" he said, and grabbed a towel.

Evie smiled and rubbed her skin dry. "Who would have imagined it?"

He looked at her. "I think a person could spend a lifetime getting to know you, Evie, and still be surprised."

Her belly rolled. *Oh...I'm in so much trouble here.*

She did her best to ignore the ever-growing awareness and minutes later they had their clothes back on and were headed for the surf club to return the gear. When they got back to the clubhouse, there was a police car parked outside.

"Trouble?" Scott asked.

Evie shrugged, and then changed to a shake of her head when she spotted Cameron Jakowski, dressed in his regulation blue police uniform, walking across the threshold of the automatic doors.

"Hey, Evie," he greeted, juggling a few tins of paint, some brushes and a roller.

He was charming, handsome, Noah's best friend and she'd known him all her life. "What are you doing here?" she asked, stopping in front of the building.

Cameron motioned to the equipment in his hands. "We've had some graffiti problems at the community hall," he explained. "A few of the kids from the Big Brother program are giving me a hand with a quick-cover paint job." He smiled. "I ran out of paint and paintbrushes."

"Did you catch the culprits?" she asked.

"Not yet," he said, and looked at her companion inquiringly.

Evie didn't miss the look. With the sailboard between them, towels flung over their shoulders and sand-encrusted feet, she was certain Cameron's curiosity was in overdrive. She quickly made introductions and they talked for a short while about the upcoming wedding until Cameron said he had to get back to the trio of teenage boys he mentored.

"You know," he said to Scott as he opened the car door, "if you've got some free time while you're here I'm sure the boys would like to hear something about your job. We meet every Wednesday night at the community hall around seven. Guests speakers are always welcome." He dumped the equipment into the passenger seat of his police vehicle. "Evie will show you where." He looked at Evie and winked. "Let me know."

Once he'd left and they'd returned their gear, she followed Scott back to the motorcycle and waited while he tucked the towels beneath the seat. He hesitated passing her the helmet.

He looked at her oddly. "Old boyfriend?"

Evie frowned. "Cameron? God, no," she replied. "He goes through women like they're...well, let's just say he has a short attention span and leave it at that."

"And you'd like someone with a long attention span?" he asked. "Is that it?"

Evie's skin warmed and she tugged the helmet from his hands. "As much as the next woman," she said. "I'd like to think I could at least *hold* his attention for longer than one night."

Scott's heart thundered in his chest. Because Evie Dunn *had* his attention. Every last bit of it. He got on the bike and didn't move a muscle when she slid behind him and rested her hands on his waist. But he felt the heat of her touch as if she were branding him with her fingertips.

Scott sucked in a breath and started the Harley. The sooner he took her home, the better. And there would be no more sailboarding. No more skin-to-skin contact. No more having to try to keep his hands to himself. And definitely no more of that damned sexy swimsuit that revealed just enough of her to turn him inside out.

When they got back to the house, Scott heard her faintly thank him for the lesson. She took off quickly and he was glad for it. He remained outside for a while, thinking. Thinking that a hotel would be a good idea. At least it would take him away from the temptation that was Evie Dunn.

He walked around the garden, determined to get his body in check. He couldn't remember the last time he'd felt like this...maybe never. It sure as hell had snuck up on him from out of nowhere. He was lusting after something...*someone*...he couldn't have. And it was damned inconvenient.

Scott walked around the garden some more, inspecting things with more than his usual detail. Okay, so gardens weren't his thing. Evie obviously liked it, though—he could tell that by the extraordinary array of greenery and foliage and flowering plants that curved around pathways and climbed over small rock walls. There was a small wishing well in the center of the garden. An old timber plaque leaned against the edge, inviting those inclined to drop in a coin and make a wish.

"It all goes to charity."

Scott swiveled on his heel. Evie had come up behind him with the stealth of a cat. She'd changed her clothes, too. The skirt was long but somehow sexy the way it moved across her legs as she stepped closer. And her hair was loose and hung like a crown around her head, highlighting the amazing color of her eyes and perfectly shaped mouth. He couldn't drag his gaze away from her, couldn't seem to make himself look elsewhere.

"Sorry?" he heard himself say, and wondered why she'd followed him into the garden.

She pointed to the well. "The money from the wishes," she explained. "I scoop it out once a year and donate it to a charity."

"It's not making you rich, then?"

She smiled. "Hardly. People don't seem to believe in wishes all that much anymore."

Scott crossed his arms. "Do you?" he asked, feeling hot and tense all of a sudden, and knowing it was because he couldn't stop thinking about Evie's incredibly kissable mouth.

"Do I believe in wishes?" She took another step toward the well and peered into it. "I'm not sure. I guess that would be like saying I believe in magic." She stepped back. "I haven't thought about magic for a long time."

"And did you have magic with your husband?" Scott had no idea where the question came from, or why he was asking it. It was intensely personal—and way out of line. And he was even more astounded when she responded.

"A kind of magic, I suppose." She pushed a stray pebble back between the cracks in the stone pavers with her sandal. "Loving someone can feel like that—like you can do anything, achieve anything." She stopped, looked at him and gave a wry smile. "I'm not normally so sentimental."

Neither was he. But being around Evie pushed his buttons—all kinds of buttons. And some of them seemed to border on sentimental. Romantic, even. He looked at her, felt the vibrations coming off her pierce through him. Whatever he was feeling, he was pretty sure she was feeling it, too.

Somehow, she was suddenly in front of him. She looked as though she wanted to say something but stopped. Then her gaze lifted up to meet his. It was all he needed. His arms moved around her and after a flash of resistance, her palms rested against his chest.

And because he knew that at that moment there was nothing else for either of them, Scott took a breath and then kissed her amazing mouth.

Chapter Five

At some point a voice of reason was going to interrupt and tell Evie to stop kissing Scott Jones. Or get him to stop kissing her. Either way, she knew it had to end. Kisses like this weren't real. They were the stuff of fairy tales and silly movies. The kind of kisses her friend Fiona swooned over and insisted were so worth waiting for.

Okay—so being kissed by Scott *was* worth waiting for. In fact, as his mouth slanted over her own to deepen the contact, the thrill of it jolted every inch of skin covering her bones. The man certainly knew how to kiss.

But it really has to stop…

Only…when his hands moved across her hips and drew her against him, Evie lost all coherent thought. She felt his breath, his lips, his tongue, and she returned the kiss, wary at first, giving a little, taking more and really *feeling* for the first time since…forever. *No woman could resist this,* a faraway voice taunted. *No flesh-and-blood woman would want to.*

And Evie was quickly discovering she was very much a flesh-and-blood woman—and that she liked kissing Scott. She liked it so much her skin was searing and her blood felt molten hot in her veins. *Desire*...the little voice sang out again. That's what this was. *Lust. Hunger. Sex.*

Sex without love? Could she do that? Making love when love had nothing to do with it? Evie knew she simply wasn't built that way. No matter how divine his mouth felt.

He must have sensed her growing reticence because he ended the kiss and gently released her. "I'm guessing you don't think this is a good idea?"

Evie's skin heated. "Do you?"

"It's just a kiss." He said the words casually.

Evie frowned. "I'm not indiscriminate," she said as she turned her head to look back at the house, wondering if the Manning sisters were peeking through the curtains. The last thing she wanted was to get caught making out with Scott. "Anyway," she said, catching her breath and trying valiantly to look in control. "The reason I came out here was to tell you that Callie called. She's expecting you tonight about six."

He nodded. "She asked me over for dinner. Would you like to come with me?"

Sensible Evie came quickly to her rescue. Thank goodness. Otherwise she might have been tempted to say yes. "I'm teaching a class tonight."

"Too bad for me, then."

Her heart skipped, then flipped, then almost got caught in her throat. "Okay—so I'll see you later." She turned and left, not quite running, but close enough to it to look like a first-rate idiot.

Evie buried herself in her studio for the following couple of hours and waited until she heard the loud rumble of the motorcycle leaving before she returned to the house. The Kellers were out for the evening and she made swift work of preparing a light supper of soup and buttered herb bread for Flora and Amelia before heading back to the studio by seven o'clock for her class.

In her studio Evie usually found a kind of peace. Only she was so distracted the peace she craved didn't come. All she had was a head full of thoughts about Scott. She'd forgotten how good kissing was and how much she'd missed it. And she'd forgotten how it felt to be held. She'd forgotten strong arms and broad shoulders. She'd forgotten everything. No, not forgotten, but shut out…left to linger along with memories of a husband she'd loved and never imagined she could replace.

Kissing Scott had felt good. Too good. But it wouldn't go anywhere. It couldn't.

He's twenty-seven. I'm thirty-six. A math genius she wasn't—but no amount of thinking could make her see their ages as anything other than an impossible divide between two people with completely different lives. *He's all wrong for me.* A firefighter. A man with a dangerous occupation had no place in her structured, orderly world.

Evie put herself to work and began cleaning paintbrushes to fill time before her class began. She had five regular students, including her youngest sister, Mary-Jayne, and their good friend Fiona Walsh. Once her students began to arrive, she managed to clear her head and concentrate on teaching the women how to texture paint on the canvas.

"So, what's with you?" Mary-Jayne asked when the class had concluded and the last of the students had left. She always lingered for coffee and a chat.

Evie shrugged and kept pushing stools in front of empty easels. "Not a thing."

"Really? You looked about as into the class tonight as I look when I go for a dental checkup."

Evie looked at her sister. Bubbly, effervescent and lovingly indulged all her life, Mary-Jayne, or M.J. as she was affectionately called by anyone who knew her, had a history of asking completely inappropriate questions and hounding for an answer with the tenacity of a terrier.

"I'm fine."

M.J.'s incredible brows rose. "Are the hormones acting up?"

A breath stuck in Evie's throat. "What does that mean?"

"Oh, just that I heard a rumor you were shacking up with a drop-dead-gorgeous fireman."

Mortified, Evie swiveled on her heel to face her sister. "I'm not shacking up at all," she said in her best big-sister voice. "You know exactly why he…" She stopped, paused, looked at her sister and faked a smile. "It's a favor for Callie," she explained. "Her place is under renovation. Noah's got Callie's mother arriving next week and our parents' house will be packed with relatives right up until Christmas and the wedding."

"So he *is* gorgeous?"

Evie ignored the thump of her heart. "Drop by tomorrow and see for yourself."

M.J. gave a chuffed laugh. "Ha—you're not fooling me with the casual act. If your face glowed any brighter you could be used as a beacon."

Evie held her ground. "Haven't you got somewhere to be?"

M.J. laughed louder and brighter. "Of course," she replied. "Actually, I do need to get going. I've had a big order through my website and need to start on the pieces," she said, referring to her jewelry design business.

After her sister left, Evie spent some time in front of an easel. Dabbling with watercolors, she relaxed a bit and tried to lose herself in the creative process for a while. But her tension returned the moment she heard the familiar rumble of Scott's motorcycle coming up the driveway. The engine cut out quickly and before she had the opportunity to move, Evie heard a rap on the door. With only a mesh screen between them, Evie knew hiding was out of the question. She took a deep breath, and invited him inside.

"Am I interrupting?" he asked when he saw she was midbrushstroke.

Evie dropped the brush and shifted off the edge of the seat. "Not at all," she said. "I'm just playing with color—nothing serious." She stood and wiped her hands down her paint-dotted jeans. "How was your evening?"

Scott placed his helmet and keys on the bench near the door and took a few strides into the room. "Good." He smiled. "Except for Callie's cooking."

Evie smiled back. Her friend and soon-to-be sister-in-law's reputation in the kitchen was well noted. "Well, thankfully Noah can flip steaks and burgers on the barbecue if the need arises."

Scott shrugged lightly. "Your brother doesn't seem to mind that she can't cook."

"No. In fact, I think he finds it endearing," she replied.

"Well, there's certainly no doubt he loves her."

Evie nodded. "Yes, no doubt. They're very happy together. And my brother is a good man," she said directly. "He'll treat her right."

Scott's gaze narrowed fractionally. "I wasn't suggesting otherwise."

Evie lifted her shoulders and then dropped them

quickly. "Sorry—habit. Sometimes I'm overprotective of my family."

"You shouldn't apologize for that." He grabbed a stool in one deft move and placed it against the wall. "Actually," he said as he sat, "*I find it endearing.*"

Evie didn't miss the hint of intimacy in his words. In fact, she knew he was being deliberately provoking. While she was trying her best to *not* think about him in that way, he didn't appear to feel the same need.

Youth and bravado.

Or just plain old male egotism running riot.

Either way, Evie knew it had to stop. Because if it didn't, she knew any moment she was going to start thinking about that scorching, toe-curling kiss again. Which simply would not do.

"I hope the bike didn't wake your guests."

She snatched a look at him, not wanting to notice the way his jeans stretched across his thighs, but noticing anyway because he was impossible to ignore. "I doubt it," she said quietly. "Trevor's staying over at Cody's, and the Manning sisters can sleep through anything." She checked her watch. "And the Kellers have gone into town for dinner and a movie."

"So we're all alone?"

More intimacy. More curled toes. More everything. Evie fought to catch her breath before it left her throat. "Like I said, Amelia and Flora are inside asleep."

"And they can sleep through anything?"

Her heart skipped. "What did you have in mind?" she asked, although she couldn't believe the words came out.

"Come for a ride with me?"

She straightened, narrowed her gaze and automatically looked at her watch. "It's ten o'clock."

"Do you have a curfew?" he asked.

Evie shook her head. "Of course not. It's just that I couldn't—"

"I promise the bike won't turn into a pumpkin after midnight," he said, smiling just enough for her to see his dimple. "And I won't turn into a frog."

"You're mixing your fairy tales," Evie said. "*Cinderella* and *The Frog Prince*—both favorites of mine—but both very different stories."

"The ending's the same, though, isn't it?"

Evie drew in a breath. "Yes."

"So come with me?" He looked at her with searing intensity. "I feel like a walk on the beach."

Evie squashed back the feeling of anticipation weaving up her back. But she willed herself not to be tempted. "Not a good idea."

He chuckled and it was such a sexy sound Evie could barely stand still in her own skin. "Evie, there's something unique about you that makes me want to get to know you better."

Evie held her breath. The man was seductive and mesmerizing. And she was in serious trouble of falling head over heels in lust. "We agreed that we wouldn't get involved."

"It's just an invitation to walk along the beach," he said easily. "Not a marriage proposal."

She twisted her fingers together, determined to do something with her ridiculously unsteady hands. *I am behaving like a first-rate fool.* But her resistance lingered. Evie knew what would happen if they were alone together on a deserted beach late at night. They might kiss again, and touch... Scott might take her in his arms and she would go willingly to wherever he led her. Perhaps they would make love on the sand.

He studied her face, absorbing every feature and making her hot all over. "Okay," he said so quietly Evie took a small step toward him. If he was going to speak she wanted to hear what he had to say. When he pushed himself off the stool, they were only a few feet apart. "Evie..."

She looked up, met his gaze and swayed forward.

"You're very talented."

Not what she was expecting. And he now looked above her head and at the many paintings hung around the room, and she hadn't expected that, either. "Thank you."

He stepped to the side and walked between the free-standing easels. "Do you sell much of your work?"

"Not really."

"Why not?" he asked, and stood in front of a trio of watercolor landscapes on one wall. "These are excellent."

Evie followed his steps. "Do you have an interest in art?"

He shrugged. "I know what I like. Although I'm no expert. You have an amazing gift."

A gift? It had been such a long time since anyone had called it that. Gordon had, a lifetime ago. He'd been her greatest supporter and in many ways her muse. He'd pushed her to work harder, to give her best every time she put brush to canvas. But his death had killed off something inside her, too. Evie hadn't stopped painting completely, although the need to showcase her work had been left behind with all the rest of her ambition. Nowadays she only painted for herself, and with the B and B, her son and the classes she taught occupying most of her time, painting for herself had become little more than an occasional whim.

"I don't get to paint as much as I used to."

He half turned and faced her. "Why not?"

Evie shrugged. "No time."

"Although you used to have time," he said quietly, and motioned to the nearly two dozen frames hanging around the room and the stack of unfinished pieces lying against the wall in a dark corner. "Judging by the look of things."

She shrugged again, feeling the bite of criticism. "Do you mean before I became a single mother and had to run this place by myself?"

He turned back to her immediately and both brows shot up. "Is that your way of telling me to mind my own business?"

Evie glared at him. "Would it make much difference?"

"I can be as sensitive as the next guy," he said easily, looking her over in that way which made her skin burn. "Try me."

She went to reply, and then stalled. Evie rarely talked about her work. Actually, she *never* talked about her work. But there was an edge of something she couldn't quite recognize skirting the mood between them, and she felt reluctant to break the link. Evie clutched her arms around her waist and wandered toward an unfinished piece on a large easel.

"I don't paint like I used to. I don't seem to have the heart for it anymore." She let out a heavy breath. "I don't think I've admitted that to anyone before."

He came beside her and looked at the picture. "You lost your drive?"

"I guess. When I was young I lived to paint. I couldn't wait to create the next piece, to see where the brush would take me. I'd spend hours in here, mixing colors, sketching and thinking up new ways to be bold and innovative. And then I stopped. After Gordon…well, I just couldn't seem to…" She paused and looked at the unfinished pieces in the corner. "I just couldn't finish anything."

"Do you still enjoy painting?"

She glanced sideways. "In here I do." She tapped her temple softly. "But in here…" Her hand came to her chest.

"I don't have the feeling in here. And that's where it really comes from. Creativity is all about heart."

"And your heart is still broken?"

Evie swayed sideways. The need to be held by his strong arms suddenly overwhelmed her. She'd never ask it. Never show it. But it pierced through her with razor-sharp precision. "My heart is full," she said quietly. "With my son, my family, this place I've been blessed to live in. Plus, I have my students, and teaching gives me great satisfaction."

He looked at her, meeting her gaze head-on. "There's a 'but' in there, Evie. And there's no shame in that. If you love to paint, then that's exactly what you should do. You owe it to yourself to try and find your heart again."

She felt the sting in his words, although she was certain he hadn't meant it that way. She knew she was being overly sensitive, but she bit back anyway. "I wouldn't expect someone like you to understand."

"Why not?" he shot back quickly. "Because you think I'm just a grunt who runs into burning buildings for a living?"

He was stung by her comment, and part of her couldn't blame him. Her words *had* sounded condescending and she wondered why she'd said them. Normally she was rational and sensible. But she was mad at him for making her explain her thoughts and feelings about her painting. It wasn't open for discussion. Not ever.

"I don't want to talk about it," she said, and pushed herself to move away from him. She grabbed a bundle of paintbrushes, took them to the sink and dropped them into a plastic container. "I don't talk about *me*," she admitted, still by the sink and without the courage to turn around and face him. "Not to anyone."

"Then I guess we're a lot alike."

She snapped her neck around and managed a tiny smile.

Were they alike? Was that why she sensed an invisible thread of connection between them? And why it felt like way more than physical attraction? She felt something, a kind of link with Scott, but it was hazy, like drifting through fog while listening to the sound of someone's voice.

"Do you ever envy those people who can express every emotion and feeling they have whenever they're having it?" she asked. "Sometimes I do. My sister M.J. says whatever she wants regardless of the consequences—and she gets away with it. While my other sister, Grace, is about as uptight and closed off as you can get."

"And you?"

She shrugged, turned around and rested against the bench top. "I'm somewhere in the middle. Reliable and predictable, following rules, making sure everyone else is taken care of."

"There's nothing wrong with following rules, Evie. Or being reliable," he said, and crossed his arms. "You don't have to be reckless to lead a fulfilling life."

Evie stared at him. It seemed a strange thing for him to say. He was a firefighter. He lived his life on the very edge of danger. What would he know about following the rules? Unless she'd completely misjudged him.

"You sound as if you're talking from experience."

He lifted his shoulders and dropped them with a heavy breath. "I just know that sometimes being reckless hurts people. Risking everything can be disastrous. Often someone else is left to pick up the pieces, and that's not a great legacy for anyone to leave behind."

He was right. And it was exactly why she always lived her life in a sensible, orderly fashion. Sure, there were no risks, but there was also no chance of hurting the people she loved. Strange, but she'd imagined Scott as a risk taker.

"I didn't think you'd be so...so..."

"So what?" he asked.

"So sensible," she replied. "Your job, your age, I thought you'd be—"

"I'm twenty-seven," he said, cutting her off. "Not seventeen. In fact, I'll be twenty-eight in a couple of months. As for my job, sure, it can be dangerous—but so can working on a high-rise or driving a truck. I haven't any illusions and I don't take the potential dangers of my job lightly. And I certainly wouldn't expect anyone..." He stopped, looked at her and twisted his mouth for a moment. "I wouldn't expect anyone...*any woman* to wait around for that late-night call saying I'd been injured, or worse."

Her chest tightened. She knew that call. She'd experienced it firsthand. "Is that why your last relationship didn't work out?"

"We worked together, lived together—I couldn't treat her like the rest of the crew. I wanted to keep her safe. She put up with twelve months of what she called my outdated macho crap and left."

Evie had always secretly liked that outdated macho crap. "And you won't get seriously involved with anyone while you're a firefighter?"

He shrugged. "No."

Part of her was acutely disappointed—the other was impressed by his integrity and she admired his principles. A niggling thought suddenly attached itself to the back corner of her mind. *If only Gordon had thought like that. I wouldn't be a widow—my son would still have his father.*

"You might fall in love?"

His blue eyes seared into hers. "I might."

"And if you do?"

He shrugged again. "No point worrying about something that hasn't happened."

Evie read between the lines. So there was no middle road. He was a man with strong convictions, and her admiration spiked. She was like that, too. She'd made a commitment to raise her son and be the best mother she could be after Gordon had died. All her energy, all her love had gone into her parenting. The good daughter, the good mother, the good widow.

And now Scott had walked into her life and she felt like abandoning every single of one of her principles and allowing herself to get swept up in his arms. Evie had never experienced anything quite like it before. Certainly she'd had desire for Gordon and enjoyed making love with him. But this feeling…this low-down-in-her-belly kind of slowly building craving was suddenly all she could think about. All she could want.

"I have to go," she said. So quietly she wasn't sure he heard her.

But he had. He grasped her arm as she made a move to leave. "Don't run away."

Evie's breath caught in her throat. "I have to," she whispered.

"You act like I'm some sort of threat to you," he said, and rubbed the underside of her arm with his fingers. "I'm not. At least, not intentionally."

"That's not it. I'm a threat to myself," she admitted, hypnotized by his gentle caress. "I'm feeling so… I'm not sure what exactly. But I know I shouldn't be feeling whatever it is. Maybe that doesn't make sense—I don't know. I only know that you'll be gone in three weeks and I'll still be here. And I have to make sure I'll be here with myself and with my life intact."

His touch continued to hold her captive. "I have no intention of taking advantage of you, Evie," he said softly, his voice as seductive as the soft stroke of his fingertips.

"And if you feel like you've been suddenly hit by a freight train—well, frankly, so do I."

She looked up. He wanted to kiss her…and Evie wanted it, too. She willed herself not to feel such a longing, to look at him and not see a man she desired more than she'd imagined possible. But her body was in control. Her body was calling all the shots.

Her breasts felt heavy, as if they knew she wanted him. Still, he only touched her arm, gently rubbing the soft skin. But it was enough. Her nipples peaked, tightening so much she knew they were clearly visible through the thin cotton of her T-shirt and lace-cup bra. Her belly dipped and rolled on a wave of desire so strong she wondered if her legs might give way.

"I can't…I want to…but I can't," she whispered. "I'm an ordinary woman and I lead an ordinary life… Don't ask me to be something other than who and what I am."

Scott's fingers stilled. "I wouldn't. I won't. I get you, Evie," he said as he released her. "I get the way you live your life—I get that you had to do whatever it took to work your way through losing your husband. I understand why you always do the right thing, the sensible thing. And because you're right—I am only here for three weeks and the two of us getting involved would not be sensible. It might be incredible…it might be mind-blowing. But it wouldn't be *sensible*."

He stepped back and put space between them. Then he stepped away and grabbed his helmet and keys. When he reached the door he stopped and half turned. "And, Evie— there's *nothing* ordinary about you," Scott said quietly.

Once he'd gone through the door, Evie's shaky legs found a chair and she slumped back with a heavy breath. Scott Jones was one heck of a nice guy. *And I'm falling for him hook, line and sinker.*

Chapter Six

On Saturday morning Evie headed into town and shopped at her favorite organic grocery store. When she got home Scott's motorcycle was notably absent and she experienced a mix of emotions. He'd gone for an early run that morning and they'd barely crossed paths over breakfast. She attended to her guests during lunch and, after catching up on a few domestic chores, spent the afternoon in her studio.

By the time she'd showered and changed her clothes, it was nearly five o'clock. She heard Scott's motorcycle return and then the sound of feet on the stairwell followed by a couple of doors opening and closing and the distinct hiss of the shower in the guest bathroom.

She walked into the kitchenette and saw her son. "Are you getting ready soon?"

He half frowned from his spot near the sink. "I wish I could stay home."

"No chance. Your grandparents are expecting you."

Trevor's lanky shoulders popped up and down. "It was just a thought."

"And I *thought* you liked your grandparents?" she suggested quietly, smiling.

He grinned. "You know I do. But there are basketball tryouts coming up before the school terms out and I figured I should practice if I want to make the team for next year."

A team? And sports? She planted her hands on her hips. "Okay…where's my son and what have you done with him?"

Trevor laughed. "It's still me. I just thought I might try out, that's all… You know, get outdoors for a while."

Her smart, computer geek son certainly surprised her. "I think…I think it's a great plan."

He shrugged, looking embarrassed all of a sudden. "Yeah, well, it was just an idea. I probably won't make the cut. You know I suck at sports. But Scott said he'd help."

Scott…

Of course. Her fatherless son would think Scott Jones hung the moon.

She ached inside thinking about it. "You're a shoe-in, I'm sure. Now go and get dressed. You've got fifteen minutes."

He dragged his feet as he left, and Scott came into the room a couple of minutes later. Evie pretended to busy herself by mopping up a nonexistent spill on the draining board. The air between them was thick. Stupid, she thought, to have tension when there were no words said and barely any eye contact. Evie slanted a look in his direction while she folded a tea towel. He looked so good in dark olive chinos and pressed white shirt. Too good. Everything about him oozed sex—the way he moved, the way he spoke, the way his hair flicked across his forehead.

"What time are we expected?" he asked.

She collected her thoughts. "Around six," she replied. They were going to her parents' house for a barbecue and Evie liked that he'd dressed up a bit. He looked older somehow. And then she felt absurd for daring to admit such a thing mattered to her. *I shouldn't be thinking that.* They weren't dating, they weren't anything really. Barely acquaintances who would soon be related only because of a marriage between their siblings. *One incredible kiss doesn't make a relationship.*

"Trevor was telling me how you're helping him to get on the basketball team."

He glanced at her and shrugged. "Just giving him a few tips."

"You were a jock in high school, right?" she asked directly. "And good at everything?"

Scott looked at her oddly. She wished she knew him better. Wished she could figure out what he was thinking behind those glittering blue eyes.

When he didn't respond she continued. "It's just that Trevor isn't usually a...sporty sort of teenager. He's more at home with his video games or computer. But I understand why he'd want to spend time with you."

He didn't move. "You do?"

"Sure. I mean...he doesn't get a lot of adult male company. Other than Noah and my dad. And you're so...so..."

"So?"

She ignored his question. Ignored the way her heart pounded like a jackhammer. And she stuck to her point. "I don't expect you to entertain my son while you're here, that's all."

He swayed fractionally on his heels, and a semismile tucked at the corner of his mouth. "He's a good kid."

"I know that."

"So I don't mind helping him out."

What if I don't want my son getting attached to you?

Thankfully Trevor loped through the doorway and announced he was ready to go. Her son wore the clothes she'd put out on his bed and had managed to tame his unruly hair with what looked like a bucket of hair gel. Evie grabbed her tote, ran her hands down the front of her pale green dress and grabbed the car keys from the table.

Once they were outside she held out the keys toward Scott. "Why don't you drive? I'll sit in the back," she explained. "You've both got longer legs than me." She pointed to her son's lanky pins but refused to ogle Scott. "So let's go. I'll give directions."

The drive to her parents' sprawling double-story home took only minutes. Scott was out before her and quickly opened the back door. He took her hand to steady her as she got out, and Evie felt the electricity coursing between them as their fingers connected. She caught her breath as a rush of blood raced across her skin. He saw it though, and even if he hadn't Evie was certain he could have felt the heat from it. And he didn't release her, at least not straightaway. And Evie didn't pull away, either. She remembered the vow she'd made to keep him at a distance, to not get involved, and all her resolutions disappeared. He was simply holding her hand, and all Evie could think about was how much she didn't want him to let her go. Not ever.

Trevor said something and Scott dropped his hand and closed the passenger door while Evie made a quick escape around to the other side of the car. She made it into the house in record time and didn't wait for either Scott or her son, figuring they could find their own way to the back patio. For now, Evie simply wanted to get away.

Her mother, Barbara, was in the kitchen and she headed straight for her and hung on to a hug a little longer than normal. She apologized for not helping with the cooking, and her mother quickly brushed off her concerns and told her that Grace, who'd arrived from New York a few days earlier, had helped her prepare the food for the thirty or so guests expected to arrive within the next half hour. Evie immediately began decorating a cheesecake.

"Have you spoken to your sister recently?" her mother asked, passing Evie an apron.

"Not since the day she arrived home. Why?"

Barbara shrugged. "She doesn't seem herself."

She's not the only one. "I'll talk to her," she assured her mother, and got the chance about five minutes later when her sister entered the room.

It was hard not to notice when Grace Preston entered a room—because she was simply stunning. Beautiful in a classic, old movie star kind of way. Beside her, Evie spent most of her time feeling about as plain as an old shoe. In designer jeans, three-inch heels Evie knew would have cost the earth and a red blouse that looked as though it wouldn't dare crease because Grace simply wouldn't allow it, her sister was a picture of elegance. No one pulled off wearing jeans like Grace. Four years younger than Evie, she worked for a large brokerage house in New York and had arrived in Crystal Point a few days earlier. She was successful, well educated and to those who didn't know her, about as warm as an Arctic winter. But Evie knew her and loved her and had always been able to get past her sister's cool reserve.

"This is the first time you've been home for Christmas in a while," Evie said once their mother had left the kitchen.

"I promised Noah I'd be here for the wedding. And the office closes down over Christmas," Grace explained.

Evie nodded. "Will you be back for Dad's party?" she

asked, thinking about their father's sixty-fifth birthday coming up in a few months.

"I'll do my best," Grace replied.

Evie began her task of piping cream onto the cheesecake. "Is anything wrong, Gracie?"

Grace looked at her. "Not at all."

"Work's okay?"

She shrugged again, but Evie wasn't fooled. "The same."

"And Erik?" she asked of her sister's lawyer boyfriend.

"Gone," Grace replied. "Months ago."

Typical that her sister hadn't mentioned it. "Bad breakup?"

"Not especially. What about you?" Grace asked, raising both her immaculate brows. "Are *you* okay?"

Evie stopped her task. "Of course. You know me," she said with a small laugh. She put down the piping bag. "Why do you ask?"

"M.J. mentioned something," Grace replied. "About Callie's b—"

"Not you, too," Evie groaned, cutting off her sister's words. "It's nothing. There's nothing going on. Nothing at all. Absolutely nothing."

"So it's *nothing?*" Grace asked with a wry smile. "Despite his obvious attributes?"

Evie colored hotly. "You met him, then?"

Grace nodded. "Noah introduced me. He seems…nice."

Evie managed a smile. Her sister didn't hand out compliments often. "My son thinks so, too."

It sounded snippy and sour put like that and she was instantly ashamed of herself.

Grace didn't let up, either. "But you don't?"

Evie made a face. "Well, of course I think he's…" She stopped and her voice trailed off. She quickly took a breath and tried again. "Okay, he's...*fine,* obviously," she admitted. "And that's all I'm going to say about it."

"Who's fine?"

They both turned their heads at the sound of Callie's voice. Her husky lilt echoed across the tiled floor, and Evie wished that same floor would open up and swallow her whole. "Um—no one. So, how's the party going out there?"

Callie made a face as she moved into the kitchen. "A few of the men have gone to the games room for a game of pool," she said, and rolled her eyes. "And you know how competitive Noah and Cameron are—they turn it into a blood sport. Although I told Scott to go easy on them because they're poor losers."

Evie's interest spiked. "He plays well?"

"My brother is one of those infuriating people who are good at everything."

Evie's insides crunched. Hadn't she said that to Scott only an hour earlier when they'd been discussing Trevor? She stole a look at Grace, and her sister raised a questioning brow before Evie turned back to decorating the cheesecake. Grace left the room a few moments later, pleading the need to observe their brother and Cameron get beaten at pool, and Evie watched Callie attempt to fill a piping bag with cream. She took pity on her and took over the task.

"Thanks," Callie said quietly and stepped back, resting her hips against the countertop. "Evie, can I ask you something?"

"Sure," she replied. "Shoot."

"Are you okay with having my brother at your house?"

Evie stilled, felt her breath get lost in her throat and tried desperately not to show it. "Of course. Why?"

"He said something about maybe moving into a hotel while he's here."

Evie's knees risked failure and she pushed herself

against the bench to stay upright. "Oh, really?" She tried to make her voice as light as possible, tried to make out as if Callie's announcement hadn't shaken her up. "I can't think why. Perhaps Crystal Point is a little tame for him." The words came out, but she wasn't sure from where.

Callie smiled. "I don't think Scott's looking for any kind of excitement while he's here. In fact, Crystal Point is probably exactly what he needs at the moment. Mike's death hit him pretty hard and after the inquest he probably should have taken some time out. But typically Scott, he went back to work straightaway."

Evie registered the other woman's words. "Mike?" was all she could get out of her mouth.

"They were friends," Callie explained. "And they worked together. I thought Scott might have told you." She pushed herself off the bench and crossed her arms. "You're easy to talk to, Evie—I'd hoped he might have opened up a bit."

Yes, usually she was easy to talk to. "Well, it's only been a few days," she said. "And we haven't spent a lot of time together." *Liar.* "Some people aren't comfortable talking with strangers."

Callie touched her arm. "You're not a stranger, Evie. You're the warmest, most genuine woman I've ever met."

"Thanks," she said, and tried to steer her thoughts away from Scott, and failed miserably. "Perhaps he's not ready to talk about it?'

Callie nodded. "Perhaps. You know, the other day, I thought…well, I thought that you and he looked kind of *close.*" Her friend sighed. "I know it's silly of me. And I don't know why I thought I had any business thinking about it. I just did."

"Well, he's your brother," Evie said gently, not daring

to disclose anything. "And we all get a little protective of our brothers at times."

"Like you did," Callie reminded her. "When you asked me how I felt about Noah."

"That seems like forever ago now." She grabbed Callie's hand and touched the bright diamond glittering on her finger. "And look how good it turned out."

Evie stared at the ring. She'd taken her own wedding band off years ago. But she missed it. She missed the idea of truly belonging to someone, and having that someone belong to her. And she didn't quite realize how much up until days ago. Up until Scott had entered her life, her world. For years she'd been in a kind of emotional hibernation, safe from wanting anything. Safe from really *feeling* anything.

Her mother returned then and quickly ushered them both from the kitchen. Evie discarded the apron and followed Callie outside. The huge patio was filled with people, and typically her mother was the consummate hostess. Two long tables were covered with starchy white cloths and held trays of canapés and bite-size morsels of food. Evie helped herself to a glass of wine from the bar and mingled for a while.

It didn't take her long to head for the games room on the other side of the patio. The pool game was in full swing and she found a spot near the door to observe the players. Only, the moment Evie saw Scott leaning against a wall with a pool cue in his hand while he waited for his turn to shoot, he was all she noticed. The room was noisy, but she didn't hear any of it. It was as if the crowd parted of its own will, urging her to make eye contact with him. He looked back, tilted his head fractionally and almost smiled. Almost, because he stopped himself, she was sure of it. It gave her a strange feeling in her chest and she turned away after a few moments, grateful she was by the door for a quick escape.

Evie headed for the pool area. She could be alone there. She could think. She made her way through the gate and closed it securely behind herself. The terraced area behind the pool was usually reserved as a dance floor when her parents had parties, but thankfully it looked as though there would be no dancing tonight. She sat on one of the bench seats and placed her drink on the timber decking.

She heard the gate click and knew she had company. Without even seeing him she felt Scott's presence as if it pulsed through her. He didn't sit at first. He stood about six feet from her, cradling what looked to be an untouched beer in one hand. The underwater lights created an inviting mood.

"Did you abandon your game?" she asked, not as steadily as she would have liked.

He shrugged and sat down beside her, stretching out his long legs. "I'll let your brother and your policeman friend fight over who's the reigning alpha male in the group. I beat them twice and figured that was enough."

"Callie said you want to leave Dunn Inn?" she asked, figuring there was little point in avoiding the topic.

"I'm considering it."

Evie's belly dipped in an all-too-familiar way. He had the most mesmerizing effect on her. She breathed a soft "Why?" and waited for his reply.

Scott felt her looking at him, felt those incredible green eyes waiting for a response. "You know why."

She didn't say anything for a moment, and when she replied he thought she sounded a little breathless. "Because we're…because…"

"Because being around you makes it difficult not being with you."

He heard her breath catch in her throat. "Oh…well… even if that's the case, I'd still like you to stay. You know, to avoid any questions from the family."

Scott knew that. He'd known it even before the words left her beautiful mouth.

"Callie told me about your friend who died."

Did she, now? "Callie shouldn't have said anything to you."

"Don't be mad at her. She's concerned about you."

"I'm fine," he said, feeling the furthest thing from fine. "It was months ago."

"Why was there an inquest into his death?"

Callie *had* been busy. "Because he died on the job," Scott replied, feeling the words like they were glass in his mouth. "It's standard practice."

"Were you involved?"

It was the kind of question Scott would normally have fielded with an effective *none of your damned business.* But he couldn't say that to Evie. "I was there," he admitted. "We'd been called out to a house fire in Orange County. We knew it was gonna be bad because the smoke was thick and black. When we got there the place was well alight."

He stopped speaking and she half turned. "What happened?" she prompted.

Scott filled his lungs with air. "Mike was working an extra shift. Looking back, I knew he was tired, knew he should've gone home. But he had a family, a mortgage he was trying to stay on top of. When we found out what street the fire was on, I could see him getting agitated. He kept saying, "No way, no way." I didn't get what he meant at first and he didn't tell me. We were the second squad to get there. Mike started yelling, screaming something about getting the kids out. There were balloons tied to the mailbox and they started popping with the heat and it became pretty obvious there was a birthday party going on at the house."

A house full of kids, he thought, as memories leached through him. Actually a backyard full of kids, all screaming, and a set of parents trying to get the children to calm down and climb over the rear fence. None of which was working very well.

"Mike kept yelling, 'Where's Isabel, where's Isabel?'— his daughter," Scott explained when he saw Evie's expression. "*His* kid was at the party. And it was pretty obvious the fire would take the house—there was no saving it."

Even in the dim light Scott could see the sudden gray pallor on Evie's face. "And the children?"

"We got a vague head count from the supervising parents," he replied. "Some were in the front yard. Some had made it to the back fence and were being helped over by a neighbor."

"And Isabel?"

He shrugged, remembering the anguish on Mike's face as he searched for his daughter. "We were told a couple of the kids could be missing."

"Were they in the house?"

"We didn't know anything for sure. But Mike was certain she had to be inside and I couldn't make him think otherwise. And he said he was going in." It had been the worst possible scenario. Made even more so when he knew his friend was about to abandon all the training he'd had as a firefighter. "Mike headed inside. We knew it wasn't safe. The whole house was engulfed by this stage and two units were working on putting the flames out. And we had no proof that anyone was inside. I tried to talk him out of it, to make him realize the risk he was taking."

"He wouldn't listen?"

"No."

Evie touched his arm. "Did you go after him?"

"No."

Her grip tightened. "Did you want to?"

Scott's chest tightened. "Of course."

"But?"

He took a breath, letting it out quickly because he felt as if his lungs would explode. "But I had to ascertain the level of danger before I could allow myself or any of the crew to go into that building. So I made the call—I did my job—and I concluded that it was too dangerous. If I'd allowed anyone to go inside, another would have followed, and then another. I couldn't risk it. I wouldn't."

"So he went inside and didn't come out?"

"That's right."

"And his daughter?" she asked.

"Safe," he replied flatly. "But now without her father. She'd been safe all along in the neighbors' yard. Which is where I told Mike she would probably be."

Evie sighed. "It's impossible to reason with a distraught parent. I don't imagine anything you said would have made much difference."

"No," he agreed. "But I still…"

"Wonder if you should have done things differently?"

Could she read his mind? "Yeah, I guess I do. I was trained to react a certain way, to respond to situations by working toward the safest possible outcome. To save lives and property is the code a firefighter lives by," he said, feeling the gentle stroke of Evie's fingers against his arm and vaguely wondering why *her* touch gave him the kind of comfort he so often longed for. "But not at the expense of breaking ranks, or protocol—that's what we're taught from day one. People die when rules aren't followed."

She drew in a quick breath and he knew he'd struck a chord. "Yes, they do."

"So, maybe in my head I know I did the right thing—and the inquest confirmed that. But sometimes, when I think about his wife and daughters, I just wonder, what if I'd gone after him? Maybe he wouldn't have gotten so deep into the house before I could talk him around."

"You might have been killed, too."

He shrugged. "Perhaps. Or I might have been able to save him if I'd relied on my instincts rather than the rules."

"Aren't the rules there to keep you safe?" she asked, the soft voice of reason.

"Try telling that to Mike's wife." He sat back, careful not to move his arm in case she released him. For now, Scott was content to feel her soft touch. "He had a chance for a desk job. He wouldn't take it. He thought he'd be selling out. It was better hours and better suited to a man in his position."

"You mean a man with a wife and children?"

"Yeah."

She took a moment to respond. "You make it sound like someone without a family is more expendable."

"Not expendable exactly. Just with fewer people to leave behind."

"I'm sure your mother and sister wouldn't think so," she said softly. "Or anyone else who...who cares about you."

He wondered for a moment if she was one of those people, and then felt stupid because they hardly knew each other. But she was still touching him, still rubbing his arm in that slow burning way which was not quite seductive, but not exactly platonic, either. "I guess that puts me in my place, then." He felt her smile through to the blood in his veins. He looked at her hand. "If you keep doing that, Evie, I'm going to forget all about my good intentions."

She removed her hand immediately. "Sorry," she said.

"Habit. I'm a touchy kind of person. I obviously need to set some boundaries."

Scott didn't like the sound of that. The last thing he wanted was a wall between them. He wanted her so much he could barely function. And she looked so beautiful in her green dress and silver sandals.

"Don't apologize," he said. "I liked it."

She looked directly ahead and spoke in a quiet voice. "Is your friend's death the reason why you think relationships and the job don't mix?"

Scott didn't bother to deny it. "I saw what Mike went through, trying to juggle the two and he never seemed to have much of a handle on either. He told me once he didn't think he was a great father or husband—and sometimes his mind wasn't on the job." Scott wished she'd touch him again, or wished he had the courage to touch her. "You know, there have been times when I've arrived at a fire and thought—this one looks bad, so is this it? But I still go in—I go in knowing I have to, I go in knowing being a firefighter is all I've ever wanted to do. Mike was like that, too, once. But he got married and had a couple of kids and he changed—he took shortcuts, he improvised, he made mistakes because he was distracted. You can't afford to do that in this job. If you do you may end up paying the ultimate price. As Mike did."

Scott felt as if a valve inside him had been released. He'd kept those thoughts to himself for eight months. And he held strong in his convictions.

"I understand what you're saying, but I'm not sure I agree with you."

He'd wondered if she would. And he respected her opinion. So he asked her a blunt question. "Do you think your husband's mind was on the job that night he went out?"

Evie's head snapped around. She went to say something,

but stopped. And she looked at him for the longest time. Finally, she spoke. "No, I don't imagine it was."

"Because he would have been thinking about everything he hadn't done at home. He would have been thinking about the approaching storm and wondering if you were okay. As well trained as he was, as prepared as he was, those distractions might have cost him his life."

Scott saw her stiffen. "I hope I was more than a distraction to my husband."

He'd offended her. He was an idiot. "I apologize—that didn't come out right. I can be clumsy when I'm nervous."

"Nervous?" she echoed, as though she couldn't believe it. "Of what?"

Scott managed a smile. "You," he admitted. "Being within touching distance of a beautiful woman makes every man nervous."

"I'm not beautiful," she protested. "Now, my sister Grace, she's beautiful."

"I didn't notice," he replied, and wondered how she'd not know she was the most beautiful woman on the planet. *Man, I've got it bad. I should pack my stuff and get away from Crystal Point as fast as I can. Clumsy* wasn't the word for how he felt at the moment. *Hotly aroused* was more like it. "Maybe we should get back to the party?"

Evie nodded. "Yes, good idea." She stood up and he followed. Before they reached the pool gate she stopped. "You know," she said firmly, leaning toward him just a fraction. "Your friend…he wanted to save his child." She took a breath, coming closer. "And until you're a father yourself, I don't think you should criticize his motivations. It might be okay to have your principles set in stone if you've got experience to back them up—if you don't, you just end up looking like an immature, judgmental ass."

With that, she turned on her sandals and walked from the pool area.

Scott remained where he was and stared after her. And he smiled. Evie Dunn had his number. And at that moment he wanted her more than he'd ever wanted anyone or anything in his life.

Chapter Seven

On Sunday night Evie took in a movie with Fiona. The few hours away from the inn gave her a chance to think. About herself. About Trevor. And about Scott. Thoughts of her outburst by the pool at her parents' house lingered in her thoughts. Lectures were not usually her thing.

When she returned home the lights were still on downstairs and she headed for the living room to say good-night to her guests before going to bed. Only her guests were in the dining room, scattered around the big table, playing rummy. And Scott sat at the head, dealing the cards.

"Come and join us?" Flora suggested.

But Evie was not in the mood for games. She wanted to climb into bed and go to sleep. She wanted to forget about how all she'd thought about during the romantic chick-flick was locking lips with Scott. And looking at him didn't help. He wore a white T-shirt, and the soft fabric molded to his perfectly and sinfully sculptured chest. The Kellers were holding hands at one end of the table, the Manning sisters were giving their cards serious attention and Scott was watching her with blistering intensity.

"Wh-where's Trevor?" she asked shakily.

"Bed."

Heat traveled up her back like a serpent. The very word conjured up a whole lot of images she tried desperately to ignore. "Oh, well…I think I'll—"

A chair moved and she realized he'd pushed it out with his foot. "He's a little old to need tucking in, right?" Scott gestured to the chair. "Come and sit down."

No exactly an order, but pretty close. Evie fought the stab of resentment behind her ribs and faked a smile. No scenes in front of her paying guests. Just smiles and a happy face. Right, she could do that. She sat down and took the cards Scott dealt her. She got a lousy hand and wondered if he'd done it deliberately. Then she figured someone so unyielding wouldn't consider cheating. His mouth twisted fractionally, as if he knew, and that set a determined pulse through Evie's blood. Evie was a master at rummy. She'd beat his pants off. Well, maybe not his pants—although the idea of strip rummy seemed scandalously erotic. If they were alone. Which they weren't. And if she had any intention of setting her inhibitions free. Which she didn't. So she needed to forget all about that in a hurry.

She lost the first round, won the second and third and was hyped up to make it three in a row when the Kellers and Amelia announced they'd had enough. Once the cards were packed away, the chairs pushed in and the few empty glasses placed on the sideboard, everyone said good-night and moved toward the wide doorway.

Except Patti Keller gave a delighted shriek and said, "Mistletoe!"

Evie stopped dead in her tracks. And looked up. And

nearly choked. Sure enough, there is was. Directly above her. And directly above Scott.

No way.

Four pairs of curious eyes looked straight at her. And Evie knew exactly what their look meant. She also wasn't having anything to do with it.

"It's tradition," Flora said, and both of her silver brows rose. "I thought you were a stickler for it?"

She was—usually. But not when faced with the idea of kissing Scott Jones in front of a roomful of people. Okay, maybe not a room *full*—but there was enough of an audience to rattle her usual ramrod composure. She had no intention of doing anything so ludicrous. Especially when she felt as if she'd been set up. When she *knew* she'd been set up. And the two gray-haired old ladies in front of her didn't seem to have the need to hide the fact. She looked at Scott, saw his amused, almost I-dare-you-to grin and wanted the floor to open up and suck her in.

"We'll go first," Patti announced, and promptly dragged her bewildered-looking husband beneath the doorway and kissed him.

Newlyweds, Evie thought with an inward groan. She'd seen dozens of them come through Dunn Inn. All of them had possessed that same look as Patti Keller—that dreamy, I-can't-wait-to-get-my-hands-on-my-man look. *Was I ever like that?* She couldn't remember. Had Gordon's kisses knocked her off her feet? Had she let him? Had she been so immersed in her role as the sensible Preston daughter she'd forgotten to live a passionate life?

Passion…the idea of it teased around the edges of her thoughts. And sex, well, that was supposed to be passionate, wasn't it? She considered her options—the Kellers were still kissing, the Manning sisters were waiting and Scott hadn't moved an inch.

So she ditched her sensible garb for a few moments, swiveled on her heel, stood on her toes and kissed Scott Jones. Just like that. Evie could feel him smiling beneath the soft pressure of her mouth. Her body thrummed, her blood sang in her veins. Kissing Scott was like nothing on earth.

When she was done she pulled away, stepped back and flashed a kind of is-everyone-happy-now? smile.

Then she waltzed from the room without another word.

Scott had always thought he knew himself. He knew what he wanted, where he was going, where he'd been. Granted, Mike's death had shaken up his world and made him question his skills as a firefighter. But this was something else.

Evie...

He could still taste the sweet softness of her lips when she'd kissed him underneath the mistletoe. His attraction for her was consuming his thoughts. Like now, while they were in the car on their way back from Noah and Callie's. They'd gone to her brother's home for dinner and it was the first time they'd been alone for two days.

"You're very quiet."

She let out a breath. "I'm just thinking."

So was he. About kissing Evie. About the scent of her perfume. About how he couldn't get her out of his head. About how she was the most remarkable woman he'd ever met. "What about?"

"Trevor," she said softly. "I was thinking about my son."

Scott laughed silently at his own self-indulgent conceit that she might have been thinking about him. She had a son and she sounded concerned. "Is there a problem?"

"No, not really."

"But?" he asked as he turned onto the bitumen road.

"I was watching Noah with his kids," she replied, settling her arms around her waist. "It got me thinking about how Trevor must miss his dad."

Suddenly it got Scott thinking, too. He remembered the conversation he'd had with Trevor when they'd shot hoops together. "Natural he'd miss him. But he had a good father, right?"

"The operative word being *had*." The pain on her face was evident.

"He has you," Scott said gently.

She looked at him and Scott stole a sideways glance. "He's a lot like his dad."

"He's like *you*."

She smiled. "I guess in some ways. But I watched my brother with his son tonight and saw what an incredible relationship that was and wondered if I'd been…selfish."

Scott glanced at her. "Why would you think that?"

Her beautiful hair rustled. "Because…I haven't married again."

Married. He wasn't sure why the idea twisted at his insides. "You can only live the life you're meant to live, Evie," he said, and then thought he'd made no sense at all.

But she nodded as though she understood. "Maybe. Only, Trevor *should* have had a father…and I… The truth is I shut down after Gordon died. I guess I shut down so much I didn't think about what Trevor might need. I just decided that to be the best parent I could be I had to give my son *all* of me. And it made it easier, too," she admitted. "I didn't have to consider what it might do to us if I brought someone else into our life. But maybe I let him down by not…well, at least I could have considered it."

"If that's what you want…you should," he said, though the words felt like rocks in his mouth. The thought of Evie with another man made it actually hurt behind his ribs.

But he was right to say it—right to get the words out between them. He was leaving in two weeks and in no shape to offer her anything other than sex. And Evie deserved way more than that. As much as part of him wanted her more than he could remember wanting anything in his life. "Even an immature, judgmental ass like me can see that."

He turned the car into the driveway and braked outside the studio.

She twisted in her seat when the car came to a halt. "I'm sorry about that. I didn't mean to come across all bossy and patronizing."

Scott smiled and killed the engine. "Sure you did."

She smiled back. "Well, maybe. But I shouldn't have. I sometimes forget that I don't have all the answers. You came here for your sister's wedding, not lectures from someone who wouldn't have a clue what it must be like to put your life on the line every day."

"Apology accepted," he said. "Though I probably deserved it."

"Perhaps a little," she said, and smiled. "And about before…what I said about Trevor. I'm not complaining…not really…it's only that sometimes," she said, suddenly seeming incredibly young and vulnerable. "I feel like I'm stuck in this role of being a certain kind of person. A certain kind of woman. And as that woman I always do what's expected, what's the right thing. I get this sense that being… I don't know…suffocated almost…as if I've suffocated myself by being *who* I am. I've built this orderly, safe life which at times feels like a jail cell."

Scott's heart thundered beneath his ribs. "And what, Evie? You want to break out?"

She shrugged a little. "I think about it. I think what it might be like to be…I don't know…different."

Heat filled the space between them, flicking into life,

energizing the air with its tiny atoms. Even in the dim light
Scott could see the brightness of her eyes, the way her lips
parted slightly, as though she was about to say something,
as though she wanted to…to… He shook the feeling off,
knowing he was nuts to keep thinking about her in that
way. But he wanted to kiss her so much. He wanted to feel
the skin on her shoulders beneath his hands, he wanted to
taste the delicate spot behind her ear and then go lower,
past her throat and lower still, to breasts he knew, without
ever having touched them, ever having had them pressed
naked against him, were glorious and round and sensitive
and made for his hands and mouth. He wanted to kiss her
ribs, her belly, her thighs… He want to bury his mind, his
body, in the softness of her skin. He was more aroused than
he could ever remember being in his life, and she hadn't
even touched him!

"You better make a run for it," he said, more groan
than words.

She obviously heard him, but remained where she was,
drawing in breath. "I should, yes."

Scott inhaled deeply and the scent of her ripped through
his blood. If he moved a few inches she would be in his
arms. And she wouldn't resist—he felt that with mind-
blowing certainty. "Last chance."

She turned, easing toward him. Scott raised one hand
and touched her cheek. He didn't imagine the way her lips
parted, or the way her tongue rested on her white teeth.
The need to kiss her, possess her surged across his skin.
And he didn't have to wait. She came willingly, moving
her body across the space dividing them and pressed her
mouth to his. Scott responded instantly, taking her lips in
a searing kiss that rocked him to the very core. His hands
moved to her shoulders and he molded the delicate bones
beneath his palms. The kiss went on, drugging, hot, kick-

ing at his libido like a jackhammer. She moaned low in her throat as he cupped the underswell of her breast. Heat radiated through the T-shirt she wore and Scott felt her nipple peak against his thumb.

I haven't made out in a car since I was a teenager.

And I shouldn't be doing it with a woman like Evie.

The realization was like a bucket of cold water.

"Evie," he said hoarsely. "We should stop. This isn't the place—"

She wrenched free as he spoke. "You're right," she said, and pulled herself into a sitting position. She grabbed the door handle and pushed herself out of the car. He watched her race toward the house, her incredible hips swinging in her jeans. Within seconds she'd opened the front door and disappeared into the house. He stayed where he was, willing his body to play fair and return to normal.

It took a while. And it gave him a chance to think. The struggle to ignore his feelings for Evie was getting more and more difficult.

It's getting damn well impossible.

He didn't want them. Or need them. Feelings only blurred his focus. And lack of focus in his line of work could prove deadly. He'd seen evidence of that firsthand. Mike had lost his edge. Scott wasn't about to make the same mistake. Every instinct he had told him to back off from Evie. He couldn't do serious, and she deserved better.

I will not get involved.

And I really should have moved to a hotel.

Evie canceled her usual Thursday night dinner for her guests. The Kellers had left that morning and the Manning sisters were visiting a niece in Bellandale and wouldn't be back until late. She had new guests arriving the following day and needed to get the Kellers' room cleaned and prepared.

Although nothing helped stop her thinking about Scott.

I would have made love with him last night.

No doubt about it. She would have thrown off every part of herself that she'd trained to do the right thing, the sensible thing, and gone to wherever he might have taken her.

Her body screamed for the kind of release she sensed instinctively he would give her. Sex hadn't seemed so important for the longest time. And she wondered why, beyond his obvious physical appeal, that it was Scott who'd pulled her from her sexless haze. After so long, after Gordon…it didn't make sense. She wasn't the casual sex type. Making love had always been exactly that. And with her husband she'd been in the security of a loving relationship. She'd met and fallen in love with Gordon in high school, and exploring her sexuality with him had been safe.

But this feeling she had for Scott…it was *all* risk.

In the car she'd felt the burn of his possession like a brand on her skin. His kisses drove her wild. His touch sent her body to another place. And knowing that it was mutual, knowing that he'd been as turned on as she'd been, made the moment all the more potent.

Evie also knew she had to resist whatever feelings were running riot inside her.

Baring all her thoughts and feelings about her son wasn't exactly helping her cause, either. She never bared her soul. She never really let anyone in. At least, not since Gordon.

But Scott had her running on both fronts—her body and her heart. She just wasn't sure which one would give out first.

* * *

On Friday evening Evie ditched her regular class and headed for the local elementary school to watch her brother's three youngest children perform in the annual Christmas play. She hadn't seen Scott much at all over the past couple of days. She'd kept herself busy in her studio or with her guests. She often heard Scott shooting hoops with Trevor, and her son had even taken up running with Scott for the past couple of mornings.

She wasn't sure what Scott did with himself during the day and didn't have the courage to ask. And he usually returned to Dunn Inn well after dinner had been served and retired straight to his room. Their earlier routine of a late coffee and conversation had disappeared as quickly as it had begun.

Trevor had declined to attend the concert and she let her son have his way. He was spending the night at his best friend's house, where no doubt the boys would be playing video games until the small hours of the morning.

A special stage and seating had been set up on the sports field, and Evie weaved her way through the crowds, looking for her brother and Callie. Instead, she found Scott.

Callie and Noah were seated beside him and for a few extraordinary seconds he held her complete attention. The dip in her belly, the way her heart raced…what had once been long forgotten and unfamiliar feelings were now all *too* familiar.

Feelings she had no idea what to do with.

Evie hung back and walked around the rear of the seating area. The music started and a group of children dressed in variations of red and green elf costumes came onto the stage and broke into delightful versions of "Santa Claus is Coming to Town" and "Frosty the Snowman." The singing made her smile, especially when she spotted her eight-year-old nephew, Jamie, in the exuberant group. When the song changed to "Jingle Bells" several younger children joined the choir onstage and Noah's twins were among them. She looked back toward her brother. He and Callie were watching the kids with obvious pride and enjoyment. And there was a vacant seat beside them.

"Can we talk?"

She stilled. Scott was directly behind her. So close she felt the warmth coming off his skin. Evie didn't turn around. "Sure," she said in a wobbly voice. "Later. At home."

"Now, Evie," he insisted.

The music volume rose and she tilted back a little and collided with his chest. It would have been easier to refuse him. Better even. But she didn't. "Okay," she said, and stepped away.

Evie knew the school grounds well. She'd attended as a youngster, as had her son, and she still volunteered at the canteen once a week. She walked through the mill of people hanging behind the seating and headed for the old library building. The sound of children singing faded substantially once she rounded the corner with Scott in her wake. It was quiet and private and had some light courtesy of an open window from a nearby classroom. Evie turned by the steps and thrust her hands to her hips.

"So...what?"

He looked her up and down. "I'm moving out."

No great surprise. She'd sensed it from his conspicuous absence over the past couple of days.

"When?"

"Tomorrow."

So soon. It took Evie about two seconds to work out that she didn't want Scott to go anywhere. "Trevor will be disappointed." *Trevor?* She wondered why she'd said that. Wondered where it came from. Guilt trips weren't her scene. She shrugged casually. "I mean, he'll be disappointed you won't be around to help improve his basketball technique."

"And you?"

Evie stepped back and leaned against the steel stair rail. "I don't...I don't have any claim on you."

He moved forward. The jeans and black T-shirt he wore did little to disguise his infinite attributes, and her mouth turned dry. "I'm not so sure about that, Evie," he said as he reached for her and she melted against him. "Right now, at this moment...I'd say you've got more claim than anyone else."

It was a highly provocative thing to say and Evie felt the meaning through to her bones. She also felt him... His strong, lean body and wide shoulders. With his arms around her Evie had a faraway, drifting thought that she'd never felt so safe in all her life.

Scott kissed her thoroughly and she kissed him right back. Evie curved her hands over his shoulders as he pulled her close and the kissing continued. So did the soft stroke of his fingertips up and down her spine. She felt the heat of his touch through the fabric of her black dress and moaned low in her throat. Her fingers moved over his shoulders, drawing them closer, and Scott curved a hand down her hip and lower. When his fingertips touched her thigh and drew her skirt higher, Evie gasped against his mouth.

There was a vague sound of carols in the background and the echo of laughter and applause. Thankfully, it pulled her from the seductive trance long enough to come to her senses. She pulled back and drew in a shuddering breath. "Stop...please."

Scott released her and she stepped back, breathing hard. He didn't look any better off.

"I'm sorry," he said, and crossed his arms tightly. "I shouldn't have done that."

They both shouldn't have. Out in the open, where they could be seen. At a school, no less. She wished Sensible Evie would come back. Before she had a chance to say anything, he turned on his heel and walked off, disappearing into the darkness.

She should have stayed and watched the rest of the performance, should have shared the small piece of Christmas spirit with her family. But Evie was in no mood to put on fake smiles and pretend she had it all together. Fifteen minutes later she was home and upstairs, pacing the space between the sitting room and small kitchenette. She flicked on a table lamp and sat on the sofa for a while, shifting position every time she heard a car pass outside. Half an hour had inched by when she finally heard the distinctive sound of Scott's motorcycle pulling up in the driveway, and her heart almost landed in her throat. She heard the downstairs door open, heard the steady thud of his feet on the stairs as he climbed them.

He came through the doorway and made a jerky stop. He looked her up and down, taking in the short dress and low heels, and she watched as he swallowed hard. An uneasy silence fell between them. And for the first time in the longest time, Evie knew exactly what she wanted. *And who.* Even if it was only for one night. She drew in a deep breath and spoke.

"Part of me wishes I could stop wanting you," she admitted, and bit down on her lip. "Part of me wishes you'd never come here."

He didn't move. "And the other part?"

Evie shrugged, half hopeless, half confused. "I've done the right thing all my life. I've always put everyone else's needs first. I've never jumped into anything without thinking about it. And as a woman, I haven't let myself really *feel* anything for such a long time." Another breath came out. "Ten years," she said on a sigh. "I haven't…I haven't…well, since my husband died…there's not been anyone else."

He didn't say a word. He simply stared at her with such hot, blistering intensity it was as though for that moment, they were the only two people on the planet. Evie met his look head-on and felt the vibration of him directly though to her bones, and deeper, to that place where she never imagined she'd feel anything again after her husband died.

Finally, he spoke. "What do you want to happen between us, Evie?"

She drew in a long breath. "I want…I want you to make love to me."

Chapter Eight

Scott knew he had to keep his head. This wasn't a one-night-stand kind of woman. This was Evie. And as much as he ached for her, he suspected that once they became lovers, leaving her would be like losing a limb.

"You know that making love will complicate things," he said quietly. "Sex *always* complicates things."

"I know," she admitted. "And I don't expect promises or declarations of any kind. We're two very different people with different lives. But this *thing* between us is stronger than I am."

It was stronger than him, too. He'd spent the past week in a haze, knowing he probably shouldn't want her, knowing it would only ever be temporary. But he longed for Evie in ways he'd never longed for any woman before.

"What if sex turns into something else…something more?"

She moved her legs. "It won't. We'll make sure it won't.

Look, I'm not denying that I like you. I do. But we both know anything serious isn't viable."

It sounded like every man's dream. Sex with a beautiful woman and no strings attached. Only, his dreams suddenly felt as if they were shifting, morphing into something he couldn't quite figure. "So, you want to have an affair?" It sounded old-fashioned, put like that. But he wasn't sure what to call it.

She nodded. "Yes. For as long as it lasts," she said.

For as long as you are here. That's what she meant. "And no commitment?"

"That's right." Her eyes suddenly looked huge in her face. "I don't want you to think I'm looking for... Well, the other night I said some things about my son, about how I should have remarried. This isn't about *that,*" she said pointedly. "I've no illusions, Scott, and you've made it pretty clear you're not in any kind of position to be anyone's...husband. And I'm not in a position to believe in fairy tales. This is what it is and I'm okay with that."

Scott's heartbeat was erratic. He wanted her so much. *And here she is, asking me to make love to her.* But she hadn't been with anyone for ten years. To be her first lover since her husband had died suddenly seemed a huge responsibility. A big deal. And certainly worthy of more than just an affair. But to refuse her? When his body, his mind, was screaming to possess every part of the woman she was.

I could walk away right now...I could walk away and not know how it feels to touch her and love her and wake up beside her in the morning.

But he didn't walk.

"Evie," he said softly. "Come here."

By the time she reached him Scott's hands were burning to touch her. The simple black dress she wore was sleeveless and her shoulders were enticingly smooth, her arms supple and sun kissed. But it was her face that held him captive. As it had from the first moment they'd met. He'd never met anyone with lips like hers. Or such wide green eyes and provocative slanting brows.

"You're staring at me," she said when they stood no more than a foot apart.

"I can't help it," he admitted, and looked at her hair hanging loose down her back. He reached out and twirled a few strands between his fingers. "You have the most amazing hair."

She half smiled. "My one beauty."

"Hardly," he said, and continued to play with her curls.

He touched the back of her neck and drew her closer. Finally, he felt her against him, felt the soft curves of her hips and breasts against his stomach and chest. Scott looked down into her face and titled her head backward. He heard her suck in a shallow breath, felt the slight tremble of her body and instinctively drew his arm around her, settling his hand at her waist. He took his time to kiss her, knowing how her mouth would taste, but wanting to savor the feeling. Evie's hands came to his shoulders and she clung to him as their lips met. She groaned low in her throat, half resistance, half insistence, and he deepened the kiss, tracing the outline of her mouth with his tongue. When her tongue touched his Scott almost jumped out of his skin.

"Your bedroom," she muttered against his lips.

He didn't waste time thinking why she'd prefer his room to hers. He kissed her again, hungrier, deeper, before he grasped her hand and led her down the hall.

"Are you sure about this, Evie?" he asked once they were in his room. "If at any point you want to stop, just say the word and I'll—"

"Do you always talk this much before you take a woman

to bed?" she asked, flicking the lock on the door and bridging the gap between them.

Scott smiled. "Not usually. I told you I get clumsy when I'm nervous."

She placed her hands on his chest. "You're nervous about having sex with me?"

"Not exactly," he said, fighting the ever-increasing surge of arousal just being near her wreaked on his body. "You've waited a long time... I just want to be...worthy."

"Do you want me to rate your performance out of ten? If you like I'll take—"

"Now who's talking too much?" he said, and reached for her.

As kisses went, the next one didn't have a whole lot of finesse, but he made his point, because she stopped talking and just kissed him back. And then again, and again. He couldn't get enough of the taste of her or the feel of her tongue curling around his own. Her hands were at the hem of his T-shirt and she gently tugged at it. It made Scott smile and he quickly pulled the shirt over his head.

When she touched his skin Scott felt the heat in her fingertips. He let her decide the pace their lovemaking would take, and for the moment she seemed perfectly content to simply touch his chest and shoulders. Of course, he was burning to touch her, too, but he held back and clenched his fists as tightly as he could. She had a soft touch, not quite tentative, but...exploring. He liked that about her— liked that she was patient and wasn't all rush and haste.

When she was done she rested her hands on his belly and traced his abdominals with her fingers. The sensation was so powerful Scott felt as though all the blood in his body had surged to his groin. She looked up at him and smiled. "Your turn."

He liked that about her, too. She wasn't all serious and

tense about touching him. He didn't want serious between them. Her fingers inched a little lower and Scott sucked in a breath. His arms came around her and he slowly undid the zipper on the dress. It slipped down her shoulders and over her hips with a quiet swoosh and landed at her feet. She wore black lace briefs that were quite modest but sexy as hell and hit his libido with the precision of an arrow.

"You are sensational," he said in a hoarse whisper.

She smiled again and stepped back, flipping the dress aside with her foot before she discarded her heels. Scott drank in the sheer magnitude of her sexy, mind-blowing beauty. Her breasts tilted upward in the half-cup bra and his palms itched to touch them. Her waist and stomach and the curvy flare of her hips were enough to fulfill his every fantasy.

Evie walked around him to flick on the bedside light and he got a great view of her toned, shapely behind. She walked back to the door and turned off the main light. It undid him, looking at her like that, watching her move around the room in her underwear.

Scott gripped her fingers and led Evie to the big bed in the center of the room. She backed her knees against the mattress and reached for the snap on his jeans. He was hard and ready for her and she knew it. She brushed her hand across the abrasive denim, feeling his erection, and he knew if he didn't start loving her soon, if he didn't get inside her soon, he might die a slow death.

He molded her shoulders with his hands and crooked his fingers beneath her bra strap. She was looking at him, smiling, waiting. Scott moved lower and cupped her breasts. Her nipples were already hard, jutting against the stretchy lace, and he traced them with his fingertips. She groaned low in her throat, and the sound pierced through him. He reached around her back with one hand and unclipped her bra with one deft flick. Once her breasts were free, Scott bent his head and closed his mouth over one rosy nipple, and as he sucked the peak she groaned again and threaded her fingers through his hair.

When he came back up to look at her, Scott was so turned on he feared his legs might give way. He gently coaxed her onto the bed, kissing her shoulder, her neck and her bountiful breasts. She undid his jeans and Scott sucked in a breath and took about three seconds to remove the rest of his clothes. He kissed her, over and over, everywhere, anywhere, light kisses, slow kisses, and pushed her briefs off in one movement.

And then he touched her center, parting the soft curls as he inched his finger inside her. Slowly, so excruciatingly slow, she pushed her hips forward. But Scott had no intention of rushing anything. Not with Evie. She was a woman who deserved to be loved right. And she'd chosen him to love her...even if only for one night. And he would make it good for her, despite the aching hunger he felt to be inside her and stay there until they didn't know when he began and she ended. She was wet and hot and he teased the tender flesh with his thumb. She rocked against him and he found the pressure she liked, sliding his hand over her, gently rubbing the slick nub he'd found with his finger. He kissed her breasts and licked each tightly beaded nipple while he explored the heart of her and heard her breathing change as she came apart in his arms.

Watching her climax, feeling her shudder against him and say his name, was so sweetly consuming, that Scott experienced an unheralded tightness behind his eyes. He gave her a moment, pushing her hair from her face as she came back to earth.

She said something as she pressed her mouth to his chest and he caught the muffled words. "Absolutely," he said quickly, twisted one arm around to rummage in the bedside drawer with eager fingers.

"That sure of me?" she asked, tracing hot kisses down his belly.

Scott grasped her chin and urged her to look at him. "Not really."

She smiled, took the foil packet and laid it on the bed and continued her exploration of his stomach and then lower still. Not shy, as he might have expected, but a sensual, confident woman who kissed and licked his skin.

"Evie," he groaned, and grasped her shoulders. "Evie," he said again, more plea than statement.

Without a word she grabbed the condom, ripped open the packet and slowly and torturously sheathed him. She scooted up and Scott took her in his arms, rolling her beneath him as he supported his weight on his elbows. Her thighs dropped against the mattress and he found her slowly, looking directly into her eyes as they joined. She gripped around him and he rocked against her, filling her so completely he thought he might pass out.

Have I ever felt like this before? Has anything ever felt this good...this right?

"Say something," she whispered.

"I...can't," he admitted raggedly, and began to move inside her.

In all her life, Evie had never felt so gloriously free, so totally uninhibited. Being with Scott, feeling the weight of his hard body and the heat of his possession, thrilled her in ways she hadn't imagined. She had no fear, no lingering concerns about her imperfections. The moment he'd looked at her in her sensible underwear and smiled that sexy smile all her remaining body image issues faded. Whatever happened after these precious moments she didn't care to know. She felt alive, desired, confident. She felt like a woman who'd met her match, who'd been in a state of sexual limbo only because she'd been waiting... for this night...this man.

She wrapped her arms around him and splayed her hands across his strong back, matching his movements so perfectly she wondered briefly about all her past notions of awkwardness and embarrassment when she'd imagined being with a lover after so many years of abstinence. There was none of that. Just two people who knew each other, somehow, who knew how to please, to pleasure, knew how to touch and stroke and give and take. And he felt wondrous—above her, against her, inside her, so much a part of her Evie wondered how she'd lived for so long without knowing such a feeling.

When the pleasure built again she went with it, matching his thrusts, his need. He kissed her as if he couldn't get enough of her taste or her tongue and she kissed him back eagerly, their mouths mimicking the act where their bodies joined. And she held on, clinging, urging and giving. And then it came, lifting her up, taking her so high she clung to his shoulders and let the sensation pulse through her body in a wave of pleasure so powerful she felt as if she'd transcended to another level of being. When he joined her in that place, Evie gripped him with all her strength, feeling his back tense, his body shudder and finally let go to be consumed by a powerful release.

He stayed where he was for a moment, drawing in long breaths. Evie could feel the furious beat of his heart pounding. His lips nuzzled her neck and she tenderly pushed his damp hair back from his forehead. After a couple of minutes he roused and shifted from her.

"I'll be back in a minute," he said as he swung off the bed and headed for the bathroom.

Evie stretched her limbs and closed her eyes. *Well, I've gone and done it now.* She lifted her knees up, pushed back the bedclothes and wiggled beneath the sheet. When Scott returned she was respectably covered and didn't linger to imagine why on earth she'd suddenly be shy about him seeing her naked, considering what they'd been doing for the past hour. He, on the other hand, didn't seem shy in the least, because he came around the bed, still in a state of semiarousal, and sat beside her.

He grasped both her hands and held them within his own. "Everything okay?"

"Of course."

"No regrets?"

"Not yet," she said honestly.

It made him smile a little. "Fair enough," he said, pulling the sheet back before Evie could protest, and looked her over with obvious admiration. He traced the back of his hand over her rib cage and then along the curve of her waist. Evie tried to grasp the sheet, but he pushed it back. "Don't do that."

Now the lovemaking was over, she could feel the fingers of reality grabbing at her. And for the first time since she'd entered his bedroom, she felt the burning scrutiny of his blue-eyed gaze.

"I'm not twenty anymore," she said pointedly.

Scott continued to touch her. "I'd be very disappointed if you were." His hand dipped lower, touching her intimately. "You have a lovely body."

"Flawed," she said, and thought how incredible his touch was as she gave him a very deliberate once over. "Unlike you."

He grinned, probably with more modesty than he felt, and it made Evie smile. So, the man had a perfect body? Didn't that simply make her the luckiest woman on the planet? She touched his chest and traced her fingertips downward toward his navel and the line of soft hair trailing down his faultlessly flat abdomen. When her hand came into contact with his very obvious erection, her libido did a wild leap. She wanted him again. And she knew he wanted her, too.

"Flawed?" His brows came together. "Are you kidding?" His hand moved across her thighs and then over her hips and belly. "This is beauty," he said, kissing the sensitive spot near her hip. "And this," he said, moving across, going lower, sliding his lips toward the juncture at her thighs.

And then neither of them said anything else for a long while.

Evie woke up alone. The clock on the bedside table flashed the time and she squinted to get a good look. Eight-forty? Impossible. She looked at light beaming through the crack in the curtains and shoved her face back into the pillow. She had to get up. There were guests to feed, things to be done. Guests who'd arrived yesterday and who would be wondering where she was, and if it wasn't for Amelia's and Flora's advancing years she was certain they'd crack it up the stairs to find out what had kept her from attending to her usual morning routine.

What kept me from it is nowhere to be seen.

Evie doubted Scott had gone for his usual morning run. She couldn't imagine he'd have the energy for anything after their night together. She certainly felt an aching lethargy in her limbs. Even her skin felt tired.

When the door opened about thirty seconds later and he walked into the room, she was appalled to see how chipper he looked, considering that she wanted to pull the sheet over her head and sleep for the remainder of the day. He was showered, dressed in cargos and a white polo shirt and looked completely recovered.

"Breakfast," he said, and Evie noticed the tray he carried.

Food sounded good, but she had to set her priorities. "I can't," she told him. "I have guests to—"

"All done," he said, and carried the tray to the bed. "Sit up a bit."

Evie jackknifed up immediately and clutched the sheet against her breasts. "What do you mean it's all done?"

"Well, I could hardly let your paying guests starve. And you were sleeping so soundly I didn't have the heart to wake you."

"You cooked breakfast?"

He shrugged and placed the small tray on the bedside table. "I made toast for Amelia and Flora," he replied with a smile. "I'm very talented."

She knew that. Her body had experienced firsthand his many talents. "What did you tell them?"

He held out a coffee mug. "That you were laid up in bed."

Evie struggled to keep the sheet in place. "Oh, God, what must they—"

"I said you were laid up," he said quickly, grinning. "Not getting laid."

Evie took the coffee, and the sheet fell to her waist. Scott looked immediately at her exposed breasts, and a flash of desire sparked in his eyes.

"I should still start moving," she said, took a sip of coffee and placed the mug on the tray before she shimmied off the bed.

He passed her one of his T-shirts to wear. "Let's go Christmas shopping."

Evie's eyes widened. Shopping? She took the shirt and quickly covered herself. "I'm not sure I—"

"I need to buy gifts for Callie's new family," he explained, and watched as she grabbed her clothes. "You know them better than I do. And I need to get something for my mom."

Christmas gift shopping? Why not? It didn't mean they were together. It didn't add to their one-night, no-strings agreement. And it would give her a chance to prove to herself that she was completely in control.

"Okay. Give me half an hour."

Evie rushed to shower and change into jeans and tank-style T-shirt and sandals. She wrote a note for Trevor, saying she would be in town for a few hours and back before lunch, then headed downstairs. Evie avoided the Manning sisters—certain they'd ask what she'd been up to and where she was going. She swung her tote across one shoulder and walked outside.

Scott was leaning against her car. "All set?"

Evie nodded and tossed him the keys. The drive into Bellandale took fifteen minutes and she gave him instructions directly to the larger of the two shopping malls in town. They parked underneath and headed up the elevator. Within the air-conditioned comfort of the mall, it was easy to forget about the rising humidity outside. While the Northern Hemisphere enjoyed the traditional cold weather, turkey and rich puddings, an Australian Christmas usually meant blistering heat, cold ham, shrimp and salads and icy beer. But Evie still got wrapped up in the festive season. She loved decorating her tree and buying gifts and settling in front of the television to watch *Miracle on 34th Street* with her son every year. She knew Trevor only tolerated

the old black-and-white movie for her benefit and it made
her love her son just that little bit more.

The mall was busy and shoppers were milling around
retailers and freestanding stalls. There was a long queue of
children waiting for a snapshot with Santa, and the charity gift wrap bar was in full swing.

"So," Scott said, and lightly grabbed her hand. "The
kids?"

"Books," she suggested, and moved in the direction
of the bookstore. She stopped when it became clear Scott
wasn't about to follow her.

He frowned and shook his head. "No books."

She realized he hadn't released her hand. "Not cool
enough for the new uncle?"

"Precisely."

Evie took a few seconds, then rattled off a couple of
other options. Once Scott agreed to one of her sugges-
tions, they headed for the toy store. And the fact that he
still held her hand felt ridiculously natural. They walked
through the mall and Evie didn't miss how other women
blatantly checked him out. A trio of pretty and preened
twentysomethings sashayed past and one said something
outrageously flirtatious toward Scott. Another from the
group looked Evie up and down and raised her brows. At
that moment Evie felt about as old as Methuselah. She
pulled her hand from his and crossed her arms.

"Something wrong?" Scott asked, seemingly oblivious
of the attention he'd garnered as they walked into the toy
store.

"Not a thing," she lied, and wished a great big hole
would open up and suck her in.

*What am I thinking? I'm thirty-six years old... He's
twenty-seven. I'm sensible. I should know better than to
think this means anything. I don't want it to mean any-*

thing...right? It's just sex. Sex without commitment that I said I could handle. No strings. No attachment.

And thinking that, Evie realized, had suddenly become her undoing.

Scott was neck deep in trouble. He'd been determined not to get involved with Evie. And now he felt *so* involved he could hardly think straight. Evie was like...she was like the skin growing over his bones, the air in his lungs. Like no other woman he'd ever met.

Maybe it's just because last night I had the best sex I've had in my life.

Sex could do that, right? Especially incredible, mind-blowing sex. It could warp a man's reality; it could make him think things, *feel* things, wish for things.

But wishes were for fools. He was leaving in two weeks. He knew better than to start something. Two weeks and he couldn't keep his fly zipped. Scott wondered if she'd want to make love again. He wondered how he'd react if she did...or didn't.

As he bought toys for the kids, she kept her distance. Even as they headed for the gift-wrapping booth, she remained quiet. The regret she clearly felt seemed like a force field over her skin. He followed her to the music store and agreed with her suggestion of a gift for Callie's teenage step daughter, Lily. Once the kids were sorted, Scott headed for a jewelry store to purchase something for his mother.

"What about this?" he asked Evie, ignoring the pushy salesclerk who batted her eyelashes at him as he dangled a gold chain from his fingertips.

She shrugged and then nodded. "You know what your mother likes."

"I'm asking if *you* like it."

He got her attention back and she slid sideways, bumping her hip against the counter. "It's pretty."

Scott got a quick image in his head of Evie wearing the necklace around her beautiful neck and nothing else. He shook the thought off and looked briefly at the clerk. "Bracelets."

Minutes later he'd made a selection and the item was wrapped and paid for and they headed from the store. She declined coffee, cake and everything else he suggested. He wasn't sure what he wanted. Being around her messed with his concentration and determination to stay focused on getting through Christmas and the wedding before heading back to L.A. where his job was waiting. The job he was determined he could do without distraction. But *not* being around Evie didn't appeal, either. So he was screwed either way.

There was an uneasy tension between them and he didn't like it one bit.

Scott drove her home and she didn't wait for the keys or for him to haul his shopping bags from the rear seat. Back in his room he could hear her moving around the house, heard the telephone ring, heard the sound of low voices downstairs and imagined her explaining her absence to the ever-curious and relentless Manning sisters. With a brisk shake he decided to stop hiding in his room. He took off immediately and headed downstairs. The sisters passed him in the hallway, all smiles, and made their way out the front door. He waited until they were out of sight and headed for the front living room.

Evie was near the huge Christmas tree, fiddling with ornaments. She still wore her jeans and the tight tank shirt that had been tantalizing him all morning. He'd barely touched her while they were out, only taking her hand once or twice. Casual, that's what he'd thought. But looking at her shapely bottom, he didn't feel at all casual. He was aroused just by the sight of her.

"Callie called," she said, and didn't turn around. He wondered how she'd sensed he was there. "She said to remind you about your mother arriving tomorrow."

"Yeah, I know."

She straightened her shoulders, still fiddling, still with her back to him. "You can put the gifts for the kids under the tree if you like. Unless…unless you're still moving out."

Moving out? That's right. That's what he'd said. That's what he'd decided to do the day before. Move out and away from temptation. And complication. *Too little too late.*

"Is that what you want?"

She shrugged and continued her attention on the already perfect tree. "It's not up to me."

Scott took a step toward her. "Evie?"

"I don't know what I want," she said, and turned. Her green eyes shone brightly. "I'm not completely naive—I know a situation like this is different for a man than it is for a woman. Turns out I'm a whole lot more emotional about having a physical relationship with someone than I thought. We agreed it would be just sex, but I'm not really made that way. So I think it would be better if we went back to how things used to be."

Scott stared at her. *I'm off the hook.* Only, he wasn't so sure he wanted to be.

She turned back to the tree. "I'm going to be in the studio for the next few hours. Please help yourself to anything you want."

Just not me…

Scott got the message. He lingered in the living room for about three seconds before he turned on his heel and left.

Chapter Nine

While she was having her fitting for her bridesmaid dress on Monday afternoon, Evie did her best to appear as much her usual self as possible. Her friend Fiona wasn't fooled, though, and asked her straight-out what was going on with her. Evie shrugged off the question and avoided making eye contact with Callie.

But Fiona didn't give up. "You're distracted."

Evie stood in the dressing cubicle and unzipped the pale gold satin gown and allowed the strapless bodice to hang on one hip. "I'm fine," she replied.

In truth, she was so far from being *fine*, and her head hurt thinking about it.

"You know," Fiona said with a laugh, "that new teacher at school asked about you again."

The third time in as many months. Maybe she should go out with him. At least it might take her mind off Scott. "So set me up."

Her friend's eyes popped wide. "You want a date?"

Evie shrugged. "Don't look so shocked."

"I am shocked," Fiona replied.

"Me, too," Callie said, tapping on the door.

"Well, don't be," Evie said sharply, and pushed at the cubicle doors. "So, can you wrangle it?"

Fiona nodded. "For sure. I just can't believe you're actually going to go on a date with him."

"Why not?"

"Because you don't date," Fiona replied. "Ever."

She experienced a weird dip in her stomach. "Maybe I'm tired of being predictable."

"Ha…not likely. Anyway, he's nice enough. He's a little…"

"A little what?" Callie prompted.

Fiona made a clucking sound. "Dull," she said finally.

Well, what's wrong with being dull? At least he's my own age, lives in the same town and isn't likely to go running into burning buildings any time soon. "Dull suits me just fine. I like *dull*."

Fiona snorted and Callie laughed and when Evie finally emerged from the dressing cubicle, both her friends were staring at her with lifted brows.

"You don't actually believe that?" Callie asked, and took the dress from Evie's hands.

"Sure I do," she said, and stepped out to allow Fiona inside to try her gown on. "Dull isn't as bad as it sounds. Dull is…" *Safe, reliable, not likely to break my heart.* "Besides, I've met him several times when I've dropped the twins to school and he seemed friendly and pleasant and—"

"Pleasant?" Callie groaned. "Now I know you must be joking."

Evie stood her ground. "Not everyone gets fireworks," she said, holding her ground. "Or wants them."

"What about plain old he-makes-me-weak-at-the-knees lust?" Fiona piped in from behind the door. "That's gotta count."

"Overrated," Evie replied, and tried not to have a flashback about making love with Scott.

"I used to think so," Callie said with a dreamy grin. "I don't think I ever believed in all that romantic stuff before I met Noah—I was always practical and levelheaded when it came to romance. And then I met your brother and *whoosh*…all my practicalities went out the window."

Evie made a face. "Have you been reading Fiona's bodice ripper novels again?"

"You can scorn all you like," Callie said. "But when it happens…watch out."

"I believe in it," Fiona said as she opened the door and stuck out her head and looked directly at Evie. "And however much you deny it, so do you."

"Just ask him, will you?" she said flatly.

Neither woman said anything else.

When she arrived home, Trevor was in the upstairs kitchen making a snack. Evie plonked her bag on the table and took the half ham-and-cheese sandwich he offered. The school term was over, and once the wedding and Christmas were done, her son would be taking his annual trip north to spend a few weeks with Gordon's parents. She always missed him terribly but knew how much her in-laws loved seeing their only grandson. They still invited Evie every year. In the early years after Gordon's death, she'd made the trip several times. But the Dunns' grief was still inconsolable and each year it became harder to face. So she took the coward's way and used the B and B as an excuse to stay behind. She knew they adored having Trevor for those few weeks and wanted her son to have a strong relationship with both sets of grandparents.

"How's the hoop shooting going?" she asked, and took a bite of sandwich.

"Scott reckons I'm a natural," he boasted with a broad grin. "Tryouts are on soon."

"You guys seem to be getting along okay."

Trevor shrugged. "Sure. He's really cool. He knows about computers, too. And mechanics."

The hero worship in her son's voice was glaringly obvious. And she couldn't blame Trevor for feeling like that. Other than her own father and Noah, her son had spent years without having a man's regular influence in his life. "I'm glad you get along."

"Yeah…it's too bad he's leaving soon."

Too bad. Evie couldn't stop her heart tightening up. "Well, Callie lives here now, so the chances are he'll come back to visit his sister."

Even as she said it Evie didn't believe it. Maybe she didn't want to believe it. She'd put the stops on their relationship. She was the one who couldn't do casual. Now the idea of Scott returning to Crystal Point in the future wasn't something she wanted to face. Especially if he didn't come alone. That would be the inevitable future, right? He'd go home, meet someone suitable, eventually fall in love and discard all his protestations about the job and relationships not working for him.

And I'll still be alone.

"I hope so," Trevor said cheerfully.

Evie took a deep breath. "So, how about helping me wrap some gifts?" she suggested, eager to do anything to dislodge the heavy pain inside. "I picked up a few things before my dress fitting today. I could use a hand getting them done."

"Sure," her son said. "But I'm heading to Cody's to-night if that's okay. His dad got him this new computer game for Christmas."

Cody's father was a soldier on tour in Afghanistan. She knew her son's best friend would rather have had his dad home for Christmas than a game for his computer, and was glad her son could be there for his friend.

Evie didn't see Scott that evening. By the time she heard his motorcycle in the driveway, it was well past ten o'clock. She knew he'd been at Callie and Noah's. His mother had arrived from L.A. and it wasn't hard to figure they would want to spend some time together as a family. Evie knew her parents were there, too, which didn't help the tiny stab of exclusion she experienced every time she thought about it.

As it got closer to Christmas Eve she had her routine down. She saw Scott briefly each morning, though they rarely met for breakfast. He spent some time with Trevor and disappeared most days and evenings. So she got exactly what she wanted. They spent a week barely exchanging words, passing each other in the stairway or kitchen. And Evie had also spent the week pulling mistletoe down from around the house. The Manning sisters were clearly the culprits. Evie tossed the stuff in the garbage every time she got her hands on it, much to Flora's and Amelia's amusement.

She had a last-minute panicked phone call from the wedding caterers, but everything else associated with her brother's Christmas Eve wedding went to plan and Evie was convinced that the ceremony would go off without a hitch. Until the day before the wedding. And it wasn't exactly a *hitch*...just a minor catastrophe. One of the groomsmen broke his foot in a boating accident and Callie insisted Scott fill in the role, as well as giving the bride away. Which meant *she* would be partnered with him all evening…at the ceremony, at the reception…and on the dance floor.

The bride and maids were all dressing at Dunn Inn, and the ceremony and reception were being held at the local country club under a huge white silk marquee. Beneath the marquee were hundreds of tiny lights, tables, chairs, a dance floor and a team of smartly attired wait staff.

At the house, Grace was on hand, helping the attendants with hair and makeup. Evie's dress fit like a glove and as Grace fussed with her hair Evie stood compliant and silent. But her sister wasn't fooled.

"Why do you look like you want to be somewhere else?" Grace remarked in a soft voice close to her ear. "Trouble in paradise?"

With Callie on the other side of the room, looking perfectly beautiful in her pale ivory organza gown, Evie knew it wasn't the time for a heart-to-heart with her sister. Fiona and Lily were fiddling with Callie's veil, and Noah's youngest daughter, Hayley, stood by the armoire in the corner twirling on her gold slippers.

There was a short rap on the door, and Grace invited whoever it was to open up. The door swung back and Scott stood beneath the threshold. Evie's skin warmed instantly. He looked incredible in the dark suit, shirt and pale gold tie, and his gaze traveled over her in that way she'd become accustomed to. It had been days since they'd shared such a look, and the silence that overtook the room was suddenly deafening. Everyone noticed. *How could they not?*

Grace said something and Evie quickly scrambled her wits together. "Yes…we're all ready," she said, and ushered Hayley from the corner.

Callie came forward and took his arm. "You look

amazing," Scott said to his sister as he kissed her cheek. "Noah's a lucky man."

Eve's throat tightened. She knew how much Noah and Callie loved each other. She'd watched their relationship blossom barely months ago and couldn't be happier for her brother and soon-to-be bride.

And that thought only made her yearn, suddenly, for happiness of her own.

Watching his sister get married, Scott experienced varying degrees of emotion. As he gave the bride away and stepped aside to stand next to Evie, tightness uncurled in his chest. They were close and he couldn't push away the need to touch her. So he rested the back of his hand against her arm and traced a little path up and down. She shivered but didn't move, didn't do anything that might distract from the bride and groom exchanging their vows.

Once the vows were over, the bridal party disappeared for an hour with the photographer. They were ferried away in golf carts to a spot in the grounds of the country club where they could get the best shots. When they returned to the marquee, most of the guests were already seated.

After dinner there were speeches, the traditional cutting of the cake and then dancing. His sister and new husband took to the floor before the rest of the bridal party followed. To have Evie in his arms felt good.

"I have two left feet," Evie warned, moving to the dance floor with him.

Scott grinned when she began to move in an awkward way. Okay, so Evie couldn't dance. She had other talents. She could cook. And paint. And she was a great kisser.

"You're smiling," she said, and tightened her grip on his shoulder. "Am I that bad?"

"Yep." He chuckled. "Follow my lead and no one will notice. Besides, the bride and groom get all the attention."

She looked across the dance floor to where Noah and Callie swayed together. "Yes, I suppose they do."

He heard a break in her voice. "Evie," he said softly. "Are you all right?"

"I'm fine. Just tired, I guess."

He wondered if she was thinking about her own wedding. That was normal, right? She looked lost and a little sad. She was probably thinking about her husband. The one man she'd loved. The urge to make it better for her drummed through Scott's blood. Not that he knew how. He didn't know much of anything when it came to Evie. The last week had been hell. Living with her but barely speaking, walking into rooms that held the lingering scent of her fragrance, working out ways to avoid being alone with her...the whole damn thing had become exhausting.

The truth was he missed her.

And hadn't a clue what to do about it. Another week and he'd be gone. Back to his life and his job and he could forget all about Evie Dunn. He could forget how she felt in his arms and the taste of her kiss. Every ounce of good sense he possessed warned him away from Evie. But the pull back toward her was intense and impossible to ignore.

They danced for a while longer, not speaking, only moving together. At one point he switched partners with Cameron, the best man, and ended up dancing with a bubbly redhead whose name he didn't quite recall. Later he tried to get Evie alone again. Instead, his sister cornered him by the drinks table.

"Is something going on you're not telling me?" she asked suspiciously.

Scott shrugged and took an imported beer from the bar attendant. "Not a thing."

"You always were a terrible liar."

"Nothing to tell," he assured his sister. "Wanna dance?"

Callie gripped his arm. "I just don't want to see anyone get hurt."

Neither do I. "No one's getting hurt," he said, and took Callie's arm. "Promise."

But as he took his sister to the dance floor, the word felt flat and empty. Because people *were* getting hurt. He was hurting Evie simply by being himself. She'd let him off the hook and he was glad for it…right? He didn't want commitment or anything resembling a relationship.

Only…watching Evie beneath the marquee, shimmering so beautifully in her gold dress, with her magnificent hair curling around her shoulders, it sure as hell felt as though he did.

Because it was Christmas Eve, the wedding was over by nine o'clock. Callie and Noah had planned to spend the next few days at home and were flying out to Hawaii for their honeymoon after New Year's. While they were gone, Mary-Jayne and Callie's mother, Eleanor, would be staying at their place to look after the children.

Evie arrived home at nine-thirty, achingly aware of Scott's presence beside her as he drove her car, and with Trevor in tow, complaining about the penguin suit he'd been forced to wear all afternoon. The Manning sisters were still awake, eager to know all about the wedding, and she remained downstairs for a while to chat with them. Scott and Trevor headed upstairs, presumably to ditch the suits in favor of something less formal. But Evie was reluctant to take off the pale gold satin dress she knew was a flattering fit and color. And the pumps on her feet gave her an extra three inches of height.

The Manning sisters were well into the Christmas cake

and cranberry punch Evie had left out earlier, and she joined them for a glass. When Trevor returned downstairs he swiped some cake and dropped into a chair. It was their usual Christmas Eve tradition—drinks with Flora and Amelia, the retelling of old stories, the exchange of gifts with the sisters and then bed at a respectable hour.

Scott came back downstairs, still in his suit minus the tie, and Evie's pulse jumped about erratically. She wondered how she'd ever find any man attractive again after he disappeared from her life. He held a carry bag and she recognized the name of the gift store in Bellandale. The sisters were delighted he had joined them and they all found a spot in the living room around the big tree and began exchanging gifts.

Trevor was blown away by the newest computer game Scott gave him, and the sisters appreciated the trinkets he gifted them with. Evie was touched, imagining him selecting presents for the elderly women. She didn't say much as she accepted a beautiful linen tablecloth from the sisters and watched as each opened the set of small watercolors she'd painted years earlier of various scenes from Crystal Point.

"This is for you."

Evie looked up. Scott held out a small parcel and she took it with tentative fingers. Instead of ripping open the wrapping as she was tempted to do, she passed him the gift she'd bought him, but had wondered if she'd have the courage to give him. It was nothing particularly personal—a traveler's guide to historical facts of the local area, but he seemed to like it. Once everyone had finished unwrapping she felt all four sets of eyes focused on her. The gift in her hands remained unopened.

"Oh, of course." She pried open the paper and then lifted the lid on the small box. On a cushion of blue velvet lay a ball of crystal, with an image of a woman cleverly engraved within. "How…lovely."

"It's Catherine of Bologna," he explained. "Patron Saint of Artists."

Evie's heart flipped over. "Thank you." She popped the lid back and stood. "Trevor—time for bed." She looked toward the Manning sisters and not once in Scott's direction. "Well, good night. I'll see you in the morning. Breakfast will be at nine."

She walked from the room with a stiff back, clutching the gift against her ribs. *Any moment now,* she thought… *any second and I will burst into tears.* She got to the kitchen in record time and didn't relax until she heard the familiar thud of feet heading upstairs and the sound of doors closing at the front of the house.

Now I can breathe.

She snuck another look at the crystal globe and shut the box just as quickly. It was too much. That he should know her like this and enter her world with a gift so personal to her, a gift she somehow knew he'd chosen because it *was* personal. No one did that for Evie. No one saw deep inside her or thought to wonder what she needed. Her family and friends gave her crockery and linen and CDs. People who'd known her forever but didn't really know her at all. Didn't know how much pain she felt because her creativity had been zapped. Didn't know how much she longed to be able to put all of her heart into her painting again and feel the passion in each brushstroke.

"You look really beautiful in that dress."

She swiveled around. Scott stood in the doorway.

"I should have said so earlier."

Evie clutched the gift and shrugged a little. "It's okay. Everyone looks at the bride."

He leaned against the doorjamb. "I was looking at you."

Her feelings for him lurched forward, catching her breath with an unexpected intensity. "I thought you might have spent the evening at your sister's. Your mother's there and Callie would—"

"I wanted to be here," he said quietly, cutting her off. "I'll see my mom and Callie tomorrow."

Evie swallowed hard. "Well, I'm glad you're here. And I know Trevor appreciated it. He doesn't get a lot of adult male company. Well, except for Noah and my father."

And he misses his dad... But Evie didn't say it, she didn't imply that her son was longing for another father figure in his life. Or that she wanted Scott to fill the role. She wasn't about to start wishing for what could never be.

"You look really beautiful in that dress."

She placed the gift on the bench top. "You said that already. Thank you for my gift."

He smiled. "I thought she might watch over you while you paint. You know, to help with your muse."

"I hope it will," she replied. "I want to get back into it. I want to find myself in it again."

He hadn't moved. She looked up and spotted a piece of mistletoe hanging above his head, and it made her smile. "Looks like Flora and Amelia have been at it again."

He looked upward. "I guess we shouldn't disappoint them."

She didn't budge. He still hadn't moved, still remained in the doorway, arms crossed, shoulder against the architrave, looking as if he knew she wanted him.

And she did. So much her whole body hurt.

"What if I can't let you go?" she asked shakily.

"You will," he replied. "You're a strong woman. Stronger than you think."

"I'm a fraud," she admitted, taking a step toward him.

"I'm not really the sensible sister. In fact, right now I don't feel the least bit sensible."

"Because you know the odds of a long-distance relationship working out are virtually zero?"

Yes...that's why. And because she wanted it to work, the idea shocked her. Lust and desire had morphed into something deeper—something so deep she knew she was in danger of having her heart broken into inconsolable pieces. She tried to marshal her thoughts and feelings and tame the wildness within her blood. But she failed.

"Because I said I couldn't do casual," she said, and took another step. "And because I know that when this is over, I will have to let you go."

He reached for her in three strides and hauled her into his arms, not roughly, but with enough force that Evie sucked in a startled breath as his mouth found hers. His kiss was hot and hard, his tongue a driving force against the softness of her lips. And she craved it. She craved it and took everything, every slide, every slant, every part of him he was willing to give her. She was hot all over, like a raging furnace, and she'd never been more alive in her life.

His hands gripped her shoulders, molding her against him, and still he kissed her. Evie pushed herself against him, wanting to feel as close as she could with clothes on. He groaned low in his throat and deepened the kiss, drawing her into his mouth.

Scott's hands roamed down her body and settled on her bottom. "Did I tell you how beautiful you look in that dress?" he asked against her mouth, and ground their hips together.

Evie smiled. "You may have mentioned it."

"But right now," he growled, "I just wanna get you out of it."

It took about two minutes to get to Scott's room and

about thirty seconds to remove their clothes. They made love quickly, passionately and without words. Evie clung to him, taking and giving, feeling him all over her, around her and finally inside her. She gave herself up to the pleasure and came apart in his arms. When he lost himself, too, she clung to him tightly, watching in amazement as his strong body shuddered and then lay still against her.

She touched his back, trailing her fingers up and down his spine. He was breathing heavy and took a few gulps of air before he rolled from her and flung himself onto his back.

In the darkness, with only the sound of the waves crashing against the rocks along the foreshore intruding on them, Evie let out a long sigh of contentment. She felt a lovely sense of lethargy. She touched his arm and was startled to feel the tenseness in his muscles.

"Evie?"

She held her breath for a second. Did he regret their lovemaking? "Yes?"

"I didn't protect you." His words echoed around the room. "I'm sorry."

They hadn't used a condom. She quickly did a math calculation in her head. "It's fine," she assured him, but tiny fingers of concern clutched at her veins. She stroked his arm. "No need to worry."

"I don't have unprotected sex, ever."

She twisted her lips. "Except for just now."

"Well...yeah. Is there any chance you might get—"

"No," she said quickly. "No, I don't think...no," she said again. "Very little chance."

Very little chance? Just what did that mean? Scott couldn't believe his carelessness. He never played roulette with birth control. He sat up in bed and flicked on the light. "You're sure?"

Evie rolled onto her side and raised both brows. "I know my cycle."

His stomach turned over. She looked so calm and it annoyed the hell out of him. "You'd tell me?" he asked, almost holding his breath. "If something happened?"

"Well, it's not the sort of thing I could keep a secret, is it?"

She had a point. And the knee-jerk terror he'd felt gradually dissipated. He reached into the bedside drawer and grabbed a foil packet. "No more roulette," he said, and tossed it onto the bed. "For next time."

"Next time?" Evie picked up the protection and held it between two fingers. "You're that sure there'll be a next time?"

Scott smiled, rolled over and pinned her beneath him. "I'm sure," he said, trailing kisses along her collarbone, "that I won't get through the next hour unless I can make love to you again."

Evie kissed his jaw. "So stop talking and get to it."

Shortly afterward they made love again, this time with protection, and then they took a shower together.

"I have a spa bath in my ensuite bathroom," she told him as she blotted her skin dry with a towel. "That could be fun."

"Is that an invitation to enter the inner sanctum of your bedroom?"

She stopped toweling. "What does that mean?"

Scott wrapped a towel around his waist. "You know exactly what it means."

She draped the towel around herself toga-style. "You think I'm keeping my bedroom off-limits?" She frowned. "And why would I want to do that?"

Suddenly, the steam in the room was coming off Evie and not from the hot water. "You tell me?"

"You know," she said, twisting her hair free from the towel she had wrapped around it to keep it dry, "that's a pretty adolescent answer."

Scott felt the bite of her remark. "Are you denying it?"

"I'm saying I haven't consciously acted that way."

Scott didn't push the issue, but he certainly felt her reluctance to share her room with him. "Okay. Let's forget it."

Evie tucked at her towel. "I should probably go to my room anyway," she said quietly as she walked from the bathroom and into the bedroom. "Trevor normally comes to see me first thing—you know, it being Christmas in about an hour."

"Sure," he said with about as much enthusiasm as a rock.

He stayed by the door and watched as she collected the dress he'd stripped off her earlier. She grabbed her shoes and underwear and headed for the door. She turned before she grabbed the handle. "Well, good night."

Scott remained where he was and pushed back the fierce pounding inside his chest and the urge to ask her to stay, and the need to take back his stupid comment about her bedroom. He'd never been the jealous type—maybe because he'd never cared enough to feel the gut-wrenching emotion before this...before Evie. But he was jealous. He was jealous she'd kept that part of her from him...from *them*.

At that moment, as if he'd been hit with a thunderbolt, Scott realized just how powerful his feelings for Evie had become.

"When this is over I will have to let you go."

He knew that. She wouldn't make a scene. She'd don her Sensible Evie hat and send him on his way, back to his life in L.A., back to everything and everyone who was familiar to him—and not one of them, he knew, could hold a candle to the woman in front of him.

"Good night, Evie," he said. "Merry Christmas."

She left the room without another word.

Chapter Ten

Christmas at Barbara and Bill Preston's house was a day-long celebration that started in the morning and only finished when Evie's dad fell asleep in his favorite recliner and the kids started dozing off because they'd consumed copious amounts of pop and candy. But it had been a good day. With her entire family in attendance, plus the whole Jakowski clan, the Manning sisters and a few other people long regarded as family, it was a day to remember.

Of course, Evie hardly spoke to Scott. She made sure she was well away from him at the long table when dinner was served, and avoided eye contact as much as possible. No one could know they were lovers. No one could know she craved him in ways she hadn't imagined possible. There was no point. He'd be gone in a week and she'd go back to the structured and predictable life she'd had before he'd entered her world. And she fooled everyone.

Except Grace.

Her smart, mostly aloof sister was onto her.

"You've been to L.A., haven't you?" Grace asked quietly. She'd sidled up to Evie as she scraped plates of uneaten food into a plastic bag. "I went to a conference there a few years back. Good weather, friendly people. Quite a lot like here, actually. You'd probably like to go back and revisit the sights, right?"

Evie continued her task and didn't flinch. "Is there a point to this conversation?"

Grace raised her perfect brows. "Of course. You'd need someone to show you around. Quite the coincidence that Scott is—"

"Would you stop," Evie demanded. "We're not—"

"Oh, spare me," Grace said, cutting her off. "Despite how hard you've tried not to show it, if you two were any more into each other I'd have to get the hose out."

Evie's face burned. "I can't believe you just said that." She tied the plastic bag in a tight knot. "It's impossible, anyhow."

Grace moved alongside her. "So you're involved?"

"We're something… I'm not sure what."

"Lovers?" Grace asked.

Evie's cheeks flamed. "It's new for me. I've never had a lover before. I mean, other than Gordon. But Scott makes me feel so…so…" She shrugged. *"Whoosh."*

Grace's faultlessly beautiful face creased in a frown. "What?"

"You know," Evie explained. "That thing…that feeling. Not that I'm an expert, but Fiona and Callie assured me it's called *whoosh.*"

Her sister looked mildly amused. "So what are you going to do about it?"

"Do? Nothing. Just get back to my real life when it's over."

"Perhaps this is your real life," Grace said.

Evie gave her younger sister a startled stare. No, she thought. Her real life was the B and B and being a mother and a friend and a sister and a daughter. Being Scott's lover was only ever going to be temporary. She raised her hands and twirled them in the air. "This is my real life."

Grace smiled and exposed perfectly white teeth. "Don't sell yourself short."

She found it a strange comment from her usually tight-lipped sister—it was Mary-Jayne who always dispensed advice on romance. "I won't."

"Not that I'm an expert in the area," Grace said. "In fact, forget I said anything. Perhaps I'm feeling more optimistic than usual at the moment."

"Really?" she asked, knowing there was something going on with her sister. At another time she would have asked. She would have donned her *sympathetic* cap and listened with an open mind and heart. But not today. Her heart was full. Her mind was muddled.

And later that night as she lay snuggled up to Scott after making love with him, Evie experienced the profound realization that she wanted to stay in his arms for the rest of her life.

Scott was certain the days got shorter the closer he came to leaving Crystal Point and returning to Los Angeles.

"I like your mother," Evie said to him one night, curled up against him after they'd made love. "We got to talk a bit today. She's nice."

"Did you?" He trailed his fingers along her shoulder. "Do you think she's worked it out? Us, I mean?"

Evie shrugged. "I'm not sure. Would she mind?"

"About you?" He smiled. "Hardly. She's happy if I'm happy."

Evie's inside jumped. It sounded so incredibly intimate. Scott was happy with her? She didn't dare imagine what that meant. "And she never remarried after your dad passed away?"

"Nope."

"She must have loved him deeply. I mean to never have another man in her life."

"She did," he replied, and suddenly he was thinking about Evie and not his mother. Evie hadn't remarried. Evie had stayed true to her husband. Except for now, he thought, feeling the smoothness of her lovely skin against him. Feeling Evie all over him, inside, as if she were the air in his lungs. How would he ever breathe again once he left her?

"How did they meet?"

Scott shuffled his thoughts to her question. "They met when they were twenty. My dad and his twin sister moved to L.A. when they were twenty and got jobs working with a telecommunications company. They were only meant to be gone twelve months. Turns out they stayed for good."

Eve cuddled closer. "Was he sick for a long time?"

Scott's chest tightened. "Yes. He'd been in a bad accident a few years before and afterward was plagued by the side effects and related illnesses."

"What kind of accident?"

"He was a climber," he said, thinking that would be enough. "A mountaineer."

Evie shifted on her side and looked at him. "Tell me about his accident."

Scott closed his eyes for a moment, remembering what had happened as though it were yesterday. "He was on an expedition to Nanga Parbat, the second highest peak in Pakistan. He suffered from high-altitude edema and almost lost his life. Fortunately his team got him down in time. He came home to us and died a couple of years later. He didn't have the lungs to climb again. Sometimes I think that *not* climbing was more responsible for his death than the peak itself."

"I didn't realize he was an—"

"Adrenaline junkie?" He cut her off gently. "Yes, he was."

"Did you ever climb with him?"

"I did not." It came out harsher than he liked, but a swell of feelings washed up in his chest, mixing with the sudden desire *not* to talk about his father.

Evie picked up on it immediately. "You didn't approve?"

Scott shrugged. "It wasn't my place to approve. It was his life."

"A life he risked?"

Scott felt the truth burn through his blood. And the lingering resentment for a man who was essentially a good father—although sometimes a reckless one. "Like I said, it was his—"

"You don't believe that," she said, cutting him off as she sat up. "I don't get it—you obviously have a problem with what your dad did and yet you chose to become a firefighter."

"One has nothing to do with the other."

Evie made a huffing sound. "Yeah—right. One is *all* about the other."

"My father climbed mountains for the thrill of the climb—I do not fight fires for that reason." He pushed at the bedclothes and sat up. "It's a job, Evie."

She scooted across the bed until she was in front of him. The light of the half-moon shone through the open curtains and when the sheet she'd been trying to hold slipped away, Scott got a great look at her rose-tipped breasts. His body stirred instantly and he grazed the back of his hand over one nipple.

"Stop doing that," she said, probably not as sharp as she wanted as she pulled back. "I want to talk with you. Don't distract me."

Scott's eyes widened. "You're distracting me," he assured her as he looked at her breasts.

Evie unexpectedly reached out and touched his face, lifting his cheek upward so their eyes met. "Tell me why you really became a firefighter."

Scott took a breath. "Because I wanted to run into burning buildings."

"And that's all?"

"Isn't that enough?" he asked. "It's what you believe, anyway—isn't it?"

"I'm not so sure anymore."

"Believe it," he said, but the truth suddenly jumped around in his head. He reached for her, dragging her against him as he pushed back against the pillows. Enough talk, he thought. Enough truth. He took her mouth in a searing kiss that was so hot it practically scorched the air between them. Her mouth was sweet and tempting and luscious. He'd kiss her and forget the days were closing in. He'd make love with her and disregard the taunting voice in the back of his mind reminding him that the heaven he'd found in Evie's arms was only ever going to be temporary. She *would* let him go. And he would have to leave and return to reality.

Evie got home to an empty house on the Tuesday after Christmas. When she reached the upstairs kitchen she found a note stuck near the telephone written in her son's neat handwriting. *Have gone out with Scott—be back later.*

Evie's heart stilled. Trevor was with Scott. And Scott, she knew, was at the Emergency Services Station, speaking with the volunteers and the local Rural Fire Brigade.

Anger quickly filled her blood and she grabbed her car keys.

He wouldn't do that. Surely he'd know I'd never agree to that.

The drive took only a few minutes. Evie parked outside and jumped out of the car. She saw Scott's motorcycle and the vehicles of the other volunteers. Her blood pumped, her thoughts suddenly centered on Trevor being here, with these people. *These people I've considered the enemy for ten years.* Maybe not consciously, but in her secret place, her darkest heart.

She reached the doorway and stood beneath the threshold. The big shed was filled with people and she felt the gut-wrenching pain she always felt when confronted with this place. She always stayed outside, never going into the big, cold building with its corrugated walls and concrete floor. Memories bombarded Evie's thoughts. Memories of Gordon's lifeless body lying on the floor—and thoughts of well-meaning colleagues hovering around him, trying to revive him, trying to bring him back.

By the time Evie had arrived, he'd gone. There were no goodbyes. Just his battered body left stretched out on the cold floor, covered in a plastic tarp so she wouldn't see the extent of his injuries.

She hated this place.

There was a group of people behind the fire truck, positioned in a half arc. Scott stood in the center beside a long white board and was talking to the Rural Fire Brigade volunteers in a quiet voice. She loved his voice, loved hearing him whisper things to her as they made love. Loved hearing him say she was beautiful, desirable…loved the soft pleas of encouragement against her skin when she touched him a certain way or in a certain place.

But he wasn't speaking those words now. Now he was

all-business, pure firefighter and every inch the man who risked his life daily because that was his job. Evie watched for a moment, half absorbed, half repulsed. Until she spotted Trevor. Her son was listening intently and wearing a yellow jacket, the same type of high-visibility gear the volunteers wore.

She saw red immediately. "Trevor?" About a dozen sets of eyes zoomed in on her, including her son's. But it was Scott's gaze she felt snap through her with blistering intensity. He stared at her, frowning, and she turned immediately back to her son. "Let's go home."

The silence continued. Everyone there knew her of course—she was poor Evie Dunn who'd lost her husband. They offered pity in their stares and it made her so mad she wanted to shout and tell them they were all reckless fools.

"But I was just—"

Evie raised her hand and beckoned him forward. "Come on," she said, before she swiveled on her heels and headed back to the car with Trevor in tow. He was complaining, but Evie was in no mood to listen. She told him to take off the jacket and he handed it to her after a few seconds of resistance.

"Evie, wait up."

She stilled instantly, told Trevor to get into the car and then turned and took the dozen or so steps to reach Scott. "How could you do it?" she demanded, her voice higher than she wanted, her heart pounding the blood through her veins.

"How could I do what?"

Evie glared at him, so angry she could barely get the words out. "How could you bring my son here?"

He looked at her oddly. "I don't—"

"You had no right," she said, and pushed away the hotness behind her eyes. "I don't want him here with these people."

"What people?"

Evie pointed toward the building. "The people who knew his father. People who did what Gordon did. People who were with him *that night.*"

"Evie," he said quietly, "I had no intention of—"

"Don't you get it?" she snapped, and tossed the jacket into his chest. He caught it immediately. "I don't want him here." She waved her arms. "He can't want this like his father did. I don't want him to be like Gordon. And I certainly don't want him to be like you."

The pain in Evie's voice cut through Scott. *"I don't want him to be like you."* He wasn't sure what to think. He heard her anguish and fought the instinctive urge to take her in his arms.

"Evie, I'm sorry if I've upset you. I didn't realize you'd have a problem with Trevor coming with me."

She made a huffing sound. "You should have asked permission. He's *my* son."

"He asked to come with me," Scott explained. "I didn't drag him here."

"He's a child. My child!" She crossed her arms jerkily, her anger palpable. "And I decide where he goes and who he goes with."

"Okay," he said, feeling less than agreeable but refusing to trade any more heated words with her while they were out in the open and at risk of being overheard, not only by Trevor but also by the dozen volunteers inside the shed. "We can talk about this later."

She seemed to calm for a moment, and took a step forward. But she wasn't calm at all, he noticed; she was furious—and all her fury was absolutely aimed toward him.

"Don't try to pacify me, Scott." She planted her hands firmly on her hips. "You can play superhero with these people all you like—but don't ever involve my son."

"Superhero?" he echoed incredulously. "What does that mean?"

"You know exactly. I saw you in there. You were holding court with the volunteers, and they were listening to you like you're some kind of fire god. Well, maybe to them you are. But not to me." She tossed her hair. "To me you're just…just…you're…"

Scott wasn't sure he wanted to hear. "I'm what?"

She glared at him and whispered, "A mistake." With a spin, she turned away and stomped toward her small car. Scott watched wordlessly as she flung herself inside and drove off.

He remained where he was, feeling her words like a fist to his gut. After a moment, he turned around to find Cameron Jakowski standing a few feet away. He shrugged.

"If it makes you feel better," Cameron said quietly, "it's more about what happened here than you letting Trev tag along. Gordon was brought here the night he died."

Scott's stomach rolled. He pointed to the building. "Here?"

Cameron nodded. "Yeah. It was a pretty bad scene that night. There was no chance of the paramedics getting to him in time—his injuries were too extensive. He was crushed between two trailers at the holiday park. They brought him here and this is where he died."

Scott felt a burning pressure gather behind his ribs. He left about an hour later determined to straighten the mess out with Evie.

It was well past six o'clock when he returned to Dunn Inn. The big house seemed eerily quiet. The lights from the Christmas tree blinked through the front window, and he headed for the room when he spotted Evie's unmistakable silhouette moving back and forth through the curtains.

"Can we talk?"

She was by the sofa, fluffing cushions, and didn't stop her task as she spoke. "I'd rather not."

Scott took a few steps into the room. "Well, how about I talk and you listen?"

That got her attention and she stopped what she was doing. "Okay...talk."

Scott pushed down the annoyance in his throat. "I'm sorry."

"Fine," she said tersely, and continued moving pillows. "You're sorry."

"Cameron told me about your husband."

She looked across the room. "He did? And what did he say? That Gordon's body was left at that place for seven hours? That I wasn't allowed to see him because his injuries were so bad? That his blood-soaked jacket was lying on the floor for everyone to see? The same kind of jacket Trevor was wearing tonight. Or that I had to tell my five-year-old son his daddy wouldn't be coming home?"

Scott chose his words carefully. "It must have been a difficult time."

"It was the worst moment of my life."

"And seeing Trevor there brought it all back?"

"Yes. And I don't want my son involved in that life."

Scott took a few steps toward her. "But if that's what he chooses, Evie, all you can really do is support him."

"Are you a parenting expert now?"

It was such an unlike-Evie thing to say that Scott felt the sting of it through to his bones. "No—but I know you can't make someone be something they're not."

Evie raised her chin. "My son is going to college, and

then he'll choose whatever career suits him. He won't be risking his life pursing pointless adventure."

A kernel of resentment sprouted inside him. She was so wrong. "I hardly think that an Emergency Services volunteer is looking for pointless adventure—it takes a certain kind of selflessness to risk one's own life to ensure the safety of someone else."

"Well, you would think that," she said, not looking the least bit convinced. "But I know most of those people that were there this afternoon. They were Gordon's friends—they're the same people he used to bungee jump with and deep-sea-dive with and when they had a chance would climb every rock face they could find. They have the same rogue gene he had—that need to push to the limit, to try something purely because it was dangerous." She sat down on the sofa. "That's not a legacy I want my son to inherit."

So her husband had an adventurous spirit. It began to make sense to him now. "It was a bad storm that killed your husband, Evie, not extreme sports."

"It was the thrill," she said coolly. "The thrill of beating human mortality. Wasn't your own father one of them? I should think you'd understand my determination to keep Trevor away from those people."

"I do understand. But I also know that the volunteers I was with this afternoon are good people who care for their community and want to give something back. They're not thrill seekers, Evie."

"*I* know them," she said quietly. "I know what makes them tick. I know that on the night of the cyclone, Gordon couldn't wait to get out there—he couldn't wait to put on his jacket and face the elements. Because he had no fear and no concern for the consequences. He wanted to fix everything, and in the end he couldn't do the one thing he should have done...kept himself safe...kept himself part of our family. He broke our family apart because he had this need to protect everyone around him."

Realization landed squarely on Scott's shoulders. "Is that why you're so angry? Because he left you that night? Are you mad at him because he went out when he should have stayed home to protect you?"

"No," she said quickly. "Yes. I don't know."

She wrapped her arms around herself and seemed so incredibly vulnerable Scott had to fight his urge to hold her. "I imagine the last thing he expected was that he wouldn't come home to you."

She looked up and met his gaze head-on. "You think I'm being irrational?"

"I think you're…hurting…and maybe a bit misguided."

His words clearly struck a chord because her eyes shone with tears. "I knew you'd never really understand how I feel about this stuff."

"I do understand, Evie."

"How could you? You're a firefighter. Your whole life is a risk. You said yourself that you'd have to quit if you wanted…if you ever wanted something else…more than just the job."

The idea of having more than just the job suddenly seemed very real. And quitting? Scott felt the weight of his words stomp between his shoulder blades. "I know what I said. I watched my friend die because he wanted both…and I watched my father give up time with his family because he was obsessed with his mountains. But the people you think are going to corrupt your son into wanting to risk his life—they're just out to do their bit for their community. I don't think they have lofty ideals about adventure or pushing themselves to the limits for the thrill of it. You're wrong about them, Evie. And you're wrong to not allow your son to get to know his father's friends."

She took a deep breath and glared at him through her tears. "I'm wrong because I want to keep my son safe?"

"You're wrong because you assume everyone's motivation is the same." Scott rested his hands on the back of the sofa. "Do you want to know why I joined the fire department, Evie? Not so I could fulfill some desire for adventure or because I wanted to put my life on the line to satisfy an egotistical need to prove I'm immortal—I joined because I wanted a profession my father would be proud of."

The words seemed truer now than they ever had before, and Scott forced back the lump of emotion suddenly clogging his throat. "He worked behind a desk his whole life, and a couple of times a year he'd take off for his mountains. And each time I'd wonder if this was the last time I'd see him. He wanted me to go with him, he wanted to share it with me, but I was just a scared kid who spent most of my time with my head in a book or playing football. I never went with him. I never got to understand what drew him to risk his life every time he climbed. By the time I'd gotten past my boyhood fears and thought that maybe I *could* go with him, he was dead. So I joined the LAFD and I thought in some way, from wherever he was, he might know I wasn't afraid anymore."

Evie felt the hot sting of tears behind her eyes again and blinked a couple of times. She had a hard time imagining this strong, confident man being afraid of anything. Her feelings for him...her love for him suddenly felt like a powerful, overwhelming force—more intense than anything she had ever known.

But loving him wasn't enough. She'd had a life before Scott entered her world—a life she had to get back to. Sensible Evie was about to make a comeback. She couldn't change who she was—at least not forever. Perhaps for a few stolen weeks. But afterward she would be left with only memories and the knowledge that they were as incompatible as oil and water.

"I need to stay angry with you to help me get through these next few days. I can't sleep with you anymore. I just can't. Good night, Scott," she said quietly, wanting nothing more than to fold herself in his arms and stay there for the rest of her life.

He touched her arm as she walked by him. "Evie," he said, taking her hand. "Is this really how you want it to be?"

"Yes," she said, but wasn't sure how. "I think we both know it's for the best."

His expression was unreadable and he released her instantly. "For the record, Evie, I'll *never* consider what's happened between us a mistake."

Chapter Eleven

Evie stayed downstairs for a while, thinking about Scott, thinking about Trevor. Her son deserved an explanation, so she headed directly for Trevor's room when she got upstairs. He was sitting on the edge of his bed, a handheld computer game at his fingertips.

"Can I come in?"

He shrugged. "Sure."

Evie took a couple of steps into the room. "I'm not mad at you or anything," she said quietly.

He looked up. "You're mad at Scott, though."

She didn't disagree. "He should have asked me if it was okay for you to go with him."

"He didn't force me to go. I tagged along," Trevor said. "I didn't think it would be such a big deal."

A big deal? Evie suddenly felt like an overprotective, cloistering parent who wasn't prepared to give her child the freedom to spread his wings. "I'm sorry if I embarrassed you. It's just that I—"

"Don't want me to end up like Dad," he said, and tossed the game onto the bed. "Yeah, I know."

Shame crept along her spine. "That's not exactly it," she said. "I just want you to have other opportunities."

"I wasn't joining up," he told her. "I wouldn't do that without talking to you about it first. I was just listening. Cody's thinking of volunteering and I thought I'd go along and see what goes on there. But Scott told us we should think about finishing school first because that's our priority at the moment." He raised his brows. "It made sense. So, like I said, I wasn't joining up—I was listening."

Evie wanted to hug him close. Instead she took a deep breath. "I should have trusted you. But when I saw you wearing that jacket I—"

"I was only trying it on. Scott told me to wear it so I could feel how hot it gets inside one of those things. Then he told me to imagine wearing that and a heavy hat and oxygen and then walking into a fire." Trevor held up one skinny arm. "He said he reckoned I needed to do a whole lot of push-ups before I could carry all that equipment."

Evie tried to shake the powerful pounding of her heart. "He's right."

Trevor made a face. "I know he is. You shouldn't be mad at him. I wish he was hanging around."

But he's not.

Three days later Evie said goodbye to Scott. Callie was taking him to the airport and Evie barely registered his quiet farewell. She didn't touch him, didn't kiss him, didn't hang on to him and tell him how much she would miss him, even though the need to do so pumped through her blood with a molten fury. She stood back as he shook Trevor's hand and said goodbye to Flora and Amelia. She didn't look at Callie as he collected his bags and left, terrified her friend would see the truth in her eyes.

Once he'd left she headed directly for her studio. She had managed about ten minutes alone when Flora Manning tapped on the door and didn't wait to be invited inside.

"I'm sorry to see that young man leave," Flora said pointedly.

"His life is in L.A.," Evie said as she grabbed a couple of pots filled with brushes.

Flora raised her silver brows. "Is it?"

Evie dropped the pots into the sink. "I really don't want to—"

"I'm not fooled, you know," she said, cutting her off. "If you had any sense you'd jump into that car of yours and chase after him."

Evie's cheeks flamed. "I *do* have sense," she said quickly. "That's why I'm staying exactly where I am."

"You're stubborn," Flora said. "That's your trouble."

"It's better this way. He can get on with his life...and so can I."

Flora looked around the room. "This isn't your life— this is the place where you hide from life." She tutted. "But enough said. Amelia and I are leaving tomorrow."

And the house would be even quieter. With no new guests arriving for a few weeks, Evie had plenty of time to think about Scott. Plenty of time to remember everything they'd shared. But right now she had to pull herself together and not give in to the dreadful pain in her heart.

"I've enjoyed having you here," Evie said. "And thank you for...well, you know." She reached out and hugged the elderly woman.

"So stop being a damned fool and take what's in front of you," Flora said into her ear.

He's not mine to take...

And knowing that hurt her so much she could barely breathe.

The end of January and all of February were unusually quiet for the B and B. But having only one guest gave Evie an opportunity to get stuck into some necessary cleaning and repair work. She hired a handyman to replace window hinges that had corroded from the salt in the air, a requirement when the ocean was at the doorstep, and set about to do some of the minor painting and yard work by herself.

She went on a date with the schoolteacher, experienced not a single bit of *whoosh* and decided to forget about dating for the next couple of decades.

Summer had arrived with a vengeance. The days were hot, the nights long and balmy. Trevor had gone north to visit Gordon's parents, and without him the big house seemed empty.

To make things worse she caught some kind of bug and was laid up in bed for a few days. Afterward, once the nausea abated, she still couldn't kick the fatigue, and her plans to spend long afternoons in the garden, pruning hedges and repotting geraniums around the wishing well, took a backseat to her sudden need to take a nap almost every afternoon.

And then three weeks after he'd returned to Los Angeles, Evie got an email from Scott. It wasn't particularly personal, just a few short lines asking how she was, and he mentioned that he'd returned to work. After dwelling on it for two days, she wrote back.

January 23
Pleased that you've settled back into your routine. It's

quiet around here at the moment, without any guests and Trevor's away. Take care, Evie.

Twenty-four hours later he sent one back.

January 24
Trev emailed me a few days ago and said he was heading off to his grandparents'. He also said you'd been sick. Are you okay now? Scott.

Evie hadn't realized her son was communicating with Scott. But she wasn't surprised. Trevor was addicted to his computer and had genuinely liked Scott. And Evie had to admit, Scott had been generous with his time in regard to her son. She wrote back a few hours later.

January 24
I'm fine, just the summer flu. Lucky you left when you did or you might have caught my germs. Evie.

January 25
I could think of worse things.

It continued like that for a week. Emails about nothing in particular. Nothing important. He asked how she was doing; she said she was fine. She inquired about his work; he said it was okay. But beneath the surface, something simmered…a kind of tension filled with words unsaid. Finally, on the seventh day, he sent her a message she obsessed over for three days.

February 1
I've been thinking, Evie…and I regret the way things ended between us. I'd like to think we can be friends. Scott.

Friends? Evie wasn't so sure she had the fortitude it would take to remain friends with a man she'd known only as her lover. A man she had fallen in love with and whom she could never have. Between the years that divided them and the career he'd chosen, their differences seemed impossible to overcome now that an ocean lay between them. But he was Callie's brother. He was family. And family was important.

So she garnered her resolve and replied.

February 4
I agree. And I've been thinking too. I overreacted that afternoon. And I'm sorry we didn't really get to say goodbye. Evie.

February 5
Me too. But I'm not sure I could have managed to say goodbye to you.

After that, the emails they exchanged became friendlier and she found herself sharing stories about what was happening in Crystal Point, about her guests who had just arrived and the slow progress being made renovating the surf club. In turn, he told her about his close circle of friends and how the football team he supported was doing and what he'd been creating in the kitchen. He asked if she'd been painting and she admitted that she had been spending time in the studio.

She slept a lot, sometimes in the guest room where she'd spent her magical moments with Scott. She lay on the bed and hugged a pillow, imagining the sheets still had the scent of him in them. But she didn't cry—despite feeling so emotional and wrung out. By the end of February the nausea returned and she began to wonder if something was seriously wrong. Trevor noticed it, too.

"You're sick again?" he asked one afternoon when he loped through the door after school.

Evie shrugged and sat down wearily. "I'm just tired."

Trevor grabbed an apple from the fruit bowl and placed it in front of her. "And you're hardly eating."

That wasn't exactly true. She did eat. Dry toast and crackers seemed to have become her staple diet to combat the wretched nausea. And she was so tired that eating huge meals seemed like way too much effort.

She grabbed the apple and smiled. "I eat," she said, and to prove her point took a tiny bite. "See."

"You've been like this for a month or so. Maybe you should see a doctor?"

Evie looked at her son. A month? Had it been that long? But what would a doctor tell her—to drink fluids and rest? Wasn't that the usual remedy for the flu?

Only, the more she considered it, the less like a flu it seemed. Besides the nausea and fatigue, she didn't feel sick. She felt…like…like…

Evie dropped the apple and quickly excused herself. She headed for her bedroom and grabbed the desk diary in her bedside drawer. She looked at the calendar pages with urgent fingers. The empty pages stared back at her.

I missed my period.

Not once, but twice. *How did I not notice that?*

Oh…God…could it be true? *Could I be pregnant with Scott's baby?* She did the calculation in her head and worked out the weeks. She remembered the time they'd made love without protection. She dropped the diary and placed her hands on her abdomen. A baby? Tears pitched behind her eyes and she shook herself. There was no point in imagining what a baby would mean to her before she had proof.

She took about ten minutes to change her clothes and

grab the keys to her Honda. The trip into town was forty-five minutes there and back, with a quick stop at a pharmacy to purchase an over-the-counter pregnancy test.

She took the test and waited. Three of the longest minutes of her life. Once the time was up, Evie stared at the strip. Two blue lines. She sat on the edge of the bathtub.

Oh, sweet heaven...

"I'm pregnant." She said it out loud. "Oh, my God, I'm pregnant."

I'm having Scott's baby...

Joy and fear mixed together and created a vortex of feelings inside her so intense she stood no chance of stopping the tears. So Evie let them come. When it was over she felt better, stronger somehow, to deal with the inevitable fallout when news of her pregnancy came out. Because it *would* come out. Another month or so and she'd be showing. Her family would ask questions, they'd speculate and she knew it wouldn't be long before they worked it out.

And Scott had a right to know he was about to become a father before the rest of the world did. Only...she wasn't sure how to do it.

Over the following days she picked up the telephone a dozen times and started emails she didn't send. But how did she tell him something like that? Especially when their fledgling relationship was over and all that remained was a courteous, forced friendship held together because they were now obscurely related by the marriage of their siblings.

So, as the days morphed into a week, and then another, her courage dwindled. Evie knew she was living in a vacuum of borrowed time. Trevor kept asking her what was wrong. So did her mother and Noah.

Physically she felt good. The nausea was gone, and her appetite had resumed with a vengeance. She remembered her wanton addiction to toffee ice cream when she'd been pregnant with Trevor, and this time appeared to be no different. She had her first appointment with her obstetrician and scheduled a time to have her first ultrasound the following month.

And still she didn't tell Scott. In fact, she'd been so preoccupied with not telling him, she hadn't responded to any of his emails for a couple of weeks.

In March she received another email.

March 15
I haven't heard from you lately. Is everything okay? Scott.

Evie stared at the computer screen and fought the urge to hit the delete button. But she didn't.

March 24
I'm fine.

March 25
Trevor said you've been sick again? I'm worried about you. What's wrong?

She deliberated for an hour. But she knew it was time for the truth. He had rights and she had an obligation to tell him what was happening. They'd both made love that night, and her resulting pregnancy was a shared responsibility. Whatever Scott chose to do with the information was up to him. All Evie knew was that she wanted the baby. She wanted this precious gift more than she'd ever dared imagine. She took a deep breath and wrote.

March 26
I'm pregnant.

Chapter Twelve

Scott wandered around his apartment that night, barefoot, in jeans and a worn T-shirt; he walked from room to room, trying to soothe the crushing ache behind his ribs.

A baby...

Evie was having his baby. But he felt as if he'd been punched in the gut. That she would tell him like that...it seemed so outrageously callous he could barely get his head around it. And Evie wasn't callous. Of course, he knew she was notoriously hardheaded about some things... but he couldn't believe she would send an email containing two words and think that was adequate.

Scott headed for the kitchen and grabbed a beer from the refrigerator.

His head felt as if it were about to explode. He gulped some beer, winced as the cold liquid froze his brain for a few seconds and tried his best to be as mad as hell at Evie.

But no use. He'd spent months in a kind of dazed

limbo—missing her, wanting her so much he couldn't think about anything else. He'd gone back to work and gone through the motions, determined to keep his head because he knew what the consequences could be if he let the distraction take hold of him.

But the nights were impossible. He hurt all over just thinking about Evie.

I'm going to be a father.

And he didn't quite know what he felt. Shock, definitely. And fear. And the absolute certainty that he wanted to share this child with Evie. And not just as a distant, absent parent. But how could it work? His life was in L.A.... Evie's was in Crystal Point.

He dropped his half-empty bottle into the trash and walked back into the living room. The laptop still sat on the coffee table in the center of the room. He should call her. Scott picked up the telephone, thinking of her number that he couldn't remember memorizing but somehow had. The telephone stuck to his hand. What would he say— *Thanks for the news...let me know when our kid arrives?* Yeah, as if that was gonna happen.

The doorbell rang and he shook himself. A few seconds later three of his friends piled into his apartment, carrying six-packs of Bud and pizza boxes.

"The game's on, remember?" Clint Dawson reminded him as he stood as if he were a statue and let them pass. "And you're the one with the big flat screen."

The game? Flat screen? Right...he vaguely remembered agreeing to an evening in with his friends, sharing the tab for takeout and watching the game on TV.

He shut the door and watched Clint, and then Marcus Crane, drop into the pair of recliners that had prime position in front of the flat screen. Gabe Vitali, his first cousin and closest friend, was the only one of the trio who thought to ask him if he was all right. Scott only shrugged, thinking the last thing he wanted was a night in with his friends. He wanted to get his thoughts together. He wanted to speak with Evie, to hear her voice, to tell her what he felt...

Which was what, exactly?

The constant ache in his chest, the lack of pleasure he got from doing anything, the almost robotic way he'd been living since he left her...what did that mean? And what they'd had together felt like more than he'd experienced before...more feeling...more passion...more everything.

He looked at his friends—newly divorced Clint, commitment-phobic Marcus and his cousin, whose fiancée had run off the year Gabe had been diagnosed with a serious illness. What did any of them have beyond the job and an apartment? Scott felt the meaninglessness of his existence through to the marrow in his bones.

And now Evie was having his baby. He wanted to shout it to the world. The shock had dissipated and was replaced by a sense of calm so acute it felt almost euphoric. Suddenly, like a shard of glass striking through his blood, Scott knew what he wanted.

Everything. Evie—the baby—a life scratching at his fingertips.

He wanted Evie. He wanted their baby. Nothing else mattered.

He stalked across the room and grabbed the remote, then flicked off the TV and turned to face his startled friends.

"I'm in love," he announced, watching as three broad jaws dropped. "And I'm going to be a dad."

Evie covered herself in the baggiest smock she could find, hiding itself in the archives of her old maternity wardrobe. At four months along she was really beginning to show. For the past few weeks she had managed to avoid too many interactions with her family and friends—but she knew she couldn't keep up the pretense forever. Especially to Trevor. Being a hermit would last only so long. Her mother wouldn't be held at bay for too much longer. Grace was calling her every few days. And Fiona was doing what friends do by trying to leech the truth from her. Her family would come around, mob fashion if need be, and she had to be prepared for the onslaught. They would mean well, but they would also demand answers to questions she was not prepared to consider.

Okay, so her pregnancy would be revealing itself to the world soon. But she had no intention of admitting anything about her baby's paternity until she spoke to Scott again. And he hadn't communicated with her at all.

Too apprehensive to email him again, or call, she caged herself into her house like a hibernating bear. And as the cold fingers of doubt climbed over every inch of skin with each passing day, Evie convinced herself that telling Scott about the baby was the worst thing she could have done.

He obviously doesn't care one way or another. And it hurt. It hurt so much she could barely stand thinking about it. And it wasn't that she had any kind of expectations— she simply couldn't believe he'd drop contact altogether.

So she was to be a single mother. Wasn't that what she'd planned anyway? From the moment she'd discovered she was pregnant, Evie had known she would be going it alone. And she was fine with that. Perfectly fine. She'd been a single mother for ten years, after all.

Only…she remembered those first precious moments when Trevor was born…she remembered the look in Gordon's eyes, the tears of pride and wonderment toward the new and perfect life they had created together. Evie instinctively placed her hands on her growing belly, and a hot surge of love washed over her. *I'll love you,* she promised her baby. *I'll love you and keep you safe.*

Without Scott. Besides, he was only her temporary lover and someone she shouldn't have fallen in love with. The fact that she had was her burden to bear. He'd broken no promises to her. He was too young…too much the kind of man she didn't want in her life and a risk she could never take. Especially now that she had a new baby to consider.

She would get on with her life, as she had always done. And once her family knew, she was certain they would support her decision to raise her child alone. Besides, nothing could dampen her joy at being pregnant. She was happy.

It was three days later that the downstairs doorbell woke her up from her usual afternoon nap. Evie checked her watch and clambered off the bed. Two o'clock. She remembered that Noah was coming around to hang a few of her paintings in the downstairs living room. To be *really* painting again had been a surprise—but strangely, her passion had returned with a vengeance. She had finished a few pieces she'd started years before, ever mindful of the small crystal globe and Saint Catherine watching over her from its spot on a shelf near her easels.

And maybe she would tell her brother about the pregnancy. She'd always been able to share things with Noah. They'd been there for one another over the years—when his wife had walked out on him and the kids, when Gordon had died, when Trevor had needed a father's influence. Evie trusted her brother with her news.

Evie reached the door and flung it back wide on its hinges. "You're two hours early," she complained with a laugh as she flipped open the security screen. "And you interrupted my afternoon—"

She stopped and caught her words in her throat. It

wasn't her brother standing on her doorstep. It was the father of her baby.

Scott's gaze dropped instantly to her belly. He lingered there for a moment and she heard him suck in a sharp breath. "Hello, Evie."

She took a step backward. "What are you doing here?"

"You really have to ask that?" he replied as he met her eyes. "I want to talk to you."

Evie absorbed everything about him in a second—the jeans and cotton Henley he wore so well, the duffel at his feet, the way his hair flopped over his forehead, the travel-weary look on his face. Her insides lurched and she instinctively laid her hands on her stomach. "I...I—"

"Can I come in?"

She took a second, thought about all the reasons why she shouldn't let him inside and couldn't come up with a single one. "Of course."

He grabbed his bag and walked across the threshold. Evie headed for the living room and sat down on the sofa. She gripped her hands together and waited. Scott stood by the doorway and dropped his duffel. A few seconds past and he moved toward her. Evie got a good look at him and noticed he'd lost weight. There was a ranginess about his lean frame and she wondered if perhaps she was responsible for it. His eyes were dark, like the color of an indigo sky. And his mouth was pressed into a thin line. He looked so tired. She touched her stomach and saw his gaze immediately follow the movement of her hands.

"Scott, I—"

"How could you do it?" he demanded, running a hand through his hair. "How could you tell me like that?"

Evie choked back a gasp. He wasn't tired, she realized. He was angry. "I can—"

"Two words," he said, throwing his hands up. "Two

words to announce the most important thing that's ever been said to me."

"I'm sorry," she said quickly, feeling the bite of shame snap at her heels. She *was* in the wrong, and they both knew it. "You're right. I shouldn't have told you like that. I should have called you and told you about the baby."

Scott let out a breath and turned, then paced across the room until he reached the window. His back was straight and Evie knew him well enough to recognize the tension searing through his body. He took a few long breaths and stared out the window for a moment before finally twisting around to look at her.

"So, how are you?" he asked, clearly back in control now. "I mean…how's the… How are you feeling?"

Evie patted her stomach. "I'm good," she replied softly. "*We're* good."

"You've been ill?"

She shook her head. "Just the normal pregnancy things."

He expelled an exasperated breath. "Well, considering this is my first experience with pregnancy, you might consider being a bit more specific."

"Nausea," she explained a little stiffly. "And fatigue. And my doctor is keeping an eye on my blood sugar, considering my age. Other than that I feel fine. The baby is healthy and growing normally. I had my first scan last week—I have a picture if you like."

He looked as if she'd slapped him in the face and she knew immediately how exclusive and selfish it sounded. She wanted to explain to him how she'd felt seeing their baby on the screen for the first time, how her heart had constricted so tight with love and joy and how she'd longed to share the moment with him but had thought it impossible.

"A picture?" he echoed softly. "And do you know…" He

paused and swallowed hard. Evie watched his throat move up and down. "Do you know the baby's sex?"

She shook her head. "I wanted it to be a surprise. If you're keen to find out, I can schedule another ultrasound."

"I'm happy to wait. But I would like to come with you next time."

"Of course," she whispered. "So, you're staying for a while?"

He nodded. "I'm staying. Have you told anyone?" he asked. "Your family?"

"No. Although I don't imagine I'll be able to keep it a secret for too much longer. I think they're all suspicious about why I've been avoiding them for the past few weeks."

He looked at her stomach. "You're already showing."

Evie spread the cotton smock across her abdomen. "Yes. I'd like to tell Trevor—and my parents."

"We'll do it together."

Evie wasn't sure what to think. He looked so far away, still angry but fighting it. She felt like caving in and crawling into his arms. But she had to keep her head. "That's not necessary. I can do it alone."

"Yeah," he said quickly. "I'm sure you can. But you're not alone, Evie," he said, and pointed to her belly. "You're not alone in this."

But she'd felt alone. For weeks she'd felt like the only person on the planet. "But you didn't respond to my message," she said on a shallow breath. "I thought…I thought you didn't…"

"You thought I didn't what?"

Emotion clogged her throat. "I thought you didn't want… I didn't hear from you, so I assumed you—"

"It's hardly the thing to be discussed in an email," he said, cutting her off. "Or over the telephone."

"But for the past two weeks—"

"For the past two weeks I've been organizing extended leave from my job and subletting my apartment."

She stilled. What did that mean? He was here, but for how long? And what kind of role did he want to play during her pregnancy? And afterward? What then? Would he expect shared custody of the child they had made together?

"Why have you done that?"

He gave her an odd look. "You can't be serious?" He shook his head. "You're having a baby, Evie...my baby... What did you expect me to do, hang out in L.A. until the kid was born and then send you flowers?"

"I'm not sure what I expected," she said frankly. "Nothing really. Only for you to know. I haven't really thought that far ahead."

"Well, you need to think about it. *We* need to think about it."

He came across the room and sat beside her and took her hands in his. Evie didn't move. She couldn't feel anything other than the strong clasp of his fingers against her own. "I want...I want this baby, Scott," she said in a shaky voice.

His grip tightened. "So do I."

Hot tears burned behind her eyes. "I'm glad. And you can see as much of the baby as you like for as long as you're here."

He shook her hands. "Evie," he said rawly. "You don't understand. I don't want to be a part-time parent." He turned on the seat and dropped to his knees onto the floor in front of her. "I said I was staying and I meant it. I want... I want to make this right. I want us to raise our child together."

Dazed, Evie shook her head. "Together? What do you—"

"Marry me?"

The room tilted and she swayed, leaning forward. Scott

grasped her shoulders and set her upright. She still spun, she still felt as if the carpet beneath her feet were moving from side to side, pulling her with it. *Marry me?* Evie sucked in a breath as the fingers of temptation entwined around her heart. Marry the man she was in love with? The man whose child she carried? It seemed like a dream come true.

Yes...a dream. A fantasy. Evie knew better than to rely on dreams. She had to rely on her good sense. On what was best for her baby. Marrying a much younger man who was a firefighter made no sense at all.

"No," she whispered.

He paled. "No?"

Evie shook her head. "You don't have to marry me, Scott. You can see the baby. I won't deny you the right to be a father."

"What about my right to be your husband and lover?"

She pulled her hands from his and straightened. "Look, I appreciate that you want to do the honorable thing. But you're too young for me, Scott. We're like...we're from two completely different generations."

"It's nine years, Evie—not twenty. And even if it were, I wouldn't care." He reached up and held her face against his palms. "I love you."

Evie's heart skipped a beat, and then another. *He loves me?* Could he? Or was he simply saying that to get what he wanted? Part of her longed to believe it...longed to say yes. But Sensible Evie stuck out her neck. "We hardly know each other."

He touched her stomach, and her whole body shook. "We do know each other, Evie. Intimately. And I know that I'm in love with you."

Rocked to the core by his revelation, Evie placed her

hand on his. "It's lust, Scott—desire. And maybe some sense of obligation because of the baby."

He jumped to his feet. "You're telling me what I feel?"

Evie shrugged, feeling the loss of his hands on her. "I'm just trying to let you off the hook."

"And what if I don't want to be let off?" he asked. "What if I want to be joined to you for the rest of my life?"

"Because of the baby?"

"Because I'm head over heels in love with you, that's why." He took her hands and gently eased her to her feet. "Evie…give us a chance?"

Doubt swirled through her. She couldn't do it. "There's too much against it working. The age difference…your job…"

"I'll quit," he announced, and wrapped his arms around her.

Evie moved against him. "You can't do that," she protested. "I wouldn't allow it."

He shrugged. "It's not your decision. I'll quit and find another job—here. Because wherever you are, Evie, is where I want to be."

She pulled back. "You're a firefighter. That's what you do. It's who you are."

"It's a job."

She shook her head and stepped away, determined to keep him at an arm's length. "I saw you, Scott—I saw you with the volunteers that day. I saw the way you were with those people, the way they responded to you. I knew then that your job was more than merely a job to you. It's part of you…it's part of the man you are. You love it."

"I love you more," he said simply.

Evie touched her belly. "Maybe right now, right here, when you see me carrying your child and look into my eyes and know I'm just as…that my feelings for you are just as strong."

His eyes widened. "Are they, Evie? Do you love me?"

Evie took a step back. "Loving you isn't the issue. The issue is marrying you…and I won't do it." She crossed her arms and inhaled deeply. "I'm tired. I need to rest for a bit. You can sleep in your old room or down here if you prefer, as I have no guests at the moment. You can stay until we sort something out."

"There's nothing to sort out," he said. "I've told you what I want…and in this, Evie, there can be no compromise."

She nodded. "I agree. I won't marry you. The sooner you accept that, the better."

And then Evie pulled on all her strength and walked out of the room.

As rejections went, Scott thought, this was pretty well up there. Back in his old room, he could barely look at the bed without imagining Evie in it.

Nice going, dude…nothing like a marriage proposal that sounded more like an ultimatum.

Did she love him? Had her roundabout admission actually been real? If she'd refused him because she didn't care enough, how did he get through that? He wanted to marry Evie. He wanted to be her husband and lover and protector. He wanted her love. And she hadn't exactly said she did. There were feelings there, he was sure of it. Evie was an honest, sincere woman, and not the kind of person to fake what she felt. And he *felt* love from her when they were together. And she *made love* to him as though she loved him.

He looked out the window. A car pulled up outside and he watched a pretty redhead get out. Evie's friend—

again he couldn't remember her name—locked her car and waited by the curb. Seconds later another vehicle pulled up. He recognized his sister and brother-in-law immediately.

Great. Annoyance waved up his spine. He wondered for a moment if Callie had sniffed out his arrival with her sister-radar—but he'd only told his cousin Gabe and his mother his plans and had sworn Eleanor to secrecy. This horde was obviously about Evie. He remembered how weary she'd looked and knew visitors would be the last thing she wanted. The trio came down the path and Scott watched them disappear beneath the eaves. He heard voices downstairs, heard feet walking across the threshold.

He didn't waste a second more and left the room. When he got downstairs and entered the kitchen, he felt as if he'd walked into the middle of a gunslinger's stand-off. Callie was frowning, the redhead was staring with wide eyes and hopping on her feet and Noah looked like a man who wanted answers. Only Evie appeared calm. She stood by the sink, hands on hips.

"I'm not sick," Scott heard her say as he rounded the doorway. "So stop worrying."

"We *are* worried," Noah said gravely. "You've been hiding out here for weeks now. You won't talk to anyone, you won't see anyone, you won't admit that something serious is going on with you. Our mother is convinced you've—"

"I'm not sick," she said again, and quickly spotted Scott as he framed the entry. Three sets of eyes snapped toward him instantly. "I'm pregnant."

The trio all did a good impression of a rabbit stuck in headlights.

Callie stared at him, her surprise obvious. He probably should have called his sister and told her he was coming. But right now his priority was Evie.

Callie said his name and then quickly clammed up. She

looked at Evie, and then back to Scott, then Evie again. It took only seconds for his sister to figure it out. The other two responded a little slower, but when they did emotion charged through the room.

"Pregnant?" Noah echoed incredulously.

"Well!" the redhead exclaimed. "Aren't you one for secrets?"

"It's not a secret, Fiona," Evie said evenly. "We chose to maintain our privacy, that's all."

We? Scott almost laughed. But now was not the time to challenge Evie. They needed a united front. "So I guess the interrogation's over?"

Callie moved across the room and grabbed his arm. "Not by a long shot. You've got some serious explaining to do."

Scott smiled at his feisty sister. "That's hardly appropriate," he said, and saw Noah glaring at him. "Besides, we're not teenagers. And we're not trying to hide anything. We're having a baby together and as long as we're okay with that it doesn't really matter what anyone else thinks."

He looked at Evie and saw the barest traces of relief on her face. Whatever he had to do to prove to her he was determined to make it work he would do. He'd beg and plead if he had to, to make her see sense, to make her realize what they had…what they could have together if only she'd let him into her life. He wanted to be a father to their baby…but he wanted Evie, too. He wanted her love. And he'd do whatever was necessary to get it.

"So, while you're all here for this intervention," he said, and chucked his hands into his pockets, "maybe you can all use your influence and convince Evie to marry me."

Chapter Thirteen

It was a low act. A despicable, humiliating thing to do. And Evie was so mad she seethed. She banged things around the house for the next hour, after quietly asking her family to leave. They hadn't wanted to leave at first and Callie looked as if she was ready to kill her brother.

Noah and Fiona had been a little less disapproving, with Noah saying he thought marriage was a great idea. *A great idea?* Evie had burned her brother with a red-hot glare for being so agreeable. She'd looked at Scott and he'd just shrugged and smiled and showed off that dimple.

Well, she wasn't falling for that sexy dimple and gorgeous smile anymore.

He was outside shooting hoops with Trevor—who'd been so pleased to see him when he'd arrived home from school that Evie had swallowed a lump the size of a tennis ball as her son had embraced Scott. Considering Evie had made it abundantly clear she wanted to be alone, they'd left her immediately.

So she had thinking time while she rearranged the pot drawer in the downstairs kitchen. She wouldn't be maneuvered into a corner, that was for sure. And she wouldn't marry Scott because it was what everyone else wanted.

But when a pair of skinny hands landed on her shoulders a short while later, Evie felt her resistance crumble fractionally.

"Scott told me," Trevor said quietly. "About everything."

Evie turned around and saw her son look at her stomach. "He did?"

Trevor shrugged. "I'm okay about the baby. And Scott said he's hanging around—which is good, too." Her son squeezed her arm and shuffled back on his feet. "And I reckon it'll be cool to have a stepfather."

Evie's temper surged and she wondered if Scott would be so duplicitous to use her hero-worshipping son to get her to change her mind. He wouldn't, surely? "I'm glad you and Scott get along so well."

"Families are supposed to, aren't they?"

"Yes," she replied, but didn't point out that Scott wasn't exactly family.

"And having a new baby might get you to stop treating me like a little kid?"

He was grinning, but Evie saw through his smile. "Do I? I don't mean to."

He shrugged lightly. "I know. But sometimes, when you want to know where I am every second and try to hand-pick my friends, it gets hard to take."

She took a step back and leaned against the counter. "Is that what I do?" Evie considered her son's words. "I didn't realize I was being so overprotective."

Trevor shrugged again. "It's okay. I get why you do it.

But you know, when I might want to hang out with some of my friends, even the ones you don't like all that much, I reckon you should let me make my own decision."

It seemed like a huge leap for Evie. Her son was no longer a little boy. He was growing up so fast and she didn't want to let him go.

"You know," Trevor said as he grabbed an apple from the fruit bowl, "I like Scott. I vote we keep him."

She stared after him as he left the room and was about to return to her chore of banging pots when Scott came through the doorway. She scowled at him. "Being underhanded won't get you anywhere."

He rested one shoulder against the jamb. "What does that mean?"

Eve straightened. "My son, who obviously believes you can do no wrong, told me he thinks we should keep you."

"He's a smart kid," Scott said, straight-faced.

Evie raised her brows dramatically. "He is smart. But he's easily influenced. I'd prefer it if you kept our relationship private."

"I didn't say anything about *our relationship,* Evie," he said. "I only told him about the baby."

She scowled. "I *did* intend to tell him."

"Of course you did. But, I *needed* to tell Trevor myself, man to man," he said, and pushed off the jamb. "If I overstepped the mark, I'm sorry."

It *was* a little presumptuous, she thought. "How did he take the news?"

Scott shrugged. "He was surprised at first," Scott told her quietly as he made his way around the countertop. "And he asked me about my intentions." He smiled. "But I think he understands. He's a smart kid. A good kid. You've done a great job raising him, Evie. If I'm half the parent you are, I'll be a happy man."

Evie fought the heat behind her eyes and pressed her hips against the bench. "Sometimes I forget he won't be a child for much longer. He's growing up. So, thank you for explaining it to him." He chuckled and Evie frowned. "What's funny?"

"Nothing," Scott replied as he moved into the kitchen. "But I think we both just agreed on how to parent a teenager."

It surprised her. It also surprised her that suddenly she didn't actually mind Scott running interference with Trevor. "I guess we'll have plenty of practice soon enough."

Scott was in front of her now. He reached out and placed his hand across her belly. "Do you mind?" he asked softly.

Evie shook her head. "Of course not."

"Can you feel the baby moving?"

She smiled. "Not quite moving," she replied. "More like fluttering, I suppose you'd call it. Another month or so and it will be a different story. When I was pregnant with Trevor I felt like I had a soccer player inside me."

Scott raised his brows. "Do girls play soccer?"

"Are you hoping for a girl?"

He rubbed her stomach gently. "I thought you might prefer it."

Evie felt the heat from his touch rise over her skin like a bloom. "I'm happy either way."

His touch changed slightly, shifting to something that reminded her of how it was to be made love to by this man. But she didn't pull away. His hand trailed around her hip and up her side, lingering on the underswell of her breast.

"Your breasts are bigger," he said, and moved closer.

Evie colored, good sense tugging at her wits. Only, it was useless to imagine she could pull away. "Of course."

"There's no 'of course' for me," he said, and traced the back of his hand across one nipple. "This is all new...your body changing…the incredible way you look even more beautiful, if that were possible."

"I'm not beautiful."

"You are to me."

Evie swayed. "Don't do this," she pleaded. "Don't use my attraction for you against me."

His expression narrowed. "Evie," he said softly as he grasped her chin. "Sometimes you say the damnedest things."

"I don't want to confuse the lines here, Scott. I want to stay clear about what I need to do."

He released her abruptly. "You mean by refusing to marry me?"

Evie pushed herself along the countertop. "You know why I won't."

"I do?" He stepped back. "That's news to me. I don't get you at all, Evie. We have this unbelievable opportunity to be a part of something great together. But you won't even consider meeting me halfway."

She bristled and snapped out the first thing she thought of. "You're too young for me."

"That's an old song," he said. "But if it bothers you so much I'll dye my hair gray and spend loads of time in the sun so I wrinkle up by the time I'm forty."

"And I'll be nearly fifty," she reminded him. "You'll still be gorgeous and I'll be a middle-age, menopausal wreck. You'll have younger women chasing after you and I won't have a hope of competing with them."

"That's ridiculous. And I don't believe for one minute that you're that insecure."

"I am," she announced, wishing she was a better actress. She wrapped her arms around her chest and expelled a heavy breath. "This is such a disaster."

He quickly took three steps back and shook his head as

he glanced at her belly. "I'm gonna forget you said that." He rubbed a hand over his face. "I'm also going to hit the sack because the jet lag is kicking in and I feel like hell. But I'll see you later and we'll talk some more."

She watched him leave and sank back against the counter. *What am I going to do?* Having Scott so close wreaked havoc on her good sense. With an ocean between them she'd felt stronger, as though she could do it alone. But this was like being a kid and browsing through a candy store, where everything was so close, but locked beneath a glass cabinet. She was the sugar-addicted kid, and Scott was the candy. Wanting him…longing for him in ways she never imagined she'd want any man again. It made her feel exposed and vulnerable.

Evie didn't see Scott again until the following morning. When he entered the upstairs kitchen, she'd already pushed Trevor out the door for school and refreshed the lavender bedroom for the guests who were arriving the following day.

He loped into the room in low-flung loose fitting jeans and a red T-shirt and helped himself to coffee. "Good morning."

Evie stalked across the room and sat down at the table. "You wanted to talk," she said, determined to be practical. "Okay, let's talk. First, how long are you staying?"

He sat down opposite her. "Is that a trick question?"

"What?"

Scott put down his mug. "Well, if I say I'm staying forever you'll give me one of your disapproving looks and tell me it's never gonna happen. But if I say I'm here temporarily, you'll hit me with how you'd expect nothing less from me than if I abandoned you and the baby."

Evie's spine jerked upward. "I wouldn't say that."

Scott raised a brow. "Really? What would you say, then?"

"I don't see the point of—"

"For good, Evie," he said quietly. "I might have to go back to hand in my resignation and put my apartment on the market. But I can't see that taking too long. My parents made sure Callie and I had dual residency since we were kids. I can live here or the States."

"And then?"

"And then I'll get a job so I can support you and the baby."

"I can support myself," she pointed out. "As I have done for the last ten years. The B and B is lucrative enough and I recently sold a few paintings."

"You're painting again?"

Evie nodded. "Yes. My muse is back."

"So your heart isn't broken anymore?"

She gripped her teacup. "Not like it was."

He pushed his mug into the center of the table and stood. "Good. Because I want your heart, Evie, and I'll do whatever it takes to get it. And I fully intend to support you and our baby, and be a stepdad and friend to Trevor. So get used to me being around. Get used to being loved. I'm not going anywhere."

Evie's heart lurched forward. "You can't stay here…I can't do this. I won't be manipulated into—"

"I have no desire to manipulate the mother of my child. But I know you're running scared, Evie. And I'm not sure why."

"You think everything's black-and-white," she said statically. "Nothing's that simple. You said you're going to quit your job with the LAFD and look for work over here. But as what, a firefighter?"

"I haven't—"

"Of course it will be," she said, her heart and body filled with so much pain and fear she could barely get the words out. "That's what you do...that's who you are. You'll join the fire department here and keep running into those buildings and the only difference will be geography. And I know I don't have any right to ask you to be someone other than who you are. You *are* a firefighter. And maybe for a little while you could try doing something else, but we both know your heart wouldn't be in it."

He looked at her and there was raw truth in his eyes. "I'd sweep streets for you, Evie."

"But you'd be unhappy," she said. "And because of that you'd be distracted. It would be like your friend Mike all over again. You'd be distracted and I'd be worried sick every time you left the house, every time I heard the sirens wailing." Evie stood up and pushed her chair back, fighting the tears batting against her lashes. "And then one day, something would happen, and you'd get injured...or maybe worse...and our child might be left without a father...and I'd...and I'd be left without...and I can't..."

She stopped speaking and closed her eyes. It was harder than hard. But she needed to say it. She needed to hear herself say the words.

The admission came out as a whisper as tears fell. "I just don't have the strength to bury another husband."

Scott moved out of Dunn Inn that afternoon. Evie didn't know where he went and she didn't ask before he drove off in his rental car. She had her life back. Sort of.

But true to his word, he didn't abandon her.

In fact, he became a permanent fixture in her daily routine over the following week.

At first he dropped by to see how she was doing, and not once did he repeat his marriage proposal. He hung out with Trevor some afternoons and at other times discussed the baby, or when they'd start decorating the upstairs guest room into a nursery. They talked colors and wallpaper and booster seats and cribs and pretty much everything to do with the baby and nothing about their relationship.

She should have been happy about it.

Instead she became more miserable with each day. He didn't touch her, didn't try to kiss her and didn't do anything even remotely intimate. He just talked. When he wasn't talking he was doing things around the B and B. He fixed anything she asked to be repaired and didn't voice one complaint.

At her parents' house one Sunday to celebrate her father's birthday, Evie prepared herself to endure the scrutiny of her family's curiosity about their relationship. But their *relationship* had developed into something so *lukewarm* it barely rated mentioning. More to the point, no one seemed to care. She was pregnant; Scott was the father of her baby. Even her mother, who would normally be gushing over the idea that one of her daughters was in a relationship, even if a slightly dysfunctional one, only smiled and patted her shoulder and mentioned what a nice man he was and how she was looking forward to being a grandmother again.

Nice…sure…more like a wolf in sheep's clothing.

And that was exactly how she felt. As if his indifference was deliberate. Her declarations about fearing something might happen to him had clearly struck a chord with him and he'd backed off. Or at least that's what he wanted her to think. Yeah—some disguises were used for camouflage and some for hunting. Evie wasn't fooled. He was on the hunt…and she was the prey.

Scott had said he didn't want to manipulate her. But she felt manipulated.

And by Sunday afternoon she was a mass of nervous energy, waiting for him to pounce. She would rather have met him head-on and deal with his marriage proposal and the attraction they had for each other than play this waiting game.

Fortunately, Evie found an ally in her sister. Grace was back from New York for a few days for the party, and Evie was grateful for her sister's support.

"You know he's staying with Hot Tub, don't you?" Grace told her, sitting down to share the love seat by the pool, which Evie had occupied for the past lazy hour because it was sheltered and quiet and away from Scott, who was playing pool with her brother and Trevor. Her sister handed her a long glass of iced tea.

Hot Tub. Cameron Jakowski. It made her grin. Grace and Cameron loathed each other, and their private war had been going on for years. The ultracharming police officer was the only person Evie had ever known who was able to ruffle Grace's supercool composure.

"I didn't know that," Evie admitted. "But we're not exactly talking about things that matter at the moment."

"No more declarations of love?" Grace inquired.

"Not one." She'd told her sister what had transpired between them in the eighteen hours he'd stayed at the B and B.

"Are you in love with him?" Grace asked frankly. "I mean, besides being full of hormones and the emotions tied up with being pregnant with his baby. Do you actually *love* him?"

"Yes," she whispered.

"And that's not enough?"

"Logically it is," Evie replied as she drank some tea. "But I'm afraid of who I'll become if I let myself go there."

Grace tutted and tapped her perfectly manicured nails

together. "And I thought I was the closed-off neurotic in the family."

"I don't think there's any doubt about that, *Princess*."

They snapped their necks around instantly. Cameron stood by the pool fence, beer in hand. He smiled at them both and raised his drink in salute.

"What do you want, Hot Tub?"

He grinned. "To see what a five-hundred-dollar pair of shoes look like."

Evie immediately looked to Grace's feet and the Jimmy Choo sandals she wore.

Grace stood and glared at him. Evie watched as her sister gave Cameron a murderous look and then took off back to the house. "You know," Evie said, "one day you're going to go too far and she'll come at you in all her fury."

He chuckled. "I look forward to it."

"Don't say I didn't warn you."

Cameron laughed again and asked Evie if she needed anything before he returned to the games room. Evie languished beneath the Balinese-style hut overlooking the pool and closed her eyes for a moment.

"If you fall asleep in that chair you'll get a back cramp."

Her lids fluttered open. Scott had approached with all the stealth of a leopard. "I'll have a spa when I get home to take the kinks out."

His eyes darkened. "Be careful getting in and out of the tub."

"Are you offering your assistance?" she asked, smiling.

Scott sucked in a breath. "I'm saying be careful you don't slip and hurt yourself."

"I won't," she said. "I have no intention of doing anything that might harm the baby."

He looked at her with blistering intensity. "Me, either."

Clarity washed over Evie like a wave. "Of course—

that explains the Mr. Nice Guy act you've had going all week." She pulled herself straight in the seat and then stood up. "I'm not fooled by it. And I'd rather you simply be yourself."

He shrugged. "I don't want to upset you."

"Too late," she snapped. "Do you think talking about teddy-bear wallpaper and prenatal vitamins are such neutral subjects that I won't be tempted to burst into tears and act like a hormonal lunatic?"

Scott stared at her and shook his head. "I can't do anything right with you, can I?"

"I'm only—"

"Your way or no way," he said stiffly. "And no way in between."

Evie bristled. "That's not true."

"It is true. There's no middle road with you and it's so damned frustrating." The air around him was filled with pent-up emotion so powerful Evie could only watch, fascinated and mesmerized. "I asked to be your husband and you turned me down… I'm trying to be your friend and that's not good enough. The only place I've ever felt marginally welcome in your life is between the sheets…and that…and that just…kills me."

Evie gasped. "Scott, I—"

He reached for her and took hold of her shoulders, molding her bones with his big hands. "Is that what you want from me?" he demanded, and Evie was suddenly so turned on, so hungry for him and so ashamed to admit it she could hardly draw breath. "Is that all you want from me?" His body was hard against hers and he stared down into her upturned face. "Just this?" One hand swept down her back to cover her behind and urge her closer. "Is that really all this is to you?"

Before she could say a word his mouth came down on

hers. It was hot and hard and had ownership stamped all over it. But Evie didn't mind and shocked herself by kissing him back hungrily.

"No," she said when he was done, when their breathing was ragged and their mouths were finally apart.

He released her gently. "But it's not enough for you to marry me, right? I know you're scared, Evie... I know you think I'm gonna die on the job and leave you. And you know what—maybe that will happen. Because there are no guarantees in any relationship. But if you can't get past that fear and keep refusing to marry me and let me take care of you and all we'll share together is that baby inside you—then, that's okay. Because that in itself is an incredible thing."

He stepped back, took a long breath and then left her alone without another word.

"You look like hell."

Scott jerked his gaze upward. He was sitting in Cameron Jakowski's living room, and Cameron and Noah were loafing back in a pair of recliners. He felt their scrutiny and shrugged. "Whatever."

And his brother-in-law was probably right. He felt like crap and figured he probably looked worse.

"Are you sleeping?" Noah asked, and grabbed the remote from Cameron. He flicked off the motor sports program none of them were watching.

"Not much," he admitted, and suddenly felt like spilling his guts to these two men who had quickly become friends. "Who knew, huh?" he said, and laughed at himself. "That it would feel this bad," he explained when he saw Cameron frown.

Noah looked heavenward. "I did."

Scott grinned. "Yeah—I guess my sister put you though the wringer a few months back."

"And then some," Noah said, and looked as if he was thinking stuff Scott was certain he didn't want to know about his sister. "But it was definitely worth it."

"Schmucks," Cameron said, looking mildly appalled.

"He thinks he's immune," Noah explained, grinning. "I keep telling him the harder the resistance, the bigger the fall."

"Not likely," Cameron replied. "I don't ever want to have that pathetic hangdog look on my face. Next you pair will be wanting a group hug." He scowled and took a long swallow of Corona. "Forget it."

Scott laughed. "I'm good," he insisted, and then a sharp pain pierced his chest when he realized he could certainly do with a hug from Evie. He'd backed off to give her space and felt the loss of her so acutely it was messing with his head. But he didn't want to upset her and was worried what anxiety might do to their baby. So he stayed away and endured the longest five days of his life.

And he was angry with her, too. Angry that she was afraid to give them a chance. Angry that she didn't *want* to love him. It…hurt. He'd never felt hurt like that before… never knew that pain like that could stop a man eating, sleeping, almost breathing.

"She'll come around," Noah said. "I know Evie. She's set in her ways about some things…but she's the most sensible person I know. And she's been on her own for so long. Give her some time."

"Well, I've got plenty of that."

"Schmucks," Cameron said again just as his cell phone pealed. He headed off down the hall to get the call and returned a few minutes later.

"That was one of my boys from the Big Brother program," he told them. "Giving me the heads-up. Apparently there's some trouble going down at the surf club tonight." He grabbed his keys as Scott and Noah got to their feet. "Teenagers fighting over turf."

A turf war in Crystal Point? It seemed incomprehensible. "Do you know these kids?"

"Yeah," Cameron replied. "Some of them. One group has been using the top floor for secret computer gaming parties. They weren't doing any harm, so we've let them use the place while the renovations are going on. The other group wants them out. I don't want to call it in until I know something's really going on. I gotta go."

"I'll come with you," Scott said.

Noah nodded. "Me, too."

Cameron looked at them both. "And you might want to decide if you should call Evie," he said. "Because my source told me that Trevor was there with them."

Chapter Fourteen

Evie taught her Friday night class with about as much enthusiasm as a wet sneaker. Callie had turned up for the class, with Noah's three youngest kids in tow, and the kids played happily with watercolors at their specially set up table in the corner.

Once the class had concluded, Fiona and Callie lingered in the studio drinking a second cup of coffee and Evie prepared herself for what she knew was an inevitable confrontation with her sister-in-law.

"Have you guys picked out names yet?" Callie asked over the rim of her mug.

"Not yet. But I'm thinking I'd like a family name and something traditional."

Callie nodded. "And the baby's surname," she asked, "what will that be?"

Evie stilled. The implication was clear. "We haven't really discussed it."

"Scott intends to be a hands-on parent," Callie said. "He'll be a good father."

Evie didn't doubt that for a moment. "I know."

"The thing is," Callie said as she flicked a look toward Fiona and then back to Evie. "He's always been… you know…rock-solid. When we were growing up I was always this unpredictable whirlwind, and Scott was exactly the opposite. He got good grades in school and knew what he wanted to do with his life. You'd be hard-pressed to find a man more responsible." She sighed heavily. "He's got this sensible, pragmatic way about him. Come to think of it, Evie, you and Scott are a lot alike."

Evie's heart filled up and flowed over. But she wasn't sure if their similarities were pulling them together or pushing them apart. He had offered her everything and Evie had refused him…rejected him…and still he loved her.

And I'm terrified of losing him.

But her logic made no sense. By rejecting Scott she didn't have him…so how could she lose something she didn't have?

Her eyes filled with tears and it took barely seconds for Callie to wrap her arms around Evie's shoulders. "I don't know what to do…what to think. As hard as I've tried not to be, part of me has been so dishonest with him, with *us*."

"There is an *us*?" Callie asked. "I mean is there a you and Scott?"

Evie shrugged, and then nodded. "I'm such an idiot," she admitted.

"Just a woman in love by the look of things."

Evie hiccupped. "Do you mind?"

"About you and Scott? Of course not—he's my brother, you're my friend, I'm married to your brother—it kind of makes us closer than regular sister-in-laws." Callie squeezed her shoulders. "But I think he's in pretty bad shape about this."

Evie knew it and it tore her up inside. "Do you think he still wants to marry me?"

Callie nodded. "But do you want to marry him?"

She shrugged. "His job…"

"His job isn't his life, Evie," Callie said kindly, looking at her stomach, and Evie sensed immediately that her friend knew her fears. "Not anymore. But there's no denying he's good at it. He has two commendations for bravery in the line of duty, was promoted through the ranks well before most people his age and he's always seemed to simply take it all in his stride. Even when his friend died he held it together. He's not a risk, Evie…."

Evie sucked in a quick breath. "But his job is risky," she implored. "And if something happened I'd—"

"We all die, Evie," Fiona said, quieter than usual. "It's how we live that counts."

With those few words it was as though a wave of clarity washed over her and Evie sat, too stunned to move. So many memories surged up and rocked her reality—memories of Gordon and the knowledge that with so many years of grief snapping at her heels, she'd forgotten how it felt to be loved…and to truly live. Occasionally she recalled snapshots of things she'd shared with her husband, like the birth of their son. But the everyday stuff—the often mundane, day-to-day things were the moments that made up a real life. The burnt toast in the morning, the laughter over a shared movie on television, the comfort of strong arms around her as she slept. That was the *living* Fiona spoke of.

And now a genuinely good, honest man wanted to share those things with her.

And I turned him down?

Evie wondered if they made bigger fools than her. "Do...do you really think he'll still want me?"

Callie smiled broadly and hugged her. "Why don't you ask him and find out?"

Fiona laughed and they had all lifted their coffee mugs to clink them together when Callie's cell buzzed. It was obvious the call was from her husband because a dreamy look crossed her face. The look lasted only seconds, though, and when she disconnected Evie knew something was wrong.

"There's trouble down at the surf club," Callie said quickly. "Noah said Trevor was there and you should sit tight and not worry."

Trevor? Trouble? Not worry? Not likely! Evie jerked to her feet. "Trevor's at Cody's on a sleepover."

"Apparently he's not," Callie said. "Cameron and Scott are dealing with it."

Evie's blood ran cold. "I have to get down there."

Callie grabbed her arm. "Noah said you should stay here and he'll call the minute he knows—"

"I'm going," Evie said firmly.

Callie's grip tightened. "Well, I'm coming with you."

Fiona stood. "You both go. I'll stay here with the kids."

Evie was by the door in seconds and her sister-in-law followed closely on her heels.

With scaffolding as the only access point while the building was still undergoing renovations, Scott followed Cameron and they climbed up the outside to investigate.

There were two groups of boys embroiled in a standoff on the top floor of the surf club—one group was clinging to their laptops and backed into a corner, the other group was fueled with aggression while the ringleader held a crudely assembled Molotov cocktail. There didn't appear to be any other weapons involved, but Cameron still approached the scene as dangerous and Scott respected his experience enough to allow him the lead.

Through the dirty window Scott saw Trevor and another boy out in front of their group of friends. They were talking and it looked as though they were trying to reason with the leader of the other group. Scott got a bad vibe from the teenager then and his instinct kicked in immediately. The handmade device in his hand looked lethal enough to do some serious damage, and with the renovations upstairs at the painting stage, there were plenty of combustible materials available if the troubled teen decided to use his weapon.

Scott knew that surprising the boys would only fuel the tension, and followed Cameron back down.

"I'm calling for backup," Cameron said once they hit the ground. He pulled his cell from his pocket and made a call. "They're ten minutes away. I know that kid pretty well," Cameron said. "The one who's holding the weapon is likely to start something once I go in there—he's got a lot of anger issues. Wait outside until the unit gets here."

As much as he wanted to haul Trevor's skinny butt out of there, Scott knew he had to do as Cameron said. If the rules weren't followed, someone might get hurt, and the idea of that someone being Evie's son was unthinkable.

If something happened to Trevor, Evie would be inconsolable. Fear pitched inside his gut, and a deep swell of feeling swept through him. He cared deeply for Evie's son and had an instinctive need to protect him.

He thought about Mike O'Shea, faced with the idea of losing his child, and Scott remembered his friend's frantic rush to race into the house without consideration for the consequences. A father not thinking clearly—a man obsessed with saving his child... Scott had labeled Mike over and over.

I'm going in there. I will do whatever it takes to save

Evie's son. But he knew, without a doubt, that he could do it and still minimize the risks for everyone around him.

I won't lose my head...that's not me. I'm not Mike. I can do both.

A silver utility pulled up about fifty meters away.

When Evie and Callie jumped out and headed toward them, Scott's heart jumped inside his chest.

She launched at Cameron. "Where's my son?"

"Upstairs."

"I'm going up to get him."

"You're doing no such thing," Scott said, and took hold of her arm. "Let Cameron handle this."

She looked at him, all eyes, all fear. "If my son is in danger I'm not going to sit back and—"

"You won't be doing him any favors by charging up there," he said, and quickly explained about the homemade weapon. "The police backup will be here soon. They can diffuse this before it gets out of control."

"But he needs—"

"He needs you to stay calm," Scott said, and tightened his hold on her arm. She looked terrified and he was just about to pull her closer when a stream of loud shouts came from the building, followed by footsteps on bare boards and the unmistakable roar of a fireball breathing into life.

Scott released Evie and raced toward the building, barking out instructions to Cameron to keep everyone back as he moved to scale the scaffolding as quickly as possible. When he reached the top he immediately saw the orange glow of flames through a closed window and heard boys running toward the door. They raced across the threshold in a frightened group, pushing and fighting each other to get through.

He was by the door in a second and instructed the boys to stay calm and file out one at a time. Through the doorway he could see the flames kicking into life, igniting painter's drop sheets.

"Scott!"

Trevor's shaky voice echoed in his ears and he grabbed the boy by the shoulders as he came through the door and hovered, clutching his computer. "Get out now," Scott told him.

"Cody," Trevor said loudly to be heard above the formidable rush of flames. "Cody's stuck in there—he won't come out."

Once the last of the boys were through the door, Scott stepped over the threshold. "You go," he demanded to Trevor. "I'll get him out." Evie's son hesitated and Scott pushed against his chest. "Do what I tell you. Go!"

When Trevor finally turned on his heel, Scott moved into the long room. The flames were running along one wall, igniting the sheets on the floor. He covered his mouth with his forearm and headed across the floorboards. In the distance he heard sirens, and relief pitched behinds his ribs.

He saw the kid backed into the corner, clearly in shock. The flames were closing in on the boy, and Scott skidded across the floor. As he got closer, the fire changed direction, skirting the walls as it hissed and ran around in an arc, combusting a pile of old rags on the floor before it moved dangerously close to the terrified kid.

"Cody," he shouted. "Move to your right and take a couple of big steps."

The teenager coughed and remained where he was as Scott moved closer. The heat pushed him back momentarily and he heard the fire truck pull up outside. But he couldn't wait for backup. The whole room would be engulfed soon. He *had* to get Cody out. There was no time to waste.

He darted to his left, flipping across a low line of fire

that snapped at his heels. The heat smothered his skin and filled his lungs. When he reached Cody, the boy almost fell into his arms.

"Come on, kid," he said as he hauled him over one shoulder. "Let's go."

Evie saw Trevor and rushed forward, oblivious of the fire brigade telling her to stay back. The fire crew worked their way up the building and helped the scared teenagers down the scaffolding.

As soon as she felt her son in her arms, Evie held on to him tightly. "You scared me, Trevor."

"I'm okay," he insisted. "But Cody…Cody's still inside," Trevor said shakily. "Scott told me to get out. He said he'd get Cody down. But he wouldn't move. As soon as the fire started I yelled to everyone to run…but Cody…he wouldn't listen…he wouldn't…he just wouldn't…"

A sob racked her son's thin frame, and Evie hugged him close. Over his shoulder she looked up at the building. Thick smoke billowed from the top floor, and her heart thumped.

Beside her, Evie felt Callie's terror and while she clutched Trevor with one hand, Evie laid her other palm over her stomach. The moments ticked over, every one seeming longer than the one before. And then she saw Scott, illuminated by the beam of torches from the fire-fighters and the bright shadow of the flames behind him. He carried Cody over his shoulder and strode along the scaffolding without missing a step. Three firefighters waited until he'd passed before heading inside the building.

He got to the ground and moved a safe distance away from the building before letting go of Cody. The paramedics were on hand and laid the boy in an awaiting stretcher. By now news of the drama had spread throughout the community and there were people everywhere. The police had now cordoned off around the building, and Evie was held back behind a tape.

Evie heard Noah mutter a relieved "Thank God," and without thinking, she ducked underneath the tape and raced toward Scott.

He looked stunned to see her moving so fast and took a few steps to meet her near the front off the ambulance. "Evie, you shouldn't be run—"

She clutched his shirt, hauled herself against him and kissed him on the mouth. A kiss to stamp herself as his. "You're okay," she breathed, and felt hot tears in her eyes as their lips parted.

He nodded, smiling. "I'm okay."

And with that one look, Evie knew what she wanted. Because she saw...*love*.

"Thank you for getting Trevor out so quickly," she said, clutching his arm. From the light beaming from inside the ambulance she got a good look at him. He had a black smudge on his face, and his T-shirt was scorched near the sleeve. "And for saving Cody."

"It's my—"

"Your job," she said, cutting him off, and smiled. "Yes, I know. I'm glad you were here."

He looked at her oddly. "You're sure about that?"

"Positive."

Someone called his name and he turned away for a moment. Cameron and another police officer were making their way toward them. "I need to talk to these guys," he said, and touched her face. "Why don't you take Trevor home and I'll come by when I'm done?"

Evie didn't want to let him go. "But—"

"Go," he insisted. "I have to make a statement, and they

might want to talk with Trevor later. I'll see you at home."
He kissed her forehead and stepped back.

Home... The home she wanted to share with him as they
raised their child together.

He turned away to join Cameron just as Evie said his
name. He half turned back toward her. "What is it?"

And in that moment Evie gave up her heart. "I love
you, Scott."

He let out a ragged breath and stared at her, looking like
a man who'd just received the most precious gift in the
world. Whatever he was about to say didn't come out because Cameron came up beside him and quickly introduced
his colleague. He had business to finish and she needed to
give him time to do it. And she was okay with that.

Evie gave Scott one last look before she swiveled on
her heel and returned to her son.

When Scott arrived at Dunn Inn, it was close to ten
o'clock. Evie had the door open before he'd pulled himself out of his rental car.

When he reached her she didn't say a word and Scott
simply took her hand and followed her up the stairs and
into the big bedroom at the end of the hall. It was exactly
what he expected—pure Evie—there was a soft printed
cover on the bed, silky oak furniture and fresh flowers on
the armoire near the window.

She shut the door behind them and walked into the
middle of the room.

"It's nice in here," he said quietly.

"I should have invited you in here a long time ago," she
said quietly as she released his hand. "I'm sorry. I wasn't
consciously keeping it off-limits. But I've been alone for
so long...I shut off part of myself and in here..." Her arms
swept over their surroundings. "In here I could simply be

me. The closed-off me who was angry at the world but was too reasonable and sensible to show it."

She took a couple of steps and sat on the padded trunk at the end of the bed. "I had it redecorated after Gordon died. I painted the walls and hung new curtains and picked an outrageously girly bedspread. I guess I was happy in my misery, you know. And then one day you walked through that gate at the airport and smiled at me…and I knew I wasn't as happy in my misery as I'd made out."

Scott's chest tightened. He loved this woman so much. "And now?"

"Now I want…I want to take the life we could have together. The life you offered me."

He took an unsteady step toward her, wanting to fold her in his arms and hold her close. But they needed to talk first, and he needed to be sure. "I have to know something, Evie. Tonight you said you loved me…." Scott swallowed the emotion clutching at his throat. "Was that really about *me?*" he asked.

"I don't understand."

"I mean that sometimes in extreme situations, when a person is pumped on adrenaline and he thinks someone he loves is in danger, the mind can make him think something even if it's not real." He came beside her and sat on the trunk. "Your son was in danger and this feeling you have could just be a kind of misplaced gratitude."

He hated saying it, hated thinking it. But he had to know. Scott had seen it before—he'd seen the victims of accidents cling to their rescuer as if they were a lifeline. If she was only feeling appreciation and relief then he wanted her to tell him so.

And if it's only gratitude, will I take it? Will it be enough?

"Of course I'm grateful," she said, and his heart

thumped inside his chest. "How could I not be?" She grabbed his hand and lifted his knuckles to her mouth, kissing him softly. "You saved my son's life. You saved *all* those boys tonight."

"It's my job, Evie," he said quietly, feeling the meaning in the words more than he'd ever felt them before. "Whether I do it in L.A., or here…it's what I do."

She clutched his hand tightly and Scott felt the connection through to his blood. "I know. I've always known. Tonight I realized something…and I don't just mean because of the fire and saving those kids. I was here with your sister and Fiona and they said something to me that made me realize that perhaps I was wrong to imagine you'd be the kind of man who'd do something risky without thinking of the consequences."

"Not intentionally, no."

"And that's really all I can ask of you," she said softly. "I thought that I wanted you to stop being a firefighter and do something without risks."

Scott's heart settled behind his ribs. "There are no guarantees, Evie."

"I know that, too," she said. "I know what you do can be dangerous and there's no way you can ever be sure you won't get hurt…or worse. But I don't need guarantees, Scott."

"You did," he reminded her.

"I was scared," she admitted. "Scared that I'd lose you, I guess. Scared that I'd have to raise another child alone." She touched his face. "But tonight, I didn't see a man who took chances. I saw a man who was completely in control the whole time, who knew my son was in that building and still did what he had to do. Someone who kept people safe. And that…and that made *me* feel safe."

Scott grabbed her hands and held them against his chest.

"I'll always keep you safe, Evie. You and Trevor and…" He looked at her slightly swollen belly. "And our baby. I'd protect you all with my life."

Tears filled her eyes. "I know you would. And I love you with all my heart."

He kissed her softly and let emotion rise between them. She grabbed on to his shoulders and clung to him, kissing him back so hotly, so lovingly, Scott knew he'd never feel as connected to another soul as he did to this incredible woman who'd given him her heart and love.

"Just one thing," he said in between kisses. "I realized something myself tonight—I've been hanging on to this idea that I couldn't have both—that it needed to be the job, or a life with someone. But I knew when I was going into that building that I wasn't like Mike. I was like myself and I *can* do both, Evie. If you ever feel differently about this—if you're ever worried or want me to stop and find another type of job to do, promise me you'll tell me."

"I will," she said. "But you know what, I fell in love with you exactly as you are, exactly who you are. Young, gorgeous, fearless." She grinned. "That's what I thought that first day and I still think it now."

"So you're over your worries about the age difference?"

Evie pushed herself against him and smiled. "Ha—I figure I'll just be thought of as the luckiest woman on the planet." She touched his cheek. "Anyway, you wait until you've had months of night feeding and changing diapers—you'll have aged ten years by the time this baby is a toddler."

"I can't wait," he said honestly.

And it was true. The thought of raising a child with Evie filled him with such an overwhelming feeling of joy he could feel the power of it over his skin, through his blood, in the deep recess of his soul.

"We have to pick out names," she suggested. "I was thinking William for a boy."

Scott nodded. "I like that. It's a good, strong-sounding name."

"And Rebecca for a girl." She kissed him again, lightly along his jaw, and whispered against his ear. "Rebecca Jones."

Scott pulled back slightly. "Jones?"

Evie smiled. "Mmm," she breathed against his skin.

"But you turned me—"

"I'm an idiot," she said, and slipped to the floor in front of him. She perched herself between his knees. "Would you mind if I asked you instead?"

Mind? He couldn't believe what he was hearing. The woman he loved, the woman carrying his child was about to ask him the most important question in the world. Scott shook his head. "Not at all."

She took a deep breath, grabbed his hands and held them against her breasts. "Scott, would you marry me?"

"Absolutely." He kissed her, thinking it was the best moment of his life. "I love you, Evie."

"And I love you. Always. Forever." She ran her hands over his shoulders and across his chest, plucking at the smudgy marks on the fabric. "You're a mess," she said as she wiped her fingertips along his cheek. "So how about that spa bath I promised you a while back?"

Scott looked toward the beckoning ensuite bathroom. "Lead the way."

She smiled and stood, taking his hands. "How about we go together?"

Now that was *definitely* the best moment in his life.

Epilogue

Evie loved Christmas. Especially this year. The big tree in the living room sparkled with colored lights and dozens of glass ornaments and there were so many gifts underneath she couldn't stop grinning when she imagined the room come morning and how all that wrapping paper would be strewn across the floor.

"I do think this year the tree is the best it's ever looked."

Evie turned as Flora Manning came into the room. "Yes," Evie agreed. "It's all those extra lights."

Flora raised a silvery brow. "That's not it," she said, and fiddled with a stray green frond. "It's you."

"Me?"

"You're happy," Flora explained. "Happier than I've ever seen. That's why this big tree looks so special."

Evie smiled. She *was* happy. She had everything she'd ever asked for and more—a wonderful son, an adorable baby and a husband she loved with all her heart. The tree was a bonus. And as it was their first Christmas as a complete family, Evie could barely contain her excitement. They would open some gifts tonight with her mother-in-law and the Manning sisters and tomorrow her parents were coming over to share the morning festivities with them. Later they would all go to Noah and Callie's for a family celebration.

This time of year would always be special to her. She'd fallen in love with Scott during Christmas twelve months earlier and those memories were etched deep within her heart. They'd shared gifts around the tree and kissed beneath the mistletoe and this year would be the same. Only now, Scott was her husband and the tree and the plastic mistletoe had more meaning for her than ever before.

Once Flora left the room to find her sister, Evie spent a little more time trimming the tree and rearranging the gifts. She'd prepared her usual punch and fruit cake and had a tray of savories warming in the oven for later. A soft and familiar sound caught her attention and she turned around.

Her husband framed the doorway, holding their precious bundle in his arms.

"She's supposed to be asleep," Evie said gently, and walked across the room. Scott held their three-month-old daughter, Rebecca, against his shoulder as she pumped her chubby legs excitedly. Evie touched the baby's soft hair. "She'll be relentless tomorrow if she doesn't sleep tonight."

Scott smiled and kissed his daughter's head. "She was awake in her crib, talking to herself. I think she said Dada again."

Evie's brows slanted upward. "You know she's too young to speak, right?"

"Not my kid," he said proudly, and cradled her head with his hand. "She's advanced for her age."

Evie knew there was little point insisting otherwise. "Yes, darling, of course she is."

Scott grinned. "And she loves the Christmas tree lights," he said, and waited while Evie flicked the switch and the tree illuminated in a kaleidoscope of flickering color. Rebecca's blue eyes widened and she gurgled delightfully. "See?" Scott said, and smiled.

Evie watched her daughter and husband together and a surge of love rushed through her blood. He was such an incredible father to both the baby and Trevor. They'd been married for six months, and each day had been an incredible joy. Scott had joined the Bellandale Fire and Rescue Department and had settled easily into his new job.

Trevor loped through the doorway, looking very grown up at sixteen. "Are we opening presents?" he asked, and grabbed some cake.

"Soon," Evie promised as the Manning sisters came through the door. "Once everyone is settled."

Scott winked at her. They'd bought Trevor a fancy racing bike to go with his newfound interest in fitness and sports. The gift was hidden in the one vacant downstairs bedroom, and both she and Scott excused themselves at the same time so they could bring it into the living room.

"I'll take the baby," Eleanor insisted as she floated into the room wearing one of her signature silk caftans. Scott's mother had become a regular visitor to Crystal Point over the past year. One day, Evie was sure, it would become a permanent move. Especially if they continued to add to their brood. She loved the idea of having another child in a year or so.

As Scott placed Rebecca in his mother's arms, Amelia and Flora starting laughing.

"Look, mistletoe!"

Evie tilted her neck backward. Sure enough, the greenery was hanging from the door frame above. She looked at Scott and smiled, thinking how it was such a perfect moment. "Have you been decorating again?"

He chuckled and drew her against his solid body. "Who? Me?" he said, and kissed her under the mistletoe before he reached up and twirled the leaves with his fingertips. "You know, I owe a lot to this little piece of plastic."

"You do?"

"Sure. You might say it's the reason we're here. Got you to kiss me, didn't it?"

Evie laughed delightfully. "Or got *you* to kiss *me?*"

He looked into her eyes. "It got us both here—and that's all that matters."

She nodded and smiled. It was, for sure, the best Christmas ever.

* * * *

HIS MISTLETOE PROPOSAL

CHRISTY McKELLEN

Okay, Charlotte, my compassionate,
clever, beautiful girl. As promised,
this one is dedicated to you.
I love you more than words can say.
And I always will.
Mum

CHAPTER ONE

To my darling Flora—confidante, cheerleader and anchor to my universe,

So this is weird, right? Me speaking to you from the grave. But I wanted to get all my thoughts down on paper because I knew I'd get all choked up and make a mess of it if I tried to say it out loud. So here goes...

I know this is a lot to ask, but please don't be too sad now that I've gone. I feel as though I've made peace with what's happened to me and I'd hate to think of my passing as something that would hold you back from living your own life to the full. I've had a good and happy existence. All twenty-eight of my years have been blessed with love and wonderful experiences and my life's been all the better for having you in it, Flora.

I'm so proud of you for all that you've achieved. I always knew you'd be successful in whatever you did, but your drive and determination have astounded even me. I know you probably won't take a minute to step back and see the enormity of what you've accomplished, but get this: you truly are an incredible person, as well as the kindest, most generous woman I've ever had the pleasure of knowing.

Which leads me on to two favours I have to ask of you, Flora. Firstly, and I know it's a biggie, please look out for Alex now that I'm not around to do it any more. As you know, I was the only family he had left and I hate to think of him being alone in the world. He wouldn't admit it—I think he was trying to protect my last few weeks on earth so they'd be stress-free—but I think someone broke his heart recently and he's really hurting.

Secondly, check your breasts for lumps EVERY DAY. Or, even better, get a gorgeous sex-god to do it for you *wink*. Don't make the same mistake I did and shrug cancer off as something that happens to someone else. Someone older. Or less busy.

You have such a good heart, Flora. You deserve to be happy, so go easy on yourself, okay?

I love you.

Your best friend for ever,

Amy

FLORA MORGAN CAUGHT the tear on her finger before it fell onto the precious, now rather crumpled, piece of paper she clutched in her hand. She'd carried the letter around with her ever since it had dropped through her letter box nearly a month ago, and she'd taken it out regularly since then to read it, hoping to conjure Amy's spirit during her weaker moments.

She missed her friend so much it made her heart physically ache. She had no idea how she was going to live her life without having Amy around, always ready to jolly her out of a funk and lift her spirits with one of her rousing pep talks.

But she was going to have to. Because her best friend was gone.

The hum and chatter of Bath's famous Pump Room restaurant faded away as she lost herself in some of the happy memories she'd shared with Amy during the six years they'd known each other. They'd met at their first jobs after graduating from university, sitting side by side in cramped, scruffy cubicles at the blue-chip company based in Glasgow that had selected them for their highly competitive fast-track programme. They'd hit it off immediately—their mutual love of order and precision drawing them together like paper clips to a magnet. Sharing both the professional and personal exciting highs and painful lows over the years that followed had cemented their tight friendship.

Folding the letter carefully away into the Italian leather handbag she'd bought herself for a birthday present, Flora took a deep breath to centre herself. Now wasn't the time to get all emotionally tangled up. She needed to focus on her reason for being here today and for that she needed to have her wits about her.

Not that her reason for being here today had turned up yet.

Sitting up straighter, Flora became aware of a burst of movement over at the maître d's desk and she turned to see that her companion for afternoon tea had finally arrived. Eighteen minutes late. But then who was counting?

Shaking off her lingering melancholy, she straightened the neckline of her silk blouse and smoothed her fingertips over her eyebrows to make sure they were both still following the required curve. They were.

Standing up, she tried not to notice how out of place Alex Trevelyan seemed in jeans that looked about ready to lie down and die, black Chelsea boots with scuffed toes and a crumpled leather jacket. She doubted very much that he'd even glanced in the mirror that morning considering how his mussed-up chestnut-brown hair fell over his cobalt-blue eyes and what must have been a week's worth of stubble darkened his prominent cheekbones and square jaw.

A few years ago, his just-rolled-out-of-bed sexy musician charisma would have been irresistible to her naïve, overly optimistic self, but not any more. She'd learnt her lesson about men like that the hard way. If she dated anyone these days, she went for smart, business-orientated men who were just as focused on their careers as she was. Though, as Amy had regularly pointed out, that was probably why she'd remained mostly single for the last couple of years. Which Flora was fine with. She didn't need a man to fulfil her.

As he drew nearer, Alex's bloodshot eyes ringed with dark circles made her heart squeeze. She mentally berated herself for being so critical of his appearance when the poor man's twin sister had died barely a month ago. He was obviously still grief-stricken.

She'd only seen him briefly at the funeral; he'd turned up at the last second wearing casual grey trousers and a bright blue shirt that had been open at the neck and glaringly free of a tie. To be fair, Amy hadn't wanted them to wear the usual black mourning clothes. Afterwards, he'd been busy with the vicar and a group of people whom she'd guessed were old friends of the family. She, in turn, had been caught up talking to mutual acquaintances of her and Amy's. By the time she'd looked round to offer her condolences to Alex he'd disappeared, not even turning up at the wake afterwards. She'd guessed he'd been too upset to face any more sympathy from strangers.

Amy's words swam across her vision—*I was the only family he had left.* He needed her support and kindness right now, not her judgement.

Relaxing her posture so that her hands fell neatly to her sides, Flora gave Alex her warmest smile as he finally navigated past the last couple of linen-covered tables and came to a halt in front of her. Taking a deep breath, she was just about to launch into the short monologue she'd composed in her head about how pleased she was that he'd agreed to meet her so they could talk about Amy and support each other during such a difficult time, when he leaned past her to pick up her glass of mineral water and proceeded to chug the whole lot of it, not even acknowledging her presence until he'd satisfied his thirst.

'That's better,' he gasped, slamming the glass back down onto the table before finally turning to face her with a wink. 'Don't let anyone talk you into drinking whisky after four pints at the pub. It's a life event catalyst.'

She stared at him, aghast.

Instead of looking contrite, he yawned loudly into his hand. 'Sorry, I've only just got up. Late night.'

Flora swallowed back her shock before replying, 'It's three o'clock in the afternoon.'

He smiled, his expression one of wry audacity. 'Like I said, late night.'

This wasn't the grieving, broken man she'd been expecting to turn up today and the incongruity was playing havoc with her composure—something that made her really uncomfortable. She hated to be on the back foot; years of facing difficult clients in tense business situations had taught her that.

Pulling herself together, she said, 'Thanks for meeting me. I thought it might be nice for us to get to know each other, what with us being the two people closest to Amy.'

He nodded, then motioned for her to sit down, taking the seat opposite.

'You were in the States, right? New York?' he asked once he was settled.

'Yes, I was working as Head of Marketing for Bounce soft drinks,' she said proudly. 'I transferred over there when the company opened up a New York office about a year ago.'

Usually when she mentioned her job and the position she held, people would look impressed and start asking her questions about what that entailed and how she'd risen so quickly up the ranks, but Alex didn't say a word. And he didn't seem impressed either; he seemed…bored.

This didn't surprise her though; Amy had told her all about her brother's attitude towards people who worked for corporations and how he thought it was 'capitalist gluttony with a corporate greed cherry on top'. Flora privately thought that a man who had given up a perfectly good job in corporate finance to faff about as a musician had no right to judge others and their career choices. If he wanted to waste his talents just so he could sit on his high horse, looking down on others who were slogging away to make a success of themselves, then that was his business.

She wasn't going to rise to it. She had more important things to worry about—like gaining the trust and respect of her new boss. After transferring to the London-based office it was proving harder than she'd expected to do this.

Not for the first time, it had made her question whether she should set up her own business at some point, but she was keenly aware of what a big risk that would be.

She gave herself a mental shake. She really shouldn't be allowing her thoughts to wander back to work right now.

'Anyway, since I'm over here now I thought it might be nice for us to get to know each other a bit so we could support each other,' she said, waving for the waiter, who appeared not to notice her. Biting back a sigh of frustration, she refocused on Alex, who was lounging back in his chair with his arms folded and his brow furrowed.

Was it her imagination or did he really not want to be here?

She cleared her throat. 'I didn't want to be one of those people who kept away for fear of not knowing what to say to someone who's just lost someone close to them,' she said, deciding just to plough on. 'Sending flowers and cards is all very well, but sometimes you just need some human contact, you know?'

He cocked his head and gave her a slow grin. 'Is that why you came back to England? For some human contact?'

She shifted in her seat, feeling heat rise up her neck. 'I needed a change of scene,' she said, straightening the cutlery on the table.

What she didn't tell him was that *he* was the real reason for moving back here. She was determined to take Amy's last wish seriously, and if that meant living in the same city as Alex for a while then so be it. London was too far removed from Bath to keep an eye on him easily, and she certainly couldn't have done it from New York. So she'd jumped at an opportunity for a temporary transfer to the West London office, commuting in from Bath to oversee a UK-only product launch.

Alex appeared to be thinking about what she'd said, and after a short pause he leaned forwards in his chair to look her right in the eye, as if making the decision to finally engage with the conversation. 'It's good to meet you in the flesh,' he said, the corner of his mouth lifting into a grin. 'Amy talked about you a lot over the years.' He paused. 'And during the last weeks of her life.'

At last there was a flash of emotion in his eyes, which he blinked away quickly.

Flora nodded, taking a moment to relax her throat, which had tightened with sorrow at the sound of her best friend's name. 'It's good to meet you too. I—' She took a breath. 'I feel awful that I didn't make it back in time to see her in the hospice. I tried to get back to England as fast as I could, but—' She'd run out of words. The pathetic ring to her excuse made her cringe inside.

She'd thought she had more time. That Amy had more time. Her friend had told her during one of their regular video calls that she was doing better and not to worry about rushing back to see her. But then she'd taken a sudden, unexpected turn for the worse.

As if he'd read her mind, Alex leaned forwards and put his large, warm hand over hers where it lay on the table. 'Don't beat yourself up about it. None of us re-

alised she'd go that soon. She did seem to have a reprieve at one point. You couldn't have known. Amy
knew you would have come sooner if you'd been able
to. She told me that.'

Flora could do nothing but nod like one of those
tacky toy dogs you saw in the back of cars sometimes.
She was suddenly terrified she might start crying in the
middle of the restaurant and have to sit there with her
make-up running down her face and nowhere to hide.

Alex obviously read her distress because he gave her
hand a squeeze. 'Hey, let's get out of here. This place
is making my headache worse.' He glanced around the
magnificent room with a pained grimace. 'There's a
really good pub round the corner that does amazing
burgers.'

Wrestling her emotions back under control, Flora
shot him a bewildered look. 'But we've come here for
afternoon tea.' She gestured round at the magnificent
eighteenth-century room with its cut-glass chandelier
hanging from the ornate ceiling and the grand piano,
which was being expertly played by a gentleman in a
tuxedo.

He wrinkled his nose. 'For a tiny plate of overpriced
cucumber sandwiches? Sorry, but that's not going to
cut it for me today.'

'Actually, this place is known for having one of the
best—' But he'd already stood up and was waving for
the waiter to bring the bill.

Deciding not to fight him on this—she wanted to
keep things as friendly and light-hearted as possible
considering why they were meeting each other today—
she gritted her teeth and stood up, taking her purse out
of her bag ready to pay for her drink.

He spotted her pulling out a twenty-pound note and waved it away.

'I'll get this.'

'You don't have—' But he'd already taken the bill from the waiter. He proceeded to rummage in his pockets to produce a handful of coins, which he emptied into his hand.

'Thanks, man,' he said. 'Keep the change.'

The waiter gave him a tight smile, then walked away, no doubt cursing them both for being the most awkward customers of the day.

Outside the Pump Room crowds of shoppers were stopping and starting along the pavement, as every now and again someone would halt at one of the little German-style wooden huts belonging to the large Christmas market that had taken over the whole of the city centre.

'Wow, it's busy out here,' Flora said as they waited for a break in the flow so they could join the slow-moving crowd.

'Warm inside the throng though,' Alex said with a smile. 'Free heat.'

He was right. Despite the biting cold of the day, it felt cosy and comforting being encased in the large mob of people. There was an excited, almost magical, feeling in the air too, no doubt an eagerness for the upcoming festivities.

Flora had spent many years in her youth loving the excitement of the run-up to Christmas, but she felt nothing but numbness about it now. It was all too tangled up with the fallout from her last serious relationship.

Pushing away the wave of gut-churning despondency she always felt whenever she thought about that, she looked round and focused on a stall selling silk scarves in every colour of the rainbow, taking comfort in the beauty of the sight.

'So you live in Bath but work in London?' Alex asked as they walked away from the scarf stall, stopping at the next one along to peruse a tantalising display of mince pies and Christmas cakes. Alongside them an assortment of delicious-looking pastries covered in snow-white icing gleamed in the soft winter sunshine.

She nodded. 'Yes. I commute into Paddington and the office is only a ten-minute walk from there. I felt like taking a break from living in the middle of a big city,' she said, telling herself she wasn't exactly lying by saying that. Recently she'd started to think that living outside the city where she worked would be better for her health. She'd be less inclined to pop into work at the weekends and less likely to stay as late in the evenings if she had to catch a train home.

Looking round at Alex, she realised that he wasn't even listening to her, but smiling at the pretty young stallholder instead. 'Nice buns,' he said to the woman, giving her a wink and making her blush and giggle coquettishly.

Flora rolled her eyes at the stallholder's reaction to Alex's cheesy pickup line. Okay, he was a good-looking man, she supposed—he had the same smile as Amy, which could light up a room—but the guy was a rumpled mess.

He turned and caught her staring at him.

'What?' he asked.

'Nothing. It's just—'

'Yes?'

'You don't seem—'

He appeared frustrated with her lack of words. 'What? Sad, bereft, miserable? Just because I'm not bawling my eyes out in public doesn't mean I don't miss my sister.'

Prickly heat washed over her. 'I know that. I wasn't criticising the way you're mourning her.'

'Weren't you?' He gave her a look that made guilt pool in her stomach. 'I promised her I wouldn't let grief get in the way of getting on with my life and I intend to keep that promise. She'd hate it if *either of us* was sitting around moping.'

'Yes, okay.' She held up her hands as a peace offering. 'I understand that. I guess it's just taking me longer to adjust to life without her, that's all.'

His expression softened and he flashed her his beguiling smile, making something twist oddly in her stomach. 'Fair enough. I know how close you two were. I don't mean to criticise you either. Each to their own, I suppose. I've chosen to move on with my life. It doesn't mean that I don't think about her all the damn time.'

Flora gave him a sympathetic smile, her guilt dissipating a little.

'Come on, let's get to the pub,' he said, gesturing to somewhere off in the distance. 'I could really do with a hair of the dog.'

Nodding, she fell into step alongside him on strangely wobbly legs and they rejoined the crowd, moving slowly onwards.

Alex Trevelyan took a deep breath and willed his heartbeat to slow down as he and Flora pushed their way through the dense throng of Christmas shoppers.

He really didn't want to be here right now. His head

was pounding and he was having trouble keeping a smile on his face after Flora's insinuation that he wasn't mourning his sister properly.

From what he'd seen of her so far, he was surprised this rather uptight woman could have been such a good friend of his sister's, until he remembered the look of near reverence on Amy's face when she'd described Flora to him.

'She's really something,' Amy had said with enthusiasm. 'She comes across as a bit—' She'd paused, searching for the right word, her nose wrinkling with the effort. 'A bit spiky, I guess you'd say—especially if you don't know her well. All the people where we worked were intimidated by her.' She'd smiled as if remembering her friend's tyranny fondly. 'But underneath she's got a heart of gold. You'd like her. Honestly.'

It was the 'honestly' that had spoken to him. Knowing his sister as he did, Alex knew that it meant she wanted him to like Flora, but wasn't sure that he would.

Well, he could see now why Amy might have been sceptical. He wasn't entirely sure that he *did* like Flora, with her side-eyeing and staid pragmatism. Though he'd be a liar to say he didn't find her physically compelling. Who wouldn't, with her long sweep of shiny caramel-blonde hair and big grey-green eyes. She was definitely an attractive woman—though more because she made the most of her assets rather than being a stop-you-in-your-tracks beauty and she had a magnetism that kept drawing his gaze back to her. She was dressed as if she was going to a business meeting rather than getting a bite to eat with a friendly acquaintance though. And she was just so polished. Everything about her shone, from the tips of her manicured nails to the toes of her high-heeled leather boots. Wealth and good taste seemed to exude from every pore of her being.

She was not his usual type at all. He preferred women who weren't afraid to get their hair wet in the rain or get covered in mud on a long walk through the woods. He liked natural and down-to-earth and simple. Like his ex-girlfriend, Tia. The woman he'd thought he'd spend the rest of his life with.

Pushing away the sinking feeling that thinking about his ex created, he stared blankly ahead of him. He'd moved on now. There was no point in looking back. He'd promised Amy he wouldn't do that.

As they walked on, he noticed Flora turning her head from side to side, as if trying to take in as many of the Christmassy sights as possible. The magic of the season held no allure for him at all this year. In fact, it would be fair to say that he was looking forward to the month of December being over and done with. Christmas Day was only going to remind him of how alone he was now.

'Take a left here,' he said into Flora's ear, attempting to cut through the noise of the crowd as they approached the side street leading towards the pub. The expensive scent of her perfume wafted into his nose, making him shiver in the strangest of ways. It had been months since he'd been in intimate contact with a woman and his body seemed to have gone a little haywire from the absence of it.

She nodded in acknowledgement and they moved slowly towards an opening in the crowd.

He watched her sashay ahead of him—elegant but entirely self-aware.

It made him think about something else Amy had said about Flora. 'I worry she's losing herself in her ridiculous quest for perfection.' Well, that fitted with what little he'd seen of her so far.

He wondered what else he was going to discover about her before the end of the day.

CHAPTER TWO

FLORA TRIED NOT to wrinkle her nose at the smell of stale
beer that seemed to rise up in waves from the ugly red-
and-brown patterned carpet as they entered the gloomy
pub that Alex had insisted on bringing them to.

'I'm going to order a burger at the bar. Want one?'
Alex asked as she settled herself at one of the sticky
mahogany-stained tables, trying to avoid sitting on a
suspicious-looking brown stain on the vinyl padded
bench.

'Er...no, thanks. I'll just have a drink for now.'

He gave her a bemused frown, then shrugged. 'Okay.
What would you like to drink then?'

She thought about it for a moment, then decided that
alcohol might actually make this situation a little bit
easier. 'I'll have a pint of the local cider.'

His brows shot up. 'Really? It's pretty potent stuff.'

She bristled. 'I might look like a lightweight, but I
bet I can drink you under the table.'

'Now there's a challenge,' he said, grinning at her
before turning away to head over to the bar.

She watched him charm the barmaid, wondering how
on earth she was going to successfully insinuate herself
into his life without it looking really suspicious. She

was pretty sure he'd be entirely resistant to the idea of her keeping an eye on him if he knew that was what she was really here for.

He was so different to Amy, she mused while waiting for him to come back with the drinks. It was odd, considering that they'd both been brought up in exactly the same environment at the same time. But then she and her younger sister weren't exactly alike either. Violet was vivacious, artsy and beautiful, the total opposite of her: sensible, conventional and, if she was being totally honest with herself, only modestly attractive. Violet had always cast Flora into shadow whenever she was around; she was just one of those people with a natural *joie de vivre* that drew people to her.

Men, particularly.

An uncomfortable tightness had formed in Flora's throat and she coughed to clear it as Alex finally returned to the table with her cider and a pint of lager for himself.

'Thanks,' she said, forcing her mouth into a smile as she took her drink from him.

He gave her a nod and sat down in the chair opposite. 'Are you sure you don't want anything to eat?' he asked.

She shook her head. 'No, thanks. I'll have something when I get home.' She really didn't fancy eating here. Their table looked as though it hadn't been wiped in ages, which didn't give her much confidence in the state of the kitchen.

Picking up her drink, she took a few good gulps of it. The alcohol warmed her as it rushed down her throat to her stomach, lifting her spirits a little.

'So how long have you been living in Bath?' she

asked, watching him knock back half of his own pint in one go.

His eyes met hers and she saw a reaction in them that she couldn't quite decipher. Wariness, maybe?

'Just over a year. I was in London for a long time, but then I got together with the band I play with now. They're mostly based in Bath, so it made sense to move here so I could practise with them more easily.'

'Amy told me you play jazz.' She hadn't meant that to sound so derisive, but she'd never understood the lure of jazz and couldn't imagine how anyone would want to listen to it every day, let alone make a career out of playing it.

A flicker of annoyance crossed his face, but he didn't pick up on her disparaging tone. 'Yeah, we specialise in thirties-inspired jazz and blues, but sometimes we give our sets a more modern slant if we're in the mood and the occasion calls for it.'

'And how's it all going?' she asked, this time making sure to keep her tone upbeat. 'Is it fulfilling? How do you make it lucrative? Do you play at weddings and parties?'

He gave her a look that made her stomach clench with discomfort.

'It's not all about the money for me.' He rested his arms on the table. 'Look, I know jazz isn't to everyone's taste, but it's worth giving it a chance before you write it off,' he said bluntly.

She wondered whether there was an underlying meaning to that. *Don't write me off until you know me better*, perhaps. He had a point, she supposed. It was wrong of her to judge before she had all the facts.

'Perhaps I could come to one of your gigs some time?' she said, trying to pull back favour.

He nodded and smiled in a manner that made her think he was just humouring her. His food arrived then and he thanked the server, then tucked straight into it as if he'd not eaten in days.

This wasn't exactly going how she'd planned. She'd really not expected him to be like this: so...*blasé*. If she so much as thought about Amy, her whole body flooded with a heavy sort of dread and she had to think about work or something practical so as not to start welling up.

There was a good chance he was burying his pain though, so she needed to be patient and vigilant—ready to support him as and when he needed her.

'You okay?' Alex asked after finishing the last bite of his food, his satisfied expression morphing into a worried frown.

She realised with a start that she'd been staring at him.

'Fine. Just thinking about my week at work,' she lied.

'Want to tell me about it?' he asked, though she could tell from the edge in his voice that he was really hoping she wouldn't.

Pushing aside a sting of hurt, she shook her head. She didn't want him to know how difficult she was finding it to impress her new boss. 'I'd rather just forget about it,' she said, picking up her drink and taking a few more gulps of it for courage.

He nodded but didn't say anything.

'So when is your next gig?' she asked, trying to keep her tone light and conversational.

'In a couple of weeks,' he said, spinning his now-empty glass between his hands and glowering into the distance, as if picturing it unfavourably.

'You know, I really would love to come,' she said.

He turned to shoot her a look of deep scepticism. 'I got the impression it wasn't your type of music.'

She felt her face heat, embarrassed now by how dismissive her tone had been. 'Yes, well, perhaps I should give jazz a chance.' This struck her as funny for some reason. 'Hey, you should work up a marketing campaign with that as your strapline. *Give jazz a chance.*' She guffawed at her own joke, but for some reason Alex didn't seem to find it funny.

Grump.

'But seriously,' she said, rearranging her features back into a sober expression. 'I really would like to come and support you.'

'Well, that's very selfless of you, Flora, but I'm afraid the gig's sold out.'

'Oh.' This news shocked her. Perhaps he was more successful than she'd realised. She squinted at him suspiciously. Or was he just telling her that because he didn't want her there?

'Can't you get hold of extra tickets as one of the band members?' she asked. Surely he'd be able to swing something? She really wanted to show him some solidarity. She felt sure Amy would have approved of that.

'Nope. Sorry. I've already given all of mine away,' he said, standing up so suddenly it made her start. 'I'm going to the bar again—want another one?' he asked, nodding to her much-depleted drink.

'Well, I shouldn't—' she hedged. The alcohol had already had quite an effect on her, making everything look a little hazy and causing her to slur her words a little, but it was plain he was determined to have another and she didn't want to leave just yet '—but hey, it's Saturday, so why not?'

He gave her a curt nod and headed over to the bar without another word.

His denial of her request for a ticket to his gig still stung and she pondered how to get him to stop resisting her attempts at being friendly.

What would Amy have done?

She probably would have been upfront about the things he was trying to conceal and forced him to discuss them. But could she really talk to Alex like that without getting his back up? She didn't have Amy's light touch and easy wit—the woman could have talked the birds down from the trees—and she didn't want to blow her chance of getting closer to him.

It was obvious that he needed a friend right now though, judging by the way he wasn't taking care of his appearance.

She watched him slouch back over to where she sat, his body language self-assured but just a little bit weary.

He gave her a questioning look and she realised that she had been staring at him again.

'Are you sure you're okay?' he asked with one quizzical brow raised.

She gave herself a mental shake. 'Yes, fine. Are you?'

He blinked slowly. 'Yes. I'm fine, thanks, Flora.'

'I was just thinking you looked a bit worn out.'

He sat down, rubbing a hand over his eyes. 'Yeah, well, I've not been sleeping well recently.'

'Hmm, I'm not surprised. It's been a difficult few months for you, hasn't it?'

He shrugged, then took a sip from his drink. 'I guess.'

Apparently subtlety wasn't going to cut it. She considered hedging around the subject of his failed relationship, which Amy had alluded to in her letter, but decided she might as well just go for it and see what happened.

'So are you seeing anyone at the moment?' she asked, attempting an offhand tone.

His shoulders stiffened at the question. He folded his arms, then frowned, as if something had just occurred to him. 'Amy asked you to keep an eye on me, didn't she?'

'No!' The lie came out before she had time to modify it. 'I was just wondering, that's all. Being friendly and taking an interest.'

'Mmm-hmm.' He looked at her steadily for one long, loaded moment and she felt her cheeks start to heat.

'Okay, yes!' she burst out defensively, unable to handle his intense scrutiny any longer. 'Amy mentioned that you'd recently split up with someone and that she thought you were a bit cut up about it.'

'I see. So that's why you really called me, is it? To make sure I wasn't about to jump off the Pulteney Bridge?'

Flora shook her head jerkily. 'I wanted to see you so we could talk about Amy. You were the person that knew her best after all.' There was an uncomfortable beat of silence while she took a shaky breath. 'And I miss her.' She felt the tears start to well in her eyes again and blinked them back. No way was she going to cry in front of him now.

Her words seemed to have had some sort of effect on him, because his posture relaxed and he reached over the table to put his hand on her forearm. Her skin tingled alarmingly under his touch, but she didn't pull away. He probably needed some human contact too, she reminded herself.

'Okay, yes.' He sighed, a rueful smile appearing on his face.

'Yes what?' she asked, a little lost.

'I am fairly recently out of a relationship, but I'm fine. I was cut up for a while because I thought it could become serious, but it didn't work out. It's okay though. I'm fine. Still in one piece,' he said, taking his hand off her arm to thump his chest right over his heart.

His bravado had a false ring to it though. Maybe it was the repeated use of 'fine' or perhaps it was the flash of pain in his eyes that he hadn't quite managed to conceal.

Her resolve strengthened. Obviously he was still hurting but wasn't willing to talk about it with her. Well, she could bide her time. Perhaps once they'd got to know each other a bit better he'd soften and let her in. He probably needed to talk it all through with someone he trusted, and she was more than willing to become that person.

If only he'd let her.

Alex sat back in his chair with a sigh, feeling the burger and beer boosting his blood sugar levels and improving his irascible mood.

When Flora had questioned his relationship status he'd been ready to close her down fast, but had checked himself at the last minute. It was pretty clear she wasn't the sort of person to take a brush-off lightly—she had fire and determination in those big, bright eyes of hers.

He'd decided that an approximation of the truth would be the best course of action.

Hopefully she'd leave it at that now. He didn't feel like rehashing the pain and misery of the last few months to satisfy the curiosity of a near stranger. Just because she'd been Amy's closest friend didn't mean she deserved his total trust and honesty.

Except it sort of did.

He sighed to himself, thinking back to the conversation he'd had with his sister in the hospice, the day she'd passed away.

'She may seem as tough as nails,' Amy had said, her voice weak and slurred from the painkillers they'd been pumping into her, 'but she'll need a friend once I've gone. Promise me you'll be kind to her, Alex, especially if she comes to you looking for atonement. She'll beat herself up about not being here to say goodbye.'

And it seemed his sister had been right.

It also looked as though he was going to have to keep the hurried promise he'd made to her as he'd watched her life ebb away.

He remembered now how her request had seemed like the only positive thing at a time when he'd felt so horrifically impotent, unable to do anything to save his sister. It had given him just a little sliver of power over the situation. He suspected Amy might have known that too.

'I'm just going to the bathroom,' he said, suddenly feeling an overwhelming need to escape from the poignant memories that were pressing in on his head like a vice.

'Okay,' Flora said, producing an overly bright smile, as if sensing his pain.

In the gents bathroom he stared at himself in the mirror, noting the dark rings around his bloodshot eyes and the unhealthy pallor of his skin. He'd not meant to get so drunk last night, but he hadn't had the willpower to say no when his bandmates had suggested going to the pub after rehearsals. He'd also not been entirely straight with Flora earlier when he'd suggested that someone else had persuaded him to drink whisky until the early hours of the morning.

He'd done that entirely of his own volition.

Yesterday had been a difficult day and he'd felt the overwhelming need to get out of his head for a while and drown his raging thoughts. Music was usually his salvation, but it had become increasingly difficult to lose himself in it over the last few months and it was slowly driving him insane.

He slapped his cheeks, seeing colour bloom on his pale skin. Time to pull himself together.

Returning to the table, he bit back a wry smile as he noted how uncomfortable Flora looked perched on the edge of the bench, as if afraid that sitting on it fully might sully her impeccable image.

'I swear that's the last time I drink whisky straight from the bottle,' he said flippantly as he sat back down, noticing Flora flinch a little. It reminded him of her less than impressed reaction earlier when he'd told her he'd only just got up. He'd laughed it off at the time but, truth be told, he'd found it virtually impossible to drag himself out of bed today.

They sat in awkward silence for a moment, both sipping from their nearly empty pints.

'It's no wonder you're depressed if you spend all your time in places like this,' Flora said suddenly in a voice that she'd perhaps meant to be jokey but actually came off as a little officious.

'I'm not depressed,' he stated firmly, feeling discomfort flood through him.

'Really? Are you sure? From what you've told me it sounds like you could be.'

He sighed in frustration, wishing she'd change the subject. 'If I need a shrink, I promise you I'll give one a call.'

She ignored his pointed sarcasm and waved a hand at him, her movements suspiciously exaggerated. 'You know, it can be a great help to get out and socialise after ending a relationship.' She took an audible breath. 'Perhaps if you went on a couple of dates? It might give your spirits a bit of a lift.'

He stared at her in disbelief. 'Are you serious?'

Fixing him with a cool stare, she said, 'Totally.'

'Yeah, well, I don't seem to be having much luck in the dating department at the moment,' he muttered, his mind spinning back to the way he'd crashed and burned last night when he'd drunkenly attempted to chat up a woman at the bar. Not that his heart had really been in it.

She seemed to be studying him closely now, her eyes narrowed. 'Is that how you usually dress when you go out?' she asked after a beat.

'Yes,' he replied gruffly, guessing where this was going and trying not to grind his teeth.

'Maybe if you smartened yourself up a bit you'd have more luck.' She waved her hand at his favourite T-shirt. 'I always find a new outfit and a haircut does my confidence the world of good.'

He dug his fingers into his thighs under the table. 'I happen to like the way I dress.'

She shot him a patronising smile. 'Well, I don't mean to be rude but your clothes look so old I suspect they're about to get a telegram from the Queen any day now.'

A heavy pulse had begun to throb in his head. 'Oh, really? Well, at least they have personality. You look like every other fashion victim on the street.'

She blinked at him in shock before regaining her composure. 'At least I made an effort with my appearance today,' she replied tightly, her words sounding more slurred now. 'It's clear you couldn't care less. You didn't even turn up on time to meet me, just left me sitting there like a lemon on my own for twenty minutes, only to turn up looking like a vagrant.'

He leaned forward in his chair, aware of his heart thumping hard against his chest, and matched her fierce gaze. 'Look, I get it. You feel some misplaced obligation to "take me in hand" and alleviate your guilt about not being there at the end for Amy.' He pointed a finger at her. 'But I don't need another sister figure and I certainly don't need some uptight do-gooder telling me how to live my life!'

'I'm only trying to help, Alex,' she snapped back.

'I don't need your help, Flora.'

'Is that right?'

'Yes!'

'Well, you know what? Since we're being so honest with each other now, perhaps you should know that Amy really struggled with your arrogant determination to keep everyone at arm's length,' she bit out, the increased volume of her voice causing the couple at the next table to turn and stare at them. She seemed to have hit her stride though, so didn't appear to notice. 'And it was incredibly frustrating for her that you found everything you did so easy when she had to work so hard for success. Then she had to watch while you just squandered your brain and your talents when she would have killed for them!' she hissed, her tongue obviously completely loosened now by strong cider and frustration.

Anger and guilt battled inside him. He was acutely aware of what a risk he'd taken, jacking in his steady job to follow his ambition to be a professional musician, but he didn't need to be reminded of it right now. 'I think what you really mean is that a slacker like me should have been the one to die, rather than my hard-working sister,' he bit out defensively.

'What? No!' She looked absolutely horrified that he could even suggest that.

He sighed, feeling his conscience prick, then held up a weary hand in recognition that he'd gone a bit too far with that statement. 'Okay, okay.' He took a steadying breath. 'Actually, I did know she felt like that—we talked about it before she died. But she told me to do what made me happy. She realised there was more to life than selling your soul just so you can wear overpriced designer clothes to eat at overhyped restaurants.'

Her eyes widened as if his words had hit her right in the solar plexus. 'So now you're having a go at me for enjoying the fruits of my success?'

He sighed in exasperation. 'No, that's not what I'm doing.' A voice in the back of his mind pointed out that it was exactly what he was doing.

'Well, it seems like it to me!' She took a deep, juddering breath. 'You know what? I'm going home. I know when I'm wasting my time.' Picking up her drink, she downed the rest of it, then stood up, wobbling a little on her heels. 'I was just trying to be friendly, Alex!'

she said in a strangled voice. With that parting shot, she spun on the spot and stormed away from him, only just avoiding stumbling into the wall on her way to the door.

Alex dropped his head into his hands and cursed under his breath.

He really shouldn't have had a go at her like that, but when she'd started her character assassination of him something inside had snapped. He'd had just about enough of women telling him what was wrong with him.

The look of hurt on Flora's face had brought him up short though. Clearly she was still struggling to come to terms with his sister's sudden death and was desperately trying to find a way to give her life some meaning—by attempting to fix his.

Sighing, he got up from his chair and pulled his coat on. He couldn't just let her storm off in that state. He at least needed to make sure she got home safely, even if she refused to speak to him again.

After giving the barmaid a wave of thanks he followed Flora out of the pub. It was cold outside and he pulled his lapels across his throat and folded his arms against the icy wind as he trudged after her lone figure, watching in alarm as she swayed along the pavement, almost bumping into a couple coming the other way. He had no idea where she lived, but he hoped it wasn't far.

It wasn't.

She turned into the next street along, which housed a row of grand terraces, and strode up to a pillared entrance a few doors down. Fumbling in her handbag, she pulled out a key, which she proceeded to stab at the lock.

He watched her, half amused, half exasperated, as she failed to get the key into the lock over and over again. Shaking his head, he walked up behind her and took the key from her hand, feeling her jump in surprise at his unexpected presence.

'I don't need your help,' she said archly, but he ignored her, sliding the key into the lock and swinging the door open for her.

'After you,' he said, gesturing for her to go first, then rolling his eyes when she snatched the keys from his hand and swept past him with her head held high. This time, she managed to get the key to the inner flat into the lock on her second try. She barrelled inside, shrugging off her coat and haphazardly kicking off her shoes in the small but elegant hallway. Her whole posture was stiff now as if she was desperately trying to keep her composure under control and as he followed her inside the flat—just to make sure she wasn't going to walk into a wall and knock herself out—he saw her shoulders slump as if she'd lost the battle.

'Are you okay?' he asked quietly, worried that he'd gone too far in his anger and really upset her.

She turned back to look at him and his stomach dropped at the dejection he saw in her eyes.

'I'm sorry,' she said, surprising him with the genuine tone in her voice. He hadn't been expecting an apology.

'I've had such a terrible week. My boss doesn't trust me to do my job properly and you think I'm annoying and stuck-up.' She rubbed her hands over her eyes, smudging her make-up. 'I just wanted to do something good, Alex.'

'I know, I understand,' he said, moving towards her.

'I miss Amy so much.' Her voice broke on his sister's name and he swallowed in empathy.

'Don't you have other friends to talk to?' he asked gently.

'Yes, I have other friends! But I've grown apart from a lot of them since moving to the States and getting so swamped with work.' She flapped her hand in an overly dramatic gesture that gave away just how drunk she was. 'And anyway, none of them understand me the way that Amy did.'

Feeling out of his depth, he held up a hand, palm forward, to gesture for her to stay there. 'I'll get you a drink of water,' he said, backing away to find the kitchen. After locating a clean glass in the cupboard and filling it from a bottle of mineral water in the fridge, he returned to the living room to find her pacing up and down.

He held out the glass and she took it from him with a nod of thanks.

'She was always so good at giving it to me straight, then finding the perfect way to cheer me up,' she said, as if needing to get it all out now that she'd started talking about Amy. 'I need that.' She let out a big sigh, then looked at him beseechingly. 'Who's going to tell me to stop getting so wound up about nothing and "take a step back and breathe" now? Who's going to tease me about buying the exact same outfits year after year, whilst also complimenting me on my good taste? Or roll her eyes at my terrible jokes whilst also making me feel loved and respected? Who will ever understand me the way Amy did?' she finished on a whisper, her voice heavy with pain.

He had no idea how to make things better for her so, despite his frustration, he remained silent. It didn't seem as if Flora was really asking him for answers though. They both knew there weren't any right now.

She cocked her head to one side and gave him a smile that was full of anguish. 'We're never going to see her again, Alex. How can that possibly be? She was so young; she had so much to live for. I'll never see her cuddle the babies she wanted so desperately. She would have been such a good mother. I was going to be their favourite honorary aunt. It's such a waste of a good life. She had so much to offer the world. It's not fair. It's just not fair, Alex.'

'I know,' he said quietly, fighting back the swell of emotion he'd kept firmly under wraps since Amy had died. He had a horrible feeling if he let it go he'd lose himself completely.

Her eyes glimmered with tears as she looked at him, shaking her head.

'I hate the idea of moving through life without having any kind of a clue about what's lying in wait for me. When Amy was around I felt like I could cope with that fear because she'd always be there, at my back, ready to catch me. But I'm all alone now.' Sloshing water out of the glass with her drunken gesticulations, she put it down onto a side table next to her.

'Yeah, I know what you mean,' he said. And he did. It was something that terrified him too.

She put her head in her hands. 'Oh, God, I'm sorry. I must sound so selfish. I know I'm not the only person to lose someone, but that's how I feel when I wake up in the dark in the early hours—swamped with this cloying sense of dread and anger at the world.' She fisted her hands and shook them as if trying to throttle her emotions.

'Yeah, well, grief affects people in all sorts of ways.'

Looking back at him, she gazed right into his eyes, as if searching for something specific there. 'It doesn't seem to have affected you in the same way though. And I don't mean that as a criticism.' Her posture slumped now. 'I guess I'm just a weaker person than you.'

He moved towards her, putting his hand on her shoulder.

'I was lucky. I got to spend a lot of time with her at the end of her life,' he said quietly, realising now just how grateful he was to have had that opportunity.

'You see, that's the thing,' Flora said, then swallowed hard, as if forcing back her tears. 'I didn't get to say a proper goodbye and it's eating away at me. If only I'd booked my flight a day earlier. Twenty-four hours. That's all it would have taken to have been there to hug my best friend one last time.'

Her pain reached right inside him, twisting his guts. He drew her towards him, wrapping his arms around her and holding her tightly to him, at last feeling a real connection to her—that they were in this together.

She hugged him back with a fierceness that nearly broke his heart, as if she was hoping that touching someone associated with Amy might bring back the peace she'd felt when his sister was around.

And then, as she drew back to look at him, the atmosphere switched in a second. Her pupils were blown in the dim light, making her eyes look huge. There was a strange expression in them now. Of longing. At least he was pretty sure that was what it was.

She raised her hand to his face and slid her fingertips along his jaw, frowning as they juddered across the bristles.

'You're a good person, Alex. Amy was so lucky to have you as a brother. I wish I had someone like you looking out for me.'

Before he realised what she was about to do, Flora lurched forwards and pressed her mouth against his, her lips warm and soft. The sweet scent of her invaded his senses as he stood there, stunned and rooted to the spot. His blood pounded hard through his veins as he fought off the strongest impulse just to let himself sink into the kiss.

But he knew he couldn't do that.

Carefully, reluctantly, he drew back from her, feeling her hands instinctively tighten around his back for a second before she realised he was deliberately pulling away.

'That's a really bad idea, Flora. One I think you'll regret in the morning when you're stone-cold sober.'

She shook her head, looking a little bewildered. 'I won't—'

But he wasn't prepared to argue this with her when she was drunk and hurting. 'Come on, it's time for you to go to bed.'

Her shoulders slumped as if all her energy had drained away now and she meekly allowed him to lead her out of the living room and into what he correctly surmised was her bedroom.

'Just sleep it off, okay? Things will seem a bit better in the morning. We just need to take each day as it comes.'

She nodded, then yawned loudly. 'I'm so tired,' she murmured.

'I can tell,' he said, pulling back the duvet so she could crawl into bed, still wearing her clothes. He figured it was probably better to leave her like that than attempt to undress her—that could only lead to more misunderstandings. Once she was settled, he pulled the duvet over her and went to fetch her glass of water from the living room. By the time he returned with it she seemed to be asleep already, her breathing soft and regular in the quiet of the room.

He watched her for a moment, just to make sure she really was asleep, feeling a sudden swell of compassion for her. Shaking off the weird twitch of nerves this produced, he crept out of the room, letting out a big yawn of his own. His insomnia seemed to have well and truly caught up with him today. Moving over to the sofa, he lay down, pulling a blanket he found neatly folded on the arm over his body.

He'd stay here for an hour or so, just to make sure she wasn't ill. He knew how evil that local cider was—he'd been caught out by it himself before.

Shifting onto his side, he felt the waistband of his jeans dig in to him, so undid them and shucked them off. Yes, that was much more comfortable. Though he was pretty hot now. She seemed to have her heating turned up to full. He tugged his T-shirt off too, feeling relief at the sensation of cooler air on his hot skin. His whole body felt overstimulated after the kiss she'd planted on his mouth.

Pushing the memory far out of his head, he let out a deep sigh to expel the tension. After the soul-crushing end to his relationship with Tia, the very last thing he needed right now was to get caught up in something new. He had a strong suspicion, from what he'd seen of Flora so far, that someone as intense and focused as her would be the kind of woman who would want to go all in on a relationship too. He needed to look after himself right now, so there was no space for anyone else in his life.

Fluffing up the cushion, he flopped back down and let out a groan of tiredness. There, that was better. He'd just close his eyes for a minute, then get out of there once he was sure she'd be okay on her own.

CHAPTER THREE

BRIGHT WINTRY SUNLIGHT playing against his eyelids
woke Alex up from a deep sleep. Peeling his lids open
he looked around him, wondering where the heck he'd
woken up. He didn't recognise the cornice on the ceiling or the glass chandelier hanging from it. Turning his
head, he looked around the room to find he was lying on
a large red velvet sofa, surrounded by expensive-looking
antique furniture. There was a large Christmas tree in
the bay window adorned with tasteful decorations and
sprigs of holly jauntily arranged in an elegant vase on
the mantelpiece. Well, this definitely wasn't his place.

Then it all came rushing back to him. He was still
at Flora's flat.

Sitting up, he rubbed his hand over his skull, attempting to get the blood flowing to his brain. He'd not
meant to stay all night, but her sofa had been so comfortable he hadn't woken up after the two-hour stretch
he usually managed these days.

His mouth felt as if someone had rubbed it with sand-
paper. Too much beer again last night. Swinging his
legs off the sofa, he stood up and stretched, feeling the
air on his sleep-warmed skin. He'd grab a quick drink

of water, then get dressed and out of there. She didn't need to know he'd stayed the whole night.

As he moved towards the doorway his gaze caught on a framed photo on the sideboard. Stopping to pick it up, he examined the picture of Flora and his sister, arms flung around each other, smiling at the camera. They both had deep, healthy-looking tans and sunglasses pushed jauntily back on their heads. They looked so carefree it made something tighten uncomfortably inside him. The photo must have been taken during one of the summer holidays to Greece or Italy or France that they'd taken together each year. Something Amy had loved doing.

The sight of his sister looking so happy brought a lump to his throat. He thought about what Flora had said last night about how unfair it was that Amy's life had been cut so cruelly short. She'd died before she'd had time to do all the things she'd wanted to do. Particularly have a family of her own.

He'd never really been that interested in having kids himself, but Amy had wanted them desperately ever since they were little. It had probably been something to do with not feeling as if their own family was as complete and functional as it should have been, what with their father running off to Thailand when they were six and never getting into contact with them again. Their mum had been a trooper, giving them every material thing they'd ever needed, but he knew how hard it had been for her on her own. She hadn't always had the patience or the time to give him and Amy the hugs and love they'd craved. Or perhaps it had been down to her having a broken heart, which had failed her when she was only forty-seven, leaving them parentless aged nineteen.

At least he and Amy had had each other to lean on.

Not wanting to dwell any longer on that thought, he put the photo back with a trembling hand. There was a gasp of surprise behind him and he twisted round to see Flora standing there, blearily rubbing the sleep out of her eyes.

'Alex!' she said, her eyes widening as she ran her gaze up and down his nearly naked body. *At least I left my boxer shorts on*, he thought wryly, taking in the thunderstruck expression on her face.

She slumped against the door frame, as if needing it to hold her up. *Hangover*, he thought, though he didn't say it. He didn't think she'd appreciate him pointing out the obvious right then. She'd changed out of yesterday's clothes and was now wearing a blindingly white fluffy bathrobe. He guessed she hadn't looked in the mirror yet though because she had panda eyes from her smudged make-up and her hair was a mess. She looked like a completely different person from the polished perfectionist of yesterday. He actually found her much more attractive like that, rumpled and sexy, not that he was going to admit it out loud.

'What are you doing here?' Her eyes widened even more as a thought seemed to strike her. 'Oh, God, we didn't—?'

Her hands flew to her face. 'Oh, no, we *didn't*, did we?'

He shook his head, riled by her over-the-top alarm. 'No. We didn't. You tried to kiss me, and I stopped you. You passed out on your bed—alone—and I slept on your sofa.'

'I tried to *kiss* you?' She looked even more horrified by this. 'Oh, God, I must have been really drunk.'

'Gee, thanks.'

She flushed and held up an apologetic hand. 'I just mean I wouldn't normally do something like that. You're a lovely guy, but I think we can safely say we'd never naturally date. We'd make a very odd couple.'

'Very odd,' he said, though he felt a strange reluctance about agreeing with her. They weren't that dissimilar, not really. His sister never would have been friends with Flora if she hadn't seen the good in her.

Not that he was interested in her in a romantic way, of course. The way he'd instinctively responded to her when she'd kissed him had been a shock, sure, but she was right—they would never work as a couple. He'd only reacted like that because he'd been missing human contact recently.

'Hey, speaking of dating,' Flora went on, pulling her robe more tightly around her body, 'I meant to say last night—before I messed up by being really rude to you about your clothes and—' she paused as a sheepish look flashed across her face '—the other things.' She produced a strange sort of grimacing grin, clearly hoping that would suffice as an apology.

'I have a friend who lives just outside Bath. I think you'd really get on with her,' she went on quickly before he could get a word in. 'She's big into music—she plays the harp, I think.' She flapped her hand as if annoyed with her less than perfect memory. 'Anyway, I met up with her for a coffee the other day—we hadn't seen each other since school—and she's single at the moment. I mentioned you to her and she seemed really interested in meeting you.'

His heart sank. 'You're trying to set me up on a blind date?'

'Sure, why not? Isn't that how most people meet their partners these days? Internet dating or through a friend of a friend?'

'I don't think so, Flora.'

Folding her arms, she fixed him with a concerned stare. 'Well, I think you should put yourself out there again. Didn't you say yesterday that you'd promised Amy you'd get on with your life and not mope about?'

She looked so expectant now he couldn't bear to refute it. Maybe if he agreed to go along with this nonsense she'd feel that she'd fulfilled her duty to Amy and leave him the heck alone.

Sighing, he nodded wearily in agreement. 'Okay. Fine. I'll meet her.'

'Really?' she asked, as if she thought she'd imagined him agreeing to it.

'Yes, really. Just don't expect to hear wedding bells any time soon. I'm not up for anything serious at the moment.'

'Sure, sure, that's fine,' she said, but he could tell from the gleam in her eye that she was hoping they'd hit it off.

God help him.

Flora tried not to think about how she'd kissed Alex.

She tried not to think about it at work when she was supposed to be leading a meeting and at home when she was heating up a meal for one from the freezer. She definitely tried not to think about it when she was lying in bed finding it hard to sleep.

She'd pretended to Alex that she didn't remember

doing it. But she did. It had been wonderful to be held like that: to feel so close to him. He'd smelled of spicy aftershave and leather and comfort, and it had made her heart flutter to feel that connection with him.

Obviously drinking cider on an empty stomach had been to blame for her uncharacteristic slip-up, but she was also unnervingly aware that it had seemed like exactly the right thing to do at the time. Perhaps in her drunken haze she'd thought they could comfort each other or something. She realised now what a crazy idea that had been, but at the time it had seemed so simple and logical.

In the cold light of day she didn't think for a second they should actually do something like that though. As she'd pointed out whilst desperately trying to keep her cool in the face of his half nakedness and hide her discomfort at him seeing her in such a bedraggled, bedheaded state, they'd make a very peculiar couple indeed.

It wasn't that she couldn't see what women found attractive about him. She wasn't blind—she appreciated his square-jawed handsomeness and ultramasculine, hard-muscled body—something that a slovenly musician who spent most of his time drinking beer in the pub had no right to have. But she really didn't see him like that. Like a potential partner. He was just Amy's scruffy, work-shy brother.

No. Her friend Lucy was a much better fit for him. They both had a love of music in common after all. And if he and Lucy hit it off, she'd be able to go back to New York with a clear conscience, knowing that someone who lived nearby was looking out for him. Even if the two of them only became friends she'd be able to check with Lucy about how he was doing. She certainly didn't expect Alex to tell her the truth over the phone, based on his reluctance to discuss his feelings last night.

She was determined not to regret the kiss they'd shared though. Why should she? It had been acknowledged as an aberration and they'd moved on from it. And she'd learnt an important lesson—no more of the local cider for her. It seemed as though that stuff was her 'life event catalyst' as Alex had called it, and she preferred not to put herself in such a vulnerable position again, especially in front of Alex. Although, to give him his due, he had been incredibly kind to her, making sure she got safely home and even sleeping on the sofa to keep an eye on her. She was grateful for that. He'd been a gentleman about it too. He hadn't teased her about her imprudent drunken behaviour and had even agreed to a date with Lucy before making a quick exit that morning.

So things were looking up.

She just needed to keep her fingers crossed that he and Lucy got on.

With that in mind, she'd put in a call to her friend as soon as Alex had left. Lucy had been delighted with the idea of meeting him the following Friday night.

Tonight, in fact.

Flora checked her watch for the umpteenth time, wondering what the two of them were doing right now as she lay on her sofa half watching an old film and half working on her laptop. Lucy had suggested meeting Alex at a local bar on the edge of the city, so it was unlikely she'd bump into them if she wandered into town. Not that she was going to do that.

She jumped as her phone made a loud beeping noise to signal a text arriving. Scooping it up from the arm of the sofa, she was a little alarmed to see it was from Alex. It was only eight-forty. Wasn't he supposed to be on a date right now?

We met. It went fine. I hope you're happy. Alex.

Fine? Fine! He thought that 'fine' was a good enough result, did he? Scrolling through to his number in her contacts, she pressed the icon to connect them and waited impatiently for him to pick up. It took five rings before he finally answered with a curt, 'Hello, Flora.'

'What do you mean, "It went fine"? What went wrong?'

'Nothing went wrong. It was a nice evening. She seems…nice.'

'Ugh. "Nice" is even worse than "fine".'

'What do you want me to say? That we're engaged and getting married next week?'

She caught her huff of breath just in time. 'No, of course not. I was just hoping you'd make a bit of an effort.'

There was a short silence before he spoke. 'How do you know I didn't make an effort?'

'Just a hunch,' she muttered in frustration.

'Well, I did, Flora. I listened to all her stories about her ex-boyfriend and all the awful things he'd done to her and how he was still in contact with her and should she speak to him or just ignore him. It seemed to me that she needed a relationship counsellor, not a date.'

Flora closed her eyes and bit back a sigh of defeat. 'Damn. Okay. Maybe I miscalculated. I thought it seemed like she was ready to start dating again.'

'You knew about the recent ex?' His voice was heavy with accusation, as if he thought she'd deliberately set him up with a no-hoper.

Flora felt her face heat. 'She mentioned him a couple of times, yes, but I thought it would be fine.'

Fine. There was that word again.

His sigh of annoyance sent a shiver of guilt through her. 'Look, I thought the best thing for her would be to get out and meet someone new. To be honest, her ex sounded like a bit of a loony to me.'

'That's great, Flora. So now I need to look over my shoulder in case her stalker ex is on my tail looking for retribution because I went out on a date with his woman.'

'Don't be ridiculous. That won't happen,' she cajoled.

'It'd better not,' he growled back.

There was a tense pause where they both breathed heavily down the line.

'Okay, look, I'm sorry,' she said, sighing. Deep down, she knew that it had probably been a crazy idea all along. She'd wanted to be able to fix this easily and she'd got a bit carried away. But this was Alex's heart she was trying to shore up, not a flagging brand of soft drinks.

'It was a stupid idea. Of course you're not going to want to embark on a new relationship so soon after everything that's happened to you recently. I just wanted to do something to try to help in some way.'

There was another loaded pause before he spoke. 'It's okay. I appreciate the sentiment behind it. But can we please agree right now that you won't attempt any more matchmaking?' He let out a gentle snort. 'It seems we've found the one thing you're not very good at.'

Pushing away the perplexity this comment provoked, she forced herself to laugh. 'Yeah, I promise I'll keep those urges to myself from now on.'

'Probably best.'

She sank back onto the sofa, grateful that at least he wasn't angry with her any more. 'So what are you going to do with the rest of your evening?' she asked tentatively.

'I thought I'd go for a swim to clear my head,' he said, sounding fed up.

'Where are you going? Is there a good pool near here?'

'I usually use the one at the Thermal Spa. It's closest to my flat and there's a heated outdoor pool on the roof.'

'Ooh, I've heard about that but I've not had chance to go yet.'

'It's great, you should check it out some time.'

'Maybe I should come with you now,' she blurted out. She really didn't want him to be alone when he was in such a bad mood. He'd probably go home afterwards and drink too much whisky again and she didn't like the thought of him doing that. Not on her watch.

There was a pause. 'Uh…okay, if you like.' He sounded as if he was really hoping that she was joking.

'Great,' she said assertively, ignoring his reticence.

She'd not put on a swimming costume in a very long time. Swimming always seemed such a lot of hassle for so little gain, what with having to wash and blow-dry her hair and apply make-up twice in one day—but this was for a good cause. He might not think that he needed her right now, and he clearly wasn't ready to date again, but she wasn't giving up on her promise to Amy to look out for him.

'Okay, I'll meet you there in ten minutes,' he said gruffly.

'What? Why so soon?' she asked, a little panicked about the lack of time to get herself organised.

'It closes at ten so we'll need to be there for the last session at nine o'clock.'

'Ah. Okay. In that case I'll see you there in ten minutes,' she said.

'Great,' he replied, not sounding like he genuinely thought it was, before cutting the call.

She had a moment of panic when she realised that she didn't have a swimming costume here in Bath, but after a quick bit of online research she discovered that a few of the clothes shops were open late for Christmas shopping.

Luckily it was only a five-minute dash from her flat into town so she was able to run into one of the stores and grab a swimming costume in her size from the sale rack, before dodging her way through the still-heavy crowd of shoppers to the Thermal Spa. She spotted Alex waiting for her outside the glass-fronted entrance with a rolled-up towel tucked under his arm.

Alex waved to Flora as she dashed towards him with an expensive-looking tote bag slung over her shoulder, wondering again how he'd found himself meeting her here tonight.

After it had become obvious that he and Lucy weren't going to hit it off, he'd made up an excuse about a rehearsal and legged it out of there as fast as he could. He'd been intent on sinking a couple of beers he had in the fridge at home when it occurred to him that Lucy might call Flora to tell her how he'd disappeared on

her and he'd decided it would be best to head her off
at the pass.

Mistakenly, it seemed, he'd chosen an activity he
thought Flora would never be interested in when she'd
asked him what he was planning to do with the rest of
his evening. He'd not banked on her determination to
maintain control over the situation.

It was obvious now that she had made it her mission
to stick to him like glue and he wasn't going to be given
any choice in the matter.

Once they'd got through the short queue at the spa
they went their separate ways at the communal changing rooms, arranging to meet at the pool on the roof.
Alex had already been swimming for ten minutes in
the warm water, with the cold air stinging his cheeks,
when Flora finally made an appearance. The complimentary robe was wrapped tightly around her and her
hair was tied in an elegant topknot.

He gave her a somewhat reluctant wave, hoping that
she'd choose not to brave the cold out here and swim
in the indoor pool instead. She spotted him and waved
back, a little mechanically he thought, and shuffled
towards the cubbyholes provided to stash robes and
slippers.

As she turned back to survey the pool he saw apprehension flash in her eyes. He guessed that she was
determined to hang out with him, but the thought of
doing it semi-naked didn't massively appeal.

Well, she was the one who had insisted on coming
with him.

His eyes widened and his pulse stuttered as he
watched her slide off her robe to uncover the most re-

vealing swimming costume he'd ever seen in his life. The material was cut high on her hips, forming a deep V that barely covered her modesty. The same went for the top of the costume, which was cut so low the flash of skin down her chest stopped just above her belly button. He found he was having a hard time tearing his eyes away from the gentle swell of her breasts, which were barely covered by the tight material.

From the look of trepidation on her face she wasn't entirely comfortable wearing it. Not that it had stopped her from coming out in public in it.

The woman certainly had guts.

His mouth suddenly felt inexplicably dry as he watched her saunter down the steps into the pool, keeping her head held high, despite the flush of colour that stained her neck and cheeks. Once fully immersed, she swam towards him with a lofty look on her face, appearing less embarrassed now that her body was hidden under the water.

'Nice cossie,' he quipped, finding it impossible not to tease her and biting back a grin as he watched the colour return to her cheeks.

'I didn't bring one to England with me so I only bought it five minutes ago. It didn't look like it'd be so revealing in the shop,' she shot back.

He couldn't help but laugh at the odd mix of superiority and mortification on her face.

'Well, you can pull it off,' he reassured her, feeling the urge to be kind now. And it wasn't as if he was lying either. She had an incredible body—curvy but toned, as if she ate healthily and spent plenty of time exercising.

'Er…thanks,' she said, looking a bit shocked at the

compliment and a little unsure about how to react to it. She must have decided that he was still teasing her because she swam away without another word, over to the other side of the pool where there were benches under the water and jets making bubbles like a hot tub.

Shrugging off her abandonment of him, Alex did laps of the pool, dodging around the few other people courageous enough to venture up there in the dead of winter. The water was wonderfully warm once you were in it, but he knew from experience it took a brave soul to get out afterwards with the cold wind whistling across your damp skin.

Once he'd got rid of the weird rush of adrenaline the sight of Flora in that swimming costume had brought on, he swam over to where she was crouching under a small waterfall. He watched as she moved from side to side, letting the strong jet of water massage her shoulders. Her make-up had begun to run down her face, but he thought that if he pointed it out he'd probably get dunked for his trouble.

'How's that working out for you?' he asked once she'd opened her eyes and noticed him there.

'It's absolute bliss,' she moaned in a voice so full of pleasure it made his stomach do a weird kind of flip.

'Here, come under—it's great,' she said, moving to one side to give him room to experience it too. She was right—it was wonderful to feel the water pounding hard on his shoulders, pummelling away the tension from the last few days. He closed his eyes and let himself feel the pleasure of it, allowing his thoughts to drift away to nothingness, a state that was rather alien to him at the moment. It had been a long time since his head had been clear of swirling chaos.

When he opened his eyes, Flora was staring at him with a strange expression on her face, as if trying to figure out what was going through his mind.

'How was your week? Did rehearsals go well?' she asked, glancing away to watch her hands as she swished them through the water in front of her.

His mood dimmed at the memory of what a joke his musical skills had been this past week.

'They went okay,' he muttered.

'Oh, dear.'

She looked back at him with sympathy in her eyes and on the spur of the moment he decided to trust her with the problems he was having. Perhaps talking about it would actually help. 'To be honest, I'm finding it hard to feel the joy in playing at the moment,' he said with a sigh.

She gave a sage sort of nod. 'Well, that's not entirely surprising; grief can knock the stuffing right out of you.' Bouncing gently on her toes, she flashed him an empathetic smile. 'I'm sure your muse will come back soon enough. You just need to work through this rough patch,' she stated with an authority that made him suspect she'd been telling herself the same thing.

He continued to look at her for a moment, and it suddenly occurred to him that she was the only person in the world who knew exactly how he was feeling right now.

She gazed back at him, the intensity in her eyes doing strange things to his insides.

'Hey, have you lain on your back and looked at the sky yet?' he asked, to break the unnerving mood that had fallen between them.

'Uh…no,' she said, looking a little discombobulated by the sudden change in subject.

He waved for her to follow him. 'Come on, it's really worth it. You can actually see some of the stars, despite the light pollution.'

They floated on their backs, side by side, staring up at the velvety midnight-blue sky, pointing out the star clusters that twinkled faintly above them.

'This reminds me of the holiday to the south of France I went on with Amy a couple of years ago,' Flora said, lifting her head out of the water to look at him. 'We were staying at this gorgeous little *gîte* near St Tropez and we spent most of the week floating around in the outdoor pool because it was so hot.' She smiled, the look in her eyes faraway but happy. 'One night we got so drunk Amy fell over a small wall in the garden and didn't realise she'd broken her toe until the next morning.'

'I remember her telling me about that,' Alex said with a grin.

'It was so swollen she couldn't wear anything but flip-flops for a couple of weeks afterwards.' Flora smiled widely. 'Unfortunately the English weather wasn't as clement as it had been in France, so she looked completely ridiculous walking around in the pouring rain with her feet bare and pink from the cold.'

She giggled at the memory, the sound of it making something fizz in his belly.

'She didn't complain though,' Flora continued. 'She never complained about anything. Just got on with it.' He could hear in her voice how much she'd loved his sister and he suddenly understood what had drawn Amy to her. She was clearly a fiercely loyal friend once you got past her hard shell.

'Yeah, she was a trouper all right,' Alex said, thinking back to how his sister had remained her cheery, positive self even during her last week in the hospice. 'She was telling jokes right up until the end of her life,' he said, swallowing a hard lump that had formed in his throat.

They talked for a while longer as they floated around in the water, about memories they had of Amy and all the times she'd cracked a joke, even though the situation had seemed desperate to everyone else. She'd always had a way of seeing light in the dark.

It was wonderful to conjure up memories of his sister like this and hear things he'd never known about her too. Having always been so wrapped up in his music he'd not paid as much attention to what was going on in Amy's life as perhaps he should have done. He knew that. Flora had been bang on when she'd accused him of keeping people at arm's length. He did do that. So hearing about a previously unknown side of Amy's life from her best friend made him feel closer to his sister.

The whole experience was so enriching that Alex felt the first lift of positivity for the future he'd had in months. So it was with regret that he dropped his feet back to the floor and stood up, aware of Flora doing the same next to him.

'I guess we should get out before they close the place,' she said, tugging on the straps of her swimming costume and looking a little uncomfortable about the idea of leaving the refuge of the water.

'Yeah, I guess so.' They looked at each other for a moment and he was aware that a subtle shift had occurred in their relationship. 'I tell you what,' he said, motioning for Flora to stay where she was. 'Wait there a minute.' After swimming to the steps he hauled himself out of the water into the freezing air and moved briskly to the cubbyholes to grab her robe. He held it open at the edge of the pool, averting his gaze so he was staring out over at the view of the cityscape instead of directly at her. He heard her wade quickly out of the water and as soon as he felt she was close enough he wrapped the robe around her, hiding her from any prying eyes.

'Thanks,' she said, looking up into his face and giving him a smile of genuine humility.

'You're welcome,' he replied, taking a step back from her. He had the strangest compulsion to tie the belt tightly around the gown for her to make sure her modesty remained intact, but he stopped himself from reaching towards her. He wasn't sure whether she'd appreciate such an intimate and domineering gesture coming from him.

They stood there for a moment, smiling at each other, before Flora broke the moment by gesturing towards the steps that led back down to the changing rooms.

'Okay, well, I'll see you at the front desk. Unless you want to get going straight away?' she said, clearly trying to sound unbothered either way.

'No, I'll wait for you. See you there in a few minutes,' he said, not wanting to end their night together just yet. Not when they were finally starting to find common ground.

In actual fact, he had to wait a while longer than he'd anticipated at the front desk before Flora appeared with her hair blow-dried back to perfection but her face free of the heavy make-up she'd been wearing earlier.

She looked younger and more approachable like that and it triggered instinctive warmth towards her that hadn't been there previously. She wasn't such a bad person to hang out with, he mused, and it was actually great to be able to talk to someone else who knew Amy well. None of his friends here in Bath had even met his sister. She'd cited being too busy at her job up in Glasgow to make it down south to see him when he'd first moved here, and then of course she'd become too ill to travel.

'Sorry to keep you,' Flora said as she reached him, not quite meeting his gaze.

'No problem,' he said. 'I barely recognised you. You look different without all that make-up on,' he joked.

She shot him a startled frown.

'In a good way, I mean,' he said quickly. 'I prefer you without it. You really don't need it.' He shrugged. 'I always think the natural look is sexier on a woman.'

For the first time since he'd met her she looked a little uncertain about what to say next.

'I guess I'd better let you get home,' she said after a beat, giving him a tight smile and making a move towards the exit. He followed her, noticing how stiff her posture seemed again now.

'You're welcome to come back to my place for a drink,' he said, realising that he didn't want to be on his own right now.

She turned to give him a look of surprise. Evidently she'd been expecting him to stride off without even a backwards glance. His stomach did a flip at the pleasure on her face.

'That would be great, if you're sure you're not too tired?'

'Exhaustion seems to be my permanent state of being

at the moment,' he joked. 'But seriously, you're most welcome,' he added when he saw her face fall a little.

'Well, okay then,' she said, recovering quickly. 'Lead the way.'

CHAPTER FOUR

ALEX LET THEM into his ground floor flat, which was housed in one of the elegant golden stone-fronted Georgian terraces that the city was so famous for, and gave a wry smile at the look of shock and disorientation on Flora's face as she realised he hadn't led her into a hovel of iniquity.

'This is—' She gazed around at the high-ceilinged room, taking in the squashy leather sofas and the sharply designed high-quality furniture he'd collected throughout his year of living here. His pride and joy, a black lacquered grand piano, stood proudly in the bay window, while his other instruments—a guitar, zither and accordion as well as various other accompaniments—leaned neatly against the wall next to it.

'—quite something,' she finished, turning to give him an earnest smile. It seemed that he'd finally been able to impress her.

'Thanks. I bought the place as soon as I moved here from London.'

She nodded slowly, her eyes narrowing in thought. 'You used your half of the money your mum left you from the sale of her house in Richmond.'

He grimaced to himself, realising there could be

other moments like this, where she told him things about himself that he had no idea she knew. Of course Amy had always been a blabbermouth and was bound to have talked about him, but the realisation that she knew him much better than he'd realised made him a little nervous.

'I made a lot of money when I was working in corporate finance in my early twenties and made some sound investments, so I'm in a pretty good financial position now. I give piano lessons too, though I mostly do cut-price deals for people who wouldn't normally be able to afford them.'

'Not just a pretty face then,' she said, then looked pained as if embarrassed by blurting that out.

'Would you like a drink?' he asked, shaking off his sudden discomposure and moving towards the door that led through to the small kitchen at the back of the flat.

'Do you have peppermint tea?'

He turned back to fix her with a look of disgust. 'No. I don't drink that muck.'

She frowned. 'Fruit tea?' she asked hopefully.

'Nope.'

'Anything without caffeine?' she asked with a small sigh of exasperation.

'No. I have coffee or builder's tea.'

'I'll take a glass of water. Mineral if you've got it.'

'Tap water it is,' he said, smiling as he turned away from her comical eye-roll to stride away to the kitchen.

When he returned a few minutes later with a mug of strong coffee for himself and a pint of tap water for her, she was drumming her fingertips on the arm of the sofa while her gaze darted around the room.

If he didn't know better he'd think she was nervous

about being here with him. But why would she be? Apparently she knew him better than he knew himself.

He put the tray down on the coffee table before sitting on the sofa next to her. She flashed him a smile of thanks and reached for the water, taking a delicate sip before replacing it on the table.

Why was the atmosphere suddenly so awkward? he wondered as he sipped at his scalding coffee.

Perhaps because they were letting each other get closer and it was a bit unnerving. After all, she was his sister's best friend and under any other circumstances they'd probably never have crossed each other's paths. He was glad he'd met her out tonight though. It felt like a small but significant development in his life.

'So Lucy told me you weren't always the polished paragon of fashion I see before me today,' he said in an attempt to lighten the atmosphere, gesturing to the designer outfit she'd worn to the swimming pool.

Was he imagining it, or had her face paled a little? She certainly looked a bit self-conscious all of a sudden as she raised her hands and surreptitiously ran her forefingers over her perfectly arched eyebrows.

'Oh, really? What exactly did she say?' she asked in what was clearly intended to be a nonchalant tone but fell well short of the mark. At least it came across that way to him.

He didn't want to make her uncomfortable, so he shrugged and said, 'Just that you were a bit of a rock chick when you were younger.'

'Yes, well, we all have our ridiculous phases. I had a thing for musician types for a while, but it never suited me.' Her back was ramrod straight now. 'Is that all she told you about me?'

'Yes, even though I tried to get all the dirt on you I could,' he joked, wondering what her uneasiness was all about. Didn't everyone have embarrassing clothing faux pas in their past?

'Well, I was pretty boring apart from that,' she said tonelessly, not playing along with his jokey manner, which made him suspect there was more to this than she was willing to admit. He had a gut feeling that if he dug deeper he'd discover something a little more painful in her past.

'You know, I can't picture you as a child,' he said, flashing her a playful grin, hoping to lift her mood. 'You're such a grown-up.'

She raised a reproachful eyebrow, but he could tell from the smile in her eyes that she'd taken his teasing as a joke this time. 'Somehow I don't think you mean that as a compliment.'

He just grinned back.

Getting up from the sofa, she walked towards his piano and sat down on the stool, gently pressing a couple of the keys.

'Do you play?' he asked, nodding towards the instrument that had given him so much pleasure in his life. The day he'd bought that piano had been the happiest of his life.

'No.' She shook her head. 'I took some lessons when I was younger, but—' She paused, as if pulling herself back from the brink of saying something a little too revealing.

'But?' he prompted, getting up from the sofa and joining her, fascinated to hear what she'd say next.

Clearing her throat, she gave a little shrug. 'It never really stuck with me. My sister got all the creative and musical genes. According to her, I'm completely tone-deaf.'

'That's a shame,' he said, sensing there was more to this story than she was giving up.

'I know, right? And I have the perfect hands for playing the piano.' She held her hands up, spanning her long fingers to show him. 'Piano player's hands, or so I've been told.'

'It's not too late to give it another go,' he pointed out.

Her returning smile was tight. 'I don't have time for anything outside of work at the moment. It's pretty intensive, especially with the commute on top.'

A question about why she'd chosen to live in Bath and commute all the way into London was on the tip of his tongue, but he stopped himself from asking it at the last moment. He didn't really want to get into a boring conversation about train delays and ticket prices.

In fact, he'd rather not think about London and the life he'd moved away from at all.

'Hey, what are you doing for Christmas?' she asked, breaking into his unsettling train of thought.

'Er...' He had to think fast. No way was he admitting that he was planning to spend it alone getting slowly sozzled in front of the TV. It was a matter of pride. And he didn't want her thinking she had to invite him to do something with her either. 'I'm getting together with my bandmates. None of us have family nearby so we're all going for a pub Christmas lunch.'

This answer seemed to please her because she gave him a bright smile. 'Oh, good. I was afraid you might be on your own. I'd have invited you to spend it with me, but I promised my parents I'd go up to Derbyshire to see them this year.'

He wondered why this had produced a pinched little scowl on her face.

'I'm glad you've got somewhere to go,' he said, pushing away his concern. Perhaps her family got up each other's noses when they got together over Christmas. He leaned back against the side of the piano and smiled down at her. 'I bet your parents will be pleased to see you. Amy mentioned that you've not been back to England since moving to the States.'

Her cheeks flushed with colour. 'No, well, it's so expensive to fly over, and my boss is pretty strict about how much holiday we can take.'

She got up from the piano stool as if wanting to call a halt to this particular conversation and gave what he could have sworn was a fake yawn. 'Anyway, I'd better get home. It's getting late and I'm exhausted after that swim.'

He pushed away from the piano and straightened up too. 'Sure. Well, thanks for keeping me company.'

Making her way towards the door, she turned back to give him a friendly smile. 'No problem. It was fun.'

He had a sudden urge to make some sort of a gesture to show her he really did appreciate the effort she was making to get to know him.

'Hey, guess what?' he said, following her into the hallway.

'What?' she asked, turning back from opening the door to look at him expectantly.

'I managed to get a spare ticket to my gig next weekend. If you're free, it'd be great if you could come.' He held up both hands. 'No pressure though.'

The delighted smile she gave him made his insides heat.

'Sure, I'd love to, if you really want me to come?'

From the wobble in her voice he suspected she thought he might just be offering it to be magnanimous. Which wasn't the case. He really did want her to come and support him. It would actually be pretty great to have someone there just for him.

Sighing, he rubbed a hand over his face. 'Look, I'm sorry if I gave you the impression I wasn't interested in being friends the other night. It's just that my head's been full of this gig and there hasn't been much room for anything else in there.' He tapped the side of his head with two fingers and grinned at her.

She smiled back, her eyes soft with understanding.

His stomach did a weird flip.

'It's fine, I get it.'

'And I appreciate you making the effort to arrange a date with Lucy for me, even if we didn't hit it off,' he added with a wry grimace.

She flashed him a shamefaced smile, then swung the door open and exited into the cold night air.

He was just about to shut the door behind her when she turned back and said, 'Thanks for letting me come with you tonight. I had fun.' And with one last sincere smile, she went striding off down the street.

He stared after her, his insides feeling a little churned up, stunned to acknowledge that, despite all his expectations to the contrary, he'd had fun tonight too.

Flora spent the next week battling with her boss to give her the autonomy she needed to do her job properly. It was only the thought of seeing Alex again at the weekend that kept her from a complete and utter meltdown at the end of each day.

While the thought of sitting through a couple of hours

of jazz didn't exactly appeal, she was actually quite glad to be getting out and socialising on a Saturday night. When she was on her own she had a tendency to go over and over the issues from her working week and it always sent her into a downward spiral of anxiety— a mental state she'd struggled with on and off all her working life. It had been worth putting up with for the kudos of the position and the generous pay packet her job offered, but sometimes she felt desperate for a re- prieve from it. At times like those, she imagined how great it would feel to be her own boss—primarily for the enhanced sense of control it would offer.

Their jaunt to the swimming pool and the subse- quent softening in Alex's attitude towards her had left her feeling much more positive about being able to ful- fil Amy's last wish though. To her surprise, she'd found herself actually enjoying his company. He wasn't such a bad person to hang out with once you got past the glib flippancy and the tendency to flirt with anything that moved. His comment about her looking good without her make-up had surprised her too. It had been a long time since she'd gone out in public without a full face of make-up, but in her haste to meet him there on time she'd forgotten to put any in her bag. His kind words had given her shaky confidence a much-needed boost.

Saturday finally came around and, keeping his com- ments in mind, she kept her make-up light and chose her outfit carefully. She didn't want to stand out like a sore thumb, she told herself as she pulled on a pair of boot-cut jeans and a cashmere jumper in a beautiful sapphire blue that she hadn't been able to resist buying that morning. It wasn't as if they were going out on a date—it was just one friend supporting another—but she wanted to look as if she'd made a bit of an effort.

After pulling on her high-heeled boots and sliding her arms into her long, satisfyingly heavy woollen trench coat, she let herself out of her flat and set off towards the venue where the gig was happening on the other side of the city.

Bath's centre was so small it only took her around fifteen minutes to reach her destination, so she walked through the doors of the old converted railway station where the gig was being held a few minutes earlier than she'd planned. While she hated unpunctuality, she also feared turning up too early for things, then having to hang around on her own like a saddo before they started. Thank goodness for being able to hide behind the safety of a mobile phone these days, she thought as she stepped through the door of the mostly empty venue.

And what a gorgeous venue it was.

It was as if she'd stepped back into the early nineteen-thirties.

The whole place was done out in the art deco style, with the sharply defined geometric motif of a sunrise decorating the large steel and glass bar at the back of the room and the long mirrored wall behind it reflecting a mind-boggling array of colourful spirit bottles. Groups of black lacquered tables and chairs, decorated with holly and silver stars in a nod to the Christmas season, faced the long, low stage at the other end of the room where the band's instruments were set up. To the left of the stage, strung with glinting white fairy lights, sat a black, highly polished upright piano.

And sitting on the stool in front of it, looking intently at a sheaf of sheet music, was Alex.

Except he hardly looked like the man she'd got to know over the last few weeks. He was dressed in a sharp black suit, with a black shirt open at the neck and a starkly white tie hanging loosely against his broad chest. He'd slicked his long fringe back with some kind of wax and it sat neatly against his head, apart from a couple of rogue strands which fell across his forehead, for once allowing his amazing bright blue eyes and strong jaw the exposure they deserved.

Flora's heartbeat thumped loudly in her ears as she stood staring at him, marvelling at how very different he looked. And how very different she suddenly felt.

But this was just Alex, she reminded herself sternly. Amy's scruffy, totally unsuitable brother. Who she was just friends with.

Just friends.

Realising that her mouth had become inexplicably dry, she swallowed hard and dragged her gaze away from Alex, making her way over to the bar to get herself a drink.

She'd just been served a large glass of white wine when she felt someone approaching from her right. Turning to look, she saw Alex making his way towards her, his usual confident swagger very much in evidence.

'Hey, you came,' he said as he drew close, giving her one of his stunning wide smiles.

For some reason her mouth didn't seem to want to do as it was told, so she just stood there grinning at him like a complete fool.

'You okay?' he asked, looking bemused.

Giving herself a mental shake she nodded, then cleared her dry throat. 'Yes, great. You look fantastic. Very dapper. Are you nervous? You must be. It's a big old place to fill. Not that I'm sure you won't fill it—' She finally managed to curb her babbling and gave him an apologetic smile. 'Sorry, I guess I'm a bit nervous for you.' The weird squeaky laugh that came out after that statement made her cheeks flush hot with embarrassment.

He just grinned at her, his eyes twinkling. 'Well, it's kind of you to take my nerves on for me, but I've got it covered.' She was sure she caught a momentary flash of trepidation in his eyes.

'Are you okay?' she asked, reaching out to rub his arm in a friendly gesture of solidarity, feeling a shock of concern at how tense his muscles were beneath his suit.

'Yeah, I'll be fine once we get started.'

In her peripheral vision Flora became aware of a man, also dressed in a sharp suit, walking towards Alex with stern intent written across his face. She gestured in his direction to draw Alex's attention to him. 'I think someone might need you.'

The man came to a stop next to them and she saw Alex give him a somewhat reluctant nod of acknowledgement.

'Alex, we need you backstage,' the man stated in a curt voice.

'Yeah, okay, I'll be there in a minute.'

His bandmate sighed. 'No, now, man. We don't have much time before this place is jammed.'

Alex's jaw flexed as he appeared to clamp it together hard. 'Yeah, I know that, Zane,' he said with ironic slowness, 'but I'm talking here. I'll be there in a minute.' He emphasised the repeated sentence with such force that Flora wondered what the problem was between them. Because there clearly was one.

Before the other man could respond there was a flurry of sparkles beside them and a woman appeared at his side.

'Hey, guys. Everything okay here?' she cooed in a beautiful gravelly voice.

Flora turned her full focus to the woman and her eyes involuntarily widened. She was dressed in an ornately decorated flapper-style dress, which shimmered under the lights as she stood there gazing at them all with catlike yellow eyes. She was beautiful. Utterly stunning, with honey-coloured skin, full red-stained lips and glossy jet-black hair that had been styled into soft waves pinned away from her face, like they used to wear it in the nineteen-thirties.

'Yeah, we're fine,' Alex muttered with a scowl, only shooting the woman the most perfunctory of glances.

'And who's this?' she asked, giving Flora a curious smile.

'This is Flora,' Alex said, but from the sound of his voice he really didn't want to extend the introduction any further than that.

Was she really that embarrassing to be around? The thought made a prickly shiver rush across her skin. Perhaps he was only being chivalrous when he'd said that she didn't need to wear make-up to look good.

Gritting her teeth, Flora flashed him a covert frown before turning back to the woman. 'Nice to meet you. I'm guessing you're part of the band too?'

'Yeah, I'm on vocals,' the woman said, extending a hand, which Flora shook, trying not to crush it as she felt how limp it was. Flora had never been one to hold back on a handshake, but this woman obviously didn't set the same store by them.

'So are you a friend of Alex's?' the woman asked with a strange inflection to her voice that made Flora think there was an undercurrent she wasn't a party to. Had they all been arguing before she got here? Or was there some sort of tension between this woman and Alex? The thought made her stomach sink in a peculiar way. Not that it wouldn't be great for Alex if he found someone new to fall in love with. Especially if she was musical too.

Her guess was thwarted though when the woman slid her arm around the other bandmate that Alex had spoken to so curtly and pressed herself against his side, smiling up at him in what was clearly a possessive and adoring manner.

Ah, so these two were a couple then.

So why had she been looking at Flora in such a strange way? It had actually felt a little unfriendly, if she was being honest. Was she worried Flora was going to break Alex's heart like his ex-girlfriend had?

When Flora turned back to glance at Alex she was surprised to see that he was deliberately avoiding looking at the overtly affectionate couple next to him. In fact he looked incredibly uncomfortable, as if he'd rather be anywhere but there.

Then it hit her, so hard it made her suck in a sharp breath, which she rushed to cover with a small coughing fit.

This was the woman who had broken Alex's heart.

And, to make things a million times worse, she was the lead singer of his band.

CHAPTER FIVE

ALEX HAD REALLY hoped to avoid a situation where Flora and Tia would come face-to-face, hence his reluctance to get Flora a ticket for the gig tonight in the first place. But the fates, it seemed, had had a very different idea.

He realised his mistake now, of course. He should have anticipated that Flora would turn up early and suggest she not come until the gig was just about to start, but in his state of comfortable equanimity after they'd been swimming last week it hadn't occurred to him.

Looking out over the large crowd while there was a short pause between songs and Tia did her usual cooing and joking around with the audience—something he used to love listening to but now made him want to chew his own hands off—he spotted Flora sitting at one of the tables in the middle of the room. A wine glass in hand, she watched Tia's performance with a quizzical frown pinching her brow. She had to have guessed who Tia was by now, he realised as the drummer started up the beat for the next song and he readied himself to play, but would she be bold enough to bring it up with him later?

Who was he kidding? Of course she would.

This was Flora we were talking about.

His cue came then and he lost himself in the music again, feeling for the first time in a while that he was getting his groove back. Despite his worry that his musical ability had completely deserted him recently, he was pleased with the way he was playing tonight. Every now and again he'd glance over to where Flora sat and see her smiling in what seemed to be mesmerised awe and it would give him a little boost that would carry him through to the next song.

Ironically, it turned out it was pretty great having her here to support him.

After they'd played their last song and Tia had bowed them off the stage, he rushed to say goodbye to the other members of the band, waving away their suggestion of a drink so he could go find Flora. He was going to suggest that they hightail it out of there and grab something to eat somewhere a bit quieter in the hope she and Tia wouldn't end up in the same vicinity as each other again. He'd noticed the strange tension coming off his ex-girlfriend in waves earlier and he didn't want to expose Flora to any more of it.

Except Flora wasn't in the seat she'd been sitting in throughout the whole performance. Perhaps she was in the bathroom. He lingered there, tapping his fingers against his leg impatiently as he waited for her to reappear.

One of the audience members came up to him as he waited, congratulating him on a great set, and he fell into a conversation with him, his attention still half-focused on the corridor leading to the bathrooms. As soon as the guy moved on to get a drink at the bar, someone else came over, then someone else. He found himself fielding congratulations left, right and centre, which gave him another lift he'd not expected from tonight. He was just finishing up a conversation with a fan who turned up at all the band's gigs, and who told him she thought he'd played his best ever set tonight, when he spotted Flora walking towards him.

Politely excusing himself, he walked over to meet her. 'Hey, there you are,' he said, letting out a grunt of surprise as she walked into his arms and grabbed him round the waist, giving him a tight squeeze. When she pulled away his stomach lurched as he saw there were tears in her eyes.

'Oh, my goodness, Alex, you totally blew me away! You were amazing! I had no idea.' She looked a little sheepish now, as if admitting that she'd been anticipating a boring evening only to be utterly confounded by actually enjoying herself.

He grinned, pleasure pooling in his belly and heating his skin. 'Thanks for "giving jazz a chance",' he teased, smiling as he noted a flush rising to her face.

'We should get out of here,' he said, gesturing towards the door where a large crowd of people were now exiting the venue.

'Really?' she said. 'Don't you want to stick around and have a celebratory drink with your bandmates?'

'What a great idea,' came a voice from behind him and he turned to see Pete, the band's trumpeter, with a tray of drinks in his hand. 'Let's grab this table while it's free,' he said, nodding to the one they were standing next to. He put the tray down on it, making the glasses rattle as they bounced against each other.

'I was going to take Flora out for some food,' he began to protest, but Pete waved away his excuse, picking up a pint of beer and thrusting it towards him.

'Don't be an idiot. You have to stay and have at least one drink with the band. We were stupendous tonight!' Alex caught the meaningful look in his friend's gaze and gave him a tight smile. Pete was well versed in the whole Tia debacle and clearly thought that running off now would be akin to letting her win.

'And here's one for your gorgeous lady,' Pete said with emphasis, giving Flora a wink and passing her a large glass of wine, which she accepted with a smile of startled surprise.

'Oh, thank you! Well, I guess we should stay just for this one,' she said, looking at Alex for confirmation.

Obviously they couldn't leave now, not without it seeming really rude—or cowardly—so he raised his eyebrows and said, 'Yeah, sure. We can move on after this one.'

They all sat around the table and just as Pete started to ask Flora whether she lived in Bath, Zane and Tia came over to join them, taking the two seats next to her.

Alex tensed as he forced himself to look over at Tia, only to find her staring at Flora with a strange speculative look on her face. There was something a little hostile about it, not that she was being overt in any way, but he knew her too well not to pick up on things like that.

Perhaps she wasn't too happy with Flora crashing the band's celebratory drinks. Not that she had any right to complain about him bringing someone else. She'd been the one to call a halt to their relationship, after all.

'So, Flora, how did you and Alex meet?' Tia asked suddenly, leaning towards Flora a little and giving her that concentrated smile that he knew meant she was on the warpath about something.

Flora, to her credit, didn't even blink. Instead she

sat perfectly still in her chair and fixed Tia with a cool, formidable sort of stare. 'Alex's twin sister was my best friend.'

So she'd definitely figured out who Tia was then.

There was an uncomfortable beat of silence during which the two women looked intently at each other, as if willing the other to look away first.

'Hey, Alex, what are your plans for Christmas?' Pete asked loudly, breaking into the strained atmosphere. Out of the corner of his eye he saw Flora turn away from glaring at Tia to look directly at him.

Heat began to creep up his neck as he remembered he'd told her he was spending Christmas Day with the band, which in retrospect had been a little foolish, especially now he was about to be caught out in his lie. He hated to think how Flora would react when she realised he'd deliberately misled her. Especially when she was being such a loyal friend to him right now.

'Er...' he began, racking his brain for an answer vague enough to get him out of trouble.

Luckily the drummer, Des, shouted over him, 'Hey, Zane, I meant to ask, are you and Tia off to London on Christmas Eve or Christmas Day? 'Cos I'll hitch a lift with you if it's Christmas Day. I've promised my dad I'll go over there for lunch now.'

'Sorry, man, we're going on Christmas Eve,' Zane answered, glancing at Tia for her agreement.

'What *are* you doing for Christmas, Alex?' Tia asked, completely ignoring her boyfriend. 'I hope you're not spending it all on your own.' She was eyeing him now in a way that made him think she suspected he'd dug himself into a hole and was intent on exposing him for it. He wasn't sure why she thought she had the right

to be so prickly with him, but he sure as hell could do
without it right now.

He felt Flora shift in her seat next to him and he
glanced round at her in panic, praying she wasn't going
to have a go at him for fibbing to her and expose his
pathetically lonely Christmas to the rest of the band.

'Actually, he's coming up to Derbyshire with me,'
she said loudly, looking him right in the eye and giving him a slow wink that no one else could see. She
turned back to Tia. 'I'm introducing him to my parents.'
Looking back at Alex, she purred, 'They haven't had
a chance to meet you yet, have they, honey?' The term
of endearment was clearly proprietorial.

Tia's mouth fell open for a second before she caught
herself and snapped it shut, forcing it into an artificial-
looking smile.

'Wow, that's quick,' she said with a slight wobble
in her voice. 'We had no idea he was even seeing anyone.' She ostentatiously slung her arm around Zane's
shoulders. 'Did we?' She gave him a swift kiss before
looking back their way again.

Flora gave a nonchalant shrug. 'Yes, well, it's been a
bit of a whirlwind romance, to be honest. But we both
knew it was right between us straight away, didn't we,
gorgeous?' She turned to look at him now, giving him
a wry but warm smile.

Before he could answer her, she looped her arm
around his neck and pulled him towards her, pressing
her mouth against his. He knew she was only doing it
to show solidarity in the face of his awkward situation
with Tia, but as she moved her mouth gently against
his he had an intense sensory flashback to the last time
she'd kissed him, remembering how she'd tasted the

same way, sweet and sensual. For one fleeting second he wished this affection was actually real. His stomach did a weird swoop as he felt her lips part a little and the tip of her tongue sweep across his. And then, just as suddenly, she drew away from him and he was left staring into her sparkling green eyes in bewildered surprise.

'You're such a good kisser,' she cooed and his heart lurched with exhilaration until she gave him another covert wink and he knew for sure she was just laying it on thick for Tia's benefit.

There was a loud scraping noise as a chair was pushed back from the table. He tore his gaze away from Flora to see that Tia had stood up and was staring at him with such hurt in her eyes it took his breath away.

'I'm hungry,' she croaked, glancing away as soon as she noticed him looking at her. 'Let's go and get some food, Zane.'

Zane looked less than impressed with this sudden change in pace and tried to protest about being dragged away before he'd even finished his pint.

'I'll get you another one at the next place,' she snapped, spinning on her heel and walking stiffly away from the table, leaving Zane no option but to abandon his half-drunk pint and chase after her, calling a hurried goodbye to the rest of them.

When Alex glanced back at Flora she flashed him a pseudo-innocent *What's her problem?* look, before breaking into a gleeful smile.

'I guess it's just us now then,' she quipped.

In that moment he felt something knit together inside him and he gave her a wide smile back, experiencing a sudden, forceful urge to take her away from here so they could be on their own. While he cared about his other bandmates and wanted to celebrate their success, he'd spent more than enough time with them recently.

'We should go and find somewhere to grab a bite to eat too,' he said to Flora, feeling a rush of relief when she nodded in agreement. He wouldn't put it past Tia to come storming back with a plan to disrupt the evening even further and he wanted to do everything in his power to avoid that.

As soon as they'd knocked back the dregs of their drinks and said a fond farewell to the rest of the group, they pulled on their coats and made for the venue's exit. Once outside, he turned to look at her with one incredulous eyebrow arched.

'What?' she asked, her eyes all wide and innocent.

'You kissed me again.' He shot her a look of mock consternation, mentally pushing away the small voice of hope that it hadn't all just been for show. She was being a friend, he reminded himself, carrying out Amy's last request of her. He felt pretty sure there hadn't been any more to it than that. 'You seem to be making a habit out of it,' he added with a smile.

Her cheeks looked a little flushed now. 'Er...yeah, sorry about that, but I wanted it to look authentic.'

'Well, thanks for stepping in and doing your duty as a friend.'

She gave him a slightly odd look, somewhere between a grin and a grimace. 'You're welcome.'

He gestured for them to start walking in the direction of the river, where there was an eatery with a roof terrace that had amazing views over the city.

'Tia seemed pretty annoyed by it,' Flora piped up as they strolled side by side along the pavement, turning to flash him a mischievous grin.

He couldn't help but snort with mirth, his insides warming at the thought that they had a private joke between them now. It felt good. Now that he thought about it, he was surprised to find himself less concerned about what Tia was doing without him tonight than about how much fun Flora was having in his company. He'd been really made up with her effusive praise about his playing earlier and the euphoria seemed to have stayed with him.

'Where are we going anyway?' Flora asked as he motioned for her to take the next road on the right.

'There's a nice restaurant near the river. I thought we could try there. It's not the fanciest of joints, but I think it might fit even your exacting standards,' he joked.

He felt his stomach sink as he saw her frown, her eyes losing their smile.

'You must think I'm really stuck-up,' she said, letting out a loud sigh.

'Not at all.' He checked himself. 'Well, perhaps when I first met you. It was pretty obvious you weren't very comfortable in the pub I took you to, especially as I dragged you away from the Pump Room.'

'I just wanted to try it out. I'd heard loads of good things about it.'

He nodded, holding up his hands. 'I get that. And I'm sorry for pulling you out of there. As I'm sure you noticed, I wasn't in the best of moods that day.'

Her mouth twisted as if she was trying not to say something rude back about that.

'Hey, I tell you what. I'll take you there after Christmas to make up for it,' he offered. 'And I'll pay. You can't say fairer than that.'

He gestured for them to cross the road and led her

past the sweeping grandeur of the Royal Crescent and on in the direction of the Assembly Rooms. 'It's not too much further up here,' he said.

'Good, because now that I've started thinking about food I'm suddenly starving,' she said with an emphasis that made him suspect that those glasses of wine on an empty stomach were beginning to have an effect.

He'd really rather avoid another incident like the last time they'd been drunk. Except for the kissing, perhaps.

Forcing that last rogue thought out of his head, he flipped her a grin. 'I'm sure they'll have something on the menu to suit even the most finicky of diners.'

He stepped to one side, laughing, as she slapped him playfully on the arm for his impudence.

'I'm not too proud to make you pay for that, you know,' she warned him. And he almost wished she would.

Three minutes later they reached their destination and hurried inside the boxy old brewery building, the rush of heat a welcome change from the biting cold.

'Let's go up to the terrace—they have great views up there,' he suggested, pointing to the wood and glass stairs that led up to the rooftop. 'Don't worry, they have heaters,' he assured her when she shot him an unsure look.

As luck would have it, there was a couple leaving a table right underneath one of the paraffin heaters as they walked onto the terrace. As they sat down, he caught Flora's look of pleasant surprise at the view laid out before them. The colourful lights of the city twinkled merrily against the heavy dark of the night sky and the river glided along gracefully in the distance.

'See, I don't just hang out in depressing pubs all the

time,' he teased, catching her sheepish expression as the memory of their first meeting obviously came flooding back to her.

'Yes, it's really lovely up here,' she said, regaining her composure quickly and flinging him an apologetic grin.

How far they'd come since then, he mused.

They'd barely finished ordering their food when Flora crossed her arms and leaned back in her chair, fixing him with a stare that clearly meant business. 'So you're fine, are you? Playing in the same band as your ex-girlfriend and her new boyfriend.'

The highly sceptical look she gave him from under her lashes made him squirm in his seat. He rubbed his hand over his face, then held it up, palm forwards in capitulation. 'To be honest, no. It's really not fine. But you've heard her sing—she's incredibly talented and I think the band's going to do really well. I've worked so hard to get where I am so I'd be an idiot to throw it all in now.'

'You're really set on a musical career?'

'Yes. It's what I've always wanted to do. I tried a "real" job for a while and it made me miserable. I don't care about the money and fame, I just want to make music. It's the only thing that makes me truly happy.'

She nodded slowly, keeping her thoughtful gaze trained on him. 'Well, I have to say, you're damn good at it. Your playing really got inside me. It made me *feel* things.'

He couldn't help but grin at such a personal and intimate description. If he didn't know better, he'd say she was flirting with him. 'That's high praise indeed, coming from you.'

She shrugged. 'Yeah, well, I'm sorry for being so snippy before. I think I was just a bit nervous about meeting you, what with the upsetting circumstances and all.'

'You're forgiven. And I have to say, I'm delighted the dastardly cult of jazz has claimed a new member,' he said, lifting his hands and curling his fingers to look like some kind of evil, jazz-playing ghoul.

She laughed at this, throwing her head back in a way he'd never seen her do before. Perhaps she was finally beginning to properly relax around him. The thought made him inordinately happy.

Once their food arrived they were quiet for a while as they shovelled steak, chips and salad into their mouths, smiling and widening their eyes in pleasure by way of communication instead of talking.

'Okay, you're going to have to tell me what happened with Tia or it'll keep me awake at night wondering about it,' Flora said once they'd both finished eating. She wiped her fingers on her napkin and fixed him with a pleading stare.

He sighed, knowing there was no way to avoid telling her the whole sorry tale now. Dumping his cutlery on his empty plate, he leaned back in his chair and gave her his full attention, feeling his spirits sink at the thought of dredging it all up for her. 'To cut a long story short, we got together when we were living in London after meeting at a mutual friend's gig. We were the founding members of the band we play in now, which we pulled together by finding the other members through auditions. Apart from Zane. He was recommended by Pete, our trumpeter.' He tried not to frown as he remembered how uneasy he'd felt about Zane from the start, but Tia had convinced him to let the charming saxophonist stay.

'Those were some good times, when we first started playing together. It was clear right from the off that we really got each other's style and we were destined for the big time if we could just keep plugging away at it.' He took a long sip of his wine to soothe the roughness in his throat before continuing. 'Anyway, Tia decided that we needed to move out of London and focus our efforts somewhere where the scene wasn't oversaturated. I didn't really like the idea at first, but she talked me into it.' He shot her a grimace. 'She can be pretty persuasive when she wants to be.'

Flora just nodded, seemingly fascinated and intent on hearing the rest of the story.

'So we moved here and things were going great until Amy fell ill.' He took a shaky breath. 'I was suddenly spending a lot of time at the hospital with her and Tia started getting more and more annoyed about how little attention I was paying to the band—and to her.'

'What?' Flora said, shaking her head in baffled anger. 'Your sister was dying from cancer and she was throwing hissy fits about not getting as much attention as usual?'

He held up a hand. 'It wasn't exactly like that. To be fair to Tia, I completely failed to turn up for her birthday meal because I was so distracted, so she sat in the restaurant on her own for an hour before going home alone. And there were other things too. Things I'm not proud of.' He frowned, remembering with a thump of shame how he'd totally fallen apart when Amy had first told him that the cancer was terminal and he'd plummeted into a spiral of self-absorbed pity. 'As you mentioned the first day we met, I'm not exactly great at letting people in when I'm struggling to deal with things.'

She gave him a sad, understanding sort of smile, the effects of which he felt right down to his toes.

'I just kind of mentally checked out for a while. It was hard on her. I get that.'

'She didn't need to jump into bed with your band-mate though,' Flora said hotly.

Despite his humiliation, he still managed a smile at her show of loyalty.

'Yeah, having to watch the two of them together, day after day, it's—' He paused, wondering how he could put into words the soul-sucking agony he'd felt. 'It's been hard.'

'I bet.' Her expression was so empathic he wanted to lean across the table and kiss her for it.

He didn't though, because that wasn't what this relationship was about.

'You know,' she said slowly, leaning forward and spreading her long, elegant fingers out on the table in front of her, 'when I told Tia you were spending Christmas with me—' she locked her gaze with his and took an audible breath as if unsure how to phrase what she was about to say '—I would genuinely like that. I've made a commitment to see my parents for lunch, but we can duck out afterwards and hang out at a nearby pub and drink mulled wine next to a roaring fire.' She raised her eyebrows and added, 'If you fancy doing something like that.'

The mere idea of it gave his spirits such a lift he felt a bit dizzy from the rush of blood it sent to his head. He'd actually begun to dread spending the whole day alone now so her offer was most welcome. 'Won't your parents mind you leaving right after lunch?'

She broke eye contact with him to look down at her hands, which were busily realigning the salt and pepper shakers. 'They'll understand, I'm sure.'

But he wasn't sure that she really *was* sure.

'Look, I appreciate the offer but I don't want to interfere with your family's plans.'

There was a beat of silence before she met his gaze again. 'I'm sure my mum would love it if you came for lunch too.'

'Really?' he asked, still not entirely convinced.

Flicking back her hair, she gave him a firm nod. 'Yes. I'm positive. I'll give them a call to check tomorrow, but I'm ninety-nine per cent sure it'll be okay.'

Sitting back in his chair, he gave her a smile that rose from deep down in his belly. 'That would be great, Flora, thanks. It'll be interesting to see where you hail from.'

Was it his imagination or did she just hide a grimace?

'Did you say they're in Derbyshire?' he asked.

'Yes, just north of Bakewell, in the middle of the Peak District,' she said, her brow furrowed as if the thought of it gave her pain.

'Okay, well, since you're providing the entertainment, I'll drive,' he said.

'Great.' She nodded slowly. 'I was planning on travelling up on Christmas Eve to arrive late in the evening.'

'Works for me,' he said, pushing aside the maddening little voice that whispered, *Maybe her mother will get the wrong idea and we'll end up sharing a room.*

He had a feeling that little voice was going to be the death of him.

CHAPTER SIX

ONE WEEK LATER, on Christmas Eve, Alex found himself ringing the doorbell to Flora's flat, ready to drive them both up to Derbyshire for Christmas at her parents' house, wondering how in the heck his life had taken such an unexpected turn.

Amy was probably looking down on him right now and laughing herself silly.

The door swung open to reveal Flora with a slightly panicked look on her face. 'Oh, you're here! I'm not quite ready yet.'

'You were expecting me to be late, weren't you?' he said, narrowing his eyes.

She gave a nonchalant shrug. 'Maybe.'

'Well, I'm glad I'm not entirely predictable,' he muttered, walking into the vestibule. He shucked off his coat and toed off his shoes, feeling a wall of heat hit him. 'Wow, it's roasting in here.'

'Yeah, I hate being cold,' she said, taking his coat from him and hanging it neatly on a peg on the wall next to a whole row of her own in every colour and style possible, or so it seemed.

'Why do you need so many coats?'

She looked at him in surprise. 'To go with all my

different outfits. And for the different seasons. Don't you have more than one?'

'Nope,' he said, pointing at the one she'd just hung up. 'That's it.'

She just shook her head, a mystified expression on her face.

'Why don't you go and wait in the living room? I won't be long,' she said, disappearing into her bedroom.

'Okay.' He wandered through to her living room, giving the sofa an affable nod. 'Hello there, my old friend.'

Walking over to the mantelpiece, he picked up a framed photo of Flora dressed impeccably, of course, shaking hands with an older guy wearing an expensive-looking suit. They were standing in front of the logo for Bounce soft drinks, the company she worked for.

There was an expression of pride in her eyes which made something twist in his chest, and he experienced a sudden rush of affection for her. He might not particularly value her choice of career but he was intensely aware of how hard she must have worked and how focused she must be to get to a position like that.

She really was a very impressive woman.

'That was on my first day as Head of Marketing,' Flora said behind him. He started, dropping the photo frame on the floor.

'Sorry,' he said, picking it up and checking he hadn't damaged it. 'You made me jump coming up so quietly like that.'

'I didn't realise you hadn't heard me,' she said, but she was smiling.

'Are you ready to go?'

She nodded. 'Yup. All packed. I just need to check all the windows are closed. Back in a sec.'

While she bustled around the place, clicking on a light here and pulling a blind there, he leaned against the wall, letting his gaze travel around the room.

'Is this all your furniture?' he asked when she came back in and held up her hands in an *all done* gesture.

'No. I rented this place fully furnished. Why do you ask?'

'I thought it seemed a bit old-fashioned for your taste. It's nice and all, but I imagined you as more of a modernist.'

'So you're tuned in to my taste now, huh?' She shot him a grin. 'Perhaps we've been hanging around with each other too much.'

He bristled at that, her comment making him realise it was a bit strange that he felt he knew her so well already. 'I'm just observant,' he muttered in response, shrugging off his discomfort and pushing away from the wall. They'd not spent *that* much time together, he mused. Amy had talked about Flora a lot. That was probably why he felt as if he'd known Flora for longer than he had.

Then something else occurred to him. 'So if you're renting furniture does that mean you're not staying in Bath long?'

'Uh…yeah. Once this product launch is live I'm going back to my position in New York.'

'Oh. Right.' He was surprised by how disappointed he was to hear this. He'd just assumed that she'd moved back to England for good and that she'd be around to meet up with every now and again. He'd grown to appreciate her company now and found he didn't like the idea of her leaving.

'Anyway, I'm ready when you are,' she said, a little more loudly than was necessary.

She really did like things running to schedule.

'Okay, then let's get going,' he said, grateful for a distraction from the strange sinking feeling in his chest.

The roads out of Bath were predictably busy and Flora sat back quietly, letting Alex concentrate on getting them out of the city and onto the motorway.

It would probably take them around four hours to get up to Derbyshire at this rate and she felt a little shiver of concern at the thought of having to make conversation all the way there. Hopefully he'd be happy to listen to the radio for a bit of it. Car journeys always made her lethargic and she liked to just stare out of the window and think when she was travelling. She often came up with her best ideas when she allowed her mind to wander like that. Blue-sky thinking. Or in this case, ominous grey sky. It looked as though it might actually snow this year for Christmas.

'Mind if I put some music on?' Alex asked when they were finally speeding along in the middle lane of the M4.

'Sure, that would be great.'

'We'll go for the radio rather than one of my jazz playlists, shall we?' he said with a teasing note in his voice.

'You've turned me around on jazz now, so I'm happy to listen to whatever you've got,' she said in her most magnanimous voice. She felt a bit silly now, having been so quick to dismiss a whole genre she'd hardly heard anything of. Evidently it was time to expand her horizons.

'Okay then,' he said, flicking on the stereo. 'Can you go into the music app on my phone, choose the top playlist and send it to "car" when it asks you.' He gestured towards his smartphone, which was sitting in the well between their two seats.

'Sure.' She did as he'd asked, then sat back as the dulcet tones of Nina Simone began to play through the speakers. When that track finished and Billie Holiday started singing 'Summertime', Flora's attention perked up. 'Hey, I know this one. Didn't Janis Joplin sing it?'

'Yeah, she did. I prefer Billie's version though.'

'It's beautiful,' Flora agreed, the emotion of the song sweeping through her and making her skin tingle.

To her surprise, Alex started singing along with the song, his voice a deep, sexy rumble. She turned to stare at him, utterly transfixed as the delicious sound prickled along her skin and made her heart beat faster.

'Join in if you know the words,' he said, flipping her a smile.

The thought of him hearing her less than impressive voice made her hesitate. She'd been ridiculed enough in the past about how untuneful it was to be wary about airing it in front of anyone.

'I won't judge, I promise,' he reassured her, obviously sensing her hesitation. 'I think everyone should sing. It's good for the soul. I don't care if you're not in tune. Just let rip and enjoy it. That's what music should be about. We've become too focused on getting things exactly right these days rather than doing it just for the joy of it. Music should be about bringing people together, not about being pitch-perfect.'

That struck a chord with her and in the spirit of coming together at Christmas she decided to throw caution to the wind and give herself permission to just go for it. There was something incredibly freeing about it once she'd got over the first sting of embarrassment. She turned to grin at Alex as they sang their way through the next couple of songs, which she knew quite well from other artists having covered them, though she still cringed when she hit a wrong note.

Alex didn't say a thing though; in fact he didn't seem to mind at all.

A little while later the playlist came to an end and the silence in the car made her long for more music. It had been wonderfully uplifting, singing the songs with him, and she was sorry it was over. She wanted to say something about how much she'd loved listening to his beautiful voice, but she didn't want to sound like a fawning idiot.

'Let's have the radio on for a bit now. I'd like to catch the news. That okay with you?' Alex said, raising his eyebrows in question.

'Sure.'

He nodded and pressed the button on the stereo to turn on the radio.

It took the whole of the news bulletin before she felt as if she'd gotten her composure back under control. As a song about driving home for Christmas started playing on the radio, she was able to sound casually offhand saying, 'You know, you've got an amazing voice. You should write your own songs and sing them.'

'Actually, I already do.'

'Really?' She turned to look at him, intrigued.

Keeping his eyes trained on the road ahead, he nodded. 'Yeah, I've made a few demos but I've not had any interest yet. There's a producer I've made contact with who's interested in hearing the next songs I produce, but to be honest I've not been in the mood to write for a while, what with Amy and everything…' He petered out. 'And it's a tough business. Really tough, especially trying to strike out on your own. It's pretty demoralising to keep getting knock-backs.'

'I bet. Well, good luck with it. Don't give up, okay? The people who make it are usually the ones who work really hard for years and keep getting back up after a rejection. Very few people are actually "overnight successes", but I guess you already know that.'

'Yeah, I get that.' He sighed and rubbed a hand over his brow. 'It'd be great to be able to run my own show. I love playing in the band—at least I do when my ex-girlfriend's not fronting it—' he shot her an ironic grin '—but the real satisfaction comes from writing and performing my own songs.'

'That makes sense,' she said, warming to the theme. 'It's important to maintain as much control over your brand as possible, which isn't an easy task these days, because everyone wants a piece of you when you're successful.'

'Has that been your experience?' he asked.

She snorted. 'It's a bit different for me. Marketing isn't the most sexy of professions.'

'But it's impressive how fast you've risen up the ranks.' There was genuine warmth in that statement and she gave him a smile of gratitude for the recognition. It meant much more coming from him than from anybody else because it had been so hard-won.

'I don't know how you can work in a place like that day after day though,' he said suddenly, frowning hard at the road ahead. 'I think it'd probably kill me. The years I spent after university working for "the man" were the most miserable of my life.'

'Yeah, well, there are great prospects for career development at my company,' she said, feeling her shoulders stiffen at how forced that had sounded.

'Is your boss still giving you a hard time?' he asked after a pause.

She shot him a startled look, anxiety rising like a heatwave up her neck. 'Why do you ask that?'

'The first time we met you mentioned that he wasn't letting you do your job properly.'

It came back to her now. She *had* told him that in her drunken stupor. Damn it.

'It's fine. I can handle it. I'll win him over eventually.' She wished she felt as assured as she sounded. Her sister might have got the looks and musical ability, but Flora had always been damn good at her job—that was her talent. Which was why this particular challenge to her self-confidence was so unsettling.

'I'm sure you will,' he said and the affection in his voice made her insides do a funny little dance of joy.

'Thanks for the vote of confidence,' she said.

'You're welcome.'

When she glanced at him he turned to meet her gaze and gave her such a warm smile she thought she might combust on the spot.

What was going on here? It seemed as though he was making a concerted effort to be nice to her now, but was she reading too much into it? Was it just because he was grateful that she'd invited him to spend Christmas with her?

Or was he beginning to actually *like* her?

'Hey, perhaps you could play some of your songs for

me some time?' she said, indulging an urge to maintain this new level of connection between them.

He shrugged, seeming pleased by her interest. 'Sure, if you like.'

She did like. She did like a lot.

'Great.'

They sat in companionable silence for a while after that, listening to the radio, passing comment every now and again on a song or a news article. An hour away from their destination, Flora realised with a jolt of surprise that she hadn't felt this relaxed for a very long time. It was actually really nice to have someone else take the wheel while she sat in enforced stillness for once.

It was so pleasant she eventually dozed off, her dreams skating between memories from her life back in the States and the last few weeks she'd spent here in England. Then her dreams drifted to Christmases past, in particular the Boxing Day three years ago when she'd come downstairs in the morning and found her sister with an odd look on her face. Violet had laughed it off as a hangover from the heavy drinking the night before—the drinking that had sent Flora to bed early, leaving her sister and Flora's fiancé, Evan, alone with each other.

She'd known right then, deep down, what had happened. She just hadn't wanted to believe it.

Waking up with a jolt, she turned to look at Alex, who was frowning at the road in front of him as he navigated the windy A road towards her parents' house. The feeling of dread that had been sitting heavily in her stomach for the last few days began to crawl up her chest and into her throat. She knew she should warn

Alex about the sort of atmosphere he was going to walk into and reassure him that they wouldn't have to stay for long.

Sitting up straight and taking a fortifying breath, she turned to look at his profile, giving him a tight smile when he glanced over at her.

'I should probably mention that my sister and her husband will be there as well tomorrow,' she said, hearing a shake in her voice. She crossed her arms over her chest, feeling hot and uncomfortable about what she was about to tell him.

'Great, it'll be nice to meet them too,' Alex said breezily.

She cleared her throat. 'Did Amy tell you the story about me and my sister, Violet?'

He glanced over and frowned, obviously picking up on her discomfort now. 'No.'

'Okay, well, I should warn you that there might be a slightly strained atmosphere between us.'

'Really? Why's that?'

'Because her husband, Evan, is my ex-fiancé.' She let that hang there for a second before continuing. 'We went out for eight months about three years ago and we got engaged two weeks before I brought him home for Christmas to introduce him to my family. After meeting my sister on Christmas Day, he dumped me on New Year's Eve so he could be with her instead. They got married just before I took the job in New York.'

'I see.' He nodded slowly, his expression neutral.

'I just thought I should mention it because Violet has a habit of flirting with any man I bring home—then going out with them when they decide they like her better.' She tried to sound offhand and jokey when she added the last part, but it fell totally flat.

She sighed, knowing there was no point in trying to make out she hadn't been heartbroken by it. 'It's been a bit of a repeating pattern, to be honest, going all the way back to our teenage years.'

'And you think she's going to hit on me?'

'I wouldn't put it past her, even with Evan there. She's always been a terrible flirt. And you're exactly her type. Musical and creative. And handsome.'

The heat in her face intensified as she realised she'd inadvertently admitted to Alex that he was *her* type too. At least he had been until Evan had smashed her heart to pieces and ground it into the dirt with the heel of his rock star–wannabe ankle boot.

'Take the next left,' she said, pointing to the entrance to her family's country pile, feeling nervous apprehension sink through her.

'We're here.'

They pulled up at the end of the sweeping driveway in front of what had to be a Grade II listed Georgian building, judging by the design of it. At a glance, Alex counted fourteen windows spread across three storeys. It was not so much a house as a small stately home.

'Wow, what a beautiful place,' he said to her.

Flora smiled back, her expression a little strained. 'Welcome to my not so humble abode.'

Clearly the thought of coming home for Christmas wasn't as joyful for her as it should have been.

Getting out of the car, he stretched out his back, feeling blessed relief at finally being able to get out of the cramped driving position he'd been sitting in for the last few hours. Then he went round to open the door for Flora. He wanted her to know that he was here to support her too, but didn't know how to put it into words without it sounding cheesy. He hoped his actions would speak for his intentions instead.

'Thanks,' she said with a smile, taking his proffered hand. He helped her stand up on the uneven gravel driveway in her heels.

'You're welcome,' he said, smiling back.

It made total sense now why she'd taken so much satisfaction in sticking it to Tia and why she'd invited him to spend Christmas with her: solidarity. She knew exactly how it felt to be passed over by someone you thought cared about you, then be forced to keep on seeing them whilst at your most vulnerable. In Flora's case the rejection and painful awkwardness seemed to have tainted her enjoyment of getting together with her family. He also suspected it had driven her to move all the way to the States to avoid it.

Grabbing the cases out of the car, he slammed the boot shut, then followed her as she walked stiffly over the gravel driveway towards the grand stone-pillared entrance to the house.

Her mother must have heard the car pull up because, before they had even reached the door, she'd swung it open and pulled Flora into her arms with a squeal of delight.

'Flora! It's so wonderful to see you. Merry Christmas!'

'This is Alex,' Flora said, disentangling herself from her mother's tight embrace and turning to gesture towards him.

He walked up to where they stood, noting how much

Flora looked like her tall, handsome mother, and held out his hand in greeting.

'Thanks so much for having me over for Christmas, Mrs Morgan, especially as it was so last-minute. I really appreciate it.'

To his surprise, she ignored his hand and pulled him into a tight hug too. 'Call me Diana. We don't stand on ceremony here.' She cocked her head in a sympathetic manner. 'Welcome to Winter Hall. It's wonderful to have you here celebrating Christmas with us, Alex. I was so sorry to hear about Amy passing away. It must be devastating to lose a twin sister, especially when she was so young.'

There was a heavy beat of silence in which Alex nodded in acknowledgement of her sympathy, his jaw clamping down hard as he pushed down the ever-present grief. 'It was. But Flora's been looking after me.'

He turned to smile at her and saw a pink flush rising on her cheeks.

'Er...well, we've been looking out for each other,' she muttered, not quite meeting his eye. 'Are Violet and Evan here yet?' Flora asked her mother, glancing around as if expecting them to spring out at her at any second.

'Not yet.' She paused, then fixed Flora with a pleading stare. 'Darling, please try and get on with your sister while you're here,' her mother said, her expression morphing into an anxious frown. 'She's not been herself recently. I think she and Evan might be having some problems, so she's going to need our support.'

'Like the way she supported me by whisking my fiancé away from under my nose, you mean?' Flora said, her words heavy with irony.

Her mother sighed. 'Oh, Flora, please tell me you're

not still holding a grudge after all this time? You know she never meant to hurt you. Sometimes love works in funny ways.'

'Yes, hilarious,' Flora muttered, shrugging off her coat and hanging it on a peg by the door.

Alex felt a sting of anger on her behalf. Clearly Flora's mother had taken Violet's side in all this, which had to make Flora feel as if her sister was the favourite child.

There was the sound of wheels on the gravel outside and her mother turned away from them to hurry to the door and fling it open again.

Alex took the reprieve to hang up his own coat and draw Flora to one side. 'Are you okay?' he asked, searching her face for signs of distress.

She nodded. 'I'm fine, thanks. Just tired from the drive.' Her smile looked strained though.

'Is Evan not with you?' they heard her mother say as she ushered Flora's sister into the house.

'We had a row and he refused to come, but I don't want to talk about it right now,' a soft, husky voice replied.

As Violet walked into the wide stone-floored hallway, Alex felt his eyes involuntarily widen.

Flora's sister was stunning. She shone like the fairy light stars her mother had hung around the door frame, from the tips of her petite, stiletto-heeled boots to the ends of her sexily mussed-up baby-blonde hair.

Violet came to a sudden stop when she caught sight of him and he could have sworn she deliberately straightened her spine as she flashed him an inquisitive smile. 'Now here's someone I don't recognise. Who are you then?' she asked as she sashayed towards him, all thoughts of her missing husband apparently gone now.

Despite her beauty, there was something brittle and false about Violet that set Alex's nerves on edge. This was a woman who expected to be adored. He had a sudden urge to put his arm around Flora and protect her from the discomfort she had to be feeling right this minute.

'I'm Alex,' he said, not bothering to add his relationship to Flora. For some reason he didn't want to give her sister the satisfaction of knowing anything more about him.

'I'm Violet, Flora's sister,' Violet purred back. 'I know, we don't look much alike,' she added with a self-satisfied, conspiratorial smile, as if she found herself saying that on a regular basis.

An irritated shiver ran down Alex's spine.

Seemingly unaware of her narcissism, Violet's expression switched to one of pained distress, her large azure-blue eyes wide with sorrow. 'I'm afraid my husband, Evan, has decided he doesn't want to spend Christmas with me this year, so if you'll excuse me, I'm going to go up to bed.'

She gave her mother a brief hug. 'It's been a hell of a day and I'm exhausted.'

'Yes, of course, darling. Your room's all made up. We'll have a good chat about it in the morning.'

Violet nodded, her shoulders dramatically slumped, then turned to shoot him a quick seductive smile. 'It was lovely to meet you, Alex. I look forward to getting to know you better tomorrow.'

They all watched her walk away and mount the wide oak stairway before turning back to each other.

'Oh, dear,' her mother sighed, shaking her head.

Flora said nothing, just stood there stiffly.

He noticed that her usually sleek hair was mussed at the back where it had rubbed against the headrest for the last few hours and he had to forcibly stop himself from lifting a hand to smooth it down for her protectively.

'I think I might need to go to bed too,' she said in a small, slightly strained voice, flashing him a look of apology.

'Fine by me,' he said. 'I'm pretty beat from the drive, so I'm happy to crash now.'

'Okay, well, Flora can show you where you're sleeping,' Diana said, giving them both a troubled smile. He guessed that this wasn't the joyful family reunion she'd been hoping for.

'Goodnight,' Alex said to her, nodding his thanks. Then, grabbing their bags, he turned to follow Flora up the staircase.

'Here you go, this is your room,' Flora said, gesturing towards the first door at the top of the stairs. 'I'm right next door,' she added.

Alex mentally gave the *little voice* the V-sign. There would be no sharing with Flora tonight then. Which was very much for the best. They would spend a lovely, warm and fuzzy Christmas together, then go back to their lives as even firmer friends.

Not allowing his overwrought mind to turn that thought into something inappropriately smutty, he handed over her bag and bade her a friendly goodnight. Then he let himself into his room with a shaking hand and flopped onto the bed, pulling the pillow over his head and letting out a long, low groan.

Tiredness. That was what this strange, nerve-filled tension was. He was *tired*, that was all.

CHAPTER SEVEN

THE NEXT MORNING Alex got up later than he'd intended after not sleeping well, despite the ultracomfortable bed he'd been given in the guest room. He stumbled down to the sunlit Breakfast Room to find Flora there drinking coffee and looking as though she'd been up for hours. Her hair appeared freshly blow-dried, her cashmere jumper and linen trousers were pristine and she was perfectly, and heavily, made-up. In stark comparison, he'd barely glanced in the mirror as he'd brushed his teeth and had only run his fingers quickly through his hair after showering before giving up on it.

'Good morning, or should I say afternoon?' Flora quipped good-humouredly, making a show of looking at her watch as he slumped into the chair opposite her.

'Merry Christmas,' he replied, looking around the well-appointed, high-ceilinged room that was empty of people except for them. 'Is your sister not up yet?'

She seemed to bristle at the question. 'No. She always sleeps in late.'

'And your parents?'

'They went to the morning church service.'

A young woman with a kitchen apron wrapped around her waist came in and gave him a friendly smile.

'What can I get you for breakfast? I can do eggs Bene-dict or a full English breakfast if you'd like.'

'This is Penny, my parents' housekeeper, who's very generously agreed to do the food today,' Flora said, giv-ing the young woman a kind smile.

'It's actually my pleasure to be here,' Penny said. 'Anything to get away from the rows and tetchiness at home,' she added with a grimace. 'My parents don't get on at the best of times and Christmas Day seems to bring out the worst in them.'

'Well, in that case, I'd love eggs Benedict and a cup of very strong coffee if you've got some on,' Alex said to her.

Penny gave him a nod of approval and left the room. He yawned behind his hand, hoping she wouldn't be too long with the coffee.

'Didn't you sleep well?' Flora asked, her brow wrin-kling.

'Not really. It's a very comfy bed,' he added quickly when her face fell, 'but I'm still having trouble sleeping for more than a couple of hours on the trot.' He thought back to how he'd tossed and turned all night, his blood rushing with adrenaline and his mind whirring with tangled thoughts about Amy, his career, Tia and the band—and Flora.

'I have some relaxation music I can lend you—whale song and pan pipes, very soothing,' Flora suggested with a totally straight face.

He fought back a look of horror and forced himself to smile at her instead. 'Uh…no, I'm okay, thanks.'

She flashed him a wicked grin, making it clear she was teasing him.

He narrowed his eyes at her. 'Very funny.'

To his relief, Penny came back in then with a large mug of black coffee filled to the brim, which she placed in front of him.

'You are a truly magnificent woman,' he said to her, a little bemused to see a blush rise to her cheeks as she returned the smile, then scurried out of the room.

'You're such a charmer,' Flora said with an exaggerated eye-roll.

He just grinned back and picked up his mug, raising it to his lips. Those first few sips were like liquid joy.

'I thought we could go for a walk in a bit to get some air,' Flora said, looking out of the large picture window. 'It might snow later on, so we'd better not leave it too late.'

'Sure, whatever you like. I'm happy to go whenever.'

'Great.' She picked up the newspaper she'd been reading as Penny came back in with his eggs Benedict and they sat in companionable silence while he ate his breakfast. He made short work of it, his body crying out for energy after the rough night he'd had. When he finally put his cutlery down Flora smiled at him with amusement in her eyes.

'I thought you were going to scrape the pattern off the plate.'

'Hungry,' he growled in reply.

She just laughed and he thought how nice it was to see her looking more relaxed this morning.

'Let's take the papers through to the living room if you're finished,' Flora suggested, standing up when he gave her a nod of agreement.

The first thing he noticed when he walked into the elegant, tastefully decorated sitting room was a baby grand.

'Nice piano,' Alex said, walking over to it and tapping out a couple of notes, pleased to hear it was in tune. He missed playing when he was away from his instruments.

'Violet played it when she was younger.'

'I remember you saying. But you gave up.'

She scowled at this, apparently riled by his comment.

There was a flurry of movement in the doorway and Violet entered the room, wearing a pair of tight-fitting leather trousers and a bright red tank top, her sexily mussed up hair spilling over her slender shoulders.

Out of the corner of his eye he noticed Flora stiffen.

'I need another cup of coffee,' she said tightly. 'Want one, Alex?'

'Sure, I'll have another,' he said.

'Vi? Want a coffee?' Flora asked her sister, not looking at her as she made for the door.

'Yes, please, Floor, I'm going to be running mostly on caffeine today. I slept horrendously,' she grumbled, walking further into the room as Flora exited.

Alex left the piano and went to sit down on one of the Queen Anne sofas that stood on either side of the large marble fireplace.

'So, Alex, how did you and Flora meet?' Violet asked as she came and sat down right next to him, tucking her legs under her and leaning in towards him so their heads were only a couple of feet apart.

'Flora is my sister's—' he paused and took a breath '—*was* my sister Amy's best friend.'

Violet frowned. 'Oh, they're not friends any more? I thought they were really close?'

'Amy died from inflammatory breast cancer almost two months ago. It was a vicious strain that metastasised really quickly. There wasn't much they could do for her. The treatment they gave her didn't have much of an effect because the cancer was so fast-moving. It had already spread to her major organs.'

He was aware that his voice had become rougher as he had talked.

Violet looked shocked. 'Oh, my goodness, I hadn't heard. I'm so sorry.' She tipped her head sympathetically. 'Flora and I haven't spoken for a while. There's been a bit of tension between us since I married Evan.' She paused, her brow furrowing. 'They were engaged briefly before I got together with him.'

'So I heard,' he said coolly, noting how quickly she'd turned the focus of the conversation back to her.

'I'm so pleased she's got you now though. It's great you're able to comfort each other at such a difficult time.' She gave him a kindly smile, obviously hoping to curry favour.

'We're just friends.' His voice sounded stiffer than he'd meant it to.

Her brows shot up. 'Really? I'm surprised. You two look so comfortable together. I thought you were a couple.'

He shrugged, feeling tension in his shoulders. 'We've been spending a lot of time together recently.'

There was a spark in Violet's eyes that made him uneasy. She put a hand on his leg and gazed right into his eyes, opening her mouth to say something just as Flora walked back into the room holding a tray laden with cups of coffee.

She had a pinched expression on her face as if something was giving her pain.

'Hey, great,' he said, springing off the sofa to relieve her of the tray, feeling a pull of guilt that she'd seen the weird scene between him and her sister and had probably misinterpreted it. Which wasn't surprising, considering the history of her sister flirting with her boyfriends. 'Thanks, Flora,' he said, making sure to give her a reassuring smile and hoping she'd know he was on her side here and that he hadn't been flirting with Violet.

There was more movement at the doorway as first her mother, then a man who he assumed must be her father, walked in bringing with them the scent of cold winter air from their trip to church.

'Aha, you're all up! Good. We can have a few games of charades before lunch,' Flora's mother said gleefully.

Both of her daughters rolled their eyes, but their mother wouldn't accept any grumbling protests. Flora's father walked over and introduced himself while the women argued about the rules, giving Alex a friendly smile and telling him to call him Francis.

They played a few games, with Flora, Alex and Francis on one team and Violet and Diana on the other. It was a little strained at first, but after a while they all began to get into the spirit of it. There were even a few giggling moments when someone made a particularly suggestive motion.

Just as Alex uncovered the mystery behind a strange and rather uncomfortable-looking move Diana was doing with her head, Penny came into the room to let them know that their Christmas dinner was ready.

'We'd better go and take our seats,' Diana instructed them. She hustled Violet and Francis out before her, leaving Flora and Alex alone in the room.

'I'm so sorry,' Flora muttered, wrapping her arms around her body.

'About what?' Alex asked, not sure what she was talking about.

'About the strange atmosphere.'

'It's fine, Flora. I'm having a good time. I'm glad to be here.'

She sighed and rubbed a hand over her face, then picked a bit of fluff off her jumper and threw it towards the crackling fire. 'Okay...well, good.' She paused as if she was going to ask him something, then seemed to change her mind with a small shake of her head. 'I guess we'd better get in there,' she said instead, making it sound more like they were about to attend a state execution than enjoy Christmas dinner with her family.

They made their way into the dining room and took their seats. Flora was discomfited to find herself sitting directly opposite Violet, with Alex between them at the head of the table.

'I'd like to propose a toast,' Francis said, raising his wine glass and waiting till they all did the same. 'To our girls for being here to celebrate Christmas with us. And to our guest, Alex. May the next year be a better one for you all.'

'Cheers,' they all said quietly, each apparently thinking about the difficulties they'd faced throughout the year.

'Tuck in, everyone,' Diana said in an overly bright voice to cut through the suddenly sombre atmosphere, waving a hand at them before picking up her own knife and fork.

They were all quiet for a while as they ate the magnificent meal that Penny had prepared for them.

'It's so lovely to have everyone together again,' Diana said eventually, smiling around the table. 'Apart from missing Evan, of course,' she added.

Violet gave her mother a sad little nod of acknowledgment but didn't say anything. Flora was feeling so tense sitting across from her sister that her shoulders actually ached. It was always like this when she was in the same vicinity as Violet these days.

She took a deep steadying breath, grateful for the comforting heat of Alex's presence next to her, but wishing she'd cancelled on her parents and suggested they stay at a nice hotel instead now. Not that her mother would have stood for that. She'd been upset last year when Flora hadn't come back home for Christmas, citing her job in New York being too busy to allow her to get away.

As if reading her mind, her mother said, 'I know how expensive it is to fly over from the States, Flora, so it's wonderful you've been able to come this year.'

Her mum had no idea that she earned enough to fly home every month if she wanted, but she wasn't going to point that out right now. She already felt bad enough about avoiding coming here to see them.

'Yeah, it's nice to be here,' she said and smiled, blotting out the small voice whispering *Liar* in her ear.

Penny came in then and saw that they'd all just about finished. 'We have Christmas pudding or trifle for dessert if anyone can manage it,' she announced as Alex put his knife and fork down on his empty plate.

'Yes, please. I'd love both of those, in the same bowl is fine,' he said, leaning back in his chair, patting his belly and blowing out his cheeks in a over-the-top satisfied manner, making Flora smile for the first time since they'd sat down.

After they'd finished dessert they retired to a toasty-warm living room and brought out the presents they had for each other.

Flora found she was actually looking forward to seeing her parents open the gifts she'd bought for them this year.

'Here you go. Happy Christmas,' she said, passing Violet a gift bag with a cashmere jumper and some expensive bath smellies in it. Then she handed a bulging gift bag over to her mother so she could divide her parents' presents up between them.

'Oh, darling, you shouldn't have bought us so much. We don't need anything,' her mother admonished, tipping the presents out onto the floor and picking one up to examine it.

'It's fine. I wanted to treat you.'

Her parents spent the next few minutes carefully unwrapping all their gifts. They built themselves a small pile of all the designer clothes she'd bought hastily from her favourite Internet clothing outlet because she'd been too busy at work to go Christmas shopping, giving the odd 'hmm' or 'ah' as they held each item up briefly to glance at it before adding it to the mound.

'Thank you, darling,' her mother said eventually, giving Flora what felt like a very condescending smile.

'I thought you might appreciate some new clothes,' Flora said stiffly, the anticipated excitement of them being overjoyed with the things she'd picked out quickly draining away.

'We do,' her mother said, as if she'd just begged them to say something nice to her.

'Thanks, Floor,' Violet said, pulling on the jumper she'd been given, which of course looked like a million dollars on her.

'You're welcome. Thanks for the make-up,' she said, gesturing to the little boxes of anti-ageing cream, eye gel and concealer her sister apparently thought she needed.

'Here you go. This is from us,' her father grunted, handing over the customary Christmas cheques he always gave his daughters. Their mother gave them each a small pile of wrapped presents.

Flora tore the wrapping off a framed painting by an artist she'd loved since she was a teenager and squealed with delight, giving both her parents a hug of thanks. Then she picked up a small flat package, pulling off the paper to look down at the book she'd been given: *Living the Good Life: How to grow your own food.*

'I thought it might come in handy,' her mother said.

'Er... Mum, I don't even have a garden,' she said with a bemused grin.

'But you might one day soon, once you get fed up with living in New York and move back here to England.' Her mother gave her a hopeful look.

Pushing a feeling of guilt quickly aside, she forced herself to smile at her parents. 'Thanks very much. I'm sure it's got some great ideas in it.'

'You're most welcome, my darling. Make sure you spend the money frivolously too. That's what it's for.'

'And this is for you, Alex,' her father said, turning to him and handing over a squashy parcel. 'Sorry it's only small, but we didn't get much warning about you coming,' he added, giving Flora an admonishing glance.

'Oh, wow. Thank you. I really wasn't expecting anything. That's really kind of you,' Alex said, pulling a gorgeous forest-green jumper out of its wrapping paper. He beamed at both of her parents, genuinely pleased with it and grateful for their generosity, then pulled it over his head.

'It suits you,' her mother declared, clearly delighted.

'Yeah, you look great in it,' Flora said, intensely aware of the undisguised admiration in her voice.

There was a short silence where she caught her parents smiling at each other covertly and she felt her cheeks heat with embarrassment.

'And this is just a very small present, to say thanks for having me today,' Alex said, breaking into the awkward silence and producing a wrapped gift.

'Ooh, how lovely of you!' her mum exclaimed, taking it from his proffered hand. She carefully tore off the paper to reveal a recordable CD case.

'It's a collection of some of the best jazz and blues tracks ever written,' he explained. 'Some are a little obscure, but hopefully you'll come to love them.'

'Oh, Alex, what a wonderful thought! We love listening to music. How very kind of you,' her mother gushed as her father reached across and gave him a pat on the back.

Flora stared at them all, wondering whether she'd somehow moved unwittingly into the *Twilight Zone*.

'We can all listen to that later on, whilst we're eating our supper,' her mother said, going over to the stereo system they had hidden in a mahogany sideboard and laying the CD reverentially on top of it.

'We weren't planning on staying for supper. We should probably hit the road before there's a mad rush,' Flora said quickly.

Her mother's face fell. 'Oh. Really? Can't you stay tonight? I was hoping we could keep you here a little longer.'

Flora stiffened, steeling herself against the wave of guilt she felt about making an excuse to hurry out of there, but before she could open her mouth she heard Alex say, 'That would be great, Diana.' He turned to look at her. 'We can stay again tonight, can't we, Flora? Perhaps I could play the piano after we get back from our walk and we can all have a sing-song?'

'What a wonderful idea!' Her mother sounded utterly delighted by the suggestion.

Flora covertly raised her eyebrows in an *Are you kidding?* look at him, but he held fast, keeping his expression neutral but firm.

She let out a long sigh, knowing when she was beaten. 'Okay, yeah, sure. That would be fun,' she said flatly.

'Great! That's settled then,' her mum said, sounding happier than she'd heard her in a long time. Even her usually taciturn dad was nodding and smiling with pleasure.

Flora smiled stiffly, then slapped her hands lightly on her knees. 'Okay, well, we should probably go out for that walk before the heavens open. You still fancy it, Alex?'

Gratitude poured through her when he nodded and smiled. 'Sure.'

'Great. Let's go now then.' She got up and smoothed

down her trousers, relieved at the thought of a little respite from her sister's perturbing presence.

'What's the matter?' Alex asked Flora as soon as they'd
closed the front door behind them. They were both
wearing warm coats, hats, gloves and the walking boots
she'd suggested they pack in anticipation of exploring
the fifteen acres of land surrounding Winter Hall.

She shrugged her shoulders and waved her hands
about, as if unable to form the words.

'What, Flora?'

'It's just—'

'Yes?'

'I thought you'd want to get out of here, that's all,'
she said, looking utterly exasperated.

'Nah, I'm fine. And I think your parents are really
pleased you're staying on a bit longer. It was obvious
they were hoping you would. They clearly miss you.'
He gestured for them to start walking and they set off
towards a clump of trees in the distance.

'Hmm,' was all she said to that, folding her arms
and glaring up at the sky, which looked ominous and
brooding.

The moody light made him suspect it was about to
snow. Just as he thought this, he saw a snowflake drift
down and land in Flora's hair.

'Flora?'

She looked at him with a frown. 'Yes.'

'You haven't told them that you're living in Bath at
the moment, have you?'

Embarrassment flickered across her face. 'No.'

He sighed and shook his head. 'Coming from someone who has no family left, I recommend trying to

bridge that gap. I think Amy would have wanted that for you. You shouldn't be alienated from the people who clearly love you.'

Flora sighed, pushing a strand of hair out of her eyes. 'Yeah, I know that. She was always encouraging me to see more of them.' She took a breath. 'I will tell them I'm over here for a bit. It's just that I'm not going to be here for much longer and I didn't want them to get all excited about me being back only to have me leave almost immediately again.'

His chest gave a weird throb at that, but he ignored it and just nodded sagely at her.

They were quiet for a moment as they strolled along side by side, with only the sound of distant bird chatter breaking the silence.

'Is something else bothering you?' he asked tentatively. He'd felt her tension when they were exchanging gifts and he was pretty sure something had really upset her. 'Something about the presents?'

'You gave my parents a music playlist!' she blurted, turning to glare at him now.

'Ye-e-s,' he said slowly, baffled by why that should incense her.

'I gave them a big pile of designer clothes and they were more impressed with a CD you knocked up in ten minutes.'

He couldn't help but laugh. 'It's not about how much money you spend on a present, you know.'

But his amusement only lasted briefly, draining away when he saw her face fall and hurt spark in her eyes.

'Apparently the latest fashions in luxury fabrics stand no chance against a few old songs thrown together right before getting into the car.'

'Actually it was the night before, but who cares,' he replied, taking a quick step backwards when he saw the look of mock-murderous intent this quip provoked.

'You're such a kiss-ass,' she grumbled, shooting him a wry grin to show she was only kidding around.

He grinned back. 'I'm just trying to get into their good books. I'm very grateful for them agreeing to let me come here at the last minute.'

'Well, I think we can safely say you've made it in there. My mum's going to start dropping hints about wanting grandchildren soon, thanks to you.'

'You don't want kids?' he asked.

'Sure. One day. I guess I'll think about it once I've got a steady partner. I've been too busy with my career to give it much thought.'

'But you'd consider it?'

'Yeah. If I had a partner who was willing to share the childcare and housekeeping. I wouldn't want to give up work full-time to look after kids. It just wouldn't be for me.'

'Fair enough,' he said.

There was a tense silence when they just looked at each other. The snow was coming thick and fast now, settling on the ground under their feet so it made a quiet crunching sound as they walked over it in their boots.

'We should probably head back before we get snowed under,' she said, clapping her hands together to try and warm them up.

'Yeah, sure,' he said, a little disappointed to be going back now. He was really enjoying being with her out in the winter wonderland. They turned towards the house, which was a vision of cosy comfort, its windows glowing with soft, welcoming light.

'You know, they probably only reacted like that about the presents you gave them because they'd rather have something a bit more personal from you,' he said, feeling a strong urge to change the subject back to the one that she clearly needed to talk about.

She gave him a confused and slightly irritated frown. 'What do you mean?'

Holding up his hands, he leaned away from her in an exaggerated manner. 'Hey, don't shoot the messenger; I'm just making an observation. Your parents have surrounded themselves with things that mean something to them. There are photos of you and your sister everywhere and what looks like every piece of artwork you've ever produced covering all the surfaces in the dining room.'

She shot him a pained smile at this. 'Yeah, there are some real beauties on public display.'

'What I mean is, they're probably not overly concerned with having a big pile of expensive *stuff*. They like things that speak to them. Things that make them feel.'

He saw her shoulders slump a little.

'Yeah, you're probably right.' She took a shaky-sounding breath, as if steeling herself to say something difficult. 'I guess I've always felt this desperate need to please that stems from my childhood. Violet was very clearly their favourite and I figured out that if I wanted to impress them I had to work really hard and get exceptional grades. Then, after uni, a really good job. So that's what I did. I worked and worked and worked. I buy them impressive-looking presents to reiterate my success because I'm still trying to make them proud.

Ugh!' She rubbed a hand over her eyes. 'It all sounds so pathetic when I say it out loud like that.'

'It's really not,' he reassured her. 'I understand why you'd act like that.'

Her expression looked pained. 'Perhaps my obsession with status has got a bit out of control now though.'

She came to a stop as they reached the front door to the house and turned her head to peek at him and gauge his reaction.

Twisting his mouth a little, he nodded at her. 'Yeah. It kind of seems that way.'

She let out a long-suffering sigh. 'I know I should be grateful for having parents that care about me. But my hang-ups about being second best to my sister are just so ingrained in my psyche now.'

He nodded slowly. 'Well, they certainly love you and they're delighted you came today. That's totally clear.'

'Thanks for saying that. It means a lot to hear it.'

There was something in her voice that made him look harder at her. She gazed back, her eyes filled with warmth, and his insides did an almighty flip, sending little thrills racing along his nerve endings.

She really was an incredibly attractive woman, as well as one of the kindest, smartest people he'd ever met.

And she *got* him.

The low winter light played over her refined features and for those few suspended seconds while she gazed at him he imagined what his life would be like with Flora permanently in it.

Her lips parted, as if she was about to say something else, and he leaned forwards, his own lips tingling and parting as the strongest urge to kiss her took hold of him. The look in her eyes flared, as if her pupils had darkened, and he dragged in a stuttered breath, his heart suddenly racing a mile a minute.

Then, most frustratingly, the door swung open to reveal the ever-distracting vision of her sister, dragging them both out of the intensity of the moment and back into the cold reality of the present.

'Hi, guys,' Violet said chirpily.

'Hi,' Flora answered with a strange wobble in her voice.

Alex cleared his throat, experiencing a sudden need to have a few moments on his own, to get his head round the disconcerting sensations racing around his body right now. 'I'm just going to nip up to my bedroom and change. I'm going to be too hot in all these layers,' he said, gesturing to the extra clothes he'd put on for the walk.

'Okay. I'll be in the living room,' Flora said, not looking at him as she pulled off her boots and outdoor wear, then walked off in that direction, her shoulders stiff once again.

When he came back downstairs after taking a few deep breaths to calm his raging pulse, Violet was standing at the bottom of staircase, watching him as he descended.

'How was your walk?' she asked, giving him an inquisitive smile.

'Fresh,' he said carefully.

His initial attraction to Violet had definitely worn off now. He found her need to be adored and admired tedious. Now it just came across as a glossy but utterly superficial kind of allure, unlike Flora's subtle beauty that grew on you the more you got to know her.

'You've got snow in your hair,' she said, reaching up to brush it away with her fingers.

He took a small step back away from her, not wanting to give her any encouragement at all.

'Oh, look. We seem to be standing right under the mistletoe,' she said with a twinkle of mischief in her eyes.

He smiled thinly. 'Sorry, I only kiss very special people.'

'Like my sister,' she said, raising a suggestive eyebrow.

'I told you, Flora and I are just friends.'

'Uh-huh,' she said, sounding entirely unconvinced.

'I'm sorry I didn't get to meet your husband,' he said pointedly.

'Yes, me too.' Her face fell. 'Ugh! Why does life have to be so complicated? I'm sure Flora's told you all about what a hussy I am, stealing her boyfriends. But you have to understand what it was like for me spending my whole childhood in the shadow of someone so smart and superb at pretty much everything she did. Yes, maybe I got the looks, but she definitely got the brains. Sometimes Evan looks at me like I'm completely stupid and I know he's thinking he made a mistake choosing me over my brilliant sister.'

'That's not how she sees it,' Alex pointed out.

Violet let out a loud sigh. 'No, I know that.' She gave him a pleading look. 'I feel awful about hurting her, but I really, truly fell head over heels in love with Evan.' Her eyes filled with tears now. 'He's my entire world. I don't know what I'll do without him.'

Alex took pity on her. Clearly she was in a panic about her marriage ending and just needed someone to listen and maybe point her in the right direction. Strangely, it seemed that person was to be him.

'Look, why don't you give him a call and ask him to come over and talk? He's probably sitting alone at home feeling exactly the same way as you. Someone has to be the bigger person and break radio silence, otherwise it's just going to drag on and get harder and harder to communicate.'

'You think I should?' Her voice shook now.

'Yes. Better do it sooner than later, when he's already worked his way through half a bottle of Scotch.' He took a breath. 'My sister dying so young has really brought home to me that we have to grab our chances when we can. Why waste time not being with the person you love?'

She took a deliberate step backwards, grim determination flashing in her eyes. 'You're right. I'm not giving up on this marriage. I'm going to call him and tell him I love him and say that we need to work this out.'

'Good,' Alex said, smiling as he saw her square her shoulders and tip up her chin.

But, before turning to go, she leaned in close to him, looking him dead in the eye, and whispered, 'I don't believe for a second there's nothing between you and Flora. I saw the way you were looking at her when I opened the door, and how uptight she gets every time I get within touching distance of you. It's clear you're crazy about each other. So let me give you that advice right back. Don't wait too long and lose her, because my sister is an incredible person and you'd be a fool to let her slip through your fingers.'

And with that parting shot she strode away.

CHAPTER EIGHT

FLORA STEPPED BACK from the living room door, her heart racing and her hands shaking as the conversation she'd just overheard between Alex and her sister raced around her brain.

Alex had refused to kiss Violet.

Now that she thought about it, Vi was the only woman she'd not seen him flirt with, which was surprising coming from a man who flirted with everyone—well, everyone except for her, of course, but then their relationship was complicated. He'd even been charming with her mother when they'd first arrived—but not Vi, even though she'd made a couple of deliberate plays for him.

Alex had to be the only man she'd brought home who had resisted her sister's charms.

Her thoughts flew back to a few minutes ago when she could have sworn he was about to kiss her, just before Violet had swung the door open and broken the intense moment that had passed between them. Her insides had leapt in confusion and she'd not known quite how to deal with the idea of it. She'd been relieved when Alex excused himself so she could have a moment to get her head together away from his befuddling presence.

And now this had happened and she had no idea what to think about it.

'Oh, Alex, you're back.' Her mother's voice rang out in the hallway. 'Perhaps you could play something on the piano now and we'll have that sing-song,' she suggested hopefully.

'Sure. I'd be happy to,' Flora heard Alex reply.

She quickly stepped back from the door and rushed to sit down on the sofa, her heart racing, not wanting to be found standing there eavesdropping.

Alex strolled in and sat down at the piano, turning to flash her a smile.

'You don't mind playing, do you?' she asked quietly before the others came in.

'Of course not. It'll be fun. We'll sing some Christmas songs—ones that everyone knows,' he added.

'Don't you need the sheet music?' she asked dubiously.

'Nope, it's all up here,' he said, tapping his head.

'Okay then.'

Alex began to play 'White Christmas' on the piano and she listened as music filled the room, feeling a sudden lift in her mood. It was funny, but music seemed to be having a much more intense effect on her since she'd met Alex.

Her mum came bustling in with a tray of tea and she helped herself to a mug, taking a quick sip to soothe her dry throat before putting it carefully onto the side table.

'Ooh, Alex, that sounds wonderful!' her mother cooed, going to stand next to him at the piano.

He turned to give her a smile and she beamed back at him.

'Thank you,' Alex said, still playing the tune, only a little more softly now so they could talk.

Her mother sighed. 'I wish Flora had learned to play the piano too when she was younger but because Violet was learning she steadfastly refused. Sibling rivalry, I don't know! They used to get on so well when they were little,' she added sadly.

'It was demoralising that she was so good at it when I could barely pick out a tune,' Flora pointed out.

Her mother frowned, her expression clouding with confusion. 'You would have been a great piano player, I'm sure, darling. You could always do anything you set your mind to.'

The affectionate look of pride she gave her now made Flora's chest contract, but before she could reply her dad strolled in and parked himself next to her on the sofa, slapping his hands loudly on his thighs.

'Right then. Are we going to have this sing-song now? I've warmed my voice up,' he said, rubbing his hands together. The next thing she knew he began to sing along with the tune that Alex was playing.

Taking this as a cue, Alex began to play more loudly and joined in with her dad's rather wonky rendition of 'White Christmas'.

After a beat her mum joined them and Flora had no option but to sing along too.

At the end they all smiled round at each other and her mother asked, 'Is Violet not joining us?'

'She said she needed some time out,' her father answered, exchanging a meaningful glance with her.

Flora wondered whether they knew about Alex's suggestion that Vi call Evan.

Before she could ask, Alex began playing 'Let it

Snow! Let it Snow! Let it Snow!' and she couldn't help but join in. After that it was 'Hark! The Herald Angels Sing' followed by 'Rudolph the Red-Nosed Reindeer'.

At the end of that one, they all fell about laughing and Flora realised to her absolute astonishment that she was starting to have a really good time at home with her family. And Alex. He was the crux of it, of course.

They took a short break to drink whisky cream, or sweet sherry in her mother's case, and throw a couple more logs on the fire.

There was a loud knock on the door just as Flora and her mum were arguing about which song to sing next and they heard Violet shout, 'I'll get it. It'll be for me,' out in the hallway.

Flora saw her mother and father exchange looks of relief and, to her surprise, she found that she was actually pleased that there was a glimmer of hope for her sister and Evan. Being here with her family, and with Alex, had made her realise exactly what she'd been missing whilst away on her own in the States. She was determined to put the whole Evan debacle behind her now. It was definitely time to move on.

They heard the couple's voices recede as they went upstairs and slammed a bedroom door shut behind them. Then Alex launched back into a variety of carols and popular Christmas songs which they all demanded he play in turn. About an hour after he'd started playing again, Alex finally got up from the piano stool and came to sit next to her on the sofa.

Francis let out a loud yawn, then waved a hand in apology. 'All this singing has worn me out. I think I'm going to retire to bed and let you youngsters enjoy the rest of your evening,' he said.

Diana let out what seemed like a suspiciously fake yawn too. 'You know, I think I'll come with you, Francis.' Bustling over to the sofa, she leaned down to give Flora a tight hug.

'It's been so lovely having you here today. I hope you'll be able to make it back to see us again soon, my darling. You're always welcome here, you know that, right?'

Flora nodded against her mum's shoulder. 'I do. It's been lovely today.' She actually meant it for once.

'Alex,' her mother said, letting Flora go and enveloping him in a big hug next. 'It's been wonderful to have you here for Christmas. Thank you for looking after Flora for us,' she said, pulling back to look him directly in the eye. 'I've never seen her looking quite so relaxed,' she mock whispered. She winked, then flashed Flora a cheeky grin.

Flora dug her nails into her palms, but managed a wry smile in return.

'It's been lovely, Diana. Thanks again for having me,' Alex said, grinning, as she drew away from him.

'Well, goodnight, kids,' Francis said, backing out of the room with a wave. 'And Merry Christmas.'

'Merry Christmas,' Diana called too as she followed him out. 'Don't do anything I wouldn't do.' She paused. 'No, forget that! Do everything!' she said, clearly very tiddly now on sweet sherry.

And then they were alone again.

'Sorry about my mother, the Queen of Subtlety,' she said, rolling her eyes.

Alex just smiled. 'She's great. Both your parents are. I feel really welcome here.'

'Yeah, they're okay, I suppose,' she joked nervously

as she suddenly became acutely aware of how close they were sitting in the otherwise empty room. She slapped her hands on her knees awkwardly. 'Well, that was fun. Thanks so much for all the music. I think my parents really enjoyed it.'

He turned his head to smile at her, his eyes dancing with amusement. 'You're welcome. I enjoyed it too. It's been a while since I've played just for fun. I'd forgotten how rewarding it can be.'

'Yes, I bet. That hadn't occurred to me,' Flora said thoughtfully. 'Well, it was wonderful. It gave me the tingles to listen to you.'

He arched an eyebrow. 'Ah, you're talking about *frisson*.'

'I'm sorry?'

'*Frisson*. It's a well-known phenomenon. Some people don't get it, but it sounds like you do, which is lucky for you.' He flipped her a smile. 'It's an emotional response to music. It starts as a rush of chills in the base of your spine, which then moves across your skin, making all your hairs stand on end. A bit like a skin orgasm.'

She swallowed hard. 'Er…yes. That's exactly what it feels like.'

He nodded, mercifully getting up from the sofa now and walking back over to the piano. She'd been having real trouble keeping her composure with him sitting so close and talking about something so intimate. It was a relief to have the physical space between them again.

Sitting down, he began to play what sounded like a piece of classical music, his long fingers skating elegantly over the keys.

'There are certain pieces of music and songs that are supposed to provoke more of a response than others. It happens when the music does something unexpected,' he said, segueing into a tune she realised she knew well.

'Is this "Hallelujah"?' she asked excitedly, sitting up straighter. She'd always loved this Leonard Cohen song.

He answered by beginning to sing the song in his beautifully gravelly voice, which of course suited it perfectly. She watched in fascination, noting how his body language was much more relaxed now that he wasn't performing for a bigger audience. His fringe fell down over his forehead as he dipped his head in concentration and she had the strangest urge to go over there and push it back from his face so she could see his eyes again.

As the emotion of the lyrics flooded through her she felt it again, that incredible rush of euphoria that started in her spine and cascaded out through her body in waves, making the entire surface of her skin stand up in goosebumps. It continued to wash over her, wave after wave of it, as he sang the entire song. The emotion caused tears to press against the backs of her eyes and throat and her insides to twist and swoop with poignant elation.

'Whoa!' she said, wiping away a tear that she hadn't been able to hold back at the close of the song. 'That was amazing.'

'Pretty cool, huh?' Alex said. The expression on his face made her suspect he'd been moved by it as well. She wondered fleetingly whether he'd been thinking about Tia and what he'd lost with her, before forcing the thought out of her head. It made her want to cry even more.

They sat there looking at each other for longer than was entirely comfortable, the intensity of the silence making her head throb and her chest ache.

'Well, I guess we ought to get to bed ourselves,' she said nervously, standing up and stretching. It seemed such a shame to leave the lovely warm living room now, especially when he was doing such a wonderful job of entertaining her with his playing, but it felt like the right time to turn in. In fact, she had a strong inclination to have a bit of time on her own now—to process the strange feeling of *yearning* for something elusive that was making her heart race and her skin prickle.

'I guess so,' Alex said, standing up too.

They walked to the bottom of the staircase together in silence.

'Straight to bed?' Alex asked, and she tried not to imagine that there was more to that question than he really meant.

'I think so, I'm pretty tired now,' she said, beginning to mount the stairs.

He followed her up, his presence like a benevolent shadow behind her.

When they reached his room and she turned back to say goodnight, she found he was looking at her with a strange speculative expression on his face.

'Well, goodnight,' she murmured, wondering what was going through his mind and knowing she'd be at a total loss if anyone asked her to explain how she was feeling right now.

'Thank you for inviting me here with you. I get how hard it must have been to bring me when things with Violet are so tense. I appreciate you telling me about it and trusting me with something so personal and challenging for you.' He took a small step closer. 'I had a really good time today,' he said, his voice a low rumble that made happy chills skitter along her nerves.

'You sound surprised,' she joked nervously, but he didn't smile back, just frowned a little.

Her throat felt oddly tense so she lifted her hand to massage it. He dropped his gaze to watch the movements she made.

'Well, goodnight. Have a good sleep. Don't let the bedbugs bite. And Merry Christmas,' she gabbled, dropping her hand awkwardly back to her side again.

He was looking at her with that strangely intense expression in his eyes again now. It was something she couldn't quite pin down. Something that made her insides swoop and soar.

Without saying a word, he pointed up at the mistletoe that was now hanging from the top of his room's doorway.

'I'm sure that wasn't there earlier,' he said, his lips quirking into a wry smile.

'Hmm, no. My mother is incorrigible.'

'Maybe it would be wrong to ignore it though.' He raised a teasing eyebrow. 'Isn't it bad luck or something?'

'I think you're getting it mixed up with not walking under ladders,' she said shakily.

'Ah, perhaps I am.'

'And I thought you only kissed very special people.'

His eyes widened. 'You heard all that between me and your sister, huh?'

'Yeah, I didn't mean to eavesdrop. I was…uh…just sitting near the door.'

He smiled, evidently not believing a word of it. 'I get the feeling it was something you needed to hear.'

'I guess it was.'

There was another small pause, during which the

house suddenly seemed very quiet. So quiet she could hear the rapid thump of her pulse in her ears.

'Okay, well, just in case it is bad luck to ignore it—' she pointed at the mistletoe, then waggled her finger at his face '—I'm just going to kiss you on the cheek this time.'

But as she leaned forwards, angling her head so that her lips were aiming for the side of his face, he turned towards her and their mouths connected.

She drew back with a startled gasp. 'Oh! Sorry, I didn't mean to—' But he cut her off by sliding his hand into her hair and pulling her back towards him, pressing his mouth hard against hers again so deliberately that there was no way she could misconstrue it as an accident this time.

Her insides seemed to melt as he deepened the kiss, opening his mouth to slide his tongue against hers. It was a covetous kiss, full of need and determination. She sank into it, breathing him in, basking in the passion of his hunger.

When he finally released his grip on the back of her head and they drew apart, their mouths remained only centimetres from each other's. They stood there transfixed in each other's gazes, their breathing loud and guttural in the quiet corridor.

'What—? What's going on here?' she gasped, staring into his eyes in total astonishment.

'I'm kissing *you* this time,' he murmured, gazing at her with such fierce intensity her whole body flooded with desire. 'Is that okay?'

She blinked at him. 'Um… Er… Uh—yes. Of course. Yes, it's okay.'

Because it was. It really, really was.

The corner of his mouth lifted in a smile at her inarticulateness. 'In that case, I'm going to do it again.'

She just nodded, not trusting herself to form any decipherable words this time. She let out a small gasp of pleasure as his mouth connected with hers again, his tongue sliding forcefully between her lips.

If she'd had any doubts about Alex being a good kisser they were totally quashed now. She'd never been kissed so intently, or so thoroughly. It made her toes curl with delight. His lips were soft but his mouth was firm against hers, his tongue gently exploring her mouth with possessive intent.

He pushed her gently backwards until she was pressed against the door to his room, his body hot and firm against hers, and she sucked in a breath as she felt just how into this he was.

'Perhaps we should take this inside,' he murmured against her mouth.

'Yes, yes, good idea,' she muttered back, fumbling for the door handle.

Once they were inside he lost no time in undressing her, slowly at first, then picking up speed as more and more of her body was revealed. She knew he'd seen most of it before when they'd gone swimming and she'd worn that skimpy bathing costume, but it didn't seem to stop him from wanting to reverently check out every inch of her now.

After finally shucking off his own clothes and standing still, quivering with barely controlled desire as she explored the smooth skin and the swell of the muscles on his chest and arms with her fingertips, he finally steered her back towards the bed. Urging her to lie back, he climbed over her and leaned down to kiss her mouth again.

He was so gentle with her, and so covetous, it took her breath away. She'd never felt worshipped like this before. Never felt so attractive. He kissed and touched every inch of her—some places much more thoroughly than others—and she sank back into the pure pleasure of it. Every part of her body felt connected. When he kissed her ankles she felt it in her belly, and when he moved up to press his mouth along her jaw, biting down gently on the sensitive skin there, it sent spirals of delicious sensation all the way down to her toes.

Then things got a little more intense. Then a little more, until the night blended into one big blur of pleasure and she lost herself in the kind of sexual fulfilment she'd never even dared to dream could exist.

CHAPTER NINE

So that was a fun night.

Alex lay in bed the following morning with Flora sleeping peacefully next to him, thinking that *that* had to be the understatement of the year.

The whole day had been incredible. From the deep connection he'd felt with Flora after gaining such a thorough insight into what drove her, to seeing the look of ecstasy on her face when he'd played music just for her last night.

Standing in front of his room, all he'd been able to think about was kissing her—not that the idea hadn't flitted through his head on a regular basis throughout the day. It had seemed inevitable that it would happen at some point, he mused. Clearly they were very attracted to each other and he was pretty sure Flora must have felt it too, considering the way she'd responded to him with such eagerness.

Last night he'd not allowed himself to think about how it would change things between them, unable to resist the overpowering desire to be close to her that had plagued him all evening—hell, all day. But, as he thought about it now, a niggle of alarm wound its way through him. Would she expect this connection to mean more than he was capable of right now?

He became aware of her stirring next to him and turned onto his side to smile at her as she started to blink open her eyes.

'Alex?' she murmured. He answered her with a gentle kiss, feeling her sleep-warmed skin heat his face.

'Good morning,' he said eventually, pulling back from her to see the smile he'd hoped for in her eyes.

She hid a yawn behind her hand, then grinned at him. 'A very good morning indeed.'

'Did you sleep well?' he asked, brushing a fallen eyelash from her cheek.

'I did,' she murmured. 'Did you?'

'Actually, I did for once. You wore me out,' he teased, grinning at her mock-reproving look.

'I think you'll find you were just as enthused as I was,' she said. He was relieved to hear her voice was only playfully stern.

'You're quite right, I was,' he said, bending forward to kiss her again.

When he drew back, she fixed him with a puzzled frown.

'What is this?' she asked, waving her finger between the two of them.

He stilled, genuinely not knowing how to answer that. His heart thumped hard in his chest. 'What do you think it is?'

'I don't know.'

'Do we need to put a label on it?' He held his breath, waiting for her answer.

'No,' she said slowly. 'Probably not.'

'It's unexpected, that's what it is,' he said, smiling in relief at her.

'Agreed,' she said, returning his smile. 'But if we did want to explain it—not that we need to—I guess it's just two friends comforting each other for the night at a difficult time in their lives?'

He nodded slowly, pushing away the unexpected sinking feeling in his gut. 'Yeah, sure,' he said, flopping back onto the pillows. 'Just a bit of friendly sex between…er…friends.'

He felt her shift beside him and she leaned over to push away a strand of his fringe that had fallen over his eyes.

He grimaced. 'I know, I should cut it,' he said, before she could.

'No. Don't,' she said, shaking her head. 'It suits you like that.'

'Still, it's about time I started taking a bit more care of my appearance again.'

'A shave might be good,' she said with a wry smile, delicately fingering her sore chin.

He rocked to one side, then rolled on top of her, taking her by surprise and making her gasp. 'Actually, I think the pink-chinned look suits you,' he said, bending forward to nuzzle her jaw, then kiss her throat, before moving back up to press his mouth to hers. 'It's very sexy,' he murmured against her lips.

'Hmm,' she purred as he shifted above her, making his intentions for the way he wished to spend the rest of the morning perfectly clear.

One night and one morning.

'I suppose I can put up with it for such a good cause.'

'Excellent. I love a martyr with no morals,' he teased,

moving down to kiss her neck again. Then he moved lower, hearing her half giggle, half moan with pleasure in response.

How he loved that sound.

Afterwards they talked and laughed and talked some more about their lives and their pasts and about Amy, but not about what they were doing here together.

It was better that way. As he'd told her when she'd tried to set him up with her friend Lucy, he wasn't looking for anything serious at the moment and she was back off to the States soon anyway.

So friendly, consoling, unemotional sex was all it could be.

They eventually peeled themselves out of bed an hour later and Flora slipped back to her own room, thankfully not encountering anyone else on the way, and took a long, soothing shower. As soon as she was ready, she tapped on Alex's door and they went downstairs together to grab some much-needed breakfast, agreeing they'd go back to Bath after eating and saying goodbye to everyone.

Evan and Violet were in the breakfast room, gazing into each other's eyes with their fingers entwined. When Flora walked in her stomach did a strange lurch. Not because the sight of her sister and Evan still made her intensely jealous, but because she realised she didn't feel like that about the two of them any more. Being around Alex had made her aware that she no longer had romantic feelings for Evan. Her body didn't respond in any of the predictable ways it used to when he turned to look at her with his mesmerising golden eyes.

'Hi, Flora,' he said in his low, gravelly voice and she didn't even blink.

'Good morning. I'm surprised to see the two of you up this early. You're not exactly known for being early risers,' she joked good-humouredly, taking a seat opposite Violet.

'No, well, we had an early night,' Violet said with a glint of mischievous innuendo in her eyes.

'So you're back together?' Flora asked, deciding there was no point tiptoeing around it.

They both nodded, then turned to gaze into each other's eyes again. Flora suddenly understood how in love they were with each other. She'd seen signs of it at the wedding that she'd been forced to attend, but through her haze of drunkenness she'd not seen the utter transfixed devotion she saw now.

'I'm glad,' she said, and found she really meant it.

'Thanks, Floor, me too,' Violet purred, not taking her eyes off her husband for a second.

Penny came in then and Flora and Alex gratefully placed their breakfast orders with the housekeeper. As soon as Penny had gone, Flora's parents came in and they all got caught up in a discussion about music that lasted for the rest of the meal.

Flora found, with a swell of happiness, that she was having a really good time chatting with her family. It helped that Alex was by her side, covertly running his fingertips over the back of her hand under the table. Being this comfortable in the home she'd grown up in was something she had not experienced for a very long time.

'Anyway, we're going to hit the road,' she announced as soon as their plates were cleared. 'We've got a long

drive ahead of us, especially with the roads so snowy.'
Snow had settled over the whole country overnight and
there were warnings about some roads being hazardous to drive on, which would make their drive back a
lot slower.

There followed a flurry of activity where she and
Alex packed up their bags and met everyone down in
the hallway for a send-off. Her parents hugged them
both and Alex complimented them on their fantastic
hospitality and thanked them for including him.

'I'll take the bags out to the car and see you there,'
he said to her, flashing her an encouraging smile.

Flora turned to her sister and held out her arms for
a hug.

'I'm so glad to see things are progressing with sexy
Alex,' Violet murmured huskily into her ear. 'It's amazing what a bit of rivalry and a sprig of mistletoe can
incite.'

Flora drew back to raise an eyebrow at her. 'Was it
you who hung it above his door?'

Violet shrugged casually, then smiled. 'I thought the
two of you could do with a bit of encouragement.'

'Yes, well, we're still just friends, Vi. Neither of us
are in any kind of emotional state for a relationship right
now. And anyway, I'm back off to New York soon.'

'Uh-huh,' Violet said, looking and sounding completely unconvinced. 'Look,' she said, her expression
becoming serious now, 'I know I've been a selfish cow
in the past, Floor, but I genuinely want you to be happy.'

Flora became aware of her eyes filling with tears and
blinked them back quickly. 'Thanks, Vi. I want you and
Evan to be happy too. You're good together.'

Her sister appeared to be blinking back her own tears

now. They had one more tight hug before Flora extricated herself and gave both her mother and father one last kiss on their cheeks.

'Thanks so much for having us. Merry Christmas.'

'Come back and see us again soon, darling,' her mother said, hugging her hard. 'We really miss you, you know.'

Flora nodded and said, 'I know. I miss you too. I'll be back soon.' Then she quickly walked out of the door before she began crying in earnest.

Alex was leaning against the car, waiting for her.

'Ready to go?' he asked with concern in his voice as he clocked her strained expression.

'Yes, I am,' she said, getting into the passenger side and clicking on her seat belt.

'Are you okay?' he asked as he got in beside her, turning to fix her with his bright, intense gaze.

Her stomach swooped as she gazed back at his handsome face, her eyes dropping to those firm lips she'd been kissing less than an hour ago. 'Actually, yes, more okay than I've been for a long time. I think Amy would have been pleased to see me getting on with my family so well. Pleased and relieved,' she added, flashing him a wobbly smile.

Alex grinned back with genuine warmth and pleasure in his eyes, then turned the key in the ignition, put the car into gear and set off back to Bath.

CHAPTER TEN

THE NEXT NIGHT Flora was kicking off her heels, desperate to give her poor aching feet a break after an intense day back at work, when her phone rang. Picking it up, she saw Alex's name on the screen and accepted the call with a swell of nerve-tinged pleasure. They'd texted a couple of times during the day about random things—clearly he'd been bored at home on his own, Flora had mused as she'd juggled emails and calls and demands from her staff and clients—but they hadn't actually spoken since he'd dropped her at home late on Boxing Day night.

'Hey, how was your day?' he asked without preamble. She really appreciated that. She had little enough energy as it was for conversation without being drawn into an awkward egotistical dance to see who could be the most aloof after a break from each other's company.

'A bit of a pig, if I'm honest,' she said, letting out a long sigh as all the tensions of the day came flooding back to her. Despite her hope that a break over Christmas would help her boss thaw to her a little, he still seemed determined to keep her right under his thumb.

'Still giving you trouble, is he?' Alex asked and she felt a rush of relief that he understood without her having to spell it out—and that it felt okay to complain to him about it. He'd been so lovely when she'd told him about how much she'd been struggling to keep her composure at work when they'd travelled back down to Bath the night before. He'd been both attentive and kind. Much like his sister had always been whenever she'd needed a pep talk.

'Yeah,' she said glumly. 'He's still treating me like I'm an idiot.'

'Okay,' he said, 'I'm coming over.' And he ended the call.

She stared at her phone for a good few seconds, wondering whether she was so tired she'd just imagined that happening.

Her fears were allayed, however, when there was a ring on her doorbell a few minutes later. She opened the door to find Alex standing on the doorstep holding a chocolate cake in one hand and a bottle of wine in the other.

'Now there's a sight for sore eyes,' she said, ushering him inside and taking the bottle and cake from him so he could shrug his coat off.

'It sounded like you could do with some company, but if you'd rather I just handed over the refined sugar and alcohol and left you to indulge in peace I'll understand,' he said, following her into the kitchen.

'No way,' she said, putting the offerings onto the work surface. 'You're most welcome too.'

And he was. It was lovely to have someone to talk to about what had gone wrong with her day. Before Amy died it would have been her that she'd call—though only if it had been a particularly taxing day. Most of the time she just kept all the stress to herself, locked away deep inside her.

As she turned to face Alex he flashed her one of his alluring smiles and her insides swooped with pleasure. 'Well, good, because I could do with a friend tonight too,' he said.

'Really?' she asked, worried that he'd had a bad day as well and in her self-centred state she'd totally neglected to ask him about it.

'Yeah,' he said, moving slowly but very deliberately towards her. 'I missed your *friendly* company.'

Ah, now she got it.

She grinned at him, feeling a little shiver of excitement race down her spine as she took in the look of desirous intent in his eyes.

'And, as your friend, it's my duty to take your mind off work,' he said, starting to undo the buttons on her blouse.

She let out a long hiss of pleasure as he dipped his head to kiss her throat, then pushed the blouse off her shoulders.

'Hmm, how very altruistic of you,' she mumbled, drawing in a sharp breath as his nimble fingers made short work of unhooking the clasp of her bra, which he then removed in one swift movement.

Taking a step backwards, she realised he'd manoeuvred her against the kitchen island. She gasped as he slid his hands under her bottom and lifted her onto it, moving his body between her legs to lean in and kiss her hard.

He was less gentle with her this time, which was exactly what she needed. She soon forgot all about her horrible day, allowing herself to sink into the passion and intensity of his lovemaking.

Not that they were 'making love' per se, she reminded herself hazily.

No, they'd agreed that this was nothing like that.

For Alex, the next few days passed by in a blur of intensely pleasurable time spent with Flora in the evenings and intensely focused days of composing new songs, which seemed to flood into his head as soon as she'd closed his front door behind her on her way to work.

He'd thought a lot about what Flora had said about how he was handling his music career and had come to the decision that he was going to make things happen for himself this next year, even if it killed him to do it. She was absolutely right—he couldn't just stay within the safe confines of the band in the hopes they'd have a breakthrough soon. He wasn't going to give up on his dream of going solo, no matter how hard that might be.

He wanted to play his own music.

Luckily, the band had agreed to take the week between Christmas and New Year off as a break in order to recharge their creative batteries so he was able to dedicate that time to working on his own material.

Near the end of the week he was confident enough in what he'd written to record it for a demo, so he called a friend in London who part-owned a recording studio and arranged to use a spare studio on the Friday. He didn't say anything to Flora about the new songs, wanting to surprise her with them at some point in the future. For now, he just wanted to keep the momentum of his creativity going.

To his utter surprise and great delight, his friend knocked on the studio door at the end of his session and introduced him to a music producer who was working in the room next to him. After an involved discussion about the state of the music industry, the guy asked to sit in and listen to what he'd managed to record.

After hearing the songs Alex played him, the producer was hugely complimentary about the material. He asked to take a copy of the demo away with him to pass on to a colleague, who was apparently looking for an artist like him to complement his growing client list.

In Alex's adrenaline-fuelled creative haze it seemed entirely meant to be. Not that he was going to get too excited about it. He'd had enough knock-backs by now to know not to hope for too much to come out of it. Still, he was pleased with what he'd achieved that week and had a solid demo to send to other labels off the back of it.

Maybe this year *would* be his year.

Not wanting to go home to Bath on his own after finishing in the studio, he looked up the address for Bounce soft drinks and went to meet Flora after work.

He spotted her coming out of the building alone, her shoulders a little slumped and her brow pinched into a tired-looking frown.

That idiot boss of hers had a lot to answer for.

The flash of pure anger at how she was being treated propelled him forwards in a surge of protective indignation. He marched up to her, scooped her into his arms and planted a hard kiss on her mouth, wanting her to know that not everyone was oblivious to her charms.

'Alex!' she said, once he'd pulled back from the thoroughly intensive kiss he'd given her. 'What are you doing here?'

He loved that she looked so ridiculously pleased to see him and his chest gave a peculiar throb of pleasure.

'I've come to escort you home,' he said, linking his arm though hers. 'I thought we could go straight back to your place tonight to celebrate you finishing work for the year,' he said, grinning at her.

She nodded in a pseudo-sombre manner. 'I guess if we're going out to celebrate the New Year tomorrow with friends, a quiet night in might be just the ticket,' she said, snuggling closer to him.

'Who said anything about quiet?' he teased, his whole body flooding with desire at her responding look of unconcealed enthusiasm.

CHAPTER ELEVEN

SATURDAY NIGHT WAS New Year's Eve and, on Alex's insistence, Flora turned up to his place for a meal before they hit the pubs in town with Pete and Des from the band, who were going to be out with their partners.

She walked into his kitchen to find him cooking up a storm.

'Did you have a relaxing morning?' he asked as he turned away from the stove to drag her to him for a welcoming kiss.

She'd been at a spa all day, pampering herself with massages and beauty treatments galore—a suggestion of Alex's after she'd complained last night about how much her whole body was aching from sitting at her desk and on the train.

'Yeah, your magic antidote suggestion seems to have cured me. I no longer feel one hundred and ten years old.' She leaned against the work surface and watched him stir some seasoning into the food, wishing his talented hands were on her instead of the spoon and pan. 'I'm really not looking forward to going back to work after New Year,' she said, sighing. 'But at least I'm only there for another couple of weeks.'

'Is that when the project's due to end?' he asked,

turning away from her to throw a couple of empty tins into the recycling box. Was it her imagination or was his body language a little tense?

'Yeah. Then I'm back off to my position in New York,' she said stiffly, moving closer so she could peer into the pan, feeling an uncomfortable urge to change the subject. She really didn't want to think about leaving right now. 'Hmm, is that chicken stew?'

'Coq au vin,' he said with a nod.

'Well, it smells delicious.'

'It's going to taste delicious too,' he said, with a cocky confidence that made her smile. 'I happen to be an excellent cook.'

'You're full of surprises,' she said, leaning back against the kitchen work surface again to give him an assessing glance.

There was a beat of silence.

'Is the stress really worth it?' he asked gruffly, making her wonder where the sudden vehemence had come from.

'At work?' she asked, her mind taking a moment to catch up with the meaning behind his question.

He nodded.

'I used to think so but, I have to admit, some days I wonder. It's pretty exhausting keeping up with the pace of it and I'm sick of having to work in the evening and weekends to catch up with myself.'

'Then give it up,' he said, waving the spoon at her. 'Make a change. Work for yourself. Break the routine and just do something different—something you feel passionate about.'

She stiffened, discomfort making heat rise to her

face. 'But I've worked so hard to get where I am. I can't just give it up now.'

He studied her with an irritated frown. 'Of course you could. You just have to adjust your priorities.'

His insinuation that it would be easy to just give up what she'd spent years working for sent a prickle of exasperation up her spine. It wasn't as simple as that. It really wasn't. She was too used to the security she enjoyed working for Bounce now. It could take years to get to that same position if she set up her own business. And what if she failed? All her hard work would be wasted.

They glared at each other crossly, the air crackling with barely contained antagonism.

'I'm just going to use your bathroom,' she muttered, looking away from his maddening expression. The last thing she wanted right now was to have a row with him. She was here for some light relief, not a life lesson.

She was just about to come out of the bathroom, after taking a few deep, steadying breaths to calm her racing heart, when she heard voices in the hall. She froze on the spot, a sixth sense telling her not to go any further.

'Look, it's not a good time,' she heard Alex say.

'Okay, you win,' came the urgent tones of a woman's reply.

It only took Flora's brain a second to recognise those gravelly tones.

Tia.

'What are you talking about?' Alex asked, sounding exasperated.

A little voice in Flora's head cheered him on.

'It worked, Alex. You wanted to make me jealous and I am.'

'Tia, what—'

'Don't pretend you don't know what I'm talking about,' she cut in. 'Give me some credit at least.'

'Are you talking about Flora?' The incredulity in his tone sent a cold shiver rushing down her spine. So that confirmed the fear she'd been pushing to the back of her mind ever since that morning in bed in her parents' house. He hadn't been feigning nonchalance about what she meant to him; he really did only see her as a friend.

'Look, I know you were upset when I got together with Zane, but I was having a really hard time. He was there for me when you weren't!' Tia whined.

'My sister was dying,' Alex stated in a cold voice.

'And you just pushed me away when I tried to support you. You wouldn't even let me come and meet her. It was like I didn't even exist any more.'

'So you gave up on me and moved straight on to the next band member in line.' There was a break in Alex's voice that made Flora's breath catch.

'I'm not proud of how I handled it.' There was a long pause. 'I want you to know I'm sorry.' Another pause. 'And that I regret it.'

Flora's heart was beating so fast now she felt dizzy as she waited for Alex's response.

'You regret it?' Alex asked in a voice that seemed to have lost all its anger now.

'Yes. I want you back.'

There was a long pause. Flora was aware of her pulse thumping painfully in her throat.

'What about Zane?' he asked eventually.

A wave of nausea rose through her at the discovery that he could be so easily persuaded to give in to Tia's will, even after the callous way she'd acted towards him.

'He'll get over it,' Tia said in that cooing voice Flora

had heard her use the first time they'd met and she'd thought she'd have to break up a fight between her two lovers.

'I... I don't know what to say,' Alex said gruffly.

There was a pause, then a strange *oof* sound, followed by a low moan of pleasure.

Flora felt her breath whoosh out of her. She took a couple of stumbling steps backwards, aware of her shoulder banging hard against the bathroom cupboard but not feeling the pain of it.

They were kissing, she was sure of it.

With heavy dread sinking through her, she crept forwards again to peek around the doorway into the hall. Alex and Tia were standing there with their arms twined around each other and their mouths locked together in a deep kiss.

Flora felt strangely spaced out, as if she was watching what was happening from afar, her emotions disconnected from what she was seeing.

Well, that's it then, she thought in a weirdly detached way. Alex was kissing Tia, which must mean he wanted her back.

But what about me? What about us?

She shook her head jerkily, pushing the dissenting voice out of her head. She was his *friend*. They'd agreed that whatever this thing was between them, it wasn't going to be serious.

Her hands had begun to shake. She crossed her arms and stuffed her hands under her armpits to calm the tremble in them.

It was Alex's life and his decision. She just wanted him to be happy. If that meant him getting back with Tia, then that had to be a good thing.

Didn't it?

Yes. *Yes.* He was in love with Tia and he'd been miserable without her.

Anyway, she was going back to America soon and she didn't want to leave him here on his own. She'd worked so hard for her powerful position and she couldn't give it all up now. She may not be beautiful and arty and alluring like Tia and Violet, but she could hold her own in a tough business environment and she could damn well look after herself.

She didn't need a man to make her happy. She didn't need Alex.

Eyes burning and throat tense with a sudden swell of panic at being discovered eavesdropping on their reunion, she dashed back into the bathroom. Taking a few steadying breaths, she closed the door quietly behind her.

Her thoughts were racing so fast around her head that she felt dizzy and sick with it. She longed to get out of there and leave them to it. She knew they must have a lot to talk about and didn't want to cause any more trouble between them. Her heart lurched and her stomach churned at the thought of making an uncomfortable exit past them. She didn't think she could face Alex right now. She had no idea what she'd say to him. Her mind was whirling with thoughts and emotions and she didn't want to put him in an awkward position.

Yes, that was it. That was why she was feeling so panicky and weird. The whole situation was highly emotionally complicated. Better to leave quietly and explain her absence later when they'd all had a chance to get their heads together.

Glancing round the bathroom, she feverishly eyed

the small window above the toilet and decided it was probably just about big enough for her to climb out of. Putting down the lid of the loo, she put one foot on it and boosted herself up. Pushing the window open as far as it would go, she slid quickly out into the sharp wintry air, trying not to fall over the recycling bins stacked up directly beneath the window. She felt her trousers snag on something, then rip as she jumped down, but she didn't stop to check the damage. She'd do a full assessment once she was far enough away from this place, safely back at home.

After letting herself out through the back gate with a shaking hand, she traversed the lane out to the street and hightailed it back to her flat.

Well, you did it, she told herself as she unsteadily poured herself a large glass of white wine in her kitchen ten minutes later. Her whole body felt weirdly numb now. She'd fulfilled Amy's wish to make sure Alex was okay. He was a lot happier now than when she'd first met him. If a reconciliation with Tia was on the cards, his life would be firmly back on track.

She could go back to the States with a clear conscience.

Taking a big gulp of wine, she forced it past the tight pressure in her throat.

Yes, it was all looking very good for Alex.

So why did she feel like crying?

For maybe five seconds after Tia launched herself at him and pressed her mouth hard against his, Alex had allowed himself to sink into the familiar comfort of the kiss. Her taste and smell and touch brought back intense memories of happier times, making his chest ache and his taste buds tingle with nostalgia. But then a vision of Flora's smile had swum through his mind and kissing Tia had suddenly felt completely and utterly wrong.

Before Christmas he'd longed for things to go back to the way they once were: before Amy had become ill, before his love of playing and writing music had deserted him, before Tia had left him. He missed that more simple time, when he was full of naïve excitement about all the possibilities that lay ahead of him.

But his life was different now. He was different.

He felt as if he'd grown up in the last few weeks.

While it was a powerful ego rush to experience the glory of winning Tia back, he realised in those jarring seconds that he didn't want her any more.

He wanted Flora—intensely and with a passion that he'd never experienced before. He felt that she understood him and that she genuinely cared about him. It wasn't all about her when he was with her, like it had been with Tia. Flora treated him as an equal.

That was who he really wanted in his life.

Flora.

He just needed to convince her that he was worth taking a risk on and staying here in England for.

After untangling himself from Tia's desperate grip and sending her on her way as fast as he could—which had proved a little tricky when it became obvious that she was intent on changing his mind, even going as far as producing tears, which had no effect on him whatsoever—he'd slammed the door shut behind her and rushed back to tell Flora about his revelation, only to find the flat empty.

He checked every room twice, desperately hoping he'd somehow missed her. But after a few minutes of calling her name—and experiencing a sick, sinking feeling when he noticed that the bathroom window was wide open—he came to the disturbing conclusion that she wasn't there any more. That she'd escaped out of a *window*.

But had she gone right after they'd had that tense conversation about her giving up her job or right after Tia had turned up?

Picking up his phone with a shaking hand, he called her number.

'Hey, where did you go?' he asked gruffly when she finally answered.

'I thought I'd make a silent exit so you and Tia could work things out without being interrupted.' Her strangely upbeat tone of voice sent a panicky sort of shiver across his skin.

'It didn't sound like I was her favourite person at the moment,' she went on before he could say anything, 'and I didn't want to disrupt what looked like a re-union?' She inflected her voice at the end to make it a question, the intrigued tone making it sound as if she was fishing for salacious gossip. It sounded as if she had seen them kissing—but she wasn't angry with him about it.

What the hell was this? Why did she sound so happy at the prospect of him getting back together with Tia? Did what they'd been through together recently really mean so little to her? Was she totally set on going back to her job and life in the States and forgetting all about him?

'She wants me back, apparently,' he said, trying to keep the hurt at her unexpectedly blasé reaction out of his voice.

'Well, it's great to hear she's finally come to her

senses,' Flora said, her voice jokey now as if she was totally oblivious to how much pain this conversation was causing him.

Humiliation sank to the pit of his stomach as it occurred to him that maybe hanging around with him as a friend really had just been about fulfilling Amy's last wish. That it hadn't meant anything more than that to her. That *he* didn't mean more than that to her.

'You think I should take her back?' he asked tersely, digging his nails into his palms to keep the desperation he felt at this painful revelation at bay.

There was a small pause before she said, 'Well, I guess everyone deserves a second chance. It sounded like she was genuinely sorry about the way she'd handled it all. And it would make your life so much easier if you were back on good terms with her, with regard to staying with the band.'

Was there a slight wobble in her voice now, or had he just imagined it?

'True,' he said, clenching his fists harder.

'I think you should do whatever makes you happy, Alex,' she said so breezily that he knew for sure now that she'd never change her mind about jacking in her job and staying in England. With him. It was clear she was standing aside so he could get back with Tia without any hard feelings between them.

That she didn't care enough to fight for him. For them.

He was glad now that he'd only hinted about her doing that earlier, rather than coming right out and saying it. What a humiliating and utterly devastating knock-back that would have been. The last thing he

needed in his emotionally fractured state after losing
Amy was another woman rejecting him.

'We'll still be friends though, right?' she asked. This
time he definitely detected a slightly strained note in
her voice. Did she think he'd totally drop her if Tia was
back on the scene? Was that really how he came across
to her? The idea made him feel sick.

'Of course we'll still be friends, no matter what happens,' he managed to force out. His head was swimming
now, his thoughts and feelings a tangled mess.

'Great.' She took a deliberate-sounding breath. 'Anyway, I'm going to go. I've got a banging headache—a
migraine, I think—so I'm going to cry off tonight. Wish
everyone happy New Year for me, won't you?'

'You're not coming out now?' he asked, hearing the
incredulity in his voice.

There was a small, tense pause. 'No. Sorry, I'll only
be a killjoy if I'm not feeling well. You'll have a good
time with Tia and your friends though, won't you.' It
was a statement, not a question. 'Happy New Year,' she
said, and with that decisive end to the conversation she
cut the line.

He sat there for a while afterwards, staring at the
wall, feeling a fresh new kind of grief pouring through
him. The pain of having become so close to Flora, only
to lose her so abruptly, made his heart ache. It felt like
a death, even though he knew she'd still be out there
somewhere, getting on with her life without him.

But then he should be used to losing the people he
loved by now. It seemed he was destined to be alone.

Getting up shakily, he walked into the kitchen and
reached for a tumbler and the bottle of whisky he kept
stashed at the back of the cupboard. But just as he went

to screw off the top, something stopped him. He didn't want to sink back into oblivion again. He wanted to feel. To relive all the joyful thoughts and discoveries he'd experienced whilst he'd been around Flora. To prod those emotional bruises.

To his surprise, he found that he wanted to compose a new song.

Flora threw her mobile across the room, watching with a sick sort of satisfaction as it bounced along the floor and came to rest against the stone fireplace.

There was a large crack in the screen. *A bit like my heart*, she thought wryly, though there was no real humour in this observation.

She had no idea how she'd said all those words to Alex without howling with misery-filled frustration throughout the whole conversation.

It seemed clear from the rasp in his voice that he felt bad about dropping her after all they'd shared in the last couple of weeks. But he was still in love with Tia. That was perfectly obvious. And she really couldn't blame him for how he felt. She'd seen the tension in him at the gig when Tia had been around and the way he'd looked at her. And she knew Tia could probably make him happier than she could; they had much more in common with each other. He only kissed very special people, after all.

Anyway, she was used to being second best by now. It seemed to be her default position with the men she fell for. She and Alex weren't right for each other; they were too different. They'd just been each other's emotional prop during a difficult time. The thing between them had only happened because they'd both been sad and in need of some human contact. They'd understood and soothed each other's pain, but that was all it had been about. If it hadn't been for Amy's death, they probably wouldn't have even connected.

Alex and Tia, on the other hand, had something she never would.

They made music together.

CHAPTER TWELVE

NEW YEAR'S DAY was horrendous.

Flora spent most of it lying in bed, staring up at the ceiling, not having the energy or impetus to get up and do anything with her day off.

She couldn't stop thinking about Alex and what he might be doing with Tia. Had he taken her out last night to meet up with Pete and Des in the pub? That would make sense. Tia was part of the band after all. They all belonged together.

Finally managing to drag herself out of bed at lunchtime, Flora got up and made herself a strong cup of coffee, wincing as the heat of it burned her mouth.

Trailing into the living room, she turned on the TV and stared blankly at the news, her eyes gritty and tired from a poor night's sleep. She hated being alone in bed again. Even though they had only spent a week waking up next to each other, she'd grown used to having Alex's solid form there next to her. She'd loved being able to roll over and wrap herself around him in the night, feeling the soft rise and fall of his breathing against her chest as he slept.

And he seemed to have slept much better with her in the bed too. He'd not woken up after a couple of hours like he had been doing before Christmas. Or so he'd told her.

Tamping down on a fresh swell of misery, she flicked the channel over to one that was playing music videos. She needed to hear something upbeat and positive right now to pull her out of this painful vortex of despair.

How could she be feeling this distraught after only being with him for such a short time? she wondered as a surge of hot tears pressed at the back of her eyes and throat. Was it because she'd been using Alex to fill the gaping hole in her heart that his sister had left when she'd died?

No. That hadn't been it. No one could ever replace Amy, not even her twin brother.

She'd fallen for him in his own right, this scruffy, roguish, compassionate, frustrating man.

Somehow he'd opened up her eyes and made her start to value things she'd never put any store in before. Like music. Like having a family and a home to go back to whenever she needed it. He'd made her stop and think about what she'd taken for granted for far too long—a notion that she'd been incredibly resistant to accepting in the past, even when Amy had repeatedly pointed it out.

At the thought of having lost both Amy and Alex, anxiety rose like a venomous snake ready to strike. She fought it back, determined not to give in to the constricting band of fear in her chest. She took a few deep breaths, blanking her mind.

But thoughts of Alex still managed to creep back in.

He'd had a way of making her feel calm whenever he was around. Whole. Enough.

Though she didn't feel *enough* right now. Not when she had Tia to compete with.

Inadequate. That was how she actually felt. Corporate success meant nothing to Alex and that was all she had going for her.

Tia was beautiful and talented and mysterious and had wrapped herself around Alex's heart like a vine. There was no way a woman like that was going to let someone as amazing as Alex go. She'd be a complete idiot to do that.

So what did that make Flora?

Choking back her tears, she got up and went to take a long hot shower, hoping the stinging heat of the water would distract her from the cold chill that had invaded her body ever since she'd left Alex's flat last night.

She was gently towelling dry her strangely sensitive skin when her mobile started to ring. She picked it up, glancing at the display and feeling her heart leap into her throat as she saw the name on the screen.

Alex.

She almost let it go to voicemail, before telling herself not to be such a coward. They were still friends and she didn't want to cut all ties with him, even if it meant only hearing from him now and again. It would be terrifically hard, but she'd deal with it. She was well-practised in dealing with grief now.

'Hi,' she said, forcing her voice to sound upbeat and breezy. 'Happy New Year.'

There was a short pause before he spoke. 'Happy New Year, Flora.' His voice was rough, as if he'd been out all night and only just woken up.

'So how was last night? Did you all have a good time?' she asked in a strangled voice, wrapping her arm tightly across her stomach to quell the uncomfortable ache there.

'I didn't go,' he said tonelessly.

Ah, of course not. He and Tia must have stayed in. They'd had some making up to do after all.

She fought back the swell of nausea this thought caused.

'Well, I slept through the whole thing,' she chirped, feeling like the biggest faker in the world. 'My head's a lot better now though, thank goodness.'

There was another pause on his end of the phone. 'Great,' he said.

Another beat of silence.

'So what's up?' she asked, feeling desperate to get this conversation over and done with now, before the hard sobs that were making her throat constrict painfully managed to escape and give her away.

'I just wanted to call and let you know my news.'

'Oh?' She held her breath, steeling herself to hear something about him and Tia.

'The band have been offered a recording contract,' he said.

She sucked in a breath of surprise, feeling genuinely pleased for him. 'Oh, wow, that's fantastic! When did you hear?'

'Just now. Tia's just finished talking to the record producer. Apparently we'll be expected to start touring around England pretty quickly to get our name out there.'

'I'm really happy for you, Alex. Make sure you send me photos from the road,' she said, biting her lip to stop herself from letting out a sob.

So that was it then. He'd be off soon, touring with

his girlfriend. She hoped if Amy was looking down on them right now she'd be pleased with what she saw unfolding here.

Perhaps if she hung onto that hope this horrendous feeling of anguish would go away and she could go back to her old life feeling satisfied that everyone was happy and their lives were sorted.

Everyone except for her.

Because she was in love with Alex Trevelyan, and he didn't love her back.

After concluding the call, Alex put the phone down and swallowed hard. It had taken all his courage to tap on Flora's name to connect him to her, but he was glad he'd done it. He'd wanted to hear her voice again. He'd dreamt about it. He was missing her as if one of his major organs had been ripped out of his body, and it didn't take a genius to figure out which one.

She'd sounded so happy for him about the band's contract that he'd not been able to bring himself to ask the questions that had plagued him all night, keeping him awake till the early hours.

Don't you care about me at all?

Would you be willing to stay in England for me?

Do you love me like I love you?

But of course he'd not asked her a single one of them.

He couldn't see any way to persuade her he was worth taking a risk on—that he could provide just as fulfilling a life for her here in England as her high-powered job did in the States.

She'd never intended to stay here long-term, so why would she change her mind now?

He remembered how she'd laughed about what an

odd couple they'd make when he'd first met her. But did she really still feel like that after everything they'd shared?

He certainly didn't. It seemed completely clear to him now that they were actually perfect together. They complemented each other, made each other think and experience things in a totally new way. That had to be a good thing. Didn't it?

He certainly thought so. He knew now that he wanted Flora in his life, challenging him and making him feel things he'd never felt without her. But he was keenly aware that if he wanted her to stay—and he really did, so much it made his head throb—just like with his musical career, he was going to have to take some risks and work damn hard for what he really wanted.

And never, *never* give up.

CHAPTER THIRTEEN

A FEW DAYS LATER, Flora let herself into her flat after another long, gruelling day at work. To her huge relief, the UK launch was finally live and the whole frustrating project was over and done with so she could finally get her life back. As she walked inside she noticed a small padded envelope lying on the mat below her letter box. She guessed that her upstairs neighbour must have posted it through for her so it didn't get lost in the jumble of junk mail by the door in the communal entryway.

There was something about the shape and size of it that made her heart beat faster. Tearing off the top of the envelope, she turned it on its end and shook it, watching a recordable CD case slip out of it into her hand. There wasn't a note inside, but scrawled across the inner slip under the clear case were the words:

This one's for you, Flora.
Love, Alex

Hands trembling, she went over to the stereo system that had come with the flat and slid it into the CD drawer.

She'd expected to hear Nina Simone or Billy Holiday or even Leonard Cohen—as a reminder that they'd always be friends perhaps. So when Alex's beautiful gravelly voice started playing through the speakers the blood rushed so quickly to her head she had to sit down and take a few calming breaths. Her heart thumped hard in her chest as she listened to every single song on the disc, unable to move as the beautiful piano music washed over her and his voice moved through her like a pain-relieving drug.

And she had tingles *everywhere*.

As she concentrated on the lyrics, her earlier euphoria began to drain away as she realised she was listening to Alex singing love songs about a woman who had beguiled and inspired him. Someone who had made him feel music in his soul. Tia. The songs had to be about her.

And then the final song came on and it was explicitly clear that this one was about someone else entirely.

Amy.

The lyrics were so loving and poignant that tears rushed to her eyes. She sat there, paralysed with grief, sobbing hard as memories of her friend whirled through her head in a dizzying kaleidoscope of images.

Alex had put into words exactly how it had felt to lose her best friend.

It made one thing starkly clear. He completely understood her.

Just like Amy had done.

Getting up on wobbly legs, she went over to the drawer where she'd been keeping Amy's letter recently, carefully lifting it out, then smoothing it down on the dining table to read it. Her gaze skimmed over the beginning until she got to the part she was looking for:

*I'm so proud of you for all that you've achieved.
I always knew you'd be successful in whatever
you did, but your drive and determination have
astounded even me. I know you probably won't
take a minute to step back and see the enormity of
what you've accomplished, but get this: you truly
are an incredible person, as well as the kindest,
most generous woman I've ever had the pleasure
of knowing.*

She'd always skipped over that part before, racing to
get on to the favour Amy had asked of her, but now she
stopped to think about what her friend had been trying
to tell her: that she could have whatever she wanted if
only she put her mind to it.

If she wanted to branch out and start her own business, then she could do that. She certainly had the experience and knowledge to make her own initiative a
success. She'd not done it up till now because she'd
been afraid to leave the safe confines of someone else's
business.

But it was time to stop being safe and move on to the
next stage of her life. One she was in total control of.
If she found herself working with someone who didn't
treat her with the respect she deserved, then she'd no
longer work with them. Simple as that.

She was going to be her own woman from now on.

Excitement fizzed through her at the thought of it,
lifting her beleaguered spirits. Yes, she was going to
start acting like the woman Amy had always seen her as.

It was time to stop blaming her feelings of inade-
quacy on other people and take stock of her life.

If that meant starting her own business—just like

Alex had suggested on New Year's Eve—then she'd do it on her terms and build it entirely from her own blood, sweat and tears.

Make it something to be truly proud of.

After meeting Alex and enjoying living in Bath, then making peace with what had happened with Violet and her family, she'd started having serious reservations about going back to her job in the States anyway. Perhaps this was the right time to move permanently back to England.

What was there in New York for her now anyway? A few friends she'd made over the last year or so, but no one particularly close. Not like Amy. Certainly no one like Alex. He was one of a kind.

She loved that about him.

Taking a breath, she pushed back her shoulders. Yup. She loved him.

And even if she couldn't have him, she wasn't going to let that stop her from taking the rest of her future into her own hands.

Alex was her friend and always would be, she hoped, and she wanted to let him know that she'd always be there for him too. She needed to tell him that, even if it would be the most painful, heart-wrenching thing she'd ever done.

She also wanted him to know how much he'd inspired her to make some positive changes in her life.

Yes, telling Alex all about her plans would be exactly the right thing to do to cement them. But she didn't want to do it over the phone. She wanted to look him in the eye and say it.

Giving her face a quick scrub in the bathroom, she decided not to bother putting make-up on. He genuinely didn't seem to care whether she wore it or not. In fact, he seemed to prefer her looking natural and unconcealed.

Striding into the hall, she pulled on her boots and grabbed one of her coats from the peg, not even stopping to check whether it matched with the rest of her outfit, then let herself out of her flat.

She walked quickly towards Alex's place, hoping he'd be in and on his own. She didn't fancy saying her piece in front of Tia, but now she'd made up her mind she didn't want to lose the momentum of her decision either.

When she finally reached his door, she rang the bell for a good few seconds to make sure he heard it. Waiting impatiently, she tapped her foot and drummed her fingers against her legs, her heart thumping hard in her chest.

She was a little breathless from walking so fast, and probably from the adrenaline rushing through her blood too. She took a couple of moments to compose herself, wanting to seem cool and relaxed when he opened the door.

After what felt like eons she heard the lock turn and the door swung open to reveal the breathtaking sight of Alex looking rumpled, but ridiculously sexy, in a T-shirt and jeans. His feet were bare, as if he'd just thrown on clothes after rolling out of bed.

'Sorry,' she said instinctively, 'I hope I didn't disturb anything.' Her insides did a slow, uncomfortable somersault as it occurred to her that he might have left Tia in bed.

He frowned at her, then rubbed at his eyes as if he thought he was imagining her there.

'Flora. You're here.' He said it as if he'd been waiting for her to come and was relieved that she'd finally arrived.

'Er... I just thought I'd pop over to say thanks,' she gabbled, a little panic-stricken by the thought of Tia overhearing them.

He stared at her with a bemused frown on his face, then rubbed a hand over his eyes, looking thoroughly exhausted.

'Sorry, I was asleep on the sofa. Thanks? For what?'

He'd been asleep on the sofa? So he was alone then. Relief flooded through her. 'For the music you sent me,' she said, giving him a grin that she had to work hard for.

His perplexed expression cleared, to be replaced with a dazzling smile. 'And not just any music,' he said. 'Every one of those songs was written by me.'

Her heart did a slow flip. 'I thought I recognised your dulcet tones and I suspected it was your work. There was something about the songs that felt very *you*.'

He nodded thoughtfully. 'Want to come in?' he asked, sounding a little uncertain.

She hesitated, but only for a second. Now that she was here she really didn't want to leave until she'd told him about her epiphany.

'Er...yes, great,' she said, stepping into the hallway, aware of her legs trembling with nerves.

He led the way into his flat and took her coat from her, then gestured for her to go through to the living room.

'Want a drink?' he asked.

She suspected from his slightly antsy manner that he was hoping she'd refuse.

'No, thanks.' She sat down on his sofa and breathed in the wonderfully familiar smell of him as he sat down next to her.

'So what did you think?'

'About the songs?'

'Yeah.'

She could tell from the anticipation in his face he was desperately hoping she'd liked them.

'They're wonderful,' she said truthfully. 'Very moving. In fact they all gave me *frisson* and a couple of them made me cry.'

'Really?' He seemed ridiculously pleased to hear he'd been able to turn her into a blubbering, overemotional wreck.

'Yeah, proper ugly crying.'

'That's great,' he said, flashing her his gorgeous smile again, making her drag in a painful breath at the heart-wrenching sight of it. She'd missed seeing it *so much* over the last week.

'So I have some news,' he said, shuffling back on the sofa.

'Oh? About the band?' she asked, bracing herself for him to say it was actually about him and Tia.

'No, not the band. About the songs I gave you. I've started sending them out to record labels to try and get my solo career off the ground.'

'Really? That's fantastic news! Good for you!' Despite her heartache she still felt a rush of joy for him. 'Amy would be so proud of you,' she added.

His brow crinkled into a frown. 'Yeah, I'd like to think so.'

Flora took a breath, wanting to get the painful part out in the open and over and done with. 'So I guess you're going to be really busy, touring with the band soon too.'

'I've resigned from the band.'

She stared at him. 'Really? But what about Tia? Won't it make it hard on your relationship if you're both off doing different things?'

His frown deepened and he crossed his arms over his broad chest. 'I'm not in a relationship with Tia. I told her I wasn't interested in getting back together.'

The room seemed to lurch from under her. 'When?' Her voice shook on the word.

'On New Year's Eve.'

'What? But it looked like—' She paused and swallowed, remembering the piercing pain she'd felt in her chest at the sight of the two of them kissing.

He uncrossed his arms and sat forwards, closer to her. 'I did consider taking her back, but only for a second and only because she was still going to be here when you were primed to jet back to the States.'

She blinked at him, her brain having trouble catching up with what he was saying. 'But you were kissing her,' was what came out when she was finally able to speak.

He shook his head. 'She kissed me. And yes—' he held up his hands '—I kissed her back, but only because she took me by surprise. I realised straight away what a total idiot I'd be to even contemplate getting back with her when I could have you. There was never any contest.'

The room lurched again. 'Really?' She could barely breathe with excitement.

'Yes. Really.'

'But those songs you sent me—'

He raised his eyebrows. 'Yes?'

'I thought you'd written them about Tia.'

He gave her a look that said, *Don't be an idiot*.

'They're the songs I wrote right after Christmas, when things were so good between us. You inspired them. They're about *you*, Flora.'

'But…but…they're love songs.'

'Yes. Exactly.'

She was trembling all over now. 'So you're saying—'

'Yes. I love you.'

He moved towards her and slid his hand against her jaw, cupping her face so she had to look at him.

'I don't just want to be your friend, Flora. I want to have a proper relationship with you. I know it's all happened so fast, but I've never felt so sure of anything in my life.'

'Wow.' She swallowed hard, her head spinning. 'I want us to be more than friends too. I think I have since the moment I saw you stroll into the Pump Room.'

'Looking like a vagrant,' he teased.

Heat rose to her face. 'Yes, well, I'm not exactly proud of myself for the way I acted then.' She gave him a beseeching smile. 'But we all have our faults, right?'

He smiled. 'Absolutely. I know I do. I don't know what I was thinking, expecting you to just give up everything you'd worked so hard for to be with me.' He shook his head. 'I was being totally selfish. I'm the one that should be flexible because it doesn't matter to me where we live. I can write and rehearse and record music anywhere. Technology makes it easy to do that now. And I can easily jump on a plane to perform somewhere when I need to.'

'You'd really do that to be with me?'

'Like a shot.' He stroked his thumb against her cheek and she felt the affection in it right down to her toes.

'If you want I'll move to New York. Whatever it takes to be with you.'

Heart racing with excitement, she gave him a wide, tearful smile. 'Actually, I came over here to tell you I've decided I'm going to set up my own business. Probably here in Bath to begin with. So I'm going to hand in my notice at my job in New York.'

He matched her smile with one of his own. 'Well, that's perfect, because I'm going to need someone to take care of my brand. Someone who really understands me.'

She blinked at him. 'You mean me?'

He shrugged. 'Sure, why not? I can't think of anyone whose hands I'd be safer in. I know you'd do everything in your power to make sure everything is perfect.'

'So what you're saying is that my perfectionist tendencies might actually be quite useful?' she teased, with tears pooling in her eyes.

'Yes, in this case, they really will be.'

'Well, it's nice to hear you finally admit it,' she said, grinning like a fool.

'Hmm,' he growled, pulling her in for a kiss and not letting her go until she was breathless and dizzy from it.

'You really love me?' she asked, not wanting to believe it until he'd confirmed it for her.

'Yes. I love you,' he said forcefully. 'You've brought me back from the darkest place I've ever known and made me want to live again. Really live.'

'Me too,' she whispered, her throat clogged with tears. She really meant it too. She'd been at her lowest ebb when she'd first met him, but now she could see a bright and shiny future ahead.

With him.

The man who had showed her that life was really worth living and that she deserved to be put first.

The man she loved and who loved her back.

EPILOGUE

One year later

THEY SAT IN front of a roaring fire with the Christmas lights twinkling on the large Douglas fir in the corner of the room and opened the presents they'd bought for each other: her and Alex, her mother and father, and Violet and Evan, plus the good-sized bump in Violet's stomach.

Diana lifted up the framed photo of Flora and Alex that they'd given her, which showed the two of them with their arms slung around each other and broad smiles on their faces, standing in front of the new sign to Flora's marketing business in Bath, and gave a squeal of delight.

'I'm so proud of you, my clever girl,' she said with real happiness in her voice. 'This will be given pride of place on top of the piano,' she added, already getting up to place it there reverently.

'This is for the both of you,' Alex said, handing the present he'd brought for Flora's parents over to her father.

Francis opened it and lifted it up to show his wife with a look of pleasure on his face. 'Look, Diana, a signed copy of our daughter's famous boyfriend's chart-topping album,' he said with a grin.

'Ooh, how lovely!' she said, coming over to give Alex a tight hug. 'We're so proud of you too,' she murmured. 'We'll listen to that whilst we eat our supper, but perhaps you could play the piano now and we'll have a bit of a sing-song?'

'Sure, I'd love to play,' Alex said. 'I just need to do something upstairs first.' He turned to Flora and gave her one of his disarming smiles. 'I'm going to need you for this,' he said.

'Oh, yeah?' Violet drawled, giggling and waggling her eyebrows at them.

'Excuse us,' Flora said, getting up to follow him out of the room, heat rising to her cheeks as she wondered what he had in mind.

Whatever he wanted would be fine by her though.

As they ascended the stairs she wondered again, as she had every now and again over the last year, whether her best friend had meant this to happen all along—for her and Alex to get together. Not that it mattered either way. She felt sure Amy would be pleased for them if she was able to look down from where she was and see how happy they were.

At the top of the stairs Alex stopped under the door frame of the guest room he'd stayed in the previous year, the room they'd first made love in. He pointed out the sprig of mistletoe that hung there once again.

'It looks like someone's been playing Cupid again,' he said with a grin.

'So it does,' she replied, walking into his arms and giving him a long and very satisfying kiss.

'Isn't it bad luck not to ask the person you love to marry you under the mistletoe?' he murmured against her lips. Before she could answer, or even draw in a startled breath, he dropped to one knee and pulled out a small velvet box from the pocket of his trousers and looked up at her.

'Flora, my muse, my lover, my friend—will you marry me?'

She stared at him, then at the beautiful diamond ring he showed her as he flipped open the box.

'Yes,' she whispered, her throat tight with exhilaration. 'Nothing would make me happier than being married to you.'

He stood up and took the ring out of the box, sliding it onto her finger with trembling hands.

'You bring the music, Flora Morgan, and I love you for it,' he said, leaning in to place the lightest of kisses onto her lips, sending her head spinning with pure joy. 'Now let's go celebrate by doing what everyone thinks we really came up here to do,' he said with a wink and a teasing smile. And as Flora giggled with happiness he guided her gently back into the room and shut the door firmly behind them.

* * * * *

CHRISTMAS MAGIC IN HEATHERDALE

ABIGAIL GORDON

For Robert Bonar,
a good friend and the kindest of men.

CHAPTER ONE

EMPLOYED AS A paediatric consultant at Heatherdale Children's Hospital, Ryan Ferguson was used to the demands of the job, but today had been in a class of its own. Relieved to finally be away from work he pulled up outside the elegant town house that was home to him and his two small daughters.

Rhianna and Martha would be fast asleep at this late hour, but he was grateful that they would have been tucked up for the night by Mollie, his kindly house-keeper, who in spite of the time would have a meal waiting for him.

Ryan's work centred mainly on children with neu-rological illnesses and injuries and his dedication to his calling was an accepted fact by all who knew him. His intention to bring up his children as a single father was more of a surprise, as there were many women who would be only too willing to fill the gap in his life.

Today's non-stop problems had been serious and in some cases rare, with almost a certainty that the dreaded meningitis would be lurking somewhere amongst his young patients and the battle to overthrow it would begin.

With the workload as heavy as it was, it was becoming obvious that they needed another registrar on the neuro unit to assist him and Julian Tindall, his second-in-command.

A rare shortage of nursing staff due to a bug that had been going round hadn't helped, and as he'd performed his daily miracles the hours had galloped past. Now he was ready to put the day's stresses to the back of his mind and enjoy the warmth and peace of his home for a few hours. Home was in the delightful small spa town of Heatherdale, tucked away amongst the rugged peaks and smooth green dales of the countryside, with Manchester being the nearest big city.

The moment he was out of the car and had collected his briefcase from the back seat he moved swiftly towards where warmth and hot food would be waiting for him, casting a brief glance in the direction of the property next to it as he did so, and his step slowed.

A town house like his own, it had been empty for years and he was amazed to see a car parked outside and a flicker of light coming from inside, as if from a torch or a candle. He frowned. He doubted it was thieves, as there would be nothing in there to steal. Could be squatters, though, and the thought was not appealing.

When his housekeeper opened the door to him she couldn't wait to tell him the latest neighbourhood news. When she'd returned from picking the children up from school there had been the car parked outside, and shortly afterwards a bed had been delivered from a nearby furniture store.

'Wow!' he exclaimed as he closed the door behind him. 'Surely they've had it cleaned first? It must be filthy after being empty for so many years. The amount of lighting inside has to mean that they've not had the electricity switched on and are using candles or a torch. It seems an odd state of affairs. Once I've changed into something less formal, I'll do the neighbourly thing and go and introduce myself, ask if there is anything I can assist them with.'

When he knocked on the door of the run-down house that was a blight in the crescent of much-admired Victorian town houses there was no sound for a moment. Then the door swung open slowly and his jaw dropped at the sight of a slender stranger with long dark hair that swung gently against her shoulders and a face blotched with weeping.

'They haven't been,' she cried desperately as he was on the point of introducing himself. 'The cleaners haven't been and the place is full of spiders' webs and the dust of years. I will have to find a hotel for the night.'

'Are you alone here?' he asked carefully. 'I'm Ryan Ferguson, and my family and I are your new neighbours.' He held out his hand in greeting. The tearful stranger shook it limply but didn't volunteer any information about herself. She seemed extremely distracted, which was no wonder considering the situation.

He got the impression that she wanted him gone but he could hardly go back to his own comfortable home and leave her in such a state.

'Can you recommend a hotel not too far away?' she asked. 'I just can't spend the night in here. I've had a bed delivered but haven't taken the wrappings off it so it should come to no harm for the present.'

Ryan was still standing in the doorway and would have liked to see just what a mess the inside of the house was in, but he could hardly go barging in without an invite.

'You must be exhausted. I'll take you to a hotel if you would like to lock up. My car is parked out front like yours, so I will lead the way and you can follow.'

'Thank you,' she said unsteadily. 'I do apologise for breaking into your evening. I shall be onto the cleaners first thing in the morning.'

'I'm only too pleased to be of assistance,' he told her. 'If you will just give me a moment, I'll go and get my car keys.'

When Mollie opened the door to him again he explained, 'This is our new neighbour, Mollie. I'm taking her to a hotel as the house isn't quite ready to move into.'

'Oh, you poor dear,' Mollie said, observing the strange woman standing hesitantly at the kerb edge. 'What a horrible thing to happen, and on a cold, dark night like this.' She turned to Ryan. 'I'm just about to dish up your meal before I go home for the day. There's plenty to spare, so can we not offer the young lady some hospitality?'

'Yes, of course, by all means,' he said, forgetting his weariness for a moment.

Their new neighbour shrank back.

'I couldn't possibly intrude into your evening any more than I am doing,' she said.

Ignoring her reluctance, Ryan insisted. 'You are most welcome. How long is it since you last had something to eat?'

'I can't remember.'

'If that's the case, you need food now.' He stepped back to let her past him to where Mollie was hovering near the kitchen door. 'If you want to wash your hands you'll find anything you need in the cloakroom at the end of the hall. Mollie will have the food on the table when you're done.'

'Thank you,' she croaked meekly, and disappeared.

Mollie was ready to go by the time his unexpected guest had removed the day's surface grime and once they were alone silence descended in what was a tastefully furnished dining room.

When they'd finished eating Ryan said, 'There's a fire in the sitting room. Make yourself comfortable while I make coffee.'

She nodded and said uncomfortably, 'The food was lovely. Thank you so much.'

He was observing her gravely. 'Are you going to tell me who you are? The house next door has been unoccupied for many years so it was a surprise to find signs of life there when I came home. Are you actually planning to live there?'

'Er, yes,' she told him hesitantly. 'My name is Melissa Redmond. The house was left to me by my grandmother when she died some years ago. I've had no interest in living out here in the backwoods until a short time ago when my circumstances changed dramatically.

'I'd arranged for a firm of cleaners to come in and make it liveable, and for the power to be connected, but when I got here late this afternoon nothing had been done and I was frantic.'

'Yes, I can understand that,' Ryan said slowly. Melissa didn't look quite as bedraggled in the warm glow of the lamps in his sitting room as she had when she'd opened the door of the mausoleum next door. The colour had returned to her cheeks and she seemed a lot calmer. His curiosity about his new neighbour had definitely been piqued. He wanted to know more.

When he came back with the coffee cups she was asleep, overcome by the comforting warmth of the fire. So it looked as if he wasn't going to find out any more about her for now.

An hour passed and Melissa hadn't stirred out of the deep sleep of exhaustion that had claimed her. There was no way she could be allowed to go back to the chill of the house that had been empty for so long, neither did Ryan want to rouse her to go to a hotel at that hour. Instead, he went and found a soft fleece, laid it gently over her, and went up to bed with the intention of checking on her at regular intervals. That turned out to be a wise precaution as the first time he went downstairs, she was awake and about to disappear through the front door.

'Melissa, wait!' he cried. 'You can't stay in that place tonight. I have a spare room that is always kept ready for visitors. I insist you stay in it. I won't be able to sleep knowing that you're not somewhere safe, *and* I've had a very exhausting day that I need to recover from before the next one is upon me.'

'My nightwear is in my case next door,' she protested faintly.

'I'll find you some,' he offered. Was he going insane to let a strange woman wear something that had belonged to Beth?

He pointed to a gracious curved staircase and said, 'If you would like to go up, I'll show you to the guest room. While you are settling in there I'll find something for you to wear.'

Ryan dug out one of Beth's plain cotton nightshirts to lend to Melissa. He avoided taking out any of the prettier nightgowns that Beth had favoured.

Melissa took it from him with a subdued smile and said with tears threatening, 'I hope that one day I'll be able to repay your kindness, Ryan.'

He smiled. 'Don't concern yourself about that. Tomorrow is another day and it just has to be better than this one has been for you.'

With that brief word of comfort he left her and went to a room across the landing. Closing the door behind him, he looked down at his sleeping daughters and wondered just what Rhianna and Martha would think when they saw there was a visitor for breakfast.

As she lay sleeplessly under the covers of the bed in the spare room, Melissa's thoughts were in overdrive. The future that had looked so bleak seemed slightly less so because of the kindness of a stranger who had taken her in, fed her, and offered her a bed for the night.

So much for keeping a low profile in her new surroundings! The hurts she had suffered over recent months had made her long for privacy, for somewhere to hide. But her meeting with a man with the golden fairness of a Viking and eyes as blue as a summer sky had put an end to those sorts of plans.

It seemed Ryan had children who no doubt were fast asleep, and was in sole charge of them, so where was their mother? Wherever it might be, it was not her business. She had to fix her thoughts on tomorrow and the cleaners, the electricity people, and accepting the delivery of her few remaining belongings some time during the day. With those thoughts in mind she drifted into an uneasy sleep.

The sound of children's voices on the landing mingling with her host's deeper tones brought Melissa into instant wakefulness in the darkness of a winter morning. She dressed quickly in yesterday's clothes and prepared to go down to where she could hear the sounds of breakfast-time coming from the kitchen.

Pausing in the doorway, she saw that Ryan was at

ABIGAIL GORDON

15

the grill, keeping an eye on sizzling bacon, and two little girls were seated at the table with bowls of cereal in front of them, observing her with wide eyes of surprise as she said, 'Thank you so much for last night. I feel a different person this morning after the meal and the rest. I'm off to find out what happened to the cleaners and the electricity services.'

He smiled across at her. 'Not before you've eaten. You have no facilities for preparing food next door, so take a seat.'

Rhianna, at seven years old and the elder of his two young daughters, was not a shy child, and burst out, 'Who is this lady, Daddy? She wasn't here when we went to bed.'

'No, she wasn't,' Martha, two years younger, chirped beside her. At that point Ryan took charge of the conversation.

'Her name is Melissa and she's going to live next door to us,' he explained. 'Melissa, these are my daughters, Rhianna and Martha.'

'She can't!' Rhianna protested.

'Why not?' he asked.

'It's haunted!'

'No way,' he said laughingly as he pulled out a chair for Melissa to be seated, as if there had been no hesitation in joining them on her part. 'There aren't any ghosts in Heatherdale, I promise you that, Rhianna. Now, who would like a bacon roll?'

'Me!' the children both cried.

With the day ahead momentarily forgotten, Melissa smiled as the memory surfaced of how, when she'd been at junior school, she and her friends used to pass a creepy-looking empty house on the way there. They had been convinced that there was a human hand on the inside window ledge. It had only been when one of their fathers had gone to investigate that it had been discovered that the 'hand' had been a pink plastic glove. There had been much disappointment amongst the children.

She had done as Ryan requested and seated herself opposite him. As she smiled across at his children she saw that they both had the same golden fairness as their father, but their eyes were different—big and brown and fixed on her.

Making her second contribution to the occasion, Martha asked, 'Are you some children's mummy? We haven't got one any more. Ours was hurt by a tree.'

Ryan had just put cereal and a bacon sandwich in front of Melissa and was about to join them at the table. He stilled, and she saw dismay in his expression.

'Just get on with your breakfast, Martha,' he said gravely, 'and no more questions.'

'It's all right,' Melissa told him. 'I don't mind. They are delightful.' She turned to his small daughter.

'No, Martha, I'm not a mummy, but I do love children. My job is all about making them well when they are sick.'

Their interest was waning to find that she didn't fit their requirements, but not their father's. The stranger at their table was full of surprises. What kind of a job was it that she'd referred to?

Bringing his mind back to their morning routine on school days, when the children had finished eating he told them to go and put their school uniforms on and have their satchels ready for when Mollie came to take them to school.

'Will Melissa be here when we come home?' Rhianna asked.

She answered for Ryan. 'I'm afraid not, Rhianna. My house needs cleaning and sorting. But once that's done everything will be fine and you can come to see me whenever you like.'

Rhianna seemed happy with that answer and she and Martha hopped off to get ready for school.

'Your daughters are adorable, Ryan,' she said with a warm smile.

'They're the light of my life. A life that would not be easy if Mollie wasn't around,' Ryan replied. 'She's a good friend as well as my housekeeper. I have a very demanding job but it's totally rewarding and somehow I manage to give it my best, while organising things at this end to make sure that Rhianna and Martha are happy, though the result is not always how I want it to be. Still, I mustn't delay you. We both have busy days ahead of us.'

She couldn't have agreed more. As she looked around her at his delightful home, the gloom of yesterday came back. Dreading what the day would hold for her, she wished Ryan a stilted goodbye and went to ring the cleaning firm and the electricity company.

As Melissa waited for the cleaners to arrive, her mind drifted back over her recent past. She recalled how only yesterday, stony-faced behind the wheel of her car, she had driven away from the house that had always been her home in a select area of a Cheshire green belt without looking back.

The doors had been locked, the windows shut fast, and as a last knife thrust she'd put flowers in the hall-way, a huge bunch of them that would be the first thing that the new owners saw when they arrived to take over their recently acquired property.

The purchase had been completed early that morn-ing, the money was already in her bank account, but the thought of it brought no joy. It would be a matter of here today and gone tomorrow.

'I'm sorry, sweetheart,' her father had said as the last few moments of his life had ebbed away. 'So sorry to be going like this before I'd sorted things.'

'You have nothing to be sorry for,' she'd told him gently, thinking that he must be delirious. 'You have always been there for me, making me laugh, indulg-ing me, keeping me safe, and David will do the same. I know he will.'

He'd tried to speak again but the mists had been closing in and the nurse at the other side of the bed had said a few seconds later, 'He's gone, Melissa. His injuries were too severe for him to overcome. There will be no more pain for your father.'

Max Redmond had been a charmer, and a wealthy one at that. Melissa had lost her mother to heart failure when she had been eleven and Max had given her everything she could possibly have wanted to make up for the loss. He'd taken her on fantastic holidays, bought her the kind of car that most young people could only dream of when she had been old enough to drive, and had given her a generous allowance that had been more than some families had had to feed their children and pay the mortgage.

The two of them had lived in a smart detached house amongst the rich and famous, not far from the city, and when she'd gone to fulfil a dream and enrolled as a medical student, it had been at a university in nearby Manchester so that her father wouldn't be lonely, although it hadn't seemed likely.

Max had never remarried, but he'd made lots of women friends in the circles in which he'd moved, where wining and dining was the order of the day. However, he had always cancelled any arrangements he'd made if his daughter had been free to socialise with him.

That had been until she'd got engaged to David Lowson, the son of one of her father's women friends. After that, he'd watched benignly as most of Melissa's time away from her career had been taken up with the delights of being in love.

She'd qualified as a doctor in paediatrics in the summer, and on receiving her degree had been employed at a nearby hospital. Life had been good in every way,

with all of it centred around the big city that she knew
so well and would never have wanted to leave, until her
father had walked in front of a speeding car on a road
not far from where they lived after a lively lunch in a
nearby hotel, and had died from his injuries.

Since then Melissa had experienced all of life's
worst emotions: grief at the sudden tragic loss of the
man who had loved her so much; sick horror to discover
that his last words to her had been referring to a huge
mountain of gambling debts that he had accumulated.

There had also been the aching hurt of betrayal from
an engagement that had fizzled out when her fiancé had
discovered that she was no longer the wealthy heiress
that his mother had urged him to propose to, and was
going to be poorer than a church mouse by the time
she'd sorted out Max's frightening legacy.

Everything Melissa could lay her hands on had been
sold, and most of her salary each month had gone into
the bottomless pit, with the sale of the house as the
final heartbreaking humiliation.

During the time that the sale had been going
through, those who knew her had seen little of her.
Grief stricken and panicked about the future, Melissa
had chosen to hide away from her friends.

Her father had given no inkling that he'd had money
problems. Always a man about town, as generous host
to all his friends, he hadn't been able to admit to his
failings, and she now understood fully his weak apology as he'd lain dying.

Incredibly, there'd been no life insurance to fall back

on, or other safeguards that were usually in place regarding the death of a person, but thankfully the money
from the sale of the house would clear the last of the
debts.

She supposed it would have been sensible to rent
herself a small apartment in Manchester and bring the
shattered remnants of her life together again somehow.
But with her father now resting with her mother in a
nearby cemetery, and an ex-fiancé who had cast her
aside living not far away, she had been intent on moving to some place where she wasn't known.

Having left the hospital where she'd been employed,
she'd headed for the small market town of Heatherdale,
where her paternal grandmother had lived and where
her house, which had been empty for a long time, was
there for her if she wanted it.

The old lady had willed it to her and, though grateful for the thought, it was the last place she would ever
have contemplated moving to in the past, but the present was proving to be a different matter. Alone and
lost, she'd needed somewhere to hide from the pity-
ing looks she'd received from her father's friends and
acquaintances when the news had got around that she
was penniless. She'd wanted somewhere to avoid the
mocking smiles of those who had witnessed the plight
of the 'golden girl' and thought it would do her good
to see how the other half lived. But the thing that had
hurt most had been the speed with which her ex had
found another woman to replace her.

She had found the keys to her grandmother's house

in a chest of drawers in her father's bedroom, and as she'd gazed down at the heavy ornate bunch of them it had been as if a means of escape was being offered to her.

There had been receipts with them for payments that her father had made to the local authorities on her behalf over the years to comply with the law regarding the ownership of unoccupied housing, and she'd decided that the paperwork and the keys were heaven sent.

She'd felt as if she never wanted to see the city that she'd loved so much, with its familiar shops, smart restaurants and green parks, ever again. She'd decided to make a fresh start in a place that she'd never cared for much on the rare occasions she'd been there.

With no job, no money, and no family, she had to hope that she could find a future for herself in Heatherdale. First she had to get the house straight. Next on her agenda was finding a job. The obvious choice would be its famous hospital, but if there were no vacancies there for a newly qualified paediatrician then she'd simply have to find something to tide her over.

The internet had come up with the name and address of a firm of domestic cleaners in the Heatherdale area and she'd hired them to give the house a thorough cleaning from top to bottom before she arrived.

Apart from ordering a bed to be delivered later in the day, when she would be there to accept it, the rest of her belongings would arrive the following afternoon, when she was satisfied that the house was ready to take delivery of them.

It wasn't the best time of year to be moving into a strange house in a strange place, she'd thought achingly as the miles had flashed past. The last leaves of autumn had been scattered at the roadside or hanging limply on trees, and a cold wind had been nipping at her while she'd been taking a last walk around the gardens of what had been her home.

During her early childhood she and her parents had visited her grandmother occasionally, but there hadn't been any real closeness between them because the old lady had disapproved of her son's attitude to life in general. She hadn't liked the way he'd been such a spendthrift, although at that time he hadn't reached retirement and had been making big money in the stock markets.

'When I die I'm leaving the house to the child,' she'd told him. 'There might come a day when she'll need a roof over her head.' As the lights of Heatherdale had appeared on the horizon, Melissa had reflected that the grandmother she'd rarely seen had turned out to be her only friend.

Martha's innocent question about the stranger who had joined them for breakfast was uppermost in Ryan's mind as he drove the short distance to the hospital. It had brought painful memories with it that he only allowed himself to think about when he was alone, but in that moment in the kitchen they had been starkly clear and he'd been extra-loving with the children while they'd waited for Mollie to arrive.

His youngest daughter had described them as being without a mother because theirs had been hurt by a tree. It wouldn't have been the easiest description of her death for Melissa Redmond to understand, but did that matter? She was just a stranger who had joined them for breakfast.

He and Beth had attended the same school in Heatherdale, had both chosen medicine as a career, he in paediatrics and she in midwifery. It had always been there, the love that had blossomed in their late teens and taken them to the altar of a church in the small market town where they lived.

Heatherdale boasted a famous spa that people came from far and wide to take advantage of, and beautiful Victorian architecture built from local stone that he never wearied of. There were spacious parks and elegant shops and restaurants. Everything that he loved was here except for the wife he had adored.

When she'd died he had wanted to die too as life had lost its meaning, but there had been two small children, unhappy and confused because their mother hadn't been there any more, so he'd pulled himself together for their sakes. In the last three years his life had been entirely taken up with his children and the health problems of those belonging to others.

If it meant that he never had time to do his own thing, at least there was the comfort of knowing that his young daughters were safe and happy, and that he was serving a vital purpose in the Heatherdale Children's Hospital where he was a senior paediatric consultant.

He knew that folks found him irritating at times because he never socialised, was always too busy when asked out to dine, even though he had Mollie, who would always take on the role of childminder if needed and who checked out every available woman she met as a possible new wife for him, without actually saying so openly.

As Melissa looked around her house in the cold light of day she was hoping that today would not be quite as horrendous as yesterday. However, every day since she'd lost her father and discovered what he had been involved in had been dreadful.

For the past few weeks she'd felt lost and alone, like some sort of outcast. Ryan's kindness had been a brief relief from what had been a nightmare for her, but at the same time getting involved with anyone at the moment was the last thing she wanted to do. Especially with the man who lived next door.

All she craved for was solitude, somewhere to hide while her hurts healed, but the die was cast. She wasn't going to get the chance to be just a stranger who nodded briefly during her comings and goings job-seeking and then went in and closed the door.

But, as if to balance the scales, there were those two lovely children and it would be a pleasure to babysit them if ever Ryan felt he could trust her.

She'd also contacted the electricity people. She was informed that they were on their way with a new meter and were going to check all the primitive services and appliances in the house while they were there.

They arrived within minutes and as light began to appear in her darkness, in more ways than one, Melissa rolled up her sleeves and looked around her for what had to be her first task of the day. The guy who had just fixed the electricity meter decided it for her by pointing to an ancient but solid-looking gas fire and asking if she'd contacted the gas services yet as both the fire and an ancient cooker were gas powered.

She needed no second telling as having the fire working meant warmth and the cooker hot food, when she'd cleaned the grime off it and had the chance to shop.

The most pressing mission for Ryan, on his arrival at the hospital, was to start the search in earnest for the new registrar for their department.

The procedure with staff vacancies at the hospital was to advertise them internally first, but so far there had been no joy for the two consultants and the vacancy would soon be advertised locally

Today he had two clinics arranged for consultations, plus a slot in Theatre in the late afternoon. With all of that ahead of him he hadn't had time to check on how his new neighbour was coping at her house.

There'd been an electricity van outside and a plumber's vehicle pulling up alongside it as he'd driven past. He decided he owed her one more visit to check she was managing okay then he would step back and let her get on with her life while he got on with his.

The surgery he was committed to in the afternoon was minor compared to some of the operations he performed on unfortunate little ones and hopefully he would be home in time to have a quick word with Melissa before his special time with his children began.

As Ryan was preparing to put in an appearance at his first clinic of the day his assistant, Julian, appeared and commented breezily, 'Still no sign of a saviour in terms of over-booking, I see. Personnel need to pull their finger out and get us another doctor. I've got a list as long as my arm for today and I'm not used to it.'

Julian Tindall, with his dark attractiveness, was every woman's dream man, until they got to know him better!

Inclined to be lazy, but on the ball in an emergency, Julian was a paediatric consultant like himself and could go places if he stopped fooling around with every attractive woman he met and got his act together.

Ryan held the paediatric unit together with the kind of steadfastness that he applied to every aspect of his daily life, and if the nights spent without Beth by his side were long and lonely, only he knew that.

CHAPTER TWO

MELISSA'S SECOND DAY in Heatherdale was progressing and she was beginning to feel calmer. The neglected house was starting to come out of its murky cocoon, though not enough for her to rejoice totally. There was going to be mammoth amount of decorating and refurbishing to be done.

But the electricity was on, the plumber she'd asked to come had switched on the water and checked for leaks, and, joy of joys, the cleaners were hard at work, getting rid of the grime and mustiness of years.

Her clothes and the few belongings she had salvaged from the sale of the Cheshire house had arrived in the late afternoon. They included a couple of carpets, an expensive wardrobe and dressing table, a dining table and two easy chairs, but there was no kitchen equipment, which meant that for the time being she was going to have to manage with a solid-looking but unattractive gas cooker that was so old it would qualify as an antique.

Yet it had lit at the first attempt and as soon as the

cleaners had finished for the day with a promise to come back in the morning, she began to clean it, and was on her knees in front of it when a knock came on the door. She raised herself slowly upright.

With hair held back with a shoelace and dressed in an old pair of jeans and a much-washed jumper that the Cheshire set would never associate her with, she went slowly to answer the knock. He was there again, the Viking from next door, observing her with a reluctant sort of neighbourliness.

'I've called to see how you've fared today,' he said. 'I see that you've got lighting, but have you got heat and water?'

'Yes,' she replied, stepping back reluctantly for him to enter.

'I have light, and heat in the form of an old gas fire. A plumber has been to turn on the water. The cleaners have removed most of the dust and grime and are coming back in the morning to finish the job.'

'And I see that your belongings have arrived,' he said easily, as if she now had a house full of furniture instead of a few oddments. Unable to resist, he went on to ask, 'Do you have family who will be coming to join you?'

'No. Nothing like that,' she said in a low voice, without meeting his glance. She wished that he would go and leave her in peace. She'd seen the inside of his house and it was delightful, with décor and furniture that was just right for the age and design of the property, all obviously chosen with great care.

No doubt he was thinking that hers was going to lower the tone of the neighbourhood and for the first time since she'd arrived in Heatherdale the grim pride and determination that had helped her to stagger through recent months surfaced.

As if he sensed that she wanted him gone, Ryan moved towards the door but paused with his hand on the handle and said, 'I'm sure that you will like it here once you have made the house look how you want it to be.' He would have to be blind not to realise that she wasn't happy about coming to live in Heatherdale.

He almost asked if she would like to eat with them again but sensed the same reluctance as the night before. He bade her goodbye and, determined to put Melissa Redmond to the back of his mind, he went to join his daughters and the faithful Mollie, without whom he would be harassed full time.

'I saw you call at the house next door,' she said when he appeared. 'Is she all right? It has been all systems go in there today.'

'Yes, it would seem so,' he told her. 'I felt she was relieved that I didn't linger. I get a distinct feeling that Melissa Redmond wants to be left alone.'

'Give her time,' she said. 'The lass looked totally traumatised when we saw her last night. Something isn't right in her life. It stands out a mile, or she wouldn't have come here to live in a house that hasn't been touched for years. Don't forget the couple of times that you've seen her she won't have been at her best.'

'Yes, I suppose you're right,' he said absently, as

Rhianna and Martha came running down the stairs at that moment, and as he hugged them to him the stranger next door was forgotten in the pleasure of the moment.

When Ryan had gone, Melissa sank down onto the bottom step of the stairs. The cooker and its requirements temporarily forgotten, she gazed into space.

She wondered what Ryan did for a living. When she'd joined them for breakfast it had been plain to see that he was a loving father in the absence of a mother who wasn't around any more, yet he would have to earn a living somehow or other.

There was an air of authority about him that was noticeable and, much as she was not eager to be involved in the lives of those around her, she couldn't help wondering about him.

Still, there were more important priorities than getting to know the neighbours in this town, which would fit in a corner of Manchester. Such as turning her grandmother's house into a home and finding a job. Dared she intrude on the man next door once again by asking him for information about the famous hospital that she would love to be part of, and the local job centre in that order, so that tomorrow she would have a head start on the employment scene? No sooner had the thought occurred to her than she was acting on it.

Changing her working clothes for a stylish cashmere top, which belonged to happier days, and skinny jeans, Melissa was pressing his doorbell seconds later. When the door opened and he was framed there, looking not the least surprised, she said awkwardly, 'I wondered if you might be able to tell me anything about Heatherdale Hospital? Also, can you let me know where the job centre is? I'm going to go looking for employment tomorrow.'

'In that case, hadn't you better come in?'

She nodded awkwardly and stepped past him into the hall with its beautiful staircase, aware from the surprise in his glance that it was the first time he had seen her looking even the least bit attractive. As she waited for him to say something she felt herself reddening.

'Are you aware that Heatherdale Hospital is for children only?' he asked, breaking into the moment. 'If you feel that you need some sort of hospital treatment, you will have to go to Manchester.'

She was smiling. 'I need the information about the hospital because I would just die for the chance to work there.'

'Doing what?' he asked, with raised brows.

'I've got a degree in paediatrics. When I qualified in the summer I was offered a position at a big Manchester hospital and loved it, but that came to an end when my life fell apart. I had to resign because I intended to leave the area due to my family circumstances.'

So that was what she'd meant when she'd said she had a job making sick children well again. At the time Ryan had wondered if she was employed by some sort of charity, but it seemed she was much more hands on than that, and incredibly he and Julian needed some-one like her. Melissa Redmond might be heaven sent!

Obviously he'd never seen her in action. The offer he was going to make her at this moment would be a temporary one until he had her measure, and aware that they were still standing in the hall as she had meant it to be just a brief call on her part, he said, 'Come through to the sitting room, while I make *my* contri-bution to this night of surprises.'

When they were seated with her eyes fixed on him questioningly he said, 'How would you like to work with me at Heatherdale Children's Hospital?'

'What?' she gasped. 'I don't understand.'

'I'm the paediatric consultant for the neurology wards there and my assistant and I need another reg-istrar to help with the workload. It would be on pro-bationary terms at first but with the opportunity of permanency for the right person. What do you say? Do you want to give it a try?'

'Of course I do!' she breathed, her eyes shining. 'I had no idea that was what you did for a living.'

'I don't mean to pry, Melissa, but can you tell me something about what brought you to Heatherdale? I need to know if it would have any effect on your work and position at the hospital.'

She nodded mutely, took a deep breath. 'My father died six months ago as a result of a road accident when he'd had quite a lot of alcohol. From having a life of luxury and pampering I became penniless because, unbeknown to me, he'd accumulated huge gambling debts over the last couple of years.

'I was engaged to be married at the time and fully expected that my future husband would be there to support me as I dealt with bailiffs and demands for payment from those that my father owed money to, but I was mistaken.

'My fiancé couldn't break off the engagement fast enough, and once I'd paid all my father's debts, which meant selling the fabulous house we'd lived in, all I could think of was leaving the area and finding a bolt hole, somewhere to lick my wounds. The only answer to that was my grandmother's house, which is a far cry from the property I'd lived in before but is mine and isn't tainted. So there you have it, a sorry story worthy of a reality TV show.'

'Thanks for telling me,' Ryan said. 'We all have our nightmares to face at one time or another and you have certainly faced up to yours. Can you come to the hospital some time tomorrow and I'll show you round and introduce you to people, including Personnel, who will need you to fill out endless forms.'

'Yes, of course,' she breathed. 'Thank you for giving me the opportunity to get back into paediatrics. I love working with children and hope to have some of my own one day.'

He nodded as the memory of Rhianna and Martha's approval of their breakfast guest resurfaced. The stranger who had come to Heatherdale in the dark of a winter night would make some child a loving mother one day in every sense of the word, he imagined, just as Beth had been to their children.

'What time do you want me to come to the hospital?' she asked.

'Some time in the afternoon when my clinics are over and I'm not in Theatre, around three—unless you have something else planned at that time?'

'No, I haven't,' she told him firmly.

She'd intended spending the afternoon looking for a washing machine that would fit in with her budget but that could wait, everything could wait. He was offering her the chance to be back where she wanted to be, and if Ryan Ferguson was willing to take a chance on her she was not going to disappoint him.

Later that night, for the first time in months sleep came like a healing balm.

A wintry sun was shining overhead as Melissa drove to the famous children's hospital the next afternoon, and although her mind was full of what lay ahead she couldn't help but notice the beautiful architecture of some of the buildings she was passing.

Maybe the market town of Heatherdale wasn't going to be as dreary as she had expected it to be. Life was beginning to feel worth living again.

Walking away from her parked car, she looked around her. The hospital was another apparently ageless building, built from the beautiful local stone that seemed to be everywhere she looked. She hoped that its interior would not lack the trappings of the latest in modern medicine for the sake of its young patients.

There was no cause to be concerned about that. The inside was bright, cheerful and immaculate, with sunshine colours on the walls and lots of pictures of things that children would like.

As she followed the directions to the neuro wards Melissa's heart was beating faster. She was on home ground, within reach of being back on the job she loved once again.

She found Ryan at the bedside of a small girl, who had been brought in by an ambulance with sirens wailing, with what might be meningitis. It was a road he'd been down more times than he could count and it was never any less horrendous to have to tell a family that one of their little ones had succumbed to the dreadful illness.

There was a fellow doctor standing beside him, but his presence barely registered. Melissa's glance was fixed on the man who in a short space of time had brought some zest into her life. Not only had Ryan taken her in out of the cold that first night but he was going to be the means of finding her employment in the very place where she wanted to be.

He glanced up then, saw her standing in the doorway, and sent his assistant over to suggest that she join them as an observer of the emergency. With her adrenaline quickening, she was beside him in a flash.

'It seemed that the child had become very drowsy during the lunch hour. It had been then that her parents had noticed the tell-tale rash and it had become panic stations. While the ambulance had been speeding to the hospital the little girl had lapsed into unconsciousness.'

Ryan turned to the anxious couple at the other side of the bed and began to explain what would happen to their daughter next—blood tests and a lumbar puncture to test for bacterial meningitis.

When the parents and their sick little one had been taken with all speed for the tests, Ryan's colleague asked. 'So, are you going to introduce me, Ryan?'

'Yes, of course,' he said. 'Julian, meet my new neighbour, Melissa Redmond, recently employed in paediatrics in the Manchester area and now about to join us here on a probationary basis with a view to a permanent position. Melissa, this is Julian Tindall.'

Ryan noticed that she was looking a different person altogether today, dressed in smart clothes and with her hair and make-up perfect. She was quite beautiful in a restrained sort of way.

As Melissa shook hands with Julian she was aware of him sizing her up and immediately had him pegged as an attractive, dark-eyed flirt.

'So when do you want to start?' Ryan asked, 'To-morrow perhaps?'

'Er, yes, if that's all right with you.'

'Certainly, if you're available,' he replied.

She had never felt more 'available' in her life. He knew she was out on a limb here in Heatherdale, that apart from getting her house in order there was no one who cared a jot about her. Why wait to begin this job of a lifetime?

Melissa wished that there was someone to share her good news with, but the days were gone when she'd had a loving father, an attentive fiancé, and lots of friends to communicate with.

Her glance rested briefly on the house next door where she'd been welcomed into the home of a stranger and had been reluctant to accept his hospitality on a dark and lonely night. Ryan Ferguson must have thought her some sort of ungracious oddball.

The lights were on, which was not surprising as his children would be home from school by now and being looked after by his housekeeper. Melissa wondered again what had happened to their mother.

Whatever it was, the two of them had seemed happy enough until they'd discovered she was coming to live next door. Then had come the protest about it being haunted and she'd tried not to smile at their childish imaginings.

As afternoon turned into evening she saw there was no car outside so obviously Ryan wasn't home yet, and as she began to prepare a snack sort of meal, which was becoming the norm since life had become so drab and disillusioning, she hugged herself at the thought of tomorrow.

Ryan had phoned home to tell Mollie he would be late due to a seriously ill child with bacterial meningitis that he wanted to try to get stabilised before he left her in the care of the night staff.

It wasn't the first time he'd been late home because of his job and it wouldn't be the last, and on such occasions he was very grateful for Mollie's presence in their lives. She lived alone just down the road from them, having lost her husband from heart failure some years previously and was happy to be of use to him and his children to such an extent.

The girls were in bed by the time he arrived and after a brief chat and a cuddle he left them sleepy and contented to go downstairs to have the meal that Mollie had kept warm for him.

She wished that his life was less stressful, but knew it had been his choice to parent single-handedly after his wife's death. She admired him for the way he cared for his children. Yet she couldn't help wishing that someone would come along who would make Ryan realise what he was missing, that Beth would not have wanted him to be alone for the rest of his life, always involved with work or family when it came to the social life of the town and its hospital.

'I've found a new registrar to lighten our load at the hospital,' he told her as she placed the food in front of him.

'That's good!' she exclaimed. 'Another man, is it?'

'No, it's a woman. Actually, someone you know.'

'That I know?'

'Yes, it's Melissa from next door. She has a degree

in paediatrics and she joins us tomorrow. What do you think of that?'

'I'm amazed, but what a good thing for both of you that she has found employment so quickly and that your stresses will be lighter. It's as if her coming to live in Heatherdale was meant to be.'

Ryan smiled. 'Don't get too carried away, Mollie. I only found out about her qualifications last night and offered her the job on condition that she fits the bill, so it will be probationary to begin with.'

'Yes, of course,' Mollie agreed, thankful that something was going right for him for once.

The blood tests and lumbar puncture had shown that little Georgia had indeed got bacterial meningitis and he'd explained to her distraught parents that she was going to be given large doses of antibiotics that he'd arranged for her to have intravenously in the hope of preventing the dreaded illness increasing its hold on her.

When he'd eventually left the hospital it had been with the determination to ring the ward later for a report on her progress as the next few hours would be crucial.

The answer was what he'd hoped for when he did. His small patient was regaining consciousness and her horrendously high temperature was coming down, so with Mollie having returned home and Rhianna and Martha asleep, Ryan decided to spend the rest of the evening with a medical journal that had been languishing on the back seat of his car for a few days.

When he went out to get it he saw that the house next door was in darkness and he observed it thoughtfully. What was the bet that Melissa was having an early night so that she would be bright-eyed and bushy-tailed tomorrow?

He supposed it could be said that it hadn't been a good idea to offer her a job working with him most of the time, but discovering that she was in paediatrics had been too good a chance to miss in his busy working life. He went back into the house in a thoughtful mood and with the feeling that maybe he needed to cool it where she was concerned.

It was an eight o'clock start for day staff on the wards and the next morning Melissa watched as Ryan kissed his children goodbye with Mollie in attendance, and drove off.

As the taillights of his car disappeared she followed him at a distance, having no wish to be on the last minute on her first day at the hospital.

Today could or could not be the beginning of a new life. A life on a lower level than before maybe, when the envious had called her 'golden girl', but at least she would have some dignity, wouldn't be an object of pity or sly smirks.

In the short time that she'd been in the house she had been aware that something strange was happening. The children next door had said it was haunted and she wasn't going to go along with *that*, but one thing she did feel was that the grandmother she had never really known was somewhere near, content that the one person she had always wanted to live in her house had arrived.

Miserable and lonely she may be, but she was there in the house that had been bequeathed to her all those years ago because the old lady had foreseen what the future might hold for her pleasure-loving son's child. Today Melissa was about to take the first step towards becoming a working member of the community.

CHAPTER THREE

RYAN HAD SEEN Melissa arrive from the window of his office, which overlooked the car park. She was so different from the woman he had been confronted with just a couple of nights ago, it was unbelievable. Her hair, her clothes, the newfound calm had altered her totally.

She was still the stranger who had erupted into his life from nowhere but she was no longer nondescript. Yesterday, when she'd come to the hospital to have a look round and meet Julian and any of the nurses who were present, he'd thought that she was beautiful and still did. Not in a voluptuous sort of way but fine-boned and slender.

Still, there was the promise he had made to himself to cool it with regard to Melissa Redmond. The absence of a woman in his life in the true sense meant that never again would there be the agony of loss such as he'd suffered when he'd lost Beth.

With that in mind he wished Melissa a cool good

morning when they met at the entrance to the wards and suggested that she find herself a white hospital coat.

'I've brought one with me from my last job,' she told him, and wondered who had rubbed Ryan up the wrong way so early in the day.

It wasn't likely to be Julian as so far there was no sign of him having arrived, though on the other hand that might be the reason for Ryan's abrupt manner. Whatever it was, she was determined that nothing was going to blight this day of all days.

Julian came strolling down the corridor towards them at that moment and she flashed him a smile, and after putting on the white hospital coat followed them into the ward.

'I'd like you to do the ward rounds with Julian today,' Ryan told her. 'Watch and learn and you'll soon get the hang of things. Little Georgia is in one of the side wards where she is making a good recovery, and her parents are with her most of the time.

'We also have a ten-year-old boy with us who is a new admission. He suffered a head injury when he fell off his bike. It's quite serious, but at the moment does not require surgery.'

Then Ryan looked straight at Melissa.

'Some time this afternoon I'd like a brief word with you. In the meantime, when the two of you have finished rounds, Julian will direct you to Personnel so that you can get the processing of a new employee over and done with.'

'Yes, fine,' she said, having decided that she was

being given the hint that being neighbours didn't mean any special treatment. As if she would expect anything of that kind.

Maybe it was Ryan's way of letting her see that his efforts on her behalf since arriving in Heatherdale were now at an end, and if that *was* the case it would have no effect on the deep gratitude she felt for the kindness he had shown her.

'I wonder what's upset the boss?' Julian mused when Ryan had gone. 'He was rather abrupt. Ryan needs some light relief in his life. He's all work and no play.'

Melissa didn't comment. There was no way she would discuss Ryan with Julian, who, from the sound of it, hadn't a care in the world.

Back in his office Ryan reminded himself that from now on he would be able to relax at the thought of Melissa in the house next door with her few belongings. If she could turn up looking like she had the last two days he need not concern himself about her any more, and that being so he would find it easier to have a good working relationship with her instead of behaving like he just had.

Ryan's crustiness forgotten, Melissa enjoyed every moment of her first morning on the wards with Julian. She would have much preferred it to be with 'the boss', as his laid-back assistant called him, but it was sufficient that she was working in a hospital once more. She read the records of every young patient's treatment and progress thoroughly when they stopped by their beds and asked Julian questions if she wasn't clear about anything.

That afternoon Ryan requested her presence for the brief chat that he'd mentioned earlier in the day, and she went to his office expecting a repeat of the brisk instructions of the morning. She was surprised to see him smiling. She was unaware that he had decided that now there was no longer any need of his help as far as she was concerned, he could relax and return to what life had been like before she'd appeared in it.

'I just wanted to ask how your first day is going,' he said. 'I know how much you wanted to be back in paediatrics.'

'Fantastic,' she told him, 'The chance to work here is the best thing that has happened to me in years and it is all due to you.' She didn't want to give him the wrong impression.

'I'll be fine from now on, Ryan, with the house that I'm going to make as delightful as yours one day, and working here with Julian and yourself, I'm back to the self-reliant person I used to be.'

Still on a high on her way home, she stopped to collect colour charts for paints and some wallpaper samples and once she'd eaten she sat considering them thoughtfully. Renovating the house that was now her home would have to be carefully budgeted, but it also had to be right for the property.

She'd seen the interior design of the house next door and had been aware of how right it was for that kind of house, and though having no wish to copy it, she felt that she needed to keep to a similar kind of décor.

The first room to be transformed was going to be the sitting room so she decided on a heavily embossed wallpaper of red and gold to match the big ornate fireplace that, along with large leaded windows, dominated the room. She sat back in the chair and imagined what it would look like and excitement spiralled at the thought.

Her second day at the hospital felt less strange now she'd adjusted to the fact that Ryan was going to be around most of the time while she was working as well as living next door, but as it was she saw little of him.

His car was there so he was around somewhere, but apart from a glimpse of him at the end of the corridor, talking sombrely to the parents of a patient, he never appeared, and when she queried his absence Julian explained that he had meetings scheduled all day with the hospital hierarchy. He added that she couldn't have joined them at a better time.

On her way home that evening she ventured into the main shopping area of Heatherdale and bought a long ladder that would reach way up towards the ceiling, a large can of white emulsion paint, and the paper that she had chosen for the walls, along with the paste that would be needed to fix it.

An obliging shopkeeper offered to drop off her purchases on his way home after closing the place and he delivered them shortly after she arrived at the house.

She'd never done any decorating before, but of late that had applied to a lot of things that she'd had to face up to, and as soon as she'd had her usual scrappy meal Melissa put on the old clothes she'd worn on the day of moving in and began to climb the ladder with the can of emulsion paint and the roller she was going to use while she painted the ceiling.

Ryan had arrived home shortly after Melissa and as he'd pulled up in front of their two houses had observed the delivery of the decorating materials and the stepladder, and been amazed at the size of it. He'd sighed. What was she up to now? Whatever it might be, he wasn't going to get involved, at least not until he'd eaten the meal that Mollie had prepared for him and the children.

Melissa was getting the hang of it. The roller went back and forth across the age-old ceiling with her standing firmly on her lofty perch. As long as she didn't look down, she would be fine.

At that moment the doorbell rang and as the heavy oak door was on the latch it swung open. As she turned quickly to see who was there, the stepladder swung backwards and sent her flying through the air with a terrified scream.

Ryan caught her just before she hit the floor, absorbing the impact of her fall.

'I am so sorry to be such a nuisance.' She gasped.

He was still holding her close and made no reply,

just kept looking down at her. It was the first time he'd held a woman like this since he'd lost Beth and it was gut-wrenching. He'd always known it would be and had made sure that it never happened for his sanity's sake, but with Melissa it was as if he just couldn't avoid her—she was everywhere he turned and he didn't want it to be like that.

Putting her carefully back onto her feet, he said abruptly, 'Whatever possessed you to try something as dangerous as painting this high ceiling? You should have hired a decorator.'

'It would be too expensive,' she replied, wishing those moments in his arms had affected him as much as they'd affected her. She'd felt safe and protected as he'd held her close and it seemed like a lifetime since she'd last had those sorts of feelings.

But she'd sensed tension in him as he'd held her in his arms, a reluctance to have her in such close contact, and her morale had been low enough of late without another putdown, in more ways than one.

'That's because you're new to the area. I know someone who would do this place up for you at a very reasonable rate and make an excellent job of it. Why don't you let me give him a buzz and ask him to come round to give you a quote? You wouldn't be under any obligation.'

'Er, yes, all right,' she agreed reluctantly, 'and thank you on both counts, for catching me and breaking my fall, *and* for offering to put me in touch with some-one I can trust to do some decorating. I've had cause to discover recently that people I thought I could trust were not like that at all, far from it. Still, that's in the past. For now I suppose I'd better start cleaning up.'

'I guess so,' he agreed, 'and I'd better get back to my place. Mollie will be getting ready to go home and my children will be waiting to play their favourite game, "Hospitals". They've both got a nurse's uniform.'

He was smiling at the thought and went on to amaze himself by saying, 'Their mother was a midwife. She went out on a late-night call in the middle of a raging storm to supervise an imminent birth, and a tree that was rotten at the roots fell across the car. She didn't survive the injuries it caused.'

'Oh! How awful!' she breathed. 'You must miss her very much.'

'Yes,' he said flatly. 'I do. More than words can say. The newborn was a girl and they called her Beth after the midwife who had been true to her calling in spite of a horrendous storm.'

On that bombshell, Ryan wished Melissa a brief goodnight, and unable to believe that he had actually talked about the worst time of his life to a stranger of all people, he went back to where his motherless children were waiting for him.

When he'd gone Melissa began to clean up the mess but her mind wasn't on it. She had her answer now to the questions about the loss of his wife.

But surely Ryan wasn't intending to spend the rest of his life alone and loveless? Yet wasn't she intending to do something similar? To have been cast aside because her cash value had dropped suddenly had made her realise what a farce her engagement had been, had made her see how gullible and trusting she'd been.

She shuddered every time she thought that someone as shallow as David Lowson could have been the father of any children she might have had. What a contrast between him and the man next door who had put himself out of circulation for the sake of his children, *and in memory of the woman he had loved.*

She really would have to stop being such an intrusion in his life. It wasn't intentional, no one needed to be solitary more than she did, having lost her faith in love and friendship. If Ryan was regretting having got involved with her again about the decorating and on second thoughts decided to let it lapse, she would understand.

When the bell rang a second time an hour later Melissa was expecting it to be Ryan, fobbing her off with an excuse about being unable to find her a decorator.

It was not so. A man in his sixties stood on the doorstep, and as she eyed him questioningly he said, 'Ryan has just phoned to say that you have some decorating that you want doing.'

'Er, yes, I have,' she told him. 'Do come in. I've just moved in and the whole place has been neglected. I tried to paint the ceiling and fell off the ladder.'

'I'm not surprised,' he commented. 'These are very high ceilings.

'Tell me what you want done and I'll call back tomorrow with an estimate. If you agree to it I'll start right away. I wonder if you realise how lucky you are to be the owner of a town house in a place like Heatherdale?'

'I'm afraid I haven't seen it in that light so far,' she told him wryly.

'You will' was the reply. 'We have a well that supplies our very own spa water all the time and is available to all comers, and the most beautiful gardens and historical buildings.'

He held out a capable-looking hand for her to shake and said, 'The name is Smethurst. I'll be round tomorrow with a price if you'll tell me what you want doing. Is it just this sitting room, or the whole place?'

'Just this room to begin with,' she told him, 'but I'm sure that by the time you've done it I will be wanting you to do more.'

'Fair enough,' he agreed. 'See you tomorrow, then,' and went striding off into the dark winter night.

When he'd gone she felt ashamed for presuming that Ryan would have wanted to back out of his offer to find her a decorator, and at the risk of making a further nuisance of herself she went next door to thank him for his prompt attention to her needs.

The children were asleep and Ryan had just settled down to what was going to be his first free time of the day when the doorbell rang. He sighed and, getting to his feet, turned the television down low and went to answer it.

When he saw Melissa standing there his first thought

was that it was getting to be too much of a habit, them toing and froing between each other's houses. He'd done what he'd said he would do and phoned Jack Smethurst. What more did she want from him?

'Hello again,' he said observing her unsmilingly. 'What can I do for you this time? I hope you haven't been up the ladder again. I did tell you I would phone the decorator.'

'Yes, I know you did,' she replied with a sinking feeling that she should have waited until morning to express her thanks. 'That's why I'm here. He has been and—'

'What? Already!' he exclaimed. Regretting his churlishness, he added, 'Do come in out of the cold.'

She shook her head. The night *was* cold, but his greeting had been colder. 'No, thank you. I don't want to disturb you any further. Mr Smethurst is letting me have an estimate tomorrow and I just wanted to thank you for putting me in touch with him.'

As she turned to go she gave a gasp of pain and he stepped towards her. 'What's wrong?'

'It's nothing,' she told him hurriedly. 'Just a pulled neck muscle from when I fell off the ladder. I'll take a painkiller when I get in. Goodnight, Ryan.' And before he could reply she was gone, hurrying towards her own front door in the dark night and wishing that she'd stayed put instead of making a nuisance of herself again.

When Melissa had gone, Ryan sat deep in thought with the memory of the mixture of emotions that had gripped him when he'd held her in his arms. There had been shock at the suddenness of it, relief that he'd been able to break her fall, and uppermost there had been a combined feeling of loss and longing that had broken down the barriers of the celibate life that he had chosen for himself.

Once back in his own house he had calmed down, telling himself that the episode had just been a one off, it could have happened with anyone, and would not be referred to tomorrow as far as he was concerned.

But when he'd answered the ring on the doorbell it had seemed that the day was not yet over where he and Melissa Redmond were concerned and he'd been offhand and unwelcoming, afraid to become too closely involved in her life.

The next morning Ryan waited beside his car until Melissa appeared. He asked if she was experiencing any after-effects of the fall, knowing that it must have jarred every bone in her body.

Dredging up a smile, she told him, 'Just one or two minor aches and pains, that's all.'

She *was* experiencing after-effects but they were mental rather than physical and had kept her awake most of the night, so she was not in the mood to start mellowing at the sight of him. She'd be polite, yes, he was her boss who had saved her from what could have been serious injuries, but afterwards he had let her see that enough was enough.

Ryan changed the subject. 'I've got some catching

up to do today. Meetings are a bind when there is work
to be done and yesterday's seemed to drag on for ever.
Julian reports that you are a natural on the job, manna
from heaven, so that's good.'

He didn't say any more, just jumped into his car and
drove off, with her following once again. She didn't
know what to make of Ryan's mood swings but, then,
she was unaware that he had also slept fitfully with the
memory of her in his arms sweet torment.

As the long hours of the night had dragged by Melissa had told herself that his manner when she'd gone
to thank him for sorting out a decorator would have
told even the most unobservant of people that he felt
he was seeing too much of her, that she was forever
at his elbow.

But the realisation had been there that as far as she
was concerned it was a case of *her* not seeing enough
of *him*. That was the real reason for her seeking him
out again, and having those sorts of feelings for him
was the last thing she wanted to happen. Since her father's death her hurts had been many and she had no
wish to add to them. Being rejected by one man was
enough to be going on with.

When Melissa arrived home that evening the estimate
from the decorator was on the doormat and she could
have wept with relief at the amount he was asking for
decorating the sitting room. She phoned him immediately to tell him to go ahead as soon as possible and

did a little dance around the room in question when she'd made the call.

'I'll be round in the morning,' Jack Smethurst had said. 'Mollie next door will let me in if you give her a key.' And that was that. Ryan had turned one of her most urgent needs into something simple and it would be difficult not to do a repeat of last night's display of gratitude.

But she had got the message loud and clear from his manner on that occasion, that just because he'd done her a good turn he didn't want her to disturb him further.

Mollie had gone. Ryan and the children had finished their evening meal and after stacking the dishwasher he did what he'd been wanting to do ever since arriving home. He rang Jack Smethurst to enquire if Melissa had accepted his estimate.

'She has indeed' was the reply. 'I'll be starting in the morning. I've asked the young lady to leave a key with Mollie. Hope you don't mind.'

'No, not at all,' Ryan told him. When Melissa dropped the key in later Ryan was determined that he wouldn't be so surly when he opened the door to her this time.

But it was eleven o'clock and she still hadn't been with the key. He'd been listening for her to ring the doorbell all evening and when he went into the hall to see if her lights were still on he saw the key on the mat with a note beside it to say that she hoped he wouldn't mind passing the key on to Mollie as Mr Smethurst had assured her that it would be all right.

He groaned. The night before he'd made sure that Melissa had got the message that he wasn't to be contacted out of working hours, and she hadn't forgotten.

Of course Mollie would give the decorator the key when he came. Jack Smethurst and Mollie were dating. If they decided to tie the knot at some future date he might have to find himself another housekeeper, but he had learned to live one day at a time since he'd lost Beth. His children and the job were his lifelines, as he was theirs, and any further than that he wasn't going to contemplate.

As he went slowly up to bed the thought came that Christmas would soon begin to spread its mantle over the ancient market town that was so dear to his heart. He wondered what his new neighbour would have planned for that. She might surprise him and have a house full of relatives turn up.

It would be his third one without Beth and an ordeal to be got through, just as the two previous ones had been, but he would cope for Rhianna and Martha's sakes.

The first sign of the coming festivities would be in a couple of weeks' time when the town's brass band would play a selection of carols outside the old pump room.

There would be mulled wine and mince pies on offer with presents for the children from a bran tub, and the residents of Heatherdale and folk from far and wide would be there, keeping up the traditions of a bygone age.

But before that there would be what there always was, young lives needing a gift of another kind, that of a healthy body, and Ryan was forever thankful that he could help towards that end in his clinic, on the wards and in the operating theatre.

As he pulled back the curtains to let the light of a winter moon into his bedroom and lay back against the pillows Ryan wondered just how close Melissa was to him at the other side of the wall.

The next morning Ryan had already left when Melissa sallied forth. She'd been waved off by Mollie and the children, who were still in their nightdresses at that early hour.

It wasn't until she and Ryan met on the wards that he had a chance to speak to Melissa, and his first words were, 'Good news about the decorating. I've given Mollie your key to pass on to Jack.'

'Yes, I can't wait to see it,' she said wistfully, with a vision of the furnishings in the house she'd had to sell coming to mind, but why was Ryan suddenly so chatty? Could it be that he had decided that there was no cause for unease, that she posed no threat to his organised existence?

When Rhianna and Martha had waved her off that morning she had felt a lump come up in her throat. Ryan may have lost his wife but he still had his children to cherish, safe and happy, while she had no one.

As if to emphasise that fact, Julian had caught her up in the car park and looking around him had said, 'I see that the boss is here before us, needless to say. He's always first on the job, as if he hasn't a moment to spare.'

'If you mean Dr Ferguson, maybe he hasn't,' she'd said dryly. 'I think he's amazing.'

'So do a lot of other women,' he'd told her, 'but sooner or later they have to accept that he is a one-woman man, even though the woman in question isn't around any more. If he ever decided to get married again, they would be queuing up.'

'Really!' she'd commented, and had left it at that. There was no way she was going to discuss with Julian the man who had been her saviour at one of the darkest times of her life.

After their brief chat about the decorating the day began satisfactorily from a medical point of view. Ryan dished out instructions. 'We have two clinics today, Melissa. I'm taking one and Julian the other. I want you to sit in at mine as joining me whenever you can will be a big part of your duties until you are ready to take a clinic of your own.'

She was smiling. The job, the wonderful job, was like balm to her soul. Even if Ryan never ever did her another good turn she would bless him for ever for this chance to use the skills that she'd had to put to one side.

As adults with children appeared before them, one lot after another, he turned to her frequently and asked her advice, explaining to them that she was a doctor from a Manchester hospital who they were pleased to have as a new member of staff at Heatherdale.

The courtesy of his introduction brought the sting of tears after dealing with debt collectors and bailiffs for months, with the added pain of missing friends and an ex-fiancé.

When the clinic was over he said briskly, 'Well done. You are going to be a big help to me. When you've had a break go back on the wards with Julian for a late-morning round.' When Melissa didn't immediately answer he asked, 'Are you all right?'

'Yes,' she breathed. 'Oh, yes!'

She was, from a job point of view, but Julian's comments about Ryan earlier had taken her into uncharted territory, and she knew that of all things she must be careful where he was concerned. The last thing she would want was to become one of the hopefuls waiting in the wings.

Ryan was very pleased. It wouldn't be long before Melissa was taking a clinic of her own. Maybe an extra doctor on the unit would give him more time with the children, as well as it being the answer to some of her problems. Further than that he was not going to think. A good relationship on the unit was enough to be going on with and as he hadn't given her any cause to think otherwise it should work all right.

CHAPTER FOUR

THE DECORATING OF the sitting room was finished and Melissa was delighted with it, so much so that when she arrived home and saw it on the evening of the third day of the transformation she had to restrain herself from going to the house next door to invite Ryan and his children to come and see it.

When she'd been on the point of leaving for the hospital that morning, Jack Smethurst had asked, 'Do I take it that the roll of pale gold carpet is for in here?'

'Yes,' she'd told him, and had wondered if Ryan was also acquainted with a carpet fitter. He'd found her a decorator so maybe he was.

It was one of the two lengths of carpet that the buyers of the Cheshire house hadn't insisted be included in the sale and she'd chosen the red-and-gold wallpaper with it in mind.

And now she saw that she needn't have concerned herself about the fitting of it as the carpet had been laid and was the perfect finishing touch to the room. She could have wept with thankfulness.

On observing that no charge had been made for it

on the account that had been left for her, she vowed that the first thing she would do when the decorator came for payment would be to ask how much she owed him for the extra work.

What Melissa couldn't know was that the night before Ryan had said to Jack Smethurst, 'I saw the wallpaper that time when Melissa fell off the ladder and presume that the gold carpet is to go with it. If she says that it is, will you fit it and let me have the bill? And don't tell Mollie or she'll be shopping around for a wedding outfit. Although she never puts it into words, I know she worries about my solitary state.'

Jack had laughed. 'She's already looking for an outfit but it's not for your wedding, it's for ours, so be warned, but don't worry. She loves the three of you too much to stay away from you for long, and, yes, I'll see to the carpet, but tell me, why are you doing this? You hardly know the woman.'

'I met Melissa on the night she came to live in Heatherdale and she was in a dreadful state. The house was filthy and she'd been let down by the cleaners, but it wasn't just that. I felt that something had happened to her beyond bearing. She was like a lost soul and I can't forget it, even though she is so different now, employed at the hospital, making her house fit to live in, and doesn't seem so alone as she did then.

'But there is still something about her that worries me, that's why I want her to have the pleasure of seeing the carpet fitted and the room finished when she comes home tomorrow. So do we have a deal? And don't forget, Jack, not a word to Melissa about it...ever.'

'Yes, if you say so' had been the reply.

It was no use, Melissa decided. Whether Ryan approved or not, she just had to go and tell him how thrilled she was to have at least one room fit to live in. Surely he wouldn't object to what he usually saw as an intrusion because he was the one who had caught her when she'd fallen off the ladder and found her a decorator.

His car was outside so he was home, but she was going to restrain herself until he and his family had finished their evening meal. It wouldn't be fair to butt in before that and so she made herself a sandwich and spent the next half-hour gazing rapturously around her.

She was about to venture forth when the phone rang and she was spared having to seek him out.

'I hope you don't mind me ringing,' he said, 'If you remember, I asked for your phone number when you started at the hospital in case I had to get in touch with you regarding an emergency of some kind on our patch.'

'No, not at all,' she replied, relieved that it was Ryan's turn to cross the privacy line. 'What can I do for you?'

'You can tell me how the room looks. Are you happy with it?'

'Over the moon,' she told him with a lift to her voice. 'And guess what, Ryan? Your decorator friend has fitted the carpet for me and it looks dreamy.'

He was smiling and carried away by her delight. 'So is it all right if I bring a bottle of champagne to celebrate the occasion and the girls and I come to admire the transformation?'

'Yes, of course,' she said eagerly, and went on to tell him laughingly, 'Just as long as Rhianna and Martha won't be expecting to see a ghost. The only person here who is a shadow of their former self is me!'

When they arrived shortly afterwards Ryan was carrying the champagne and his daughters were on either side of him. He saw that Melissa was wrapped around with delight and hoped she would not discover his part in the fitting of the carpet.

While he was thinking those sorts of thoughts Melissa had been into the kitchen and had come back with the champagne in two flutes out of boxes of oddments that had survived the removal, and with glasses of fruit juice for the children.

Ryan raised his glass. 'So, now that you have an elegant sitting room, does it mean that you are going to stay here in Heatherdale and make the rest of the house as attractive as this room?'

'Yes,' she said. 'The place is growing on me. When I went into the centre the other day I was entranced by the beauty of the architecture and the pump room with the well beside it forever providing the famous spa waters. I think I might get to like Heatherdale. I am already over the moon with its hospital, and in any case I can't afford to buy or even rent another property elsewhere.'

The conversation was about to take an awkward turn. Martha had come to stand by her side and looking up at her said, 'Do you know any mummies? When you came to breakfast you said that *you* weren't a mummy, but we thought you might know where there is one.'

Although her glance was fixed on the small questioner, Melissa could feel Ryan's tension so keenly it was as if he was glued to her side, and she said with great gentleness, 'I'm afraid I don't, Martha, but you have got a lovely daddy, haven't you?'

'Yes,' Rhianna chipped in, 'but lots of our friends have a mummy as well as a daddy.'

Ryan was cringing. 'That is enough from both of you. We came here to look at Melissa's house, not to be impolite and nosey.'

'It's all right,' she assured him. 'I understand.' And to take the sting out of what he'd said to them, she went on, 'They are lovely children, Ryan, a credit to you.'

He was not to be humoured. 'I'm not looking for "credit" and now I think we shall go. Say goodnight to Melissa,' he told his daughters and as they wished her a subdued farewell, unable to help herself, she bent and kissed them both, holding them close just for a second.

In return they clung to her and when she looked up she saw pain in Ryan's expression and was immediately sorry for causing a situation that would have no joy in it for him. Ryan marched to the door, opened it, and waited for Rhianna and Martha to leave her side.

When they'd stepped out on to the drive he said in a low voice that was for her ears only, 'It would seem that I am not very successful with regard to my children's contentment, although it is only since they met you that this kind of thing has kept cropping up.'

'I'm sorry,' she said. 'I meant no harm, Ryan. They're both so appealing I couldn't resist holding them close for a moment.'

He nodded. 'I suppose that's fair enough.' And taking them by the hand he went with a brief goodbye.

When Rhianna and Martha were asleep he stood looking down at them with the feeling that he'd behaved like a complete moron by objecting to a moment's affection for them from Melissa.

Martha had never fretted about not having Beth around before. He doubted that her fixation with the subject was because Melissa reminded her of her mother as she was not like her in any way. Maybe she sensed something about her that she and Rhianna needed, something that he couldn't see but which the eyes of a child saw, and he was just going to have to live with the disruption in their lives that it was causing until it had passed. He'd felt sick inside as he'd watched them lift up their faces to be kissed. His heart broke for them all.

They left their respective houses the next morning with the same thought in mind. Whatever had been in their minds the night before, today they both had jobs to do. His far more important than hers, and as tomorrow was Saturday Melissa hoped that the weekend would give them the chance to avoid any further uncomfortable meetings.

The trouble was that Ryan knew only the brief details of her past that she'd told him on the day when she'd first gone to the hospital. Was it any wonder he was wary of his children getting too close to a virtual stranger?

Thankfully their positions at the hospital had an impersonal approach that gave them some degree of separation otherwise it could be awkward, to say the least.

Having made a good recovery from the meningitis, young Georgia was due to go home and, as was sometimes the case, her grateful parents had brought a bottle of something for the doctor who had saved her life and chocolates for the nurses. As they were ready to leave, Georgia's father said to Melissa, 'We are having a party next Saturday to celebrate having our little daughter back with us and would like Dr Ferguson to be there, but he tells us that he has other commitments. Can you not persuade him to change his mind?'

As if! she thought. She was the last person Ryan would take note of, and in any case he was certain to have something planned with Rhianna and Martha, so she smiled and said that she had no authority over him.

She didn't see Ryan again during the rest of the morning. He and Julian were both taking clinics and she'd been left to do the rounds while they were absent.

When she was taking a short lunch break in the staff

restaurant Julian appeared and for once his expression was grave. 'What's wrong?' she questioned.

'Two young lads and their respective parents were at the clinic this morning,' he informed her, 'and both of the youngsters have been diagnosed with muscular dystrophy, which, as you know, is caused by a faulty inherited gene from somewhere back in their families. Ryan had the ghastly job of telling them.'

'Not telling the children surely?' she questioned.

'No, of course not,' Julian replied. 'Just the parents. It is at their discretion what they tell the youngsters.'

'There have been some huge steps forward with regard to muscular dystrophy over the years,' she reminded him. 'Diagnosis and treatment have advanced a great deal.'

'You seem to be well informed,' a voice said from behind her, and Ryan was there, the golden Viking who was just as fierce as men of old when it came to protecting those who belonged to him.

She didn't deny it. 'Yes, I am. I've been on a course about the illness.'

Julian had been to the counter and was coming back with sandwiches and coffee for the two of them. Having no wish to intrude into their lunch break, Melissa got to her feet and left them to it.

The rest of the day passed uneventfully and so did the evening, with the only interruption the arrival of the decorator to enquire if she was satisfied with the room now that it was finished.

'It's perfect,' she told him, 'and I can't thank you enough for fitting the carpet. Do you want to add it on to the original account, or give me a separate one? Either way will be fine, but I would like to pay for all the work that you've done while you're here.'

'The fitting of the carpet is included in the first figure I quoted,' Jack Smethurst said awkwardly, with the memory clear of Ryan's stipulation that Melissa must not know about his being involved in it.

'But you didn't know then that I was going to have it put down in the sitting room,' she persisted.

'I suppose I guessed,' he replied, and thought that Ryan's concern for her was complicating what should be a simple payment for a job well done.

Still unconvinced, Melissa wrote out a cheque for the original quote and when he'd gone decided that if she asked him to do any more work for her she would insist at the time of asking that he give her a separate price for the laying of any carpets, or carpet, as she'd only brought the two pieces with her.

As it was, she could only feel that Ryan had done her a really good turn by recommending Mollie's man friend to do the job, and when he had gone she sat unmoving with the thought of the coming weekend on her own bringing no joy.

She'd seen the signs of Christmastime appearing on the wards and in the corridors of the hospital while she'd been there today, and it had been the same when she'd driven home along the quiet lanes where high in the trees there had been the rare sight of mistletoe, and down below every so often a bright red flash of holly, but there had been no joy in it. Christmas was just going to be something to be endured this year.

She'd thought of volunteering to work along with others over the Christmas weekend so that staff on the neuro unit with children could be with them, but the thought came that Ryan was one of them, and if he was caught up in any emergencies that couldn't be avoided, it would be catastrophic unless Mollie could be there for the children.

Saturday morning brought with it wintry sunshine, a chill wind, and the opportunity for her to carry on organising her new home as best she could with whatever was available in the form of resources.

She'd seen Ryan and the children go out on foot in the direction of the town centre, which was only a short walk away, while she had been putting curtains up at the dining-room window. She wished there was someone as close to her as his children were to him in spite of Martha's yearning for a mother.

Her own mother was long gone, her father had followed her just a short time ago, and she'd been an only child. As for her friends and the man she'd thought she was going to marry, none of them knew where she was and that was how she intended it to stay.

Having seen Ryan and the children strolling along happily had made her feel restless, and the chores that she'd had lined up were something that could be left for another day, so after showering and dressing carefully she ventured forth into the town centre.

It was a beautiful town, with its pump room and the well that produced the spa water from underground close by. There were hotels built out of weathered limestone that had a stately magnificence, gardens that stretched as far as the eye could see, and all around the small market town were the high peaks and green dales.

She came across Ryan and the girls on the pavement outside one of the toy shops and before she had a chance to backtrack Rhianna saw her so she had to stop.

'Hello, there,' he said easily, as if they were on the best of terms. 'Are you out Christmas shopping, too?' He then whispered, 'I've brought the children to have a look around the toy shop to get some ideas from what they show interest in, and then we're going to look for a wedding present for Mollie.'

'No,' she said in reply to his question. 'I haven't given Christmas a thought, or at least if I have they've been negative ones.'

He would have liked to ask her what she meant by that, but refrained with the children close by, and guessed that it would be something to do with her solitariness, which he supposed he could do something about if he was so inclined.

The children would love it if he asked Melissa to spend Christmas Day with them but what about him? Would having her there make the occasion a bigger ordeal or a lesser one?

Bringing his thoughts back to the present, he asked,

'Could you possibly stay here with the children for a moment while I go into the shop to check on how long delivery might be on some of the items they have on display?'

'Yes, of course,' she said, determined that there would be no repetition of the last time she'd been with them.

'We liked your sitting room, didn't we, Martha? But we think the rest of your house is ugly.' Rhianna piped up.

'Yes,' her sister agreed.

Melissa hid a smile. She was with them on that. It *was* ugly, but not for long, if not in time for Christmas maybe soon after.

'It was Daddy who told Mr Smethurst to put the carpet down on the floor for you,' Rhianna continued, and Melissa frowned. What was that supposed to mean?

'He told him not to tell you.'

'And why do you think that was?' Melissa asked gently.

'He said he would give him some money.'

So that was why the decorator hadn't wanted any extra payment for laying the carpet. Light was dawning.

Ryan stepped out of the shop at that moment, and leaving the children engrossed in what was in the window Melissa stepped quickly towards him and took him to one side.

'You paid for the carpet to be fitted, didn't you?' she choked out. 'I wondered why I wasn't charged any extra for it. It was very kind of you, Ryan, but please don't treat me as a charity case.'

'That is not how I see you,' he said levelly. 'I meant no offence. It was just a thought that it would give you pleasure to see the room finished when you came home, that's all.'

With that Ryan went to where the children were still observing the toy display and said, 'Say goodbye to Melissa.' And not allowing time for kisses and hugs this time, he walked them away from her and disappeared from sight.

There was a coffee shop nearby and Melissa went inside on leaden feet. As she stirred the drink in front of her unseeingly she was ashamed of her reaction to his kindness in one way but hurt that Ryan hadn't thought that he might have embarrassed her with his act of generosity.

He was the most attractive, amazing man she'd ever met, as well *as a paediatric surgeon* who was bringing up two motherless children with a totally selfless kind of love, and she'd dared to berate him for what to him had been just an act of thoughtfulness.

The urge for sightseeing was gone. She drank up quickly and made her way back to the crescent of town houses where they lived, feeling so ashamed of her behaviour she wouldn't be able to rest until she'd apologised. Ryan had shown her nothing but kindness since the day she'd arrived in Heatherdale and that was how she'd repaid him?

She would pop a note through his door so it was

there when he and the children arrived home from their Christmas shopping. For her part she intended to be no-where to be seen. It would be time enough to face him when they met up on Monday morning at the hospital.

With every passing day she was becoming more aware of him and didn't want it to be like that because she knew that to him she was just someone he was al-lowing briefly into his busy life.

Ryan groaned when he read the note that was on his doormat when they got home. Their relationship, if it could be called that, was like a see-saw, up and down, but more down than up, and if he had any sense he ought to let it stay that way.

He had never met anyone to make him change his mind about marrying again, and if he ever did he hoped that it would be someone he knew something about. The children were his first consideration in everything he did because they were small and vulnerable, and if he was doing them no favours by not providing them with a new mother figure, at least he wasn't blotting out what little they remembered of Beth.

Tomorrow he would clear the air with Melissa, tell her that in future he would never again interfere in her affairs, and if the promise made life less liveable he would have to stick with it.

She wasn't around on the Sunday, as he'd been expect-ing, and he felt frustrated and on edge, eager to say his piece and clarify the situation between them knowing that he wasn't going to rest until he'd said it.

But short of talking into thin air he was going to have to wait until she reappeared.

He wasn't to know that she was at the last place he would have expected. She'd seen a notice in the hospital announcing that there was to be a children's Christmas party for past and present young patients on Sunday and that volunteers to assist from staff and friends were needed.

On impulse she'd given her name to the organisers during the week and after Saturday's upset was grateful to have somewhere to go where she could be lost in a crowd, instead of being isolated in her grandmother's house.

She'd checked to make sure that Ryan wouldn't be there and been told that consultants didn't usually take part on such occasions, that it was organised by the nurses and social workers based at the hospital. It would start mid-morning and finish halfway through the afternoon.

The party was a yearly event that was held in the run-up to Christmas, and when she arrived Melissa felt as if she belonged for the first time since she'd come to Heatherdale.

For the children who were confined to bed there was special attention to their needs and she was perched on the side of the bed of a small girl who'd had surgery a few days previously after a fall that had resulted in bleeding inside her head.

They were playing one of the fun games that had been provided and the little one was forgetting her tears and fears in the excitement of the party when Melissa looked up and her eyes widened. Ryan and his children had just arrived and he was chatting to one of the nurses.

He hadn't seen her, but Rhianna and Martha had. They'd left their father's side and were coming across the ward to her.

Ryan looked up at that moment and surprise showed on his face.

This was the last place he would have expected to find Melissa. Weekdays yes, but not on a Sunday. He wouldn't be here himself if it hadn't been that just an hour ago he'd had some bad news that could affect the neurology unit during coming days. He'd driven to the hospital to check on what his clinics and surgery arrangements were for the coming week.

A phone call had come through from Julian's parents to inform him that their son had been involved in a riding accident the previous day and was in a Manchester hospital with spinal injuries.

'It looks as if it might be a long job,' Julian's father had told Ryan and he'd thought that Melissa had arrived in the unit in the nick of time. She was going to be heaven sent in his working life—*and could be the same out of it if he would only let her.*

There was no use denying it. Melissa was never out of his mind no matter how much he told himself that she was just a passing fancy. His children loved her and who could blame them? There was a gentleness about her when she was with them that pulled at his heartstrings, but did she feel the same about him? He doubted it. She seemed to have enough emotional dramas of her own to worry about, without taking on those of a bereaved father!

The phone call had brought him to the hospital to check what was on their agenda in the unit for the coming week with Julian missing, and here *she* was, conveniently already on hospital premises.

'Will you excuse me for a moment?' he asked the nurse beside him. 'I see my colleague over there, chatting to my daughters, and I need to speak to her. Dr Tindall has had a serious riding accident and we need to check what we have ahead of us in the coming week.

'Can you look after Elfrida for a few moments while I talk to Melissa?' he asked Rhianna and Martha, indicating the small girl in the bed, and when they nodded he told her in a low voice, 'Julian isn't going to be around for some time. He's been seriously injured in a riding accident so it is going to be all systems go here next week and for some time to come.

'I'm here because I need to know what I'm down for in the clinics and theatre and I can get that information from my secretary's computer, so I'm going to have a quick look. Finding you here has saved me having to disturb you at home so can I leave the children with you for a little while?'

'Yes, of course,' she told him. She had listened to what he'd had to say in stunned silence, aghast to hear what had happened to Julian, with her first thought for the hospital's Romeo. Then it dawned on her that it was going to be just the two of them working together for the foreseeable future until a temporary replacement could be found.

They were going to be in each other's company workwise much more than she'd expected. How was she going to cope with that? How was she going to keep a hold on the attraction he had for her, being near him so much in the neuro unit and only a few yards away from him at home?

But most importantly, would Ryan want her around him so much? He might feel that living next door to her was enough, especially after her having been so ungrateful about the carpet-laying incident.

After flicking through his appointment list on the computer, he returned to Melissa and the girls.

'So what do you think about Julian? What a shame, eh?' he commented.

'Yes, it is,' she said in a low voice. 'I have had no wish to go back to Manchester since I moved here, but will put all that to one side and go to visit him when I get the chance.'

'Me too,' he agreed. 'I'm going to have plenty to keep me occupied for some time to come, but will find time for that.' He looked around him. 'How long are you planning on staying at the party?'

'I'm not sure,' she told him. 'It depends on how long I'm needed.'

'Right, we'll be off, then,' he said, and with a child on either side of him he went.

Melissa could tell that Rhianna and Martha were disappointed that she wasn't leaving at the same time as them, but she knew the rules now and number one was '*no fussing please*', so she waved them off with a bright smile that faded as soon as they'd disappeared.

Outside in the hospital corridor Ryan hesitated. He was going to take the children for a meal somewhere and was tempted to ask Melissa to join them. He wanted to make amends for their exchange of words outside the toy shop. Turning, he took the children back into the ward and saw that the party was practically over. Relatives of the children were helping nursing staff to tidy the place and Melissa was ready for the off, expecting that he would have gone by now.

'What's wrong, Ryan? I thought you'd gone.'

'We're going for a meal in the children's favourite restaurant,' he explained, 'and I wondered if you would like to join us.' It was a spur-of-the-moment invitation and he expected her to refuse.

'Yes, I would like to very much,' she told him, 'just as long as you are sure you want me there.'

'I wouldn't have asked you otherwise,' he said easily. 'I'll lead the way in my car, with you following, if that's all right?'

'Yes,' she replied.

She noticed that his expression didn't alter when

Rhianna cried, 'Goody! Melissa is coming with us, Martha!'

When they were seated at a table in a bright modern restaurant with the children tucking in to fish fingers and chips and the adults something more spectacular, Ryan amazed her by commenting in a low voice, 'This is what I miss, family outings. We used to do this a lot when Beth was with us, but it all feels like a charade now.'

'Maybe it does,' Melissa said carefully, 'but you are the only one who can put that right, Ryan. You are a fantastic father, holding down a very responsible job, but you must feel the loss of your wife a great deal. What was she like? Tell me about her.'

'Beth was just Beth, medium height, slim and very active, with brown eyes like the children's and light brown hair. She was a loving mother and dedicated to bringing babies safely into the world. Wouldn't hear of it when I tried to persuade her not to go out in the storm, and that was how she lost her life.'

When he lapsed into silence Melissa asked gently, 'And would she not want you to have the joys of family life again with someone else?'

'Maybe' was the answer. 'But so far there has been no one that I've wanted enough to be ready to take that step.' Until now, maybe? But he was far from sure that it would be a good idea to give Melissa any signals that he might regret afterwards.

Even though today had shown an affinity between them that hadn't been there before. Maybe it was because this was his loneliest time of the year, and whatever her Christmastimes had been like in the past, this one looked as if it was going to be a non-event.

The waitress was at his elbow, waiting to take orders for dessert, and the conversation became general again until they were leaving the place and Rhianna spotted mistletoe above the doorway.

'Look, Daddy!' she cried, and lifted her face to be kissed beneath the white berries. When he'd bent to oblige it was Martha's turn, and as he straightened up she cried, 'Melissa hasn't had a kiss! She must have one too!'

As Melissa shook her head laughingly, Ryan stepped towards her and took her in his arms. He wished the moment could go on for ever because the feel of her mouth under his and the closeness of her was like coming in out of the cold.

When he let her go there was a round of applause from the other diners and taking her hand, with Rhianna on one side and Martha on the other, they left the restaurant with not a word between them and went to their separate cars.

On arriving home, Ryan unlocked the door to let the children in. Before going inside himself, he walked over to where Melissa stood at her own front door.

'Do I have to say sorry for what happened?'

'No,' she said lightly, 'not at all. It was only a Christmas kiss, wasn't it?'

'Yes, of course,' he replied with a tight smile, and was gone. After his door had closed behind him, Melissa went inside and sank down onto the nearest chair. She relived the moments in his arms again. Beyond that she couldn't think.

CHAPTER FIVE

IT HAD BEEN the strangest of weekends as far as Melissa was concerned. She wasn't sure what to think as she drove to the hospital on the Monday morning. First there'd been her exchange of words with Ryan outside the toy shop about the carpet-laying, and the consequent remorse on her part for being so ungracious when she'd tackled him about it.

Then, thinking she had been well away from him when she'd gone to help with the party, he had turned up there with the bad news about Julian and had left her uneasy about what it could mean for them both. Finally there had been that surprise dinner invitation, culminating in an unexpectedly passionate kiss!

Monday morning was always Ryan's first clinic of the week and even though Melissa was early he was there before her and observed her keenly for a second when she appeared.

'If you do the ward rounds, I'll get going with the clinic earlier than usual,' he said briskly. So much for their kiss under the mistletoe. He was finished before her and came to join her as she moved from bed to bed, where often anxious parents were hovering, seeking reassurance.

Ryan was impressed with what he saw. Melissa was a natural with patients and parents. Obviously he'd seen her in this mode before and was satisfied with the way she performed, but today his awareness of her was heightened. He'd spent the night tossing and turning, the memory of their kiss haunting him. It should have been a peck on the cheek and it hadn't been. It had opened a floodgate of longing that he wanted to hold back, but the more he observed her the harder it became.

Unaware of how his mind was working, Melissa was concentrating on the young occupants of the beds in the two wards. She was confident that it was here that she belonged, amongst children who were sick and needed all the help they could get to become well again.

As the young ones and the parents hovering around their beds saw her approaching they felt her reaching out to them. No matter how worrying the diagnosis they had been given previously or might be receiving, she made them feel that their child was special.

'So,' Ryan said when the rounds were over. 'Now we'll leave the wards in the care of the nursing staff and have a quick lunch. This afternoon you can watch and learn while I operate on a child with a cleft lip and palate, just as long as there aren't any emergencies brought into A and E that our unit have to deal with.'

She was expecting Ryan to lunch in his office as he'd done on other days since she'd joined the staff of the neuro unit, but when she moved in the direction of the staff restaurant he fell into step beside her and when they'd queued and been served he said, 'Do you mind if I join you?'

'No, of course not,' she told him. She hoped he wasn't going to refer to the mistletoe incident while they were eating. It would be just too embarrassing if he did as she hadn't been entirely unresponsive while he'd been kissing her.

She needn't have concerned herself. He made no mention of it. He was probably regretting it and had decided to act as if it had never happened.

When they'd finished eating, Ryan got to his feet and said, 'I usually have a quick chat with Mollie in the lunch hour to check that the children got off to school all right, so will you excuse me? They were chattering non-stop about yesterday at breakfast-time.'

Before she could ask what part of the day before he was referring to, he was wending his way towards the restaurant exit.

He was an exceptional man. Strong and caring when it came to those he loved, and professionally a doctor of complete dedication to his calling. When she compared him to the man she'd been going to marry she felt grateful now instead of bitter that David had called off their engagement. It was all because of the man who'd taken her under his wing when she'd come crawling to Heatherdale like a lost soul.

She still had no idea what Ryan really thought about her, of course. However delightful he was to work with, nothing had changed back at the town houses where they lived. When he came home from the hospital each night she didn't see him until the following morning and so she had to be satisfied with that. However, she did wish she had the chance to see the children more often, even if their father was still guarding his private life just as much as before.

On the Saturday of her second week on the neuro unit, Melissa planned to visit Julian at the hospital where he was recovering. It was against the vow she'd made never to return to Manchester, but she felt so sorry that Julian's career and future had been put at risk by such a dreadful accident that the least she could do was take him some magazines, nice things to eat, and give him a few hours of her time.

She was undecided whether to tell Ryan what she was intending, or just proceed with her arrangements. In the end decided to just go and tell him afterwards.

'Wow!' Julian said when he saw Melissa approaching his bedside and to his parents who were present.

'This is a surprise! Mum, Dad, may I introduce Melissa? She's a doctor on my neuro unit.'

They smiled across at her.

'So, how are you coping without my charm and expertise?' he teased.

She had to smile at the question. Only Julian would be so chirpy while flat on his back with a spinal injury.

'Everyone is hoping that it won't be long before you are back amongst us.'

She could hear footsteps on the polished floor behind her and children's voices, and when Julian exclaimed, 'Look who's here now!' she turned slowly and saw Ryan coming towards them with Rhianna and Martha in tow.

When the children saw her they ran to her side, and Martha asked, 'How did you know we were coming?'

'I didn't,' she told her gently, 'but it's a lovely surprise.'

'We knocked on your door to ask you if you wanted to come with us,' Rhianna explained, 'but you weren't there. Why are you never there when we want you, Melissa?'

Ryan was chatting to Julian after greeting his parents and wasn't a part of her conversation with the children, but Melissa knew he'd heard what Rhianna had said, although he was still smiling at the chirpy patient on the bed.

'I'm hungry, Melissa,' Martha said pleadingly, taking Melissa's hand.

'I'll take them to the snack bar near the main entrance for something to eat while you talk to Julian,' she told Ryan. 'And I promise not to lose them,' she teased gently. Before he had time to reply they were off with smiles from her two young companions and a level look in her direction from their father.

* * *

As Ryan watched Melissa and the girls walk away, he was filled with mixed emotions. On the one hand, it was heart-warming to see how easily and openly his girls responded to her. On the other, it made him feel things he wasn't yet ready to feel. Was he attracted to her? He thought he probably was, but was he ready to do anything about that attraction? And what about letting the girls get too close? He was on dangerous ground.

'So where are you off to when you leave here?' Julian asked, breaking into his thoughts. His parents had gone to do some shopping while he had someone to talk to and Ryan brought his thoughts back to the present as Julian continued to chat.

'They tell me that the Christmas lights are on everywhere in the city centre and that there are Father Christmases appearing in all the big stores. Your children will want to visit him, won't they?'

'Yes, I'm sure they will,' he agreed. 'I hope that you will soon be mobile again, Julian. If our hospital wasn't just for children, we could have had you recovering in Heatherdale.'

'I'll do my best,' he promised. 'Besides, you'll be all right with Melissa filling my slot. How lucky can you get?'

Ryan's smile was twisted. 'I don't know. It's debatable.'

Melissa's appearance in his life had brought chaos rather than tranquillity into the ordered existence that was the only way he could survive his many responsibilities of family and work. But at night, in the darkness, in his lonely bedroom, when all the house was still, visions of her came to mind.

The long dark mane of her hair, the mouth that was never anything but tender when she was with his children, but buttoned up if *he* ever tried to get to know her better, and the dark hazel eyes that were full of hurt and loneliness.

She was in his line of vision at the top of the ward, bringing the children back from the snack bar, and as he was going to take Rhianna and Martha to see Santa Claus in one of the big stores it seemed only fitting that he should invite her to go with them rather than let Melissa make the train journey home on her own.

'Do you want to come with us to tell Santa Claus what you want for Christmas?' he asked her as the three of them drew level.

Julian had just been taken for a scan and as Melissa surveyed the empty bed she had a question of her own. 'Where's Julian?' she asked anxiously.

'Gone for a scan. He said to pass on his goodbyes,' he replied laconically. So much for his invitation. Could it possibly be that Melissa was attracted in another direction?

Melissa smiled, the moment of anxiety past. 'Yes, I'd love to see Santa.' There were a few things she would like for her first Christmas in Heatherdale, top of the list a better understanding with her independent neighbour.

As they left the hospital, Ryan's thoughts were running on a different track. He was remembering that Mollie wouldn't be around to cook the Christmas dinner for them as she usually did. She and Jack were getting married on the morning of Christmas Eve and they were off to Italy later in the day for their honeymoon. He was going to have to polish up his cooking skills.

He was still doubtful about asking Melissa to share the most festive day of the year with them as he knew she would pick up on his sadness and see his tension. Yet for all he knew she might have plans of her own on how to spend the day. Although she hadn't exactly been bubbling with joy when Christmas had first been mentioned. But spending it in a house that had only one presentable room was not a tempting prospect.

They found a jovial Santa in the first of the big stores that they came to amongst the busy city throng. Excitedly, Rhianna couldn't wait to tell him exactly what she wanted this Christmas.

'There are lots of things we would like,' she told him, 'but most of all we want a mummy.'

Santa's white brows lifted. It was obvious he wasn't too sure how to react to that one!

'Why don't you make a list and send it to me?' he said. 'One of my fairies will give you my address.'

Rhianna seemed satisfied with that and the small party made their way from the store.

'I'm sorry that you had to be involved in yet another

awkward moment,' Ryan said. His tone was casual, as if it had been something and nothing.

Melissa was unaware that, inside, Ryan was cringing at another plea from his children for someone to take Beth's place. She smiled.

'Think nothing of it,' she told him. 'What the children are asking for is quite understandable, but anyone can see how well cared for and happy they are. You are a man in a million.'

'Most folks think I'm a fool,' he replied dryly. 'Struggling on alone.'

She was the fool for imagining that one day he might turn to her.

They worked together, doing what they'd been trained for, and it was a joy. They lived next door to each other, and if they weren't always communicating under those circumstances she was always conscious of his nearness.

Any imaginings of what it might be like to have him beside her in the night were kept under control. Ryan was a man who was travelling along a road of his own making and didn't want company on the way. What about herself? Hadn't she vowed to steer clear of the opposite sex too?

Unaware of Melissa's thoughts, Ryan was wishing that those few moments in the store when Rhianna had turned a happy occasion into a depressing one had never happened, but as they had the atmosphere between Melissa and himself needed lightening.

'Shall we go for a meal before we go for the train, somewhere bright and festive?'

'That would be lovely,' she replied. Her glance held his for a precious moment and he smiled.

'Let's go, then,' he said briskly, and with Martha holding Melissa's hand tightly amongst the crowds, and Rhianna clinging to her father, they went to find a place to eat.

'You know the city better than I do, so you choose,' he suggested as they moved along. 'How far are we from where you used to live?' He saw the brightness fade from her face.

'Not far enough,' she replied flatly, and pointed to a restaurant that had an attractive menu displayed. 'I think that your young ones will like this place.'

So much for Melissa telling him anything about herself that he didn't already know. Yet why should she tell him about her life before Heatherdale if she didn't want to? It didn't make him feel any less curious.

'Melissa!' a voice exclaimed from nearby. 'I've been wondering where you'd got to.' When Ryan looked up he saw an expensively dressed older woman looking down at them.

'And now you know,' Melissa replied coolly. 'How are you, Monica?'

'Er, I'm fine, busy getting ready for David's big day. It's going to be the wedding of the year in our set.' The other woman's glance went over Ryan and the girls. 'I see you haven't been moping.'

'Dr Ferguson is my boss, and these are his children.'

'Ah. I see,' Monica said with a meaningful smile that belied the words.

'I don't think you do,' Melissa told her. Her face was drained of colour but she remained totally calm.

Ryan was curious about the identity of this woman who was interrupting their meal. She was going, thank goodness!

'It has been nice to meet you, Dr...er... And what lovely children.'

Uninterested, Rhianna and Martha tucked into the food that had just arrived, but as the other woman floated off, Melissa's calm deserted her and she bent her head as a flood of painful memories came back of the weeks and months before she'd moved to Heatherdale.

As he watched her Ryan felt like following that Monica woman and throttling her. He didn't know who she was to Melissa, but it was clear that she was bad news as far as she was concerned.

'I wouldn't mind knowing who that was,' he said gently, and this time Melissa didn't hesitate to reply.

'She was going to be my mother-in-law until her son broke off our engagement.'

'Of course, I remember you telling me that you were escaping a broken engagement. I hope you don't think that all men are that shallow, Melissa? He obviously didn't deserve you.'

'No, of course I don't think that.' she said quickly. 'It's very kind of you to take my side so readily.'

If she didn't feel that the new rapport that the day

had brought between them might be spoilt, she would have told him that if she *had* felt like that, getting to know him would have made her think again. She couldn't help but admire the choices he'd made when he'd lost his wife, and she was deeply moved by his gentleness with sick children. She felt privileged to know him.

They finished their meal quickly, the girls' excited chatter filling any potentially uncomfortable silences between Melissa and Ryan.

On the train journey home the two of them were again silent, but the children continued to make up for it. Used to being in the car, the novelty of a journey by train or bus caused great excitement and Melissa had to smile.

She'd been brought up with expensive cars and still used that form of transport, but now it was a small second-hand car. Where at first it had been a wrench to see them go, now it didn't seem to matter as long as she arrived at her destination.

She would have liked to invite the three of them in for some supper when they arrived back in Heatherdale, basic as her accommodation was, but she knew if Ryan came up with a reason not to accept the invitation it would take the edge off the brief closeness.

As they parked their respective cars and approached their own doors, Ryan was reluctant for the day to end.

'Would you like to come in for a coffee?'

'Are you sure?' she asked in surprise. 'I'd considered

asking you the same thing but didn't want to cause embarrassment if you refused for some reason.'

He *wasn't* sure, far from it! As she'd walked along level with him he'd watched the dark swathe of her hair swing gently against her shoulders and had wanted to hold her close, tell her that she had no need to be so alone any more.

If she needed someone he would be there, next door, ready to help. Yet would he be able to fulfil that promise on a purely friendly basis and not begin to want more? If he had any sense he would let Melissa get on with her own life now that she was settled here and was no longer unemployed. He should take a back seat and take pleasure from working with her.

She was excellent at her job, quick to learn, efficient in every aspect of paediatrics, and their young patients responded well to her, without alarm, but he hadn't answered her question.

He could tell her glibly that, yes, he was sure, because he didn't want the day to end just yet. Their relationship had moved on, he'd felt it in every word she'd said, in her every movement, but he wasn't sure that he was ready to let Beth be just a beautiful memory, instead of keeping to the vows he'd made on the day she'd been lowered gently into a grave in the churchyard.

Melissa watched him, wondering when his thoughts were going to come back from where they'd gone. He'd opened the front door to let the children into the house and for what seemed like an eternity she'd been waiting for him to say something as she had a strong feeling that he was regretting his impulsive invitation.

Sure enough, he turned to face her.

'Maybe we *should* call it a day, Melissa. The children are usually tucked up in bed by this time. But I want you to know that if ever you have a problem I'll always be only too pleased to help if needed.'

'I can cope, Ryan,' she told him levelly. 'The past few months have taught me a lot about myself and I feel stronger than ever. I'm hoping that most of my problems will be over once I've got the house how I want it. So please don't feel that you need to increase your commitments by adding me to the list.'

On that comment she opened her own door and went inside, and as he watched it close behind her Ryan's heart sank. What was he playing at? He'd invited her to have coffee and then gone back on it, and had been extremely patronising with his offer of help.

He was the one in need, content on the outside unhappy on the inside. Mollie had ventured to tell him a few times that Beth would not want him to live like this and he'd just ignored her advice and let it pass.

But on those occasions he hadn't known that there was such a person as Melissa Redmond and now he did. Not only was she one of the best registrars he'd ever worked with, she was his neighbour. Were the fates telling him something? Not if they knew that once he made up his mind regarding something important he rarely changed it!

CHAPTER SIX

IT WAS SUNDAY again. This was the day that Melissa always felt was long and empty. Well, not empty—she had plenty of chores she could get to. Still, her life did feel empty of family and friends because there was no one to phone her, or come to her door, except Ryan, of course, and after her cool reception of his change of mind the night before she wasn't expecting that. Part of her was almost dreading seeing him at work in the morning, too.

What had he expected her to do once the children had fallen asleep and they had been alone? Strip off and do the dance of the seven veils? One thing was sure, he would be keeping a low profile today after her chilly acceptance of his speedy change of mind.

She was wrong. He phoned at midday.

'Have you ever done any knitting, Melissa?'

'Not since I was about twelve,' she informed him. 'Why do you ask? Are you short of something to do in your spare time?'

'Hardly! Explain to me, what is spare time?'

'I've heard it described as the time you wish you had but never get. So tell me more about the knitting.'

'Rhianna wants to knit her doll a wetsuit. But first she has to learn how to knit.'

'Has she got a pattern, wool, and needles?'

'Er...no.'

'Right, so if you will entrust her to me, the two of us will go to the shops today and sort that out, if any of those kinds of places are open on a Sunday.'

'No problem regarding that,' he told her. 'Heatherdale is a popular tourist centre. They come from miles around to see the spa, the well and the rest. Sunday is one of the busiest days for the shops, but are you sure you can spare the time to take Rhianna for the wool and stuff?'

Could she spare the time? Of course she could. Ryan was actually willing to let Rhianna out of his sight for a while *and into her keeping*!

'Yes,' she told him, 'but a wetsuit is rather ambitious for a first attempt. Beginners usually start with something simple, like maybe a scarf for their doll?'

He was laughing. 'We Fergusons always aim high—in endeavour that is.'

She didn't join in. Was he referring to his dedication to his job or his celibate life or both?

'So shall I send Rhianna round?'

'Yes, but, Ryan, what about Martha? Won't she want to come?'

'No, she's all right, watching a children's film on TV at the moment.

'Thanks for offering to take Rhianna for whatever she needs to get started, and being willing to spend some time with her.'

'Thanks are not necessary,' she told him. 'It will be a pleasure, *not a chore*,' she continued coolly.

'Yes, of course,' Ryan said hastily. He'd phoned her with the request about the knitting because he'd been desperate to hear her voice after his bungled invitation. He was getting the kind of reception he deserved, though, looking on the bright side, Melissa hadn't hesitated when she'd heard what he'd rung for. He said a brief goodbye and went to tell Rhianna the good news.

As he watched the two of them walking along the pavement in the direction of the town centre, Ryan swallowed hard. They looked so right together, with Rhianna chattering away to Melissa and doing a little skip every few steps, but not as right as if it had been Beth taking her daughter to the shops. Would that feeling of loss ever go away?

They weren't gone long and then they were back. Melissa phoned to say that she was giving Rhianna her first knitting lesson and would send her back shortly. She'd also managed to talk Rhianna out of the wetsuit and into the idea of knitting her doll a scarf for starters.

'Sounds great,' he said. He wished Melissa was there beside him so that he could have the pleasure of her company, instead of having only her voice to listen to, but thankfully there was still tomorrow to look forward to at the hospital, where they had no hang-ups around each other.

* * *

Melissa saw Mollie arrive earlier than usual while she was having her breakfast the next morning, and within minutes Ryan was on the phone.

'Emergency Services are bringing in two young-sters with serious head injuries from a pile-up on the motorway. Eleven-year-old twin boys who were in the back seat of the family car without seat belts. They were thrown forward like rag dolls when the car be-hind them in the pile-up connected with the back of theirs. It's the tail end of the night shift so they're hang-ing on for the moment. Needless to say, I want to be there when they bring them in, so I'm off now. Can you follow as soon as possible? If surgery is required, I'll want you to assist.'

'Yes, of course,' she told him, already stepping out of her nightdress on her way to the bathroom. The adrenaline was kicking in. This was what she'd trained for, and it was going to be under the guidance of Ryan Ferguson. Did anything else matter?

If he was going to throw a fit every time she was near enough for the other kind of physical contact that had nothing to do with medicine and everything to do with sexual chemistry, at least she would have these kinds of moments to treasure.

Ryan was in Theatre, scrubbed up and masked, when she got there. He pointed to a motionless young figure on the operating table.

'Both twins have frontal fractures of the skull due to the force with which they were thrown forward, but this young guy is the most serious so I'm going to operate on him first. The other lad is next door, being watched over by theatre staff. The anaesthetist is at the ready so get gowned up and then we'll begin.

'The two boys had arrived and been scanned by the time I got here. It has shown there's a subdural haemorrhage to deal with for this youngster. He has been barely conscious since it happened, so I don't want to delay as there's bleeding between the inner surface of the skull and the outer layer of the meninges. Have you been involved with anything like this before?'

'Only once, but I remember it clearly,' Melissa told him. 'Just tell me what to do and I'll do it.'

As she scrubbed up, in what could not have been a more unexpected moment, Melissa realised that she was falling for Ryan, the golden-haired consultant who had burst into her life like a breath of clean fresh air. She loved his integrity, his devotion to his children, and to those belonging to others who came into his care, and above all his loyalty to his dead wife.

Would he ever feel the same way about her? There was a spark between them that would soon become a flame given the chance.

Ryan was waiting. The theatre nurses were in position, the anaesthetist poised for action at the head of the operating table and everything became centred on saving the life of an injured child.

Later in the morning the process was repeated for the second boy with the same sort of injury as his brother.

It seemed that they'd been on their way to school, with their mother driving, and with the carelessness of youth had skipped fastening their seat belts, which had caused not only devastation for themselves but a nightmare for her too.

Just before three o'clock in the afternoon the theatre staff were having a welcome late lunch in the staff restaurant after the traumas of the morning. It wasn't unusual, they often had to eat when they got the chance. Ryan had chosen to have a bite in his office as he wanted to make his regular call home to check that Mollie had coped all right with the Monday morning rush for the children.

The two boys had been transferred to the high-dependency unit, where they were being monitored all the time by nursing staff and watched over by their horrified parents, whose normal Monday morning had turned into a nightmare.

When Ryan had spoken to Mollie he went to seek out Melissa, who was in the middle of a late ward round. He found her sitting by the side of the cot of a tearful two-year-old whose mother had just taken an older child to the toilet. She was holding his hand and soothing him gently. Melissa was fantastic, either on the job or off it. So why couldn't he act on that delightful thought and do something about it, instead of holding on to the past so tightly?

'When you've finished rounds, I'd like a quick word

in my office,' he said briskly to conceal the effect she was having on him.

She smiled up at him. 'Yes, of course, Dr Ferguson.' She pointed to the toddler who was now asleep, still holding her hand. 'I'll just let Oscar settle into a deeper sleep before I move away.'

'Of course.' When a nurse approached with the medicines trolley he went.

The nurse was middle-aged, plump with a smiley face, and as she observed his departing straight-backed and purposeful figure, she said with comic wistfulness, 'Isn't he something to make any woman's heart beat faster?

'I keep telling my husband that if he doesn't stop watching football on the television instead of taking me out, I'm going to run off with Dr Ferguson. Which might not be so easy as our doctor friend is reluctant to put any woman in place of that nice wife of his.'

The nurse went on her way, moving from bed to bed with whatever medication its young occupant might be requiring. Melissa was despondent. To be told what she had already worked out for herself had put a blight on the day.

When she went to Ryan's office the first thing she saw was a florist's delivery of beautiful flowers of the season on a side table. Picking up the bouquet, he got to his feet and came round to her side of his desk and handed them to her.

'Just to say thanks for putting Rhianna on the right track with the knitting. There wasn't a sound out of her last night. She was working away at it until the very last moment before going to bed and at breakfast before I left the house. So thanks, Melissa.'

She looked down at the flowers and swallowed hard. It was the moment to tell him that she would do lots more for his children and *him* if he would let her, that she was falling in love with him, he was in her every waking thought *and in her dreams*, but something held her back.

She was letting a nice gesture mean more than had been meant by it. Her dealings with her ex-fiancé had shown her that humiliation was a hard pill to swallow if she should be mistaken, and hadn't the medicines nurse just confirmed Ryan's devotion to his wife's memory?

'You didn't have to do this, Ryan. I enjoyed the time spent with your daughter, but thanks, anyway.'

As she turned to go he stopped her.

'There is one other thing.'

She swivelled round to face him once more.

'You were good in Theatre this morning. We work well together. Keep it up and you will have a great future before you in paediatrics.'

'Maybe,' she told him gravely, 'but somewhere along the way I want to be a wife and mother, too.'

She watched him flinch.

'Yes, of course,' he agreed stiffly, and went back to the paperwork on his desk, leaving her to make an undignified exit. Once out of his office she went through a side door that led to the car park and put the flowers in her car out of sight. There was no way she wanted questions asked about them by other staff that might set rumours off that were not true.

The twin boys from the motorway accident had regained consciousness when she returned to the neuro unit and were looking pale, drowsy, and rather the worse for wear. Unless anything unforeseen occurred, they should, however, make full recoveries.

During their separate operations they'd had burr holes drilled into their skulls and blood clots drained away, followed by repair of damaged blood vessels.

As she checked them over their father said sombrely, 'Somehow I don't think they'll forget to fasten their seat belts again.'

When Melissa went to her car at the end of the day Ryan was about to drive off in his and he rolled the window down.

'You know that Mollie is getting married to Jack on the morning of Christmas Eve and that Rhianna and Martha are to be her attendants? She was saying the other day that she wondered if you would be willing to help in the choosing of their dresses.'

'Me!' she exclaimed. 'But I hardly know your housekeeper.'

'She may not be that for much longer, I fear, certainly not in the same capacity. Come the new year I might have to find a substitute, but that's a few weeks away yet. So, getting back to the wedding and the children, Mollie would be glad of your advice as you wear such attractive clothes yourself.'

She smiled. How ironic.

'My clothes belong to a time when I was a pampered pet and I haven't been able to afford anything new since, but while I've come to live in Heatherdale I've forgiven my father. In a strange sort of way he did me a favour when I had to sell the place we had in Cheshire and come to live in my grandmother's house.' *Because if it hadn't happened I would never have met you,* she wanted to tell him, but she was still too cautious. The dread of being hurt again was like a dark shadow hanging over her

'It's good to know that you're happy here!' he exclaimed. 'I've had my doubts about that once or twice. I have always felt that this is a magical place, but I don't expect everyone to feel the same as I do.'

With an unmistakeable lift to his voice he continued, 'Getting back to the matter of Mollie's wedding, can I tell her that you'll go with her to choose the children's dresses? She is concerned that they should have something really pretty but also warm and cosy for this time of year. I can usually manage to choose their clothes myself, while giving them some degree of choice, but not when it is something like this, and in winter.'

'Yes, of course. I'll help in any way I can,' she said. Was she in her right mind, surrounding herself with the trappings of motherhood when their father ran a mile if she came within touching distance?

'Thanks, Melissa, that's wonderful. I am most grateful,' he told her, still smiling, and added jokingly, 'I've got my name down for a knitted pullover when Rhianna is more accomplished in the art.'

She smiled back at him. 'Don't tease her, Ryan. She is more like you than you realise, not to be defeated by anything, but she is only seven years old.'

He didn't reply, just gave her a long level look, and she wondered if he thought her interfering. He brought the subject back to Mollie's wedding.

'The way things are going, we Fergusons are going to be well represented on the day as not only are the girls going to be Mollie's young attendants, she has asked me to give her away as she has no close family. Her husband died a few years ago and she has no sons or daughters to do the honours, so it will be my pleasure.

'Her invitation was addressed to Ryan Ferguson, family, and friend, so if you want to tag along with us, Melissa, feel free. You will be most welcome.'

'Thanks just the same but no,' she said levelly, not enamoured by the phrasing of his invitation. 'I am not a tag-along sort of person. My life has scraped the bottom of the barrel over recent months and one of the things it has taught me is not to accept being merely tolerated by anyone.'

She watched his eyes widen and his jaw tighten. She drove off before he had a chance to comment. If he had, Ryan would have told her that he'd phrased the invitation in such a manner because he didn't know what Melissa thought of him, and a casual approach

had seemed like the best idea at this stage of their relationship.

What would she have said if he'd worded it along
the lines that she was the best thing that had happened
to him in years and he would be proud to have her by
his side in front of Mollie and her wedding guests?

The rest of the week dragged by on leaden feet.

On the day that Ryan was holding one of his clinics Melissa asked, 'Is there a chance that I could sit in
with you as I did when I first came onto the ward? I
learned such a lot.'

'I'm glad to hear it,' he said with a dry smile, 'but I
think not at present. If Julian was here there would be
no problem, but as it is I need you on the wards while
I'm taking the clinic so that all aspects of the job are
covered. I don't know if he will ever be mobile enough
to come back to us but if he eventually does…'

'What?' she asked. '*What* if he eventually does?
Are you going to tell me I might be out of a job? Do
you want me gone?'

'Now you are being ridiculous,' he told her, and almost laughed.

As if!

She was the best registrar he'd ever had. How could
Melissa ever think that he would pass her over because
of a few wrongly chosen words in the car park the other
night? He just had the feeling that he needed to cool it
for a while. After all, their small patients came first.

* * *

It was Saturday. The small town was buzzing with Christmas shoppers and a local brass band played carols in the centre of the town square beside the huge Christmas tree.

As she heard the music in the distance, Melissa remembered Ryan telling her about the musical event some time previously. When she saw the three of them come out of the house next door and move off in that direction, she decided to go to the special yearly happening herself, but from another direction to avoid being invited to *tag along*.

It wasn't likely, of course, not after the reception the wording of his invitation had received that evening in the hospital car park, but she wasn't taking any chances. She was relieved that Ryan wasn't going to be present later in the afternoon when the promised shopping trip with Mollie and his children was to take place.

There were lots of the townsfolk gathered around the tree and as the band played the familiar music and those there sang the equally familiar words, she looked around her at the beautiful setting and sent up a prayer of thanks to the fates that had brought her here.

It was as if Manchester, the place that had been so familiar to her with its smart stores and many famous restaurants, didn't exist, and neither did the millionaire's row where she had lived with her father on money owed to others.

For the first time in ages she was beginning to feel

in control of her life. That the house was still dark and dismal except for her delightful sitting room didn't matter—she would get that sorted eventually. She had the job she'd always longed for in pleasant surroundings and had met a man who made all others seem nondescript.

The only cloud in her sky was that she doubted he saw her in the same light, though why should he when he was still in love with the wife who had been taken from him so tragically?

A child's voice calling her name broke into her thoughts and when she looked up there was Ryan with his girls, all three smiling their surprise at seeing her amongst the festive crowd.

'Hello, there,' Ryan said. 'I nearly phoned to remind you of the band playing carols before we left the house as I wasn't sure if you remembered me mentioning it a couple of weeks ago.'

Unable to disguise her pleasure at meeting them, she told him, 'I'd forgotten but when the sound of the music came drifting over I realised where it was coming from and came to see what was going on.'

She turned to Rhianna and Martha.

'Are you ready for us going shopping this afternoon for your dresses for Mollie's wedding?'

'Yes,' they chorused excitedly.

Martha added, 'We already know what kind we want, Melissa.'

'Really!' she said in mock surprise.

'So be prepared,' Ryan warned laughingly, and followed it by saying, 'We are about to go for a hot drink somewhere. Dare I ask if you'd like to join us?'

There was no mention of her 'tagging along', she noticed as their glances met, but she knew he wouldn't have forgotten and she wished she hadn't been so snappy the other night in the car park.

'I'd love to,' she told him, letting the joy of being with the three of them take over. It diminished somewhat as they strolled along the high street in the direction of a café in one of the parks.

She had forgotten how well known Ryan must be in the town as a paediatric surgeon and a very attractive single father, and every time someone called across to him in greeting, she was observed with unconcealed curiosity.

In keeping with the frosty winter morning she was wearing a designer winter coat, elegant knee-high boots with high heels, and on her head was a fake fur hat the same colour as the coat. She wondered if the interest she was arousing in passersby was due to Ryan being seen with a woman, and an expensively dressed one at that.

Those observing them couldn't be expected to know that she had a wardrobe full of expensive clothes in a house that was like something out of the Dark Ages except for one room. Before leaving it, she'd stood in front of the mirror in the dressing table that had been one of the few things she'd managed to salvage from the onslaught of the bailiffs, and thought that if she sold some of her clothes, the money would buy wall-paper and paint.

Ryan had also noticed the stares and buzz of interest they were causing and suggested they go down the next side turning, but she shook her head and told him she was fine. She wished it was true.

While they drank coffee and the children sipped hot fruit drinks, Melissa and Ryan were silent. The girls, unaware of any tension in the atmosphere, chatted happily about their role in the upcoming wedding and Rhianna asked, 'Will you help us to get dressed that morning, Melissa?'

'Er, yes, of course I will, if you want me to,' she answered, somewhat dazed at the way she was being involved in their lives once more. She wasn't sure how Ryan would feel about her stepping into the mother role once again, so having offered to do as Rhianna had asked she needed to know what his opinion was.

'Would that be all right with you? I don't want to intrude on such a special day.'

'Of course. I would be greatly obliged if you would help the girls to get dressed, but only if you come to the wedding as my guest.'

'All right, I'll come!' she said levelly. 'Are you sure you want me at the wedding as your guest, though? It always feels like treading on eggshells when we are together outside the hospital. When we're there it's so different, more like being on safe ground.

'I've got to go, Ryan. I'll come for the children at the

arranged time this afternoon.' And after kissing them both lightly on the cheek, she left the café.

Ryan sighed. Melissa had kisses in plenty for his children, but no tender gestures came his way.

They worked together as if they were joined at the hip, but once away from Heatherdale Children's Hospital the spark that he'd thought was there never seemed to burst into flame. She was right to point out that things were far from easy between them outside work.

Her outfit today had been stunning but he'd hesitated to tell her so as he seemed to have developed a talent for saying the wrong thing where Melissa was concerned. His mind went back to the night when she'd opened the door of the cold, grim house next door to his, looking on the point of collapse, and had burst into tears. He hadn't known in those few seconds that his life was about to change. It was something he was finding hard to accept and until he did there would be no peace in him.

Now that Melissa had gone, the children were fidgeting, ready to go. He paid for the drinks and they set off in the same direction as Melissa. He was hoping they might draw level with her, but she was nowhere to be seen and he wondered how she could move so fast on those heels.

Melissa enjoyed the afternoon spent with Mollie and the children immensely.

Melissa liked Ryan's middle-aged housekeeper and had not forgotten how she had suggested to him that they invite her to eat with them in her distressed state on that dreadful night when she'd been so much out on a limb she'd been on the verge of collapse.

It was easy to see that the children were fond of her, which was not surprising with Mollie being the only womanly figure in their lives.

As they walked the short distance to the high street she wasn't surprised when Mollie said, 'Rhianna and Martha are staying at my house tonight. They have a sleepover every few weeks. We have a lovely time and as it's always on a Saturday night there is no rush to get them to school the next morning. It gives Ryan a few hours of freedom to do whatever he pleases, which is rarely connected with socialising, I'm afraid.

'Before he lost Beth they had lots of friends and a lovely social life. During the first twelve months after she was gone there were some of the unmarried women that they knew who would willingly have stepped into her place if he'd asked them, but there was nothing further from his mind, and as far as I can see there still isn't.'

They had stopped outside a small but select department store and while Melissa would have liked Mollie to carry on talking about Ryan for ever, the older woman's thoughts had switched to dresses for her attendants.

'They have a delightful children's clothes section in this place, shall we see what is on show?'

A display of pretty long dresses in pastel colours, obviously aimed at Christmas partying for the young, immediately attracted the attention of all four of them. And after some degree of trying on, the small attendants-to-be were fitted out with dresses in a soft turquoise fabric with matching under-slips to help keep out the cold.

As they left the store Mollie asked, 'What do you think they should carry, Melissa, posies?'

'What about if they keep their hands tucked into little furry white muffs decorated with snowdrops?' she suggested.

The bride-to-be was smiling. 'Yes, indeed. They will keep their hands warm.'

'And what are you going to wear?' Melissa asked.

'I've bought a lovely dress and jacket in apricot silk.' Mollie's face took on a dreamy expression. 'And I'm delighted to say that Ryan is going to give me away. It won't be an easy day for him, with Beth not being there beside him, but I've invited him to bring a friend.'

'Yes, he's asked me to fill the gap.'

'That *is* good news! And are you going to?'

'Er, yes. I think so,' she replied. Mollie might not be so pleased if she knew the circumstances of her agreeing to be his partner for the occasion.

When they'd completed their shopping by buying soft white satin shoes for the children, Mollie said, 'Would you mind dropping off what we've bought at Ryan's house so that I can take the girls straight to my place?'

'Yes, of course,' Melissa said, and as the three of them set off in the opposite direction she heard Martha say, 'Melissa is going to help us get dressed for your wedding, Mollie.'

And Rhianna chipped in with, 'She's going to make us beautiful.'

Melissa considered Ryan's daughters beautiful already. With a slightly aching heart she set off to deliver the afternoon's shopping into their father's keeping.

CHAPTER SEVEN

WHEN HE OPENED the door to her Ryan stepped forward to take the shopping from her and then stood back to allow her to pass.

Noticing Melissa hesitate, he said, 'I've just finished catching up on a back log of paperwork from the hospital and am about to relax over a mug of tea. Can I persuade you to join me?'

She stepped inside, knowing that she wouldn't have refused the invitation if it had been a mug of castor oil he was offering.

He saw she was wearing the same outdoor clothes as she had that morning.

'Can I take your coat and your hat?'

Melissa nodded, and he stepped forward and slid the coat off her shoulders with one hand, gently removed her hat with the other and hung them carefully on a nearby coat hook.

She had become very still while he was taking off her hat and coat and when their glances held the dormant spark suddenly became a flame and instead of ushering her into the sitting room he led her slowly upstairs into his bedroom. As they faced each other beside the bed, which to him was the loneliest place on earth, she still hadn't spoken.

'Say something, do something, Melissa, please,' he said softly. 'Show me that you want me as much as I want you, or we'll let this moment pass.'

As he waited to see what she would do, Melissa began to take off her clothes, and as the dress that she'd been wearing beneath the coat slid to the floor and flimsy underwear and tights followed, she was smiling.

When she stood before him naked she spoke for the first time. 'Now *you* show me,' she said softly.

Without a second asking he stripped off and lifted Melissa onto the bed. His mouth caressed hers and the soft stem of her neck before dropping to the firm mounds of her breasts. She gave herself to him in a huge wave of wantonness, crying out as longing was appeased and delight filled her being.

But as she lay content in Ryan's arms afterwards Melissa realised that he hadn't spoken since he'd asked her to show him that she wanted him to make love to her. Raising herself up on to one elbow, she looked down at him and saw that his expression was no longer that of the man who had just possessed her, adored her and made her feel wanted. It was as if he'd pulled down the shutters.

'Ryan, what's wrong?' she asked with deadly calm. 'Clearly what has just happened between us didn't mean as much to you as it did to me.'

He didn't deny it and it was like a knife in her heart. Instead, he put her away from him gently.

'I am so sorry, Melissa. I would never willingly hurt you. I let my guard down, sought solace from you, and should not have done. It was unforgivable. When Beth was taken from me I chose a path to follow and have never diverted from it until a few moments ago. I hope you understand.'

She understood all right. What had made her think that the magic of Heatherdale had brought the man she would love for ever into her life when he had his own agenda? Was this how Ryan coped, a brief liaison with some willing member of her sex when the strain got to be too much, and then back to the life he had chosen?

The thought brought with it the urge to be gone, back to the house of horrors next door. It propelled her to her feet and in a matter of seconds she was dressed again in the clothes she had shed so willingly. Ryan made no protest, just threw on a robe and left her to it.

When she went down the curving staircase he was waiting in the hall, and lifting her coat and the fur hat off the hook where he had hung them she walked past him and out into the winter dark.

If it wasn't for her commitment to the sick children who came into their care at the hospital and the fact that she had nowhere else to go, she would be gone. Melissa drew the curtains to shut out the night of her humiliation.

She'd convinced herself that she understood Ryan's

loyalty to the memory of his dead wife, even though it did seem an awful waste of another life...*his*. But tonight he'd taken the first step towards letting the memories be just that, and as he'd made love to her she'd rejoiced at the thought, until she'd looked down at him amongst the tangled sheets of his bed, seen the look on his face, and thought she should have known better.

After a miserable night she slept late on Sunday morning. She was brought out of sleep by the bedside phone ringing. She hoped it wasn't Ryan. He was the last person she wanted to speak to.

It wasn't, but the call *was* from next door. It was Rhianna to say that Mollie had brought them back home. They wanted to try on their dresses and the rest of their outfits to show their father, so would she come and help them to dress up for him?

She'd been finding a glimmer of comfort in the thought that she would have today to gather her wits before facing him on Monday morning, but the children were unwittingly turning that into a vain hope as there was no way she would refuse their plea.

'I'll come round in twenty minutes, Rhianna.'

After showering and dressing quickly, she skipped breakfast until later and went next door. Thankfully it was Martha who answered her knock.

'Daddy is under the shower and says he will wait until we are ready before coming down.'

Was that because he wanted to get the full effect of their outfits or because he was in no rush to see her again so soon? If that was the case, he need have no worries. If it hadn't been for the affection she had for his children he wouldn't have seen a blink of her today.

They looked delightful in the long turquoise dresses with their hands inside the pretty muffs and their feet in the satin pumps, and when Rhianna called up to Ryan from the hall that they were ready, Melissa felt her mouth go dry.

The children were standing at the bottom of the curving staircase as Melissa hovered near the front door. The longing to open it and be gone was strong, but the two small girls wanted her there and there she was going to stay no matter what, until he'd seen them dressed how they would be at the wedding.

He came slowly down the stairs towards them and she swallowed hard. Her mouth felt dry, her body weak and wilting at the sight of him with the golden thatch of his hair damp against his head from the shower and the rest of him covered by a cotton shirt and shorts. Though dry-mouthed and weak at the knees, beneath it she was in control. Last night had been humiliation time once again and she'd walked right into it, but it was not going to happen again.

On the third step from the bottom, Ryan paused and, observing her standing behind the children, stony-faced said, 'Thanks for finding the time to assist in the dressing-up parade, Melissa, they needed your help.'

'Think nothing of it,' she said levelly. 'It's nice to know that I'm needed by someone.' She placed her arms around their shoulders. 'We have two pretty bridesmaids waiting to hear what you have to say about their outfits.'

He was smiling as he came down the last steps of the staircase, giving no sign of having got the message in her first comment.

'The two of you are always beautiful to me, but in these lovely dresses, with the sweet little muffs to keep your hands warm, and the dainty shoes on your feet, you will be more beautiful than ever. What do you say to Melissa for helping you to choose them and dress up in them this morning?'

'Thank you,' they chorused, and hugged her close, then went slowly up the stairs to take off their finery.

When they'd gone Ryan said, 'I imagine that coming here this morning was the last thing you wanted to do.'

'Yes, it was,' she told him, 'and now I'm going to go and have some breakfast. I won't be available for the rest of the day.'

'Of course,' he said, and after waving to the children, who were looking down at them from the upstairs landing, she left, without another look in his direction.

The thought of spending her working day doing the job she loved had always been a pleasure to contemplate each morning as she drove the short distance to the hospital, and with Ryan nearby most of the time on the wards and in surgery it had been blissful, but not so on the Monday morning after the events of the weekend. Melissa was dreading being in his presence for any length of time.

But any awkwardness between them was avoided when she arrived because, amazingly, Julian was back in circulation, still as darkly attractive as ever but thinner, looking drawn and on crutches. She came across the two men chatting beside their cars in the staff parking area.

When Julian saw her he leant against his car and waved a crutch in her direction and she went to join them.

'This is a very pleasant surprise. It's lovely to see you. Are you just visiting, or here to take up where you left off?'

'Just visiting today,' he said breezily, with his usual aplomb, 'but I'm hoping to come back on a part-time arrangement soon. The spinal unit in Manchester have worked wonders for me. The boss says he'll have me back whenever, so we will be a happy threesome once more.'

Melissa very much doubted it!

'When I'm back in harness, maybe we could have a night out together, the three of us,' Julian continued.

Melissa just smiled and didn't let it falter when Ryan spoke for the first time to comment, 'It would have to be a twosome, I'm afraid. All my time away from here is spoken for.'

On that downbeat comment he turned in the direction of the nearest entrance to the hospital and they followed him inside. Melissa took care to stay level with Julian's slow progress on his crutches and vowed that

Ryan was not going to dampen her spirits or Julian's on his totally unexpected appearance.

He didn't stay long, just enough to say hello to everyone, and when the night shift were ready to go and day staff about to take over she walked with him to his car. On the way he stopped and, leaning forward between his supports, kissed her lingeringly while they were opposite the window of Ryan's office.

Taken aback, she didn't push him away, just told him laughingly, 'It's clear that your cheek wasn't affected in the accident. You will be getting me the sack.'

'That was for the benefit of a mutual friend of ours,' he said, serious for once, 'as I guess that nothing of that nature has been happening in those quarters while I've been away.'

'The answer is *yes* and *no*,' she told him, 'but how did you pick up on that?'

'By observing you both when the two of you came to visit me in the spinal unit.'

'Oh!' she said blankly, and before he could comment further waved him off and hurried back inside.

Ryan was in the secretary's office by the time she reached the corridor, having paused briefly to remind the tranquil middle-aged woman that an urgent appointment was needed for a child who had been diagnosed with epilepsy.

The family had missed the first appointment after the diagnosis when they would have discussed the illness in detail with the parents and explained to them what treatment was going to be given their daughter to control the symptoms and seriousness of it. Ryan caught Melissa up at the entrance to the wards.

Julian's ploy had worked. He'd seen the kiss from the window of his office. His colleague had some nerve, yet why shouldn't he come on to Melissa if he was so inclined? She hadn't exactly pushed him away.

They were both free to fraternise with whoever they liked, had no family ties or emotional hang-ups from painful memories that wouldn't go away, so it made perfect sense to Ryan that Julian and Melissa would get together. It didn't make him feel any happier, though!

'The results have been back a couple of weeks from the scan I requested for a child we saw at one of the clinics with suspected epilepsy. We gave the parents a date for an early appointment as soon as we knew what it was, but they didn't keep it. So I've just been asking my secretary to phone them.' He glanced at a clock on the wall above their heads. 'So now maybe we can get the day under way.'

'Yes, of course,' she said flatly, avoiding making a fool of herself again by explaining what had been behind Julian kissing her outside his office window. There was always the chance that Ryan had been relieved to see her turning her attention to someone else after him bringing her down to earth so abruptly when he'd just taken her to the stars, so maybe explanations were not needed.

'I was called here late last night to observe a five-year-old boy who had been brought in as an emergency,' Ryan said. 'I want him to be our first priority this morning.'

He led the way towards a small side ward that was used for seriously ill children or any who might have something contagious.

'So what time was it when you got the call?' she asked.

'Half past nine.'

'And what did you do about Rhianna and Martha?'

'Er, brought them with me.'

'You got them out of bed to come here when I was next door?' she said in an angry whisper. 'I would have thought that their welfare was more important than you not wanting to have anything to do with me again.'

He ignored the last part of her protest and assured her, 'The children weren't asleep and they were well wrapped up with cosy dressing-gowns over their night-dresses and warm boots on their feet.

'Both of them were concerned about the sick little boy and also as I was already in the dog house where you were concerned I didn't want to damage my image any further. If you remember, you had said that you wouldn't be available for the rest of the day when you were leaving us after the girls' modelling session.

'We are not here to question each other's motives in any shape or form, Melissa. We have a very sick child here. His name is Alexander.'

They approached the small figure on the bed.

'His parents have been here all night and I've suggested that they go for some breakfast while we check if the procedure I started then is working.'

At that moment the door behind them opened and Alexander's parents appeared, followed by a porter with a trolley, and while nursing staff were lifting the small boy carefully onto the trolley Ryan said to them, 'Has Alexander had anything in the nature of a cold sore recently?'

'He had one a couple of weeks ago,' his mother told him tearfully. 'An aunt of mine who is subject to cold sores had been hugging and kissing him when she called round, and it was shortly afterwards that a big blister appeared on his lip. The chemist told us what to use and it finally healed over.'

'Let's go,' his father said impatiently, with his arm around his wife. 'There is no time to lose, is there, Dr Ferguson?' When Ryan nodded sombrely they went, one on either side of the trolley that carried their small son.

In those moments Melissa's admiration for the doctor who had even put his own children second to a very sick child belonging to someone else reached new heights. She'd had no right to criticise him for bringing Rhianna and Martha out late at night for once if Mollie hadn't been able to babysit for him, which had to have been the case.

Had she been so desperate for family and friends that she'd coveted his children? Was she now hurting because he didn't want her intruding into the life he had planned for himself and his daughters? If that *was* the case, it would not happen again.

By late afternoon their small patient was showing signs of responding to the anti-viral treatment after a second intravenous infusion. It wasn't mind-blowing, just a slight improvement, but it showed there was a chance that he might be able to fight off the serious infection, and it brought tremulous smiles to the faces of his parents that hadn't been there before.

The phone call to the family of the small girl with epilepsy had worked. A slapdash sort of young mother had brought the child to Outpatients in the late afternoon and had been forced to sit up and take notice when Ryan broke the news to her that the fits that her child had been having were due to epilepsy.

'That is the bad news,' he told her, as Melissa sat in with them. 'The good news is that young children often grow out of it as they get older. The word "epilepsy" refers to abnormalities of electrical activity in the brain that can be sometimes brief, which is how you described your daughter's seizures. Any longer and it could be a more serious matter.

'You must remember never to try to bring her out of it when she has a seizure. Just make her comfortable and she will recover of her own accord. The same if she occasionally has periods of drowsiness or doesn't answer when spoken to. Don't make a fuss, just let her come back to normality in her own time.

'A couple of things to bear in mind are to try to prevent her getting overtired or upset about anything, as those are situations that can trigger a seizure. Make sure that the staff at the school she attends are aware of the problem in case something of that kind occurs while she's in their care.

'I'm going to prescribe an anticonvulsant medicine that will help to reduce the number of seizures and in time they might disappear altogether,' he said reassuringly.

The young girl's mother had listened to what he'd had to say without interruption but now she was finding her voice and the first thing she did was apologise. 'I'm sorry we didn't keep that other appointment. I had no idea that a few funny moments in a child's life could be so serious.'

'We're hoping the episodes will decrease once your daughter starts taking the medication that I'm prescribing,' he told her.

When they'd gone Ryan said wryly, 'So what do you think the chances are that the mother will remember what I've said?'

'I'm not sure,' Melissa told him. 'She sounded sincere enough when she actually had something to say.'

'I hope you're right, for the child's sake' was the reply. 'I'm going to have a word with Alexander's parents to answer any questions they might have, and if the improvement is being sustained try to persuade them to go home and rest for a while.'

At the end of the day Ryan sought her out.

'Alexander seems to be stabilising now he's on the treatment, but in case I get called back here this evening, can we call a truce?'

'In what way?' she asked.

'Can I ask if you will stay with the girls if that should occur?'

'Yes, of course,' she said immediately. 'Just give me a buzz if you need me.' He might need her help with the girls but his requirements for her didn't seem to extend beyond that.

Ryan arrived home shortly after Melissa, and after an evening that was dominated by listening for the phone to ring into the silence, and frequently checking that his car was still where he'd parked it, Melissa went slowly up to bed.

It would seem that there had so far been no setbacks in Alexander's recovery, which was good, and also good was the thought that she and Ryan had found an uneasy kind of peace. If nothing else was ever forthcoming between them, she would have to live with the memory of being naked in his arms, matching his passion with her own, and for a few blissful moments seeing a future of living and loving together with Rhianna and Martha and maybe children of their own one day. She should have known better.

Ryan was not mercenary like David, or a shallow charmer like Julian. He was a man whose life had been changed drastically on a stormy night and he'd taken it on himself to stay faithful to his wife's memory while he brought up their children.

His life was rich and meaningful. Small wonder that he didn't need any more strings to his bow, so why did she feel that she had been guided to Heatherdale for a purpose more important than having a roof over her head?

Her grandmother had been a far-seeing woman. She'd known that one day Melissa would come to the small market town that was weaving its magic around her as it did with many others. Had the old lady foreseen her finding there the man who would be her heart's desire, while she was living in the drab town house that one day she was going to turn into a dream home?

As sleep began to claim her, her last thought was that she would seek out the place where her grandmother was buried. She recalled her father once saying that it was in the graveyard of the nearest church. When she found it she would make it beautiful, as she was doing to the house after years of neglect.

On Saturday morning Melissa set forth to find her grandmother's grave.

It was a cold and clear morning with the feeling of Christmas everywhere. The large tree that the council had erected dominated the centre of the town and shops and restaurants were in full festive mode as she walked the short distance to where she'd noticed a gracious stone building not far away from where she lived.

Older by far than the town houses, it stood on a large mound high off the roadside with a tall spire pointing upwards and was surrounded by a tranquil graveyard.

It took some time to find what she sought and her surmise that she was going to find long neglect there was proved correct. Overgrown and dirty, what had once been an attractive resting place was crying out to be cleaned, and once she'd found the spot where her grandmother was buried it would be just a short journey with cleaning materials and some hard work to make it beautiful once more. With all the weeds and brambles dug out of the ancient plot, it would be one way of offering her thanks to the person whose foresight had been her only hope to cling to in recent times.

After a quick lunch Melissa was back with all the necessary tools for the job and as she walked slowly along a side path in a sheltered place next to one of the stone walls of the church her eyes widened. There was a grave of gleaming white marble there with beautiful roses on it, but it was the inscription that caught her eye.

HERE LIES ELIZABETH (BETH) FERGUSON
CHERISHED WIFE OF RYAN
LOVING MOTHER OF RHIANNA AND MARTHA
MAY SHE REST IN PEACE

Melissa put the bucket she was carrying down slowly and laid the spade beside it. On returning to the graveyard, she'd gone down a different path to reach her grandmother's grave. If she hadn't she wouldn't have seen this. It was almost as if it had been meant, but in what way?

Yet even as she asked herself the question the answer was there. 'I don't want to take your place,' she said softly. 'I just want to love Ryan and Rhianna and Martha and help them to keep your memory alive.'

At that moment the sun broke through cloud high above and as Melissa took a last look at the beautiful memorial to a midwife who had risked her life and lost it to the elements when she'd put an imminent birth before her own safety, she bent to pick up the spade and bucket, and the rest of the things she'd brought, and at the same moment heard the crunch of feet on the gravel path in the deserted church yard.

When she looked up Ryan was coming towards her, and crazy as it was she felt as if he had caught her out in some misdemeanour as he observed what she'd brought with her in astonishment.

'What on earth?' he exclaimed, with a sideways glance at his wife's grave. 'You've not taken on an extra job at weekends as a grave-cleaner, have you? Only I'm in charge of this one.'

'That's not funny,' she said stiffly. 'The things I've brought with me are to clean up my grandmother's grave. I feel it is the least I can do after her leaving me her house.

'I came earlier to inspect it and of course after years of neglect it was how I thought it would be, so I went home to collect some things to help clean it up. I must have taken the wrong path. They all look alike.

'Your wife's grave is beautiful. I'm sure that she must have been the same, Ryan.' Melissa turned to go.

'Wait!' he called. 'Give me the spade and the bucket and anything else that is heavy. Did you honestly think I was going to let you stagger off like a pack mule?'

She didn't reply, just did as he'd asked and led the way to her grandmother's overgrown grave. 'Ugh!' he said when he saw it. 'That is too much for you to tackle. Perch on the seat over there while I give it a go.'

He was taking off his jacket and rolling up his sleeves and she said, 'Before you do, I have a couple of questions.'

'What are they?' he asked.

'Where are the children? And did you follow me here?'

'Rhianna and Martha are at a birthday party that won't be over for a couple of hours. I didn't follow you here. It was an opportunity to spend some quiet moments with Beth, to feel her near in the midst of my restricted life. I came because the future was becoming unclear and I hoped that I might see the way ahead better after some quiet time with her.'

'And I've butted into that, haven't I?' she said. 'Sallying forth with my grave-cleaning equipment. I'm sorry, Ryan.'

'You don't have to be,' he told her. 'You've done nothing wrong since the moment of your arrival in Heatherdale, except perhaps make me doubt some of my decisions. Maybe I needed someone or something to take the blinkers off my eyes.

'With regard to today and us meeting like this, I can always come again as this place is so near where I live. However, before I start cleaning the grime of ages off this imposing headstone, I have a question for you.'

'What is it?'

'Are you going to partner me, as you promised, to Mollie's wedding? Only you didn't sound too sure the last time it was mentioned.'

'Yes, I suppose so,' she told him flatly. 'If you recall the occasion of my lack of enthusiasm it was when only hours before we'd made love and I was unsure whether you had just used me because I was there or if I hadn't made the grade when it came to your sex life.'

He threw the spade down with a clatter. 'I don't have a "sex life", Melissa!

'The kind of life I live doesn't allow for that. I made love to you because you were and still are totally desirable, and you are the only woman I have wanted to make love with since I lost Beth.

'The way I behaved afterwards was because I felt guilty. Because that kind of magic didn't fit in with the vows I made when I lost her, not because I didn't want you like crazy.'

He picked up the spade. 'And now, as nothing has changed, can I proceed with the job in hand? It is going to take some time, so I will have to keep an eye on the graveyard clock with regard to the birthday party.'

So Ryan *had* wanted her. To hear that was joy untold, or at least it would be if he hadn't finished what he'd had to say with a reminder that nothing had changed with regard to his commitment.

'Don't be late on my account,' she told him, bringing the moment back to reality. 'There's no rush with this. I shall persist until my grandmother's grave is returned to its original splendour. With regard to the party, I could pick the children up if you want me to.'

'It would be good if you could,' he replied. 'They will be pleased to see you and I can carry on here until the light fades. The party is at the house of one of Rhianna's school friends and Martha was included in the invitation.'

'What time do you want me to pick them up?' she questioned. 'I'll need directions on how to get there, not being a native of this beautiful place. I can't believe what I ever saw in life in the big city.'

He rested on the spade for a moment and with his vivid blue gaze observing her said, 'So you have no regrets at finding yourself living in Heatherdale?'

'No,' she said gravely. 'I am employed in the kind of work I've always wanted to do, with a first-class paediatric consultant to learn from in the process of healing sick children, and have a house that has twice as much character even in its present state as the over-the-top expensive showpiece that was in keeping with my father's vision of an ideal home.'

She didn't mention that she might also have found the man of her dreams living just next door, too.

Ryan's glance was still on her in the silence that

followed and she brought herself back down to earth by saying, 'So, when do you want me to pick up the children and where? It will be dark soon so it would be better to go now, I feel. I'd rather to be too early than too late.'

'Yes,' he agreed, and gave her the address where the party was being held and directions to get there.

'I'll take your tools home with me and see you back there later.'

As he watched her go, snug against the cold in a warm jacket and leggings with a woolly hat covering her head, he saw a different vision of her in his mind's eye, looking up at him from the covers of his bed, beautiful, wanton, adoring. What had he done?

Spoilt it, made her feel cheap because of the self-sacrificing dogma that he lived his life by. The children had more sense than he had. They already loved Melissa without any reserve. But their life with their mother had been short, while his love for Beth had been there since his early teens and it had deepened with every passing day. Never once had he expected that they wouldn't grow old together.

CHAPTER EIGHT

WHEN RHIANNA AND Martha came tripping out of the party with all the other young guests their faces lit up when they saw her, and as Melissa hugged them to her it was a moment of unexpected pleasure in the approaching dusk of a winter afternoon.

'Where's Daddy?' Martha wanted to know, and when Melissa had explained they climbed into the back of the car and talked about the party, Mollie's wedding, and Christmas all the way home. Melissa wished that *she* could visualise some joy coming her way in the weeks to come.

When they arrived back at home, Ryan had returned and had hot drinks waiting for the three of them. With the children perched one on either side of him, he was listening intently to their excited account of the party while Melissa observed the three of them bleakly.

They had something that she was not likely to ever have, a loving family bond, because she had fallen in love with Rhianna and Martha's father. He was the only man she would ever want to give her a child and as the chances of that were not good, childless she would stay.

'You look very serious,' Ryan said suddenly from beside her. 'If it's about the grave, a few more hours the first chance I get we'll have it sorted.'

The grave was the last thing on her mind but thanks were due for his assistance.

'I'm most grateful for you taking over,' she told him stiltedly. 'Any improvement will be better than it was and, now, if you will excuse me, I need to change out of these clothes into something less drab than my grave-cleaning outfit.'

'Yes, sure,' he agreed, and it was there again, the memory of when he'd made love to her, taunting him, reproving him for how he'd treated her afterwards.

The hospital was already full of Christmas cheer, with a beautifully decorated spruce in the grounds and another in the entrance hall, and for the staff there was a ball arranged to take place a couple of weeks before.

Julian was hoping to be mobile enough to attend and was expecting an enthusiastic response from Melissa at the news, but as far as she was concerned if Ryan wasn't going to be there because of his domestic duties, or for any other reason, it would put a blight on the occasion.

With Christmas being so near, Melissa was turning her thoughts to presents for the children next door and a wedding gift for the bride-to-be. With regard to Ryan it would be like trespassing into his privacy to buy a personal gift, so it would have to be something basic that didn't give off any messages other than Christmas good wishes.

From his manner after those never-to-be-forgotten moments when he'd made love to her it had been clear that he'd felt it vital to point out that it had been just a moment of hunger for her that had been the cause of it. With the hurt of that forever in her mind he need have no concern that she was going to use the magic and romance of Christmas to tempt him again.

She smiled a wintry smile. What were the least personal of gifts for the opposite sex? Socks, scarf, handkerchiefs, toiletries, book token?

What about a romp with a junior doctor? From the way he'd described it, there had been nothing personal about *that*, either.

On the Friday night before the staff ball Melissa went shopping, and as she walked past the house next door on her way to the town centre it was ablaze with light. The curtains were drawn back and she could see Ryan and children seated at the dining table, having their meal. Longing swept over her in a painful tide as any impetus to shop drained away at the sight.

For a moment she almost turned back, but returning to her empty house would make the evening seem even more desolate. Better to be among the crowds of late-night Christmas shoppers than cooped up on her own.

It turned out to be the right thing to do. The shops were ablaze with all the reminders of the time of year they could think of, and inside them the public were buying gifts that would be brought out into the open only on the day.

Choosing a present for Mollie was no problem. A wedding gift voucher from the elegant department store where they'd chosen the girl's dresses didn't take long, and neither did a talking teddy bear each for Rhianna and Martha.

About to take the escalator to the floor above that to Menswear, she stopped, her eyes widening.

Ryan and the children had been on the point of finishing their meal when Melissa had passed the house earlier looking less than happy, and he had immediately gone into the kitchen where Mollie was tidying up and said, 'I've just seen Melissa go past looking lost and lonely. Could you hang on here for a little while longer, so that I can go after her to make sure that she's all right?'

'Yes, of course,' she said immediately. 'That lovely girl has nobody else to care about her except us. Take as long as you like.'

'All right, no need to push it, Mollie. I *have* got eyes in my head, you know.' He opened the front door. 'I'm presuming she was off to do some late-night shopping, would you agree?'

'Almost certainly' was the reply. 'The shops are open late tonight. Try the department store where we shopped for the girls' outfits. It's classy and so is she!'

Groaning at Mollie's second plug in favour of the

only woman he'd ever cared about since Beth had been taken from him, he went, heading off towards the town centre.

There was only one man that she knew with hair like gold and eyes as blue as a summer sky. Melissa watched Ryan making his way towards her through the crowds. But how could that be? It was only a short time since she'd seen Ryan and his children having their evening meal.

He was beside her in seconds, relieved to have found her so quickly. Taking her arm he drew her to one side. Observing him anxiously, she asked, 'What's wrong? I saw you eating at home not long ago.'

He was smiling. 'That was then, this is now. I saw you pass and thought you looked lost and lonely so I followed you to make sure that you were all right.'

She felt tears prickle her eyes. He cared enough to come chasing after her from just a fleeting glance through the window, but not enough to want her in his home, his bed and his heart. *She* knew where she belonged but he didn't.

'I'm fine,' she told him with a brittle smile. 'I came to do my Christmas shopping for the only people I know as I'm short on family and friends. I also came to get a wedding gift for Mollie and Jack. I take it she's with Rhianna and Martha?'

'Yes, of course,' he told her evenly, and wondered if Julian was on her list. If what he'd seen outside his office window that day was anything to go by, he might have graduated to the top of it. But for the present the moment was his. He'd found Melissa, and Mollie had said there was no need for him to rush back.

'Let me take you for a coffee,' he suggested, 'or we could be more upmarket and go to a wine bar. I'm not too pushed for time.'

She was wearing the fake fur hat and coat again and was very much the elegant shopper, but there was strain in her expression, her dark hazel gaze was asking for answers to the questions that filled her mind and without setting too much store on his importance in her life he knew that he was most likely the cause of it.

'Yes, all right,' she agreed, to his surprise. 'Whatever you decide will be fine.'

'We'll go to a new place that has just opened near the pump room. I was there the other night and it is quite something.'

He'd seen her expression and said, 'It was on a private consultation. The guy and his wife who own the place are the son and daughter-in-law of the chairman of the hospital board and they'd asked for a visit to their small daughter in their apartment above the wine bar. So, you see, I wasn't living it up,' he said dryly. 'Mollie was doing the honours once again and I nearly asked you to go with me for the experience... and the company.'

'But you didn't,' she commented, as they made their way out of the store amongst the jostling crowds.

'No, I didn't. It was Tuesday night and it had been an

exhausting day for us both, if you remember. It hardly seemed fair to ask you to work on into the evening.'

It was only half-true. It had been on his mind to ask her to accompany him ever since the chairman's urgent phone call that morning. He only felt alive in her presence, and when she wasn't there he lived on the memory of her in his arms, giving herself to him trustingly, completely, only to be rejected when his sanity had returned.

And then, hoping to lessen the hurt he'd caused her, he'd got himself involved in the task of cleaning up that filthy grave with Beth's beautiful white marble gleaming not far away in a wintry sun. He doubted it was enough to earn her forgiveness.

He was steering her across the busy main street with his hand beneath her elbow and as she looked up at him questioningly he said, 'What?'

'The little girl you went to see, what was the problem?'

'I'm not sure until I get the results back from tests that I've arranged. There was something rather puzzling about her condition.'

'So are you going to tell me what you think it might be?'

'No. This is the two of us spending a short time together away from everything else in our lives.'

'We won't be away from everything if the little girl's parents are at the wine bar,' she pointed out.

He shook his head. 'They won't be. They're staying the weekend at the grandparents' place, the chairman's house. Otherwise I wouldn't be taking you there as it would seem rather tasteless, don't you think?'

'Yes, I do,' she agreed, and thought it would also be tasteless if Ryan was using their meeting in the department store as an opportunity to spare her some of his precious time, with the get-away excuse, whenever he chose to use it, of Mollie waiting to be relieved from childminding.

He had stopped outside what had to be the wine bar. Soft lights were spreading their glow onto the pavement outside another of Heatherdale's attractive stone buildings and she hoped that it wasn't going to be one of those places with low lighting and intimate corners.

It wasn't. When they went inside it was warm, well lit, and crowded. He saw her smile and thought that at least one of them was pleased.

When he'd gone through the bar area on the Tuesday night to get to the apartment above, it had been deserted, but tonight was Friday of course. 'Shall we go somewhere else?' he suggested, not wanting to forego the pleasure of some quiet time together that they weren't going to get in that place.

'No,' she told him. 'Maybe just the one drink and then home.' She glanced at the shopping that he'd been carrying for her. 'We're not exactly dressed for Friday night on the town and Mollie needs to be relieved. I'll stay with the children while you take her home.'

He almost groaned out loud. Having got her to himself for once, Melissa was all for rushing back home. She'd been wary of being alone with him ever since they'd made love. Was there ever going to be any clarity in their lives away from the hospital?

Workwise they were in complete harmony, both with the same dedication, but away from that there was nothing to hold on to. He wasn't going to let the opportunity to talk about themselves go by, even if only for a short time, and when they'd found a table and he'd been to the bar Ryan asked, 'Would you like to spend Christmas Day with us, Melissa? The children would love it, if you haven't already made other arrangements.'

She smiled a twisted smile. What other arrangements could she have made in a place where she knew no one and had no connections other than those she worked with? The alternative would be booking a solitary meal at some restaurant.

'It's very kind of you to invite me,' she said stiffly, 'and I would love to be with the children on such a special day, but I wouldn't want the invitation to be a drag on you personally at a time that will have painful memories.'

'Having you with us will help to put them into the right perspective,' he told her, and was amazed how much he meant it. 'So what do you say?' He smiled. 'Would you be willing to sample my cooking?'

'Yes, I would,' she said. 'I really would. I'd love to spend Christmas Day with your children.'

She hadn't mentioned looking forward to spending the day with him but between now and then he would work on it, just as long as he didn't allow himself to be sidetracked by responsibilities that he was hesitant about sharing with anyone else.

With a lighter heart than when he'd found her in the department store he said, 'Maybe we should make tracks. As you so rightly pointed out, we ought to be relieving Mollie.'

As they walked the short distance to their respective houses there was new harmony between them that Melissa prayed would last, and that she wasn't setting herself up for more heartache.

They found the children asleep and Mollie painstakingly retrieving dropped stitches in Rhianna's knitting when they got back. On seeing their expressions, the older woman thought thankfully that the short time they'd spent together seemed to have brought them closer.

When he came back after seeing Mollie safely home, Melissa was ready to leave, and he protested, 'Surely you have time for a coffee?'

She was turning to go and shook her head. 'I have things to do, Ryan.'

'I'm still not forgiven for what happened between us, am I? Our working relationship is second to none, but our private lives are lagging behind, and I'm to blame but, Melissa, I *am* working on it.'

She was weakening. 'It isn't your fault that you lost the wife that you loved so much, and your devotion to her memory is very special. But what about your children's needs? Do you remember what Rhianna asked Santa for?'

'Yes. I am hardly likely to forget that. She asked for a *mummy*, which was not the first time since you came into our lives, but I'm not going to fill the gap for the sake of my small daughter's request to Santa. It is the agony of such a loss that I couldn't face again that makes me hesitate. *Do you understand?*'

She was across the room and holding him in her arms. 'Yes, I do,' she told him softly. 'It would be so much easier if I didn't, but I do.'

Brushing her lips gently across his cheek, she held him closer and when he turned his head the kisses were there and everything became a blur of aching need until he eased himself out of her arms.

Looking down at her gravely, he said, 'I don't want to hurt you any more, Melissa. I'm going to make that coffee and afterwards I'll see you safely back to your place.'

She nodded, unable to speak because her heart was racing and her bones melting as he disappeared into the kitchen.

When he came back with the drinks Ryan said surprisingly, 'Am I right in thinking that our friend Julian lusts after you? I saw that kiss out there in the hospital car park and let's face it, *he* wouldn't bring any baggage with him, would he?'

'That was Julian trying his hand at matchmaking between the two of *us*, instead of his usual womanising,' she informed him with the euphoria of previous moments disappearing. 'I do not sleep around with the likes of him, neither do I like to be described as husband-hunting, and if ever you decide that we do have a future together I would feel blessed to have Rhianna and Martha to love and care for, just in case you have any issues about that.'

She was on her feet and placing the coffee cup carefully on to a nearby table when she said, 'I can see myself out.' As he came towards her she shook her head and before he could protest she was gone.

Saturday dragged by with the thought of the ball in the evening bringing no feeling of anticipation. If it wasn't for the fact that Julian was to be there and expecting a fuss from everyone at his reappearance, Melissa would have given it a miss. She couldn't even muster the enthusiasm to come up with an outfit for the evening ahead.

One thing she wasn't short of was clothes, expensive ones that she'd been loath to part with when settling her father's debts. Her smart car, her jewellery had all gone into the seemingly bottomless pit, but her clothes she'd managed to save and somewhere amongst them were a couple of evening dresses carefully protected against the chill that was ever present in her grandmother's house.

They hadn't discussed the ball since his put-down after they'd made love. When it had been mentioned before then it had seemed that it was one occasion when he was prepared to socialise and let his children do one of their favourite things—spend the night at Mollie's.

So she had half expected that they would go together for the sake of convenience if nothing else, but things had changed between them since then and if he suggested they go together now she would refuse. There was no point in starting hospital gossip when there was nothing to comment about.

She was going to go use a taxi to transport her there and back. That way her arrangements could be best controlled. The thought of an early departure might seem tempting as the evening wore on.

When she tried on the dresses the choice wasn't easy. A black low-cut number that fitted the smooth lines of her body like a glove or a high-necked sleeveless dress of pale cream silk that accentuated the dark sheen of her hair and luminous hazel eyes were the choices before her.

She was drawn towards the black with an urge to show her neighbour that she was more than the drab girl next door, much more.

But the jewellery sold to help clear the debt had left her without the kind of relief that the black dress would need, whereas the cream number's high neck needed no such adornments.

So putting the thought of sophistication to one side, when the time came to dress for the evening ahead her choice was going to be that with long elbow-length gloves to match the dress and conceal her lack of finery.

* * *

After the rebuff of the night before, Ryan had spent the day cleaning the car in the morning and then taking the girls to the cinema to see a children's Christmas movie in the afternoon. Mollie had been to collect them and a brooding silence lay over the house.

There had been no sightings of Melissa all day and as the minutes dragged past he knew that he could not let her make her own way to something like the ball in the town centre when she hardly knew the place.

It would be churlish not to offer to take her. If she refused, so be it, but at least he would have offered, and if she preferred to spend the evening with Julian and his cronies he would have to endure it because she must be weary of him forever bleating about his responsibilities.

When she opened the door to him his eyes widened. He had yet to shower and change into a dinner suit, but she was ready, beautiful, and desirable in a fantastic dress.

'I came to ask how you intend to get to the ball,' he said levelly.

'Why? I'm going by taxi. I was just about to ring for one,' she replied, hiding her dismay at the sight of him showing no sign of being ready himself. Was Ryan not going because she was?

'Forget the taxi,' he said. 'I'll take you.'

'No, thanks.' As his jaw tightened, she continued, 'You might cramp my style while I'm giving all the men with no baggage the benefit of my company, and in any case if you are driving it will stop you from drinking a toast or any other kind of alcohol.'

'So why don't we share a taxi, if you don't mind waiting until I'm ready?' he persisted.

'Yes, all right,' she agreed, relieved to know that he hadn't changed his mind about the evening ahead, that he still had every intention of attending the ball.

When he called for her half an hour later her mouth went dry at the sight of him, as it always did. Scrubbed clean with his golden fairness accentuated by a dark dinner jacket and pristine white shirt, he was every woman's dream man yet didn't seem to realise it, and if he did, he didn't care.

In that moment it was there again. The certainty that she would never want any man but Ryan, and if he didn't feel the same about her she was either going to have to stand by and watch him live his life without her or leave Heatherdale and endure a second new beginning where he wasn't forever so near but so unattainable. With that thought came the vision of a grave of beautiful white marble in a secluded corner of a nearby churchyard.

'I rang for a taxi before I left the house so it should be on its way,' he informed her, conscious that her thoughts were somewhere else, though he would have been surprised to discover where.

They sat facing each other on the drive to the hospital, each of them so conscious of the other they needed the space between them to quell the longings they sparked off in each other.

When they arrived at their destination, Melissa stood by hesitantly while Ryan paid the taxi driver. She was the one who should have given the ball a miss. It would have been so much easier for them both if she had.

He belonged there, was highly respected at the hospital, and had lived in Heatherdale all his life. She was a newcomer, also a doctor dedicated to child care but way behind him in experience, and with a past that when she looked back on it seemed so empty and fruitless she couldn't believe how she had existed without what she had found here.

As the taxi began to pull away, Julian's car stopped beside them at the kerb edge en route for the hotel car park. 'Wow!' he said when he saw her. 'Aren't you the lucky one, Ryan? I'm no longer on crutches but still need two sticks so I can't offer any competition.' With that he drove off to find a parking space.

'One can't help but admire that guy's impudence,' Ryan said laughingly when he'd gone. 'Can we stand having him back when he's well again, do you think? Julian has already been sounding me out with regard to some part-time hours, but I don't relish the idea of him hovering over you all the time to make me jealous.'

Melissa hadn't spoken since they'd arrived. Julian's appearance had lifted her out of the doldrums, but she was still not in a party mood and had no answer forthcoming to what Ryan had just said.

Instead, she led the way into the foyer and when they separated to go to their respective cloakrooms to hand over their coats she realised that this must be a rare occasion for Ryan, out on the town probably for the first time in ages.

She was wrong not to understand his lifestyle, and wrong to present such a miserable face. Tonight she would forget everything except that she loved him more than life itself, and if she possibly could was going to make it a night for him to remember.

When she appeared back in the foyer he was chatting to an older couple she identified as the chairman of the board and his wife.

As she hesitated Ryan beckoned her across.

'Dr Redmond is a colleague who has recently joined us and is proving to be a lifesaver in every sense of the word. She will be working with me as I treat your granddaughter.'

Ryan must have received the results of the test he'd ordered. She was keen to discuss the findings, but other guests were hovering, waiting to speak to the chairman of the hospital board, and as the two of them moved on she asked, 'So what is it that is wrong with their granddaughter?'

'I only got a phone call with the results of the tests a few moments before I left the house tonight,' he explained, 'and have just been informing the grandparents of what has come up in them before I told you. Are you sure that you want to talk work at a time like this?'

'Yes, if you do.'

'Then let's find somewhere where we won't be over-heard. This is a private consultation that I'm dealing with, don't forget.'

'I won't forget,' she promised. Their work with chil-dren with neurological problems was the one area of their relationship that brought no personal heartache.

'Have you heard of von Recklinghausen's disease?' he asked when they were seated at a table at the far end of the ballroom. 'Or to give it its medical title neuro-fibromatosis?'

'Only vaguely.'

'I'm not surprised with a name like that. It's an in-herited disorder diagnosed from numerous soft fibrous swellings of nerves on the trunk and pelvis in the first instance. They can be of any size and are pale brown in colour.'

'And that is what the little girl has got?'

'Yes. Fortunately they are not present in the central nervous system, which could cause problems such as epilepsy. They will not require surgery unless they begin to look unsightly.

'When I said I was confused as to whether I was right in suspecting the von Recklinghausen's disease it was because no one in either of the child's parents' families has ever had it, so little Carly seems to be what could be the first of others who might inherit it from *her* if she has any children.

'Her grandparents have been extremely worried about her and even now with a diagnosis that might have been much worse they're apprehensive. I've told them that we will see her regularly and keep a keen eye open for any signs of the illness affecting the central nervous system in the future, and there you have it.'

At that moment an announcement was made asking those present to take their places for the meal that was part of the evening, and as they seated themselves with the rest of the neurology staff Julian appeared on the other side of her.

'I saw the two of you wrapped up in each other at the far table,' he murmured conspiratorially.

'We were discussing a patient, if you want to know,' she told him. 'Don't jump to conclusions.'

CHAPTER NINE

As THE NIGHT wore on Melissa was conscious of the festive atmosphere amongst the staff of the renowned children's hospital. It was an opportunity that came once each year for them to socialise with those who, like themselves, worked endlessly towards the healing of the young.

Obviously a few were missing because the wards and emergency sections needed to be staffed, as well as having a small nucleus of theatre staff available should the need arise, but the bulk of them were there to enjoy the Christmas ball that the authorities held for them each year.

It had been noted by most of them that Ryan Ferguson, head of the neuro unit, had arrived in the company of his new registrar, and there were those there who were curious as to the meaning of it. But when she was swept in turn onto the dance floor by a couple of young medics, with an amicable smile from the man himself, their interest waned.

Fortunately, they were not able to read his thoughts,

which were a jumble of not wanting to be seen to be monopolising Melissa and the longing to hold her close and dance every moment of the night away with her. But she'd reminded him about his tactless comment regarding men with no baggage and he was giving her the chance to get to know some of them.

For her part, she'd felt sick inside at being handed over to the young hopefuls like some sort of raffle prize, and when they had each returned her to where Ryan was chatting to other staff members, she was already debating whether to go and keep a subdued-looking Julian company to make up for his lack of mobility.

No sooner had the thought occurred to her than she acted on it and as Ryan watched her cross the now deserted dance floor in that direction he groaned inwardly.

He wanted her in *his* arms, not those of someone else, to be able to forget his hangs-ups and frustrations for a while. So why wasn't he doing just that, letting Melissa's nearness banish the aching feeling of loss that was there whenever they were apart?

'So what's new?' Julian asked, when Melissa seated herself beside him. 'Is the boss blind or what?'

'I'm competing against a beautiful memory,' she told him, 'and I don't want it to be like that. I want Ryan to see me as an opportunity to move into a new relationship without causing any hurt to the past, but of all things he is a man of honour and integrity. He was the first person I met when I came to Heatherdale and he took my breath away.'

'That was because you hadn't met me first,' he teased, and as she laughed at his cheek he went on, 'Watch out, here he comes.'

The band had started to play again, smooth, languorous music to warm the blood and create desire. When Ryan stopped in front of them he held out his hand, and when she took it in hers he raised her to her feet and said, 'My turn, I think.'

It would always be his turn if he could only see the rightness of it. More likely he was only dancing with her out of some sense of duty.

She was wrong about *that*! Ryan stayed by her side for the rest of the evening. Every time the music filled the ballroom they danced and his nearness was fantastic, his touch a delight. She wondered how the night would end for them, with the children safely tucked up at Mollie's.

It wasn't going to be her in his bed, that was for sure. The pain of his rejection after they'd made love still gnawed at her. So what did it leave them, a peck on the cheek and goodnight?

Unaware of her confusion, Ryan was smiling down at her. They were being watched, talked about, and he didn't give a damn. He could imagine them gossiping about him and Melissa, but for once Ryan didn't mind.

He had gone to the bar to get them drinks and while he was waiting to be served amongst many others Melissa's unease increased regarding what was going to happen when they arrived back home with only themselves to be concerned about.

They'd danced almost every dance together; the attraction between them was at its peak. Would they be able to separate each to their own property with just a brief farewell?

She wouldn't be able to face another putdown if they made love, only for Ryan to have regrets again afterwards. It was a ghastly situation to be in, never sure whether one day he would ask her to marry him, or would keep her on the edge of his life for ever.

There was the memory of the other day when they'd met unexpectedly by his wife's grave and he'd made no secret of how much Beth still meant to him. Would *she* ever mean so much to him that he could accept her in Beth's place?

The uncertainties of the moment were crowding in on her and aware that it would still be a few minutes before Ryan was served, she rose to her feet. Moving swiftly in the direction of the cloakroom, she collected her coat and keeping out of sight went into the hotel foyer and out into the night where taxis were lined up in readiness for transporting homeward-bound revellers. It took only seconds to give directions to the driver of the first one in the queue and she was gone.

When Ryan arrived back at the table and she wasn't there he expected her to reappear any moment, but as the minutes ticked by and eyes were on him it began to register that Melissa was no longer in the building.

Julian stopped by the table and said, 'I think she's gone, boss.'

Ryan got slowly to his feet and made his way towards the taxi rank.

Was she insane? Leaving the warmth and safety of the hotel to go out into the dark winter night alone? Surely Melissa wasn't so wary of him that she was concerned that he might want a repeat of that last time when Rhianna and Martha had been at Mollie's?

All he had wanted was to have her with him at the ball, to dance with her, delighting in her nearness that always kept the loneliness he lived with at bay, and to see her safely home when it was over. Any other desires would have been kept tightly under control, but it would seem that she saw him as someone who would want it all his way and she'd panicked and gone.

When the taxi driver pulled up at the bottom of his drive Ryan saw that Melissa's house, gaunt and unpainted, was in darkness, and as the man drove off he wondered what to do next. How was he going to find out if Melissa was safely home or elsewhere without creating a disturbance?

One thing was sure: he was not going to put his key into the lock of his front door until he was sure that she was warm and safe behind hers. So first a phone call and if there was no answer it was going to be a case of hammering on it until Melissa appeared, and if she didn't he shuddered to think what he would do.

Melissa was huddled under the bedcovers when he rang and cringed at the sound, but when it continued she reached for the bedside phone and managed a weak 'Hello?'

'So you're back safely,' he said flatly, as relief washed over him. 'What was behind the sneaky Cinderella performance? You could at least have let me know that you wanted to leave so that I could have seen you safely home.'

'I didn't want you to have to do that,' she explained awkwardly. 'It wasn't as if I was your partner for the evening, even though we'd danced a lot. We'd just shared a taxi to take us there, that was all. I'm sorry if I caused you any anxiety, it was just that...' Her voice trailed away and into the silence that followed he let her see that he read her mind.

'You didn't want to risk a repeat of the last time the children stayed at Mollie's?'

'Yes, that was it, and now will you please leave me alone?'

'If that is what you want, yes,' he said coolly, and rang off.

Melissa turned her face into the pillows and wept.

She awoke the next morning with head aching and face red and blotchy from weeping, but with a decision made to leave Heatherdale, to find somewhere where she could live without hurt and insecurity and where there was a position in paediatrics.

Estate agents were open on Sundays for a few hours in the town, so she decided that later in the morning she would make an appointment for one of them to come round to value the house and set things in motion.

She just hoped that Ryan wouldn't make a fuss about her departure from Heatherdale when the time came.

A move in February or early March was not far away and wouldn't leave it too long before she went. In the meantime she wouldn't get any closer to Rhianna and Martha so that they weren't too upset when Santa didn't bring them a new mummy, or at least the promise of one.

And what of their father? She knew Ryan wanted her but in what role in his life? She'd been betrayed by her own father, discarded with all speed by a shallow fiancé, and in the wonder of meeting a man like Ryan had hoped that he might feel the same about her. Maybe a part of him did, but there were side issues, grief of long standing and children to consider. Would he ever feel ready to put someone in Beth's place?

Mollie brought the children back in the middle of Sunday morning and immediately cottoned onto an atmosphere of gloom around their father.

'So, how was the ball?' she asked. 'Did the two of you enjoy yourselves?'

'Er...yes,' he replied unconvincingly and she didn't pursue the subject.

There was no sign of anyone from next door when Melissa set off for the centre of the town at midday. Mollie's car was nowhere in sight so she concluded that Ryan must have taken the children out for Sunday lunch. If that was the case she was grateful for it. The last thing she wanted was to meet them on her way to the estate agent's.

The place was empty of customers when she got there and a smart-suited middle-aged man sprang to attention when she went inside and asked if someone could come to value a property that she wished to put on the market as soon as possible.

'I can come now if you like,' he offered. 'As you can see, we are quiet at the moment.'

On the point of taking him up on the offer she decided that it would be better if he came some time early the following day while Ryan was at the hospital, the children at school, and Mollie wasn't around, and with that in mind left a key with him.

By the time she arrived back at the house her determination was dwindling. Was she crazy to be cutting herself off from Ryan and the children in such a hurry? Suppose no one wanted to buy the house when the 'For Sale' sign went up. It could hardly be described as a desirable residence in its present state, and what about her grandmother's wish that she should live there, and the grave that she was going to sort out?

They were things that belonged to the past, she reasoned miserably. It was the present that she was running away from.

Monday was a weird day, working with Ryan in assumed harmony when she longed to be somewhere else where there was no heartache. But the children in their care had to come first and no matter what was going on in their lives away from the hospital, when they were there it took priority over everything.

When they'd come face-to-face in the corridor on arriving he'd said, unsmilingly, 'I'm told that we have had some intakes over the weekend that are going to keep us busy, so when you're ready…'

'Yes, of course,' she'd said coolly, and presented herself on the wards within minutes to find him already examining a twelve-year-old girl who had been rushed in over the weekend after drinking some kind of noxious substance and had had to have her stomach washed out.

'Do we know what it was?' she asked.

'Not at the moment,' he replied. 'Apparently the youngster was partying at a friend's house and was given a drink that caused her to start vomiting and lose consciousness temporarily. The inside of her mouth and throat is very inflamed so she's been given something to ease that, and as you see she's now sleeping normally after the ordeal of the stomach wash-out.

'Her mother is here. She thinks that one of the lads at the party thought he was playing a harmless trick on her daughter and gave her some concoction in the drink that he'd got out of the chemistry lab at school. He is now being questioned by the police.'

His voice was brisk and businesslike, as it always was when they were on the wards or in the clinics, but there was a remoteness about it that wasn't usually there, as if he was talking to a stranger. Whatever was between them was now over.

It confirmed to Melissa that she was doing the right thing in leaving Heatherdale, and when the estate agent rang in the early afternoon with a valuation figure that was better than she'd expected she told him to go ahead with the sale.

'How about a board outside?' he questioned. 'Not everyone wants that, but it is a good way of advertising.'

'Yes, please,' she told him. It would be easier for Ryan to find out what she was planning that way, instead of having to face him herself with the news.

When she'd arrived at the hospital that morning everyone except her had chatted about the ball. There'd been no sign of Ryan and she'd gone to the secretary's office to check on what the day had in store for them to avoid being involved in the small talk when they came face-to-face.

He was still annoyed by her conduct of Saturday night, when she'd left the hotel without telling him, and if his manner was remote his feelings weren't. He'd been so wrapped up in his safe lifestyle he'd given no thought to hers, living alone without friends or family in that ghastly house. Tonight he would make amends, go round to see Melissa and ask her to forgive him for his selfishness.

That determination lasted until he pulled up in front of their two houses in the evening and saw the 'For Sale' sign. 'Oh, no!' he exclaimed. Were his eyes deceiving him?

Melissa must have really meant it when she'd told him to stay away from her. Where on earth was she

planning to go? She'd told him how she loved Heatherdale. Had it been a short-lived attraction and the same
applied to him? She was writing him off like a ship
that had passed in the night.

And what about Mollie's wedding? He'd asked Melissa to partner him for the occasion and be there for
the children while he was performing his duties during the service. Rhianna and Martha loved her and
she loved them. It was just him who was the problem.

There was no sign of her car so maybe she was
avoiding him. She would have to face him sooner or
later and until then he was going to keep a low profile,
for her sake if nothing else.

'What do you think is going on next door?' Mollie questioned when he went inside. 'Doesn't Melissa
like us any more?'

'I don't think she has any problems with you and the
girls,' he told her wryly, 'but she's not too thrilled with me.'

'She won't be gone before Christmas, will she?' she
asked anxiously, without commenting on his remark
about himself.

'I very much doubt it' was the reply. 'She won't want
to miss your wedding and also hopefully the children's
excitement on Christmas morning.'

He was rallying from the shock of seeing the sale
board. House buying always took a few weeks at least,
sometimes months, and if she got a buyer who was in
no rush it could take for ever. Melissa would be around
for Christmas, unless she'd got any other dreadful surprises planned.

* * *

Melissa had called in at the estate agent's just before they closed to sign any necessary paperwork and to avoid arriving home at the same time as Ryan. When she eventually turned up she breathed a sigh of relief because there was no sign of him, which would give her a few hours' respite before having to face him the following day.

Once she'd eaten she phoned Mollie, who was back home, to assure her that she would be there for her wedding and if she needed any help with anything she had only to ask. The last thing she wanted was to cause any hassle for either the bride or her two small attendants.

'I'm sorry to see that you're intending leaving us, Melissa,' the older woman said. 'Ryan and the children need you, and I feel that you need them.'

'I can't compete with his devotion to his wife's memory,' she told her. 'He is happy as he is, Mollie.'

'Not all the time.'

'Maybe, but that is how it seems to me,' she replied, and changed the subject. 'I will see to the children getting ready on the morning of the wedding so have no worries on that score, and will be in touch before then to check if you need me for anything else. If Ryan still wants me to partner him, that's okay, too, though I have my doubts about whether he will.'

After saying goodbye to the motherly housekeeper, she settled down to browse over the day's events, aware that so far there had been no feedback from Ryan.

Maybe he was just relieved that she was removing temptation out of his way.

Ryan was far from relieved about the state of affairs. If Melissa had wanted to make him realise how much she meant to him, she was succeeding. Mollie had called to say that the two of them had spoken on the phone and that Melissa was still available to assist on the morning of the wedding and that she would still partner him on that occasion if he wanted her to.

So there was going to be time for her to change her mind over Christmas and afterwards while she was waiting for a buyer. In the meantime, he would be his normal self when they were in each other's company, without referring to her wanting to move.

The next morning on the wards Ryan talked only about their patients, which was not unusual on a normal day, but Melissa had been expecting at least some mention of her putting the house up for sale and concluded that he must see it as something of minor interest. If that was the case, she wasn't going to refer to it, either.

The days leading up to Christmas and Mollie's wedding were some of the strangest Melissa had ever known. On the last Saturday before the two events there was a knock on her door and she opened it to find a van from a local tree nursery parked in front. When he saw her the driver said, 'I've got a tree here for you.'

'There must be a mistake,' she told him. 'I haven't ordered anything from you.'

'Well, somebody has,' he told her. 'Two trees were ordered and paid for to be delivered to these two houses.' When she looked across, Melissa saw that he had already deposited a tree on Ryan's drive. 'Your neighbours are out,' he explained, and without further comment went to his truck and hoisted a fresh green spruce tree from the top of a pile and carried it to her door and through into the hall.

'Have a nice Christmas, lady,' he said, after resting it upright against the wall, and went on his way.

Where she hadn't done anything regarding decorations so far, Ryan's house already had a festive look about it, with fairy lights around the door and Christmas lanterns glowing in the garden as soon as darkness fell. No doubt the delivery of the tree would create a focal point for the children's presents to be placed around.

All of that was perfectly understandable but why go to the trouble of providing her with a tree too? Was it another example of the way he was ignoring her decision to leave him to his restricted existence?

Later the same morning, on her way to buy ornaments for the tree, she stopped off at the cemetery to put Christmas flowers on her grandmother's grave, and observed it in amazement when she got there. It was immaculate. Ryan had said he would clean it and had kept his word, but how when it was dark in the evenings and late afternoons and there would be no time before he went to the hospital each morning?

It was only the previous Saturday that they'd met there and he'd made the offer. Had it been in his thoughts that he wanted her to have peace of mind regarding it when she was gone and had wasted no time in cleaning it up?

Before continuing on her way, she stopped in front of Beth's grave. She would try to make up for their mother not being there over Christmas for the children, but couldn't promise any joy with regard to their father because he didn't want her to take their mother's place and she would have to accept that.

Ryan had gone to have a haircut in readiness for his role at the wedding and had gone to a unisex hairdresser so that Rhianna and Martha could have theirs made especially beautiful at the same time in preparation for the occasion. Only a week to go and it would be upon them.

When they arrived back at the house the tree was there on the drive, but there was no sign of Melissa's. He hoped that she'd accepted it in the spirit it had been given. Whatever happened in the new year, he was determined that her decision to leave Heatherdale was not going to put the blight on Christmas.

He saw her go past on her return from the shops and within minutes she was on the phone, thanking him for the tree and asking how he'd managed to find time to finish the cleaning of the grave.

'It was just as easy to order two as one, and no way

would the children want you not to have a tree when they come to see you over Christmas. As to the cleaning up of the grave, I'm afraid I haven't been performing miracles. The church has a facility where they will maintain a grave on a regular basis, so you have your answer to that.'

'Well, thanks, anyway,' she told him. 'If you pass the contract on to me, I'll see that it gets paid when due.' And without further comment she rang off with the thought in mind that she was supposed to be keeping a low profile with Rhianna and Martha instead of spending most of Christmas with them. But it wasn't going to be easy with the wedding and Christmas morning and everything else that gave the young excitement and delight at such a time of year.

If the morning had brought surprises with it in the form of the unexpected delivery of the tree and the immaculate gravestone, the afternoon's surprise was in a class of its own.

The estate agent phoned to say that they had a buyer for the house. 'What, already?' she croaked, as her legs felt as if they would give way under her. Yet wasn't it what she wanted, to be off as soon as Christmas was over?

'Those houses where you live are always soon snapped up,' he said, 'so don't be surprised. It amazes me that they're not listed, like a lot of the buildings in the town. The buyer's bankers are in charge of the sale as he is some busy professional guy, so we'll be dealing with them.'

'When did you show him around?' she asked, still stunned.

'We didn't. He asked for a brochure to be sent to his bank, saw that it was what he's looking for, and wants to buy it. Could be a developer, I suppose,' the voice at the other end of the line was saying, and as she listened it was all so unreal, like Ryan's calm acceptance of her leaving Heatherdale with no sign of dismay.

If anything should make her feel confident that she was doing the right thing, it was that, but if she'd been lost and lonely when she'd come to this place that had captured her heart, what she was going to feel like when she left it didn't bear thinking of.

In the early evening she went upstairs and went through her clothes to decide what was going to be the most attractive outfit she possessed to wear at Mollie's wedding.

A pale blue dress of fine wool with a matching jacket and high-heeled shoes seemed a good choice, but she had no large wedding-type hat to go with it and settled for an inexpensive fascinator that was modern and youthful and shaped to show off the dark sheen of her hair.

When she observed herself in the mirror she was smiling. She was 'poor' and 'needy', she thought, but could manage a show of prosperity when the need arose and hoped that Ryan would approve of her outfit.

* * *

The following day the 'Sold' notice went up outside the house and if Melissa was expecting any revealing comments from Ryan regarding it she was disappointed. He merely commented as they arrived home simultaneously at the end of a busy day at the hospital that someone had wasted no time and left it at that, leaving her once again with the sick feeling that she was a poor judge when it came to the men in her life.

Especially when his next comment was to remind her that he would be cooking Christmas dinner and hoped she realised how much Rhianna and Martha were looking forward to her spending the day with them. There was again no mention of *his* feelings about the invitation, and she told him levelly if that was the case with regard to the children, she would be there.

But first there was the ordeal of the wedding to get through.

It was the day of Christmas Eve, and as Ryan drove the four of them through town to the church where the wedding was to take place it was thronged with last-minute shoppers and sightseers come to share in the magic of Heatherdale at a special time of year.

When she'd gone next door earlier in the morning, in good time to help Rhianna and Martha into their pretty outfits, Ryan's heart had ached when the children had run up to her and hugged her, and he'd felt the familiar longing take hold of him, as it always did when she was near.

'You look very swish,' he'd commented.

'So do you,' she'd told him, taking in the vision of the tall figure in morning suit and smart white shirt. Would she ever be able to put him out of her mind when he was no longer only feet away from her all the time at the hospital, and almost within touching distance in the house next to hers? Lots of women would be happy with that arrangement, if only to have him in their lives, but not her. The pain of always being an onlooker would be too much to bear.

The children had been tugging at her, eager to get dressed, and she'd given them her full attention for the next half-hour, then presented them to him and had to watch the pain in his expression that had to be at the thought of what their mother was missing.

She'd wanted to go to him and hold him close again, but it had been a moment that had belonged to Ryan and his children only and she'd gone into the next room and stood gazing out of the window until his voice had come from behind asking, 'So are we ready to leave, then?'

Feeling that she would be relieved when the day was over, she'd nodded and when the children had come trooping in and had stood one on either side of her she'd taken them by the hand and followed him out to the car.

The church was full of well-wishers as both Mollie and Jack were well respected in the area. Once Melissa had positioned the children behind the bride, who was holding Ryan's arm for support, the organist struck up the wedding march and the ceremony got under way, with her hurrying to find a seat near the front.

It was like the night of the ball, curious glances in her direction. Unless they'd had cause to meet her at the hospital for some reason, she was a stranger to most of them, but it would seem not so to Ryan and his children.

When she would have seated herself at a small table amongst others at the reception that followed, Ryan went to her and raising her to her feet took her to the top table to sit beside him and the children, with Mollie beaming her approval.

The bridal pair intended honeymooning in Italy for two weeks and were leaving on a flight later that evening. Ryan was taking leave due to him from the hospital to cover the time that Mollie would be away.

Fortunately she was intending to stay on in the role of his housekeeper but Melissa thought there would always be times when there was the problem of someone to be there for Rhianna and Martha when he was working. If things had been different they could have shared those kinds of responsibilities between the two of them, but he hadn't wanted to let her into his cloistered life.

No point in wishing for the moon. She had made her decision to leave behind the feeling of being surplus to Ryan's requirements, and soon would have to decide what direction to take for yet another new beginning.

CHAPTER TEN

It was late afternoon when they arrived home from the wedding and as Melissa wished the children good-bye, with a promise to see them the next day when Santa had been, the evening stretched ahead like an empty void.

She had no wish for a continuation of the day's awkwardness between Ryan and herself, and when he'd asked her what she had planned for the evening she'd told him hurriedly that she was meeting friends in the town.

He'd eyed her dubiously and explained that he would be spending the time preparing for the Christmas dinner that he was going to cook for them the next day. She was welcome to join him if she wanted to, and if she didn't and still persisted in going into town, she must be sure to get a taxi home and to ring him if she had any problems.

'I won't be doing that,' she protested hotly, 'expecting you to leave the children on my account.'

'I wouldn't be. I would bring them with me.'

'Yes, well, that isn't going to happen because I won't need you,' she said firmly.

Under any other circumstances she would have been more than willing to be with him in the kitchen, but the thought of being alone with Ryan for any length of time, as the children would be in bed early on such a night, was not to be faced.

Never once had he said he was sorry she was leaving, that he wanted her to stay, and if that wasn't a guideline for her own attitude towards *him*, *she* didn't know what was.

He was using her fondness for his children as a lever to achieve his own ends and she couldn't believe it of him. Once Christmas was over she would be on the outside of his life, as she'd been before. Without further comment she left him to his preparations for a meal that she felt would choke her.

Melissa hadn't had any intention of going into town for Christmas Eve, but her quick-as-a-flash excuse for not spending any more time that day with Ryan was making her feel that she had to justify what she'd told him, and she *had* been invited to join a group from the hospital who were intending to wine and dine the evening away in one of the local restaurants, so maybe she would take them up on it and try to chase away the blues that way.

It didn't work. She kept thinking of Ryan and his ever-changing moods. How he hadn't wanted her to come into town, and how he'd fussed about her getting home safely, *and the rest*. Had it been that he'd felt guilty because it was because of him that she was leaving Heatherdale?

She excused herself from the gathering early and did as he had ordered and used a taxi for the return journey. She would have called to let him know she was home except that his house was in darkness and she didn't want to disturb him.

She wouldn't have done. The house lights had fused when he'd plugged the tree in and he'd been searching for a torch when the taxi had stopped in front, but he'd seen its headlamps shining in the darkness and had thought thankfully that she was back.

He had a gift for Melissa, a Christmas surprise that he would give her in the morning and hope it would last for ever, and with the lights back on, the turkey cooking slowly, and all the trimmings that went with it sorted, he went to bed, and in what seemed like no time at all the children were tugging at him to get up because Santa had been.

They'd had their breakfast and were upstairs surrounded by all the things they'd asked for when he phoned Melissa. The lights were on in the house next door, smoke was curling out of the chimney, and it was now a reasonable hour to get in touch.

When she answered he said, 'Merry Christmas. Are you up and about?'

'Er, yes' was the reply. 'I'll be over shortly. I've got presents for you and the children.' Ryan would hardly be jumping for joy when he opened his to find a book token!

'Fine,' he said, 'but I'm not phoning about anything like that. It's to tell you that the guy who is buying your house is outside and he wants a word. I think he wants to introduce himself.'

'What?' she gasped. 'It's Christmas Day, for heaven's sake.'

'So goodwill to all men, yes?'

'Mmm, I suppose so. Where exactly is he?'

'Waiting on the drive.'

'All right, thanks for letting me know.' She went to greet the stranger at her door.

But when she opened it there was only Ryan there, and looking around her she questioned, 'So where is he?'

'Quite close' was the reply. 'In fact, very close. If you reach out you can touch him.'

'What? You?' she gasped, holding on to the doorpost. 'How? Why? What do you want with two houses?'

'To make them into a home for the four of us, Melissa. Did you really think that I was going to let you go out of my life now that I've found you? Now, is it all right if I step inside? I don't want to propose to you on the doorstep,' he said gently.

Speechless, Melissa stepped aside to let Ryan in.

'When you appeared in my life on a dark autumn night, distraught and dishevelled, the last thing I felt like was having to offer you food and find you accommodation. It had been a long, busy day at the hospital and all I wanted was to enjoy the meal that Mollie had cooked and then spend some special time with my children. But for ever kind and thoughtful about others, Mollie wanted to see you fed and warm before I took you to find a hotel, and I remember that I agreed to whatever she suggested with a reluctance that must have been obvious to you.

'I little knew that I would fall in love with the stranger at my door and that the way of life I had set for myself was going to be thrown into chaos. It has taken the thought of losing you to bring me to my senses, and I'm buying your house for two reasons.

'One, because we owe it to your grandmother. Because of her generosity in leaving it to you, you came into my life, and because our two houses made into one will be delightful when the builders have finished with them. So will you marry me, Melissa? Will you let me take you next door to tell the children that their wish has been granted, that Santa has sent them a mummy who will love them always?'

'Yes,' she breathed. 'It is all I've ever wanted for weeks, to be your wife, but why buy my house when it's yours for the asking to be part of our home?'

'Because once you were rich and now are poor,' he said laughingly. 'And now you will be rich again.'

'Having you and the children will be all the riches I need,' she said softly.

'Yes, I know,' he agreed, 'but nevertheless...'

With his arms around her they went to tell Rhianna and Martha their good news, and when they ran to her and held her close Melissa hoped that somewhere not far away their mother would be giving the four of them her blessing.

'Can we phone Mollie and tell her that we're going to have a mummy?' Martha cried

'Yes, but just a quick call,' Ryan warned, as he and Melissa went to check that the food he'd prepared was cooking satisfactorily.

In a hotel in Italy, the bride of the day before was enjoying a late breakfast with her new husband when her mobile phone rang, and when she'd listened to what the childish voices had to say she cried joyfully, 'Jack! There's going to be another wedding!'

EPILOGUE

WINTER HAD PASSED. It was spring, with new life opening up in the parks and gardens of the famous market town and with the outline of the moors that surrounded it taking on a softer green than the bleak shades of winter.

The building work was finished, the two houses had been made into one, and the result was a gracious family home that was going to be a joy to live in.

Since Melissa had come to live with them, Ryan's bed was no longer the loneliest place on earth. When he held her close in the night there was always the joy of knowing that she was his, always would be, and the spring wedding that they were planning would tell the world that it was so.

The children were on cloud nine because they were going to be bridesmaids again, this time in summery dresses with pretty posies. Julian, now recovered from his injuries, was going to be Ryan's best man, and Jack Smethurst would be giving Melissa away.

Everyone who wasn't on duty at the hospital was there to celebrate the wedding of two of its doctors, and the old stone church near the town houses was full of well-wishers, amongst them grateful parents of patients.

When Melissa arrived in a white wedding gown that was stunning in its simplicity, carrying a small ivory cross that had been her mother's and with two young bridesmaids carrying her train, it felt as if she'd been waiting for this day all her life.

When she stopped for a second, framed in the doorway of the church as the organist began to play the music that announced the arrival of the bride, Ryan turned from his position in front of the altar and as their glances met it was there, the love that each of them had for the other, and like a blessing the scent of roses, Beth's favourite flowers, was all around them.

The photographs had been taken in front of the church and as the guests began to make their way to the reception at an hotel in the town, Melissa and Ryan left the children with Mollie and Jack for a few moments and went into the graveyard. She laid the small white cross she had carried beside the roses that always graced the grave in the quiet corner then, hand in hand, they went to that other grave where Ryan placed the carnation he had worn on its weathered but immaculate surface and after a few moments in the silence that was all around them they returned to where the future was waiting.

* * * * *

LET'S TALK
Romance

For exclusive extracts, competitions
and special offers, find us online:

f facebook.com/millsandboon

🐦 @MillsandBoon

📷 @MillsandBoonUK

Get in touch on 01413 063232

MILLS & BOON

THE HEART OF ROMANCE

A ROMANCE FOR EVERY KIND OF READER

MODERN

Prepare to be swept off your feet by sophisticated, sexy and seductive heroes, in some of the world's most glamourous and romantic locations, where power and passion collide.
8 stories per month.

HISTORICAL

Escape with historical heroes from time gone by. Whether your passion is for wicked Regency Rakes, muscled Vikings or rugged Highlanders, awaken the romance of the past.
6 stories per month.

MEDICAL

Set your pulse racing with dedicated, delectable doctors in the high-pressure world of medicine, where emotions run high and passion, comfort and love are the best medicine.
6 stories per month.

True Love

Celebrate true love with tender stories of heartfelt romance, from the rush of falling in love to the joy a new baby can bring, and a focus on the emotional heart of a relationship.
8 stories per month.

Desire

Indulge in secrets and scandal, intense drama and plenty of sizzl hot action with powerful and passionate heroes who have it all: wealth, status, good looks…everything but the right woman.
6 stories per month.

HEROES

Experience all the excitement of a gripping thriller, with an inter romance at its heart. Resourceful, true-to-life women and strong, fearless men face danger and desire - a killer combination!
8 stories per month.

DARE

Sensual love stories featuring smart, sassy heroines you'd want as best friend, and compelling intense heroes who are worthy of the
4 stories per month.

To see which titles are coming soon, please visit

millsandboon.co.uk/nextmonth

MILLS & BOON
True Love
Romance from the Heart

Celebrate true love with tender stories of
heartfelt romance, from the rush of falling
in love to the joy a new baby can bring,
and a focus on the emotional
heart of a relationship.

MILLS & BOON

MODERN

Power and Passion

Prepare to be swept off your feet by sophisticated, sexy and seductive heroes, in some of the world's most glamourous and romantic locations, where power and passion collide.